Praise for Earl Emerson

"Emerson, himself a [firefighter] . . . deserves a medal . . . for taking us . . . into the . . . men and women who do this dangerous work for a living."
—*The New York Times Book Review*

"A terrific read with rousing scenes of firefighters in action . . . When writer Earl Emerson takes you into a burning building, you believe it."
—Baltimore *Sun*

"The best suspense fiction . . . such chilling, utterly convincing detail that readers may wind up struggling to breathe."
—*Los Angeles Times*

"Reads like James Patterson decked out in fire gear."
—*Booklist*

"Thrilling . . . Emerson depicts [the] dangerous but alluring world of firefighting [with] skill and verve."
—*The Seattle Times*

"Earl Emerson gives the reader enormous insight into the grueling and dangerous lives of firefighters."
—JOHN SAUL

"Scarily authentic and utterly captivating . . . easily one of the most compelling books you'll encounter this year."
—*Mystery Scene*

"Emerson keeps the heat on from start to finish."
—*The Sunday Oregonian*

ALSO BY EARL EMERSON

Vertical Burn
Into the Inferno
Pyro
The Smoke Room
Firetrap
Primal Threat

THE THOMAS BLACK NOVELS
The Rainy City
Poverty Bay
Nervous Laughter
Fat Tuesday
Deviant Behavior
Yellow Dog Party
The Portland Laugher
The Vanishing Smile
The Million-Dollar Tattoo
Deception Pass
Catfish Café
Cape Disappointment

CAPE
DISAPPOINTMENT

A NOVEL

EARL EMERSON

BALLANTINE BOOKS • NEW YORK

2010 Ballantine Books Mass Market Edition

Copyright © 2009 by Earl Emerson, Inc.

All rights reserved.

Published in the United States by Ballantine Books, an imprint of The Random House Publishing Group, a division of Random House, Inc., New York.

BALLANTINE and colophon are registered trademarks of Random House, Inc.

Originally published in hardcover in the United States by Ballantine Books, an imprint of The Random House Publishing Group, a division of Random House, Inc., in 2009.

ISBN 978-0-345-49302-6

Cover design: Jae Song
Cover photographs: © Attilo Ivan (raindrops), © Craig Clements (Cape Disappointment)

Printed in the United States of America

www.ballantinebooks.com

9 8 7 6 5 4 3 2 1

It's so real the way people disappoint you.
                                        —Meg Ruley

*The power of accurate perception is commonly referred
to as cynicism by those who have not got it.*
                                        —George Bernard Shaw

ONE

WHAT I REMEMBERED MOST was the janitor's plastic helmet bouncing between the open rafters like a Ping-Pong ball, that and chunks of metal whirring past my ears. I should have dodged the shrapnel, but all I did was stand and watch the flotsam fall out of the rafters and land all around me. Fortunately, the gym had emptied out minutes earlier, or the explosion would have killed several hundred people instead of a handful of unfortunates.

Pieces of the podium and stage, scraps from the bleachers, and even parts of the bomb itself had flown outward in all directions. Some of it bounced off the walls, some struck bystanders like myself, and the rest dropped out of the rafters like forgotten props in a school play. Most of the janitor, who'd been virtually on top of the blast, landed thirty feet from me. We were told the explosion, although executed with a relatively unsophisticated device, had blown out all the high windows in the gym and spewed glass onto roofs a block away.

I remember an amazing amount of dust in the air. Nearly all the inside lighting had been shattered by flying debris or obscured by clouds of dust. I remember the relative quiet immediately afterward, too. I was dazed. I couldn't have told you what planet I was on, much less the name of the school gymnasium. Or what I was doing besides bleeding. What they don't tell you about a bombing is that the event itself is probably the least memorable chapter in the book, that 99.9 percent of the story concerns the aftermath.

I found myself standing against a wall, unable to move. With each inhalation, my abdomen throbbed. When I looked down, I found a long metal rod jutting out of my belly, nailing me to the wall, twelve inches of it protruding from my shirt like one of those fake arrows Steve Martin used to wear on his head.

As the bomb went off, hundreds of metal chairs were thrown across the room, knocking people down like bowling pins and piling debris and bodies—some living, some not—at the end of the gym. Across the room a woman whose sweater and shoes were blown off was on her knees, blood dribbling down her face. I was close enough to the center of the blast that I must have had other injuries, lots of them, but the spike protruding from my belly was all I could think about.

Whether or not I was going to die against the wall was anybody's guess.

You read about bombings every day—in Baghdad, or Tel Aviv, or Pakistan, or some other place you've never been—and if you're intelligent and engaged and empathetic, you wonder what it might be like to be involved in one of those attacks, or to have a loved one involved, but the truth is that for most of us, our eyes glaze over before we flip the page or turn the channel, for bombings simply do not happen in the United States. At least, not anywhere nearby.

Some people walked around in a daze, including several bloodied individuals in front of me, but I stood like a guard at the palace, knowing there was nothing else I could do.

I didn't recall hearing any noise when the bomb went off. All I knew was that one second I was talking on my cellphone and the next I was nailed to the wall. Oddly, it didn't hurt as much as one might suppose, though that might be what all people in my circumstances told themselves, knowing they had no choice but to brave it.

I'D BEEN WALKING across the gymnasium near the west bleachers trying to improve my reception at the moment the blast erupted. If it hadn't been for the call, I would have been even closer than the unfortunate janitor. The bleachers around the sides of the gym had been pulled out to help seat the crowd, which had turned out to be meager. In those days, that was all Maddox could draw, a hundred or so of the faithful and some of the law-and-order crowd—after all, he was an ex–police officer. I'd listened to the speech from the wings, and after it was over and the main body of the crowd filed out, had gone back inside for reasons it took some time to recall. Had I suspected a bomb? It certainly would have been part of my job assignment to watch for any suspicious activity. If so, why hadn't I discovered it before the speech, when it might have done some good? And, if I had suspected, what tipped me off? I couldn't remember.

In the weeks after the explosion, as the ATF investigation progressed, people would learn that the bomb had been placed directly under the podium. They would speculate that had Maddox, the speaker for the evening, been on the podium when it went off, he would have been blown into parts so small the medical examiner never would have been able to reconstruct him. As it was, nobody was vaporized, although the janitor came close. Later, I saw his picture in *Newsweek* among the photos of the dead. He was young, twenty-three, and lived at home with his parents. He had a girlfriend and one child with her whom he'd been doing his best to support. His life had hardly begun. Even weeks later, it was hard to fathom the enormity of the tragedy for his relatives and those of the others who died.

As the dust settled I began to feel more physical symptoms. My left eye was swollen, my vision blurry, and the fingers of my right hand were not functioning properly. My back hurt like hell. After a while, I realized I could barely hear anything—just a constant, low-level background ringing in my ears. I was too dazed to pick up on it just then, but there was the distinctive smell of recently detonated explosives, the iron tang of blood, and the smell of human entrails, as well as the overpowering odor of construction dust. Inexplicably, the worst part during those minutes after the blast was the lack of human voices. I could see people's mouths moving but could hear no words. Nearby a man on his back had been impaled by two wooden shards. There were maybe twelve or fifteen people within sight of my position, some prone, some on their hands and knees, one couple clinging to each other and weaving around like drunks in an alley.

For some idiotic reason—the same reason you always do inane things that count for nothing during an emergency—

I glanced around for my cellphone. It was on the floor next to a woman lying in a pile of twisted, metal chairs. I wanted to ask her to slide the phone over to me, but my vocal cords wouldn't respond. Even if she could slide it over, I wouldn't have been able to pick it up, nailed to the wall as I was. You'd think I would have had more important things to do than yak on my phone, but I suddenly became obsessed with finishing that last call, even though I couldn't remember who I'd been speaking to. As I stared at the woman next to my cellphone, it occurred to me that she hadn't moved an inch, that she wasn't breathing. "Ma'am," I said. "Ma'am, are you okay?"

My words sounded hollow and garbled, as if I were talking underwater. It took a long time to realize I was talking to a corpse. Thirty yards away, a group of onlookers appeared in the doorway, led by a firefighter in a white helmet speaking through a megaphone. It didn't seem possible that enough time had passed for the fire department to show up. Except for the ringing in my ears and my own muffled words, the fire chief's megaphone voice was the first sound I heard after the bomb.

"Will everyone who can get up and walk out, please do so." After about a minute, when only one or two of the twenty or so victims had begun to move toward the door, he added, "We have received information that there's a second explosive device in the gym. I repeat. We have word there's a second device that could go off at any minute. At this time we cannot allow our personnel to access this site. Anybody who is ambulatory should get out now. If you have the capability, try to help someone else out."

After his second statement, five men and one woman straggled to the doorway. Three or four others followed at a slower pace, some limping, a man hopping on one foot. A woman got up off the floor where she'd been caught in a tangle of chairs, took two steps and fell, then stood back up, spent a moment getting her bearings, and launched off in a lurching line not much straighter than a bumblebee's flight. I wished I could help her, but then, who would help me? For some time I'd been feeling something wet in my right shoe, and when I looked down I saw a puddle of blood squishing through the laces like something in a horror flick. My sock was warm with it. I was beginning to feel light-headed. Heaven only knew what would happen if I fainted on this steel rod. I might rip it out of the wall or I might just hang.

After the walking wounded evacuated the gym, I could see four prone bodies, one of whom was calling for help. From the doorway, the fireman motioned for me to walk over to him. I wanted to explain why I couldn't, but I didn't have enough air in my lungs to yell. I kept trying to remember what organs were on my wounded side, so that I might discern what the rod, which was about a quarter of an inch in diameter, might have penetrated. The wound was bleeding profusely now, my shirt and the front thigh area of my jeans sopping with it. I could barely keep awake. It was weird that my survival was dependent on a whim of physics, that if the rod had been four inches higher and a little more to the center, I would be dead. It was strange and a bit horrifying to realize I'd missed a coffin by so little. Not that I was out of the woods. Nor anywhere close.

One of the doorways led outside, and it was through this door that I saw Maddox and a redheaded woman, along with several others I recognized from the election campaign— though if you'd asked me to put a name to any of them I wouldn't have been able to. My brain was scrambled. I did notice Maddox looked very senatorial in his tidy blue suit and slicked-back silver hair. As I watched them, he and the others were ushered farther into the darkness by police officers and firemen. From time to time when the doorway emptied, I could see them out in the darkness.

It was only when I saw the looks on the anonymous faces that appeared now and then in the doorway that it occurred to me how dire was my predicament. I was impaled and I was slowly bleeding out and there was another bomb about to go off. Anybody who came in would be risking his own life.

Nobody was coming to rescue me.

═══ TWO ═══

THERE IS A TIME as you're attempting to wake up when your brain slips cogs, and I am at such a place now, straining to regain consciousness, working to transfer myself out of dreamland and into some semblance of cogent thought. It is during this twilight of consciousness, while the cognitive motors grind, that I begin to believe I may be among the living.

It is a frightening but lackadaisical time for me as I lapse in and out of consciousness, unable to distinguish between reality and the haunting morphine nightmares that have riddled my perspective. At times I sleep so heavily I think I will never awaken. I strain and fail to move a body part that is either sore or going to sleep. Every inch of my body feels as if it's encased in concrete. When I try to move my legs, nothing happens, nothing. My body craves any position other than the one I seem to have been in forever.

Through half-open eyelids I glimpse people working in the room. Bandages are changed. My temperature is taken. A hand is laid across my brow. I feel numbness and then, at times, a dull pain. There are long periods when I know I am alone, other periods when nurses and doctors fuss and fiddle over me. I am jostled, poked, washed, and gossiped over, but nobody tries to awaken me. It is as if they know the undertaking is pointless.

And then, inexorably, after what might be two days, or maybe two years, I succeed partially in regaining consciousness. As I come out of the haze into the light, I see a woman in the room. She doesn't realize I'm awake. She is tall and slender and has flaming red hair. Sunshine angles into the room from a high window off to my right. I can see the glare on the walls and ceiling and in the highlights of her hair. She has a graceful way of moving and there's a wonderful fragrance I have a memory of but can't identify.

"Thomas?"

"Kathy?"

"No. It's Deborah. How are you?"

"Okay, I guess."

"You're awake. You haven't been awake in a while."

"Where am I?"

"Swedish Hospital. Do you remember any of what happened?"

"I can barely hear you."

She moves closer, until her lips are next to my face. I can feel the heat off her body. "They said you would probably have some hearing loss. Hopefully, it will be temporary."

Her accent is vaguely southern, with just a hint of Louisiana, or is it Tennessee?

"Thomas. Are you all right?"

My voice is hoarse and the words seem to scar my throat. I know this woman and she knows me, but I cannot recall her place in my life.

"Are you all right?" she repeats.

"I can't feel anything."

"I so wish this hadn't happened."

"Me too."

"Can I get you anything? Should I call the nurse?"

"I don't think so."

"Are they giving you enough pain medication?"

"I guess."

She leans closer and kisses my cheek lightly. "Can you feel this?"

"I don't know. Where is everybody?"

"Who do you mean?"

"Everybody."

"Thomas? Do you know what day it is?"

I don't even know what year it is. I don't know this woman's name, although she may have given it to me moments earlier. I don't remember what hospital I'm in, although I know I'm in a hospital. The meager knowledge that I am conscious and speaking to someone seems like a small victory. It feels as if I have been in this bed for weeks. My bones ache as if I've been in a crypt.

A pair of warm lips press against my cheek and work their way across my face to my lips. I'm probably not the world's best kisser just now, but she seems to be doing okay on her own. "You feel any of this?"

"Not a bit." Her lips feel wonderful. I cannot help thinking it would be useful to know who she is and why she is kissing me. I have a wife, and even though I can't think of my wife's name, I know this is not her.

"Oh, but you're not married anymore."

"Did I say that out loud?"

"You *were* married," she replies, ignoring my query, then hesitating. "Your wife died."

"I am married." I want to tell her my wife's name. It's on the tip of my tongue.

"You're confused, darling. They said you would be." *Darling*.

Her green-eyed gaze is intense and close. I take a deep breath and think about what she's saying. I mull it over—my wife is dead?—and begin to lose focus, and after a while, when I open my eyes, I'm alone. I must have dozed off, I think, because the sunlight is gone and the hospital background noises seem muted. It's dark outside. I manage to turn my head and catch a glimpse of the window, where a windblown rain beats against the panes. The smell of perfume has been replaced with the tang of hospital bleach and disinfectant.

Time passes in small dollops when you're drugged and on your back and dozing twenty-three hours a day. I can hear a television down the corridor entertaining somebody whose IQ has no doubt been drugged down by 50 percent. The audience on the television reacts like the rabble at a public stoning. Eventually I realize there's somebody in the room with me, moving about briskly, working. My covers are lifted to one side, and I turn my head to catch a glimpse of an African American woman with a large, pretty face and shiny skin. Her hair is straightened and worn in a chopped style with panache. She is somebody who thinks of herself as stylish, and she is. "Oh, you awake now, are you?"

"I guess so," I mutter.

"Every news guy in town is waiting to talk to you. Oh, don't worry. Nobody's coming in until doctor says it's all right. They want to know all about the hero. We get calls at the desk from all over the country."

"Hero?"

"That's right, hon. In the bombing."

"Did anyone die?"

"Four people. Harborview saved two by the skin of their teeth. You lucky to be alive your ownself. You have a serious concussion. Made the national news. I saw your boss on Jim Lehrer. Some real heroics that night. And you were right at the center of it."

Heroics? What was she talking about? Was I a hero? The only thing I remembered was the bomb's destruction around me. I'd been nailed to a wall, as I recalled.

"Tell you what. Now that you're beginning to make sense, I'll send doctor in to take a look."

"Sure."

"You're healing up real fine everywhere else. Just that head injury they were worried about."

"Did I . . ." She'd already finished whatever she was doing under the blankets and was wheeling a cart out of the room. "I have any visitors?"

"Oh, honey, you been having a whole bundle of visitors. I don't think anybody's out there just now, but they been in and out all week."

The room is overflowing with flowers. I smell lilies, roses, and oleander. "Was one of my visitors . . . a redhead?"

"She been here a number of times."

"Was she just here?"

"Oh, no, honey. She hasn't been here in a while."

"Is she pretty?"

"All the men around here seem to think so. Don't ask me why. If I was a man, I'd be chasing the sister with the great big ol' booty." She slaps her behind and laughs uproariously.

"What's her name?"

"I haven't been introduced, but you know they wouldn't be letting her in unless you two were kin or something."

As the nurse exits, I think of another question and blurt out, "Where's my wife?" The nurse is already out of earshot and she doesn't reply. There are so many things that need clearing up. What I need is for somebody to sit beside me and tell me why I feel this need to be out of bed and walking the streets. I have a sense that there are things out there that only I can fix. I wish I knew what they were.

═══ THREE ═══

IT WAS A MILD, sunny, autumn afternoon, a day that ordinarily would have pleased me to no end, yet I was in a particularly foul mood and had been for some time. I'd fallen into the tropical hurricane of bad moods so it was really no surprise when I went berserk.

Have you ever done it?

I'm talking about when you go stark raving mad, the kind of blind rage that doesn't do anybody any good, the kind that if it lasted for more than a few minutes, would put you in the loony bin or prison.

You know what I'm talking about. You're on a two-lane highway with tons of oncoming traffic; the speed limit is sixty, which you're doing, when some dunderhead looms up from a side road, gives you a careless glance, sees that he has no chance of avoiding a collision if he pulls out, but pulls out anyway and begins to accelerate with agonizing slowness, as if he wants you to hit him. You are forced to slam on your brakes to keep from rear-ending him and killing yourself; your tires squeal and your vehicle slews out into oncoming traffic and you escape death by inches, while he cruises blithely on as if it never happened. You curse and shout and honk, and if you could somehow get him to pull over and step out of his vehicle . . . well, you're not quite sure what would happen, but it wouldn't be pretty. The newspapers call it "road rage," but it can occur anywhere. Educated people like to think they're immune to momentary insanity, but in reality few really are.

The last time I went berserk, I was driving Kathy's car through the U-district, coasting down Brooklyn Avenue past a grocery store only blocks from our house. I'd shopped at that store for eons, so what happened was particularly appalling because the people who worked there would no longer remember me as the genial man who always had a pleasant smile and a comment he thought was witty but usually wasn't, but as the maniac who terrorized the staff and customers in a freakish encounter none of them could explain or forget.

When I spotted him, he was walking along the sidewalk, behind him a group of high school kids, probably cutting school so they could stand in cold doorways in the U-district for hours and be hip. He was a short, spindly man, slightly bowlegged, wearing shabby suit trousers, scuffed dress shoes, a loose jacket, and a fedora of the type that hadn't been popular in sixty years. In short, he was dressed as if visiting from a second-world country, Estonia maybe. I slowed the car to a crawl and watched him traipse along the sidewalk, his head glued to the store windows; it was an old detective's trick, following the action on the street in the reflections. It was in the reflection on the grocery store window that he spotted me. Without turning around, he ducked into the store as if that was his destination all along. We'd never been on good terms, but the last few days had sealed it.

"You bastard," I said under my breath.

As luck would have it, a parking spot opened on the street and I swung into it, effectively swiping it from a young woman in a red Corolla, who'd been waiting patiently. As I jogged across the street through traffic, she rolled her window down and berated me with a polite rectitude that tugged at my heart for a moment because it was so like Kathy. In no mood for social amenities, I disappeared into the store without answering.

I'd half expected him to go shooting out the back door and onto the loading dock, but he was loitering inside the store pretending to read the ingredients on a can of refried beans. When he looked up, I was closing in fast, my hands balled into fists. He saw me coming and said, "I'm not him, see?" and then spat a full plate of dentures into his palm and held them up for appraisal. When his dentures didn't slow me down, he pitched the can of beans at me in a kind of atavistic reflex, then hurled another, cans bouncing off my shoulders and careening down the aisle behind me. The third can struck me on the forehead and produced a fair amount of blood that ran into my eyes. It hurt. He was running away by the time I grabbed his arm and swung him around, hitting him behind the ear as hard as I could. The blow knocked him out of my grip and across the aisle, where he skidded across the floor on his belly, coming to a halt near a rack of corn chips, his head buried in the packages. Two nearby shoppers backed away in alarm. Several others who felt they were already at a safe distance froze in place and gaped. At least one student couple fled in panic, as if I might attack any stranger I could lay my hands on. That's certainly what it must have looked like. One woman who was either blind or obtuse continued inspecting melons as if nothing unusual was taking place.

He started crawling into the rack of chips, trying to worm his way through to the next aisle. He was buried up to his belt when I grabbed one of his legs and dragged him back. He held on to the rack and we played a game of tug-of-war. I yanked on him and he yanked on the rack, which began to teeter and finally toppled, burying him in Kettle brand tortilla chips.

When his head finally popped up through the chips, I kicked it. I was wearing running shoes, so I didn't do as much damage as I wanted, but a foot to the head gets your attention. I grabbed the metal rack and pulled it toward me, reeling him in. As soon as he was close enough, I grabbed him by the back of the jacket, hauled him free of the debris, and swung again. My knuckles connected with the top of his skull. He rammed me in the stomach with his shoulder, thinking to force me backward, but he didn't have the strength or body weight to counter my fury. As he pushed into me, I grabbed him around his torso and upended him so that his head was down and his flailing feet in the air.

"You've got the wrong guy, Thomas. I'm not my brother."

"I'm not my brother, either," I said, throwing him into the melon counter. The woman shopping for melons had finally backed off when the chip rack came down, else she would have been knocked over. He landed on the counter and slid to the floor along with about fifty melons, riding them like an avalanche. As he fell I spotted a gun in a shoulder holster. It should have slowed my attack but didn't. It should have alerted me to his true identity, but it didn't.

A left hook caught him on the cheek and he went sailing backward. He got up quickly and inexplicably began unbuckling his pants. Dropping his belt, he put up both hands in a defensive posture. I knocked them away with my left forearm and punched him in the chest. His right eye was beginning to swell from one of my earlier blows. Before I could reach him again, a stocky man in a green apron came around the corner, made eye contact with me, and said, "Get out of my store right now!"

"Happy to," I said, striding forward and knocking my victim into the dairy counter. Because his trousers had fallen to his knees, he looked like he was sitting on a toilet in the margarine containers.

"No, I mean it," said the man in the apron. "I want you out of here. Now!"

"I'm not Bert. I'm Snake," insisted my quarry.

"Sure you are," I said.

The grocery store worker stepped between us. I had to give him points for chutzpah, because at that moment, I must have looked like I was on PCP. Situated as it was in the University District, the store had seen plenty of druggies and probably had its share of pilfering and shoplifting problems as well, so this store manager was used to trouble, but I was bigger than him and mad as a hornet. He was a few inches shorter than my six one and out of shape, though he had the look and stance of a former high school or college wrestler.

"Don't get mixed up in this," I said. "You don't have a clue what this is about."

He must have seen the dementia in my eyes, because he stepped aside, but not before he'd stalled long enough for my victim to climb out of the dairy cooler, turn his back to us, drop his trousers to his ankles, and bend over. "Oh, my Lord," said a woman who'd only that moment pushed her grocery cart around the corner.

"See that scar!" he shouted from between his knees. "That's from a bull named Bart Simpson. Ended up killing a rider a year later. Bert doesn't have any scars on his ass, and you know it. This is me, Snake. God damn it, I'm Snake."

We stood like that for some time, Snake with his rump in the air, the grocery store manager, the woman with the grocery cart who seemed reluctant to leave the first mooning she'd probably attended in years, and a host of additional gawkers on either side of us. It began to dawn on me that I'd just given Snake a beating meant for his twin brother.

"Geez, I'm sorry, Elmer."

"Snake. Don't call me Elmer," he said, hoisting his trousers and boxer shorts as one package. "I showed you my damn teeth."

"You threw those cans at me," I said, touching my brow and finding blood on my index finger.

"You should have seen the look in your eye."

"You're dressed like him. Where's your cowboy hat? Geez, you guys really are identical."

"We're not identical. He's got more teeth than I have."

"I didn't know that."

"Well, now you do. And next time, take a look at my ass before you begin whipping it."

We must have looked a sight, me with blood running down my face and Snake with his right eye beginning to swell shut, his clothing disheveled, hair mussed, a knot growing on the back of his head. The grocery store manager was staring at Snake's shoulder holster, which was probably the reason he'd stepped back. It was one thing to get between two students roughhousing in the store, quite another to get between two grown men, one of whom appeared to be insane and the other packing a .44 Magnum. If Snake hadn't looked so disreputable, the grocery store manager might have mistaken him for a cop. He might have mistaken me for a cop, too, but I had six or seven days' growth of beard and wore rumpled jeans and a sweatshirt with food stains all over it, and my hair hadn't been washed in days.

"Listen," Snake said, draping an unwelcome arm around the grocer's shoulder. "My friend here's been having a bad week. Maybe you could cut us some slack if the cops show up." Snake pulled his wallet open and handed the man five one-hundred-dollar bills along with his business card. "You take this and spend whatever it takes to fix all this. If no cops hassle us, I won't show up for my change. How's that sound?"

"Well . . ."

"I thought so." Before we left the store a boy of about six or seven walked up to Snake and handed him his dentures.

"Better sterilize your hands, kid," I said.

Snake took the teeth and pushed me gently. "Come, Thomas. Let's get out of here before the cavalry arrives."

Once we were outside and sitting in Kathy's car, Snake said, "Were you going to kill me?"

"I hadn't thought that far in advance. Why are you dressed like your brother?"

"I thought maybe I could pick up some leads if people thought I was him."

"You picked up a fat lip."

"Thomas, that sort of thing is going to get you in serious trouble. I've never seen you that mad."

"I've never *been* that mad. You going to be all right?"

"Maybe."

═══ FOUR ═══

THE WAY I REMEMBER IT, the afternoon light at Cape Disappointment was serene, almost ethereal. A man nearby talked on his cellphone while his wife waited impatiently beside him. I picked up my own phone and made a call, the two of us, strangers, standing side-by-side talking to people who were dozens or hundreds or maybe thousands of miles distant. It occurred to me that the cellphone was the pièce de résistance of public isolationism, enabling us to remove ourselves from the people around us in an instant, which was one reason it had been embraced wholeheartedly by the entire planet.

As I pushed buttons on the phone, I visually traced the flight of a small plane flying north over the Pacific Ocean along the Washington coast under a low cloud cover. In a few hours the sunset would be brilliant. Already shafts of sunlight were angling from the heavens in spires that hit the ocean. She answered on the first ring, as if she'd been expecting the call, or as if she didn't want anybody else to hear the phone ringing. "Hi, baby," I said.

"Hey, big boy."

"You got people around?"

"Well, sort of."

"Can you talk?"

"I can talk."

I could hear a man chattering in the background, then she replied to him but covered the phone so I couldn't hear. Also in the background were the sounds of traveling, the engines on the jet or whatever. As we spoke, I handed a small digital camera to one of the tourists standing in front of the lighthouse, gesturing for him to snap a picture of me with the ocean in the background. After he'd taken my camera, I moved around so that the plane was framed in the photo over my shoulder: the lighthouse, the plane, the ocean. It was going to make a great joke photo, our vacation together, Kathy in the plane, me a mile away chitchatting with her on the phone.

It was midafternoon and the sky was a curious amalgam of the soft grays and blues that only the Northwest can produce, and then only in autumn. I was standing on the grass under the little black-and-white lighthouse at Cape Disappointment and gazing out at the Pacific Ocean, which was a deadly shade of slate today, the water riffled by a light wind. The ocean was close enough to taste, and I could feel its vastness in a manner that made me long for another kind of life. Seattle, where I lived, was buffered on two sides by water, some salt, some fresh, the Puget Sound and Lake Washington, but this lighthouse overlooked the largest body of water on earth, and that put things into perspective.

It was chilly and I had my jacket zipped to my chin while the man with my camera tried to figure out the mechanism. I explained that all he had to do was push the button, but he needed to understand the workings of his tools—one of those guys.

"One day wasn't very long," she said. "Although we got in about a week's worth of you-know-what."

"A week? By my calculations, that was two days' worth. But we'll catch up at home."

She laughed and it charmed me the way her laugh had charmed me from the beginning. "You're incorrigible."

"I'm a guy. My job is to be incorrigible. It's in the DNA. At least where that's concerned. Kathy. I see you. You're . . . maybe a mile out."

"There's something I need to tell you, Thomas—"

The tourist was still having trouble figuring out my camera, so I stepped forward and, with one hand, pointed out the button he needed to push. Out over the ocean, the plane waggled its wings. She'd promised she would have the pilot do that, and it tickled me that she had not forgotten. "Kathy? What were you going to say? Kathy? You there?"

FIVE

I'M LEANING AGAINST the windowsill, peering out at the city skyline as it appears between several nearby tall buildings. I am a thoroughly confused man in a hospital gown wondering how long I've been here and whether or not my wife is alive. Even though I've seen and spoken with Kathy, I am convinced somewhere in the reptilian portion of my brain that it was all fantasy.

I've never had so much curiosity as I have right now. I'm wondering what I was thinking the other day when I beat the hell out of my friend Elmer "Snake" Slezak, whom I mistook for his twin brother, Bert. I'd never liked Bert, but what had he done to send me over the edge? My actions had been about two miles past the last bus stop of sanity. If Kathy is around, why doesn't she visit? My bare legs are trembling. I'm close to falling. I don't remember getting out of bed and tottering over to this windowsill, but here I am.

Outside, the wind spatters tiny raindrops against the window. I hear a familiar male voice in the hallway. He's flirting with a nurse. He's been in the room, I think, because Elmer Slezak has an unmistakable scent about him, of cologne, cigarettes, and the vague smell of leather, having been a former rodeo bull rider. There is also the odor of farts. "Snake?"

"Yeah, man." Elmer hustles in from the corridor, where he's waylaid the African American nurse. "Jesus, you're not supposed to be out of bed!"

Elmer and the nurse walk me back to the bed, one on either arm. Snake wears cowboy boots, tight jeans that make his legs look like ax handles, and one of his huge, silver world championship belt buckles. "What on earth possessed you to do that?" asks the nurse. "You fall down in here and break your skull, it's going to be my fault. I don't want you out of bed again. You understand?"

"Yes, ma'am."

"Jesus, Thomas," Snake says. "You can hardly walk."

"Gee, you think, Elmer?" I may not have all my wits about me, but I can still shovel out sarcasm.

"Don't call me that." Years ago Elmer had seen some old movie, *Escape from New York,* and afterward decided to call himself Snake. Sometimes he forgets about it for weeks or months, but most of the time he insists on the nickname. When I want to get his goat, I refer to him as Elmer.

The nurse arranges the blankets over me and I lie back, exhausted. It's uncanny how a couple of days in bed can zap your strength. When the dizziness has abated, I focus on my friend. "What happened?"

"You can't remember?" Snake asks.

"Just bits and pieces."

"You want it all?"

"Everything you know."

"That's going to take a good little while, and I doubt I know it all. You were keeping your own counsel there toward the end."

"I've got nothing but time."

"Yeah, okay, but don't fall asleep on me. You've got a serious head injury, or don't you remember that?"

"I know it but I keep forgetting," I joke.

He sits in a chair beside the bed and starts to lay out the story of my last ten days as he knows it. A couple of sentences into it, I want to tell him to stop, because it is clear right off the bat that I don't have the capacity to grasp a tale this knotty. Half the names he mentions are people I either don't recognize, can't place, or swear I've never heard of. He speaks for five minutes, and as he speaks I forget nearly all of what he's said. Instead of asking him to start over, or warning him that he's wasting his breath, I let him continue. There is something reassuring and at the same time frightening about his voice. Snake is a competent private investigator and a good friend who would do almost anything for me. I don't have many others who are so close.

Once, while watching an old Glenn Ford movie together, Snake and I invented a test of friendship: A friend is somebody you would trust to help cover up a murder. Not that either of us was planning or had planned a murder, but I have only one friend I would go to for a task like that: Elmer. It was an outlandish way of measuring friendship and an odd thing to remember when so many other memories remain missing. And then I remember the man I'd killed years earlier and what Snake had done for me afterward. The killing had been an accident, but there would have been no way to establish that in a court of law.

Old memories I had no trouble with. It was the recent stuff that was giving me the slip.

As he speaks, my mind begins drifting and I start to piece together some of the events and images from the last few weeks. It is as if some maniacal film cutter has taken all the film stock in my brain and cut it into various lengths, so that there's a two-hour film somewhere on the premises, but it's been completely disassembled. My sense of time is so skewed I'm stunned when I realize Elmer is gone and has probably been gone for an hour.

I sort through random memories. I remember reclining on a bed in a motel room at the ocean. Outside the patio slider I can hear the surf pounding on several miles of flat sand. In the small bathroom Kathy is finishing up her shower, every part of her body glistening except her voluminous dark hair, which she's pinned into a knot on top of her head. She is taking the sort of care women often do after bathing. She spots me watching from across the room, smiles, drops the towel, and strides across the dim room, climbing onto the bed and crawling toward me like a lioness. The playful look on her face is one I don't want to forget.

And then, without knowing why, I remember myself in a small boat, chilled to the bone, riding an endless series of choppy waves. Nearby, other boats of all descriptions and sizes keep us company. The Coast Guard spotlights are bobbing every which way in the dark. Several local fishing boats are there. I've hired a young man to drive me out to the site in his father's boat. We're both wearing rain slickers—he's loaned me one of his father's, which has a hole under each armpit. I am wet and cold and miserable. I hate small boats. I get seasick on a water bed, so I'm about as wretched as a human being can get. My body is ill, but my soul is worse.

"You want to go back in?" he asks when he sees how queasy I am.

"No."

"It's your call."

I'm peering into the depths with a powerful spotlight, searching for something horrible. This is the worst night of my life.

I have a vivid memory of running through the darkness. It's a rural area, and there are two of us. We're dashing through brush, large branches of Scotch broom slapping me in the face. I'm breathing hard, but the man I'm chasing is breathing harder. He runs in spurts while I keep an even pace. We've been racing some minutes now. He's beyond redline and will crap out any second. All I have to do is keep pressing on. He's dangerous. That's all I remember about him. He's dangerous, and I'm desperate to get my hands on him.

Another set of memories—or are they fantasies now?—place me in a small plane, a Beechcraft King Air, a twin turboprop aircraft that can cruise comfortably at fifteen thousand feet, though we're flying much lower. Below us the wind is whipping the ocean into a frenzy. The plane dips its wings, first to port and then to starboard. Then something goes wrong and the plane drops fifty feet in a millisecond. My stomach leaps into my throat. The plane has a single row of seats on either side. Because of the insanely rapid descent, one man falls into the aisle. A woman slides off her seat and shrieks. I fumble to fasten my seat belt. As we dive, pieces of luggage, handbags, and computer cases fly around the cabin as if floating in space. In the cockpit I can hear the pilots. One of them keeps screaming, "What's happening?" The plane levels out for a few moments, then dips steeply again, and again my stomach jumps into my mouth. We're going down. We're going to crash, and there's not a damn thing any of us can do about it. A man screeches. Somebody tries to talk on her cellphone, final words to her loved one.

In the cockpit, the pilots have become quiet. I don't take that as a good sign. We're diving in a near vertical descent. Hurriedly, I try to calculate how many seconds I have to live. I'm guessing fifteen seconds, max. When you've got fifteen seconds left, what are you supposed to think about? Is it best to mutter a prayer? Or review your life? Or are you supposed to declare your love for those closest to you? Frittering away my last moments, I'm in a dither about what to do. I've faced death before, but this time I'm terrified.

ONCE AGAIN the redhead is standing over my bed. I strain to awaken fully, but it's like swimming through wood chips. Nothing much happens. I cannot feel any part of my body. I know only that I'm flat on my back and it's night. After some struggle, I manage to speak. "Hey."

She is startled. "Oh, good. I was hoping you would wake up while I was here."

"I'm awake."

"Yes, you are."

I roll my head to the right, and there sits a beautiful young woman with lots of dark hair. Her brilliant blue eyes have puffy sacks under them, as if she's been crying, or losing a lot of sleep. Or both. The redhead is gone. Once again the morphine is playing tricks with my senses. "Are you alive?" I ask the brunette.

She smiles. "Of course I'm alive. Why wouldn't I be?"

"No reason."

"Are you awake, Thomas? We were talking and then you drifted off. Are you awake now?"

"I think."

"Would you answer a question?"

"Is there money in it for me if I get it right?"

"What's my last name?"

I have to think about it for a while. It's tough, because I'm not sure I can conjure up her first name, at least not without some time to ponder it. She looks like Kathy and that's what I want to call her, but I've been wrong lately about so many things and I don't want to take a chance. Her last name is even harder. "Driscoll," I announce, rather proudly.

"Jesus," she says.

"What?"

"Listen, honey. I know you're on morphine."

"Kathy."

"At least you got that right. You're batting five hundred. I guess in any other league that would be good."

"But not when I'm trying to identify my wife?"

"So you know I'm your wife?"

"Of course I know. Where have you been? You're never here."

"I can't hang around as much as I'd like. You know that."

"I don't know much of anything. I got hit in the head."

"Yes, you did, sweety, and it's not your fault if you have a soft skull. How are you feeling?"

"I've been trying to sort through some memories. Soft skull? Was that a wisecrack?"

"Just a little one. You're the one who always says it. Ever since that woman knocked you out with an alarm clock." She is standing over me now and leans down to kiss my cheek. "Have you had other visitors?"

"I think so."

"Ms. Driscoll by chance?"

"Does she have red hair?"

"She dyes her hair red, yes."

"Snake was here, too. Or Snake's brother. Hard to tell with those two. I'm not sure of anything. I've been having . . . flashbacks . . . I'm having a lot of trouble figuring out what happened."

"It might help if you could stay awake for a while."

"They're doping me."

"Not that much, they're not. Not anymore. It's that crack you took to your skull."

"All I know is that at some point . . . you die."

"We all die at some point, Thomas, but I'm here for you now." She kisses me on the lips.

"A woman who can kiss like that . . ."

"Does that prove anything?" she says, kissing me again.

The redhead kissed me in much the same manner. I have a foreboding about Kathy that I cannot shake. Something terrible is going to happen to her, or has happened. The thought sends a shudder through me, and I wonder if I've been talking to a ghost. We talk a little longer and I strain to believe she is actually alive, that I'm not creating her out of morphine dreams and old memories.

SIX

I'M SITTING UP, feeling more alert than at any time in recent memory, and to make things even better there's a doctor standing in front of me going over my chart. She's introduced herself and I'm having absolutely no trouble remembering her name. Miraculous. She is Miranda Swartz, and she has a beauty mark on her upper lip that gives her a sexy aspect, despite the fact that she's not exactly a beauty queen. She's not quite five feet tall, is thick through the middle, opinionated, blunt, cares not a whit about her appearance, and I'm quickly falling in love with her.

"So, how am I doing, doc?"

"There's nothing here you won't recover from."

"Can you tell me what's wrong with me? Besides the fact that by the time lunch comes around I can't remember what I had for breakfast?"

"Well," she says, putting the chart back, "you've suffered a traumatic brain contusion with subdural hematoma, which is basically severe bruising and bleeding of your brain tissue. A steel rod approximately two centimeters in diameter went through your side and came out your back. It chewed off a small piece of your liver and caused a good deal of internal bleeding, which we managed to stanch the first night you were here. Aside from that, you have a broken finger, some superficial lacerations to your face, hearing loss, and thoracic contusions. And you have a wound in your lower leg, where a splinter of wood penetrated the muscle, which we continue to monitor for infection. What we're most concerned with now is that brain injury."

"Me too. I need my brain. I use it almost every day."

A single burst of laughter erupts from her mouth, though her lips do not, I notice, curl into a smile. "I'm going to ask a few questions. I want you to quickly answer each to the best of your ability, and then we'll go on to the next."

"You mean you don't want me dawdling on a question? Because I'm pretty astute psychologically, and I might be able to glean the answer from you without you knowing it, right?"

"They're not that kind of questions." She smiles. "And yes, you probably are astute. I know that from some of the things I read about you in the paper. First question. Who's the president of the United States?"

"Well, it's . . . uh . . ." The idea that I can't name the president comes as a shock, but I quickly capitalize on my loss as only I can. "I know it's not Calvin Coolidge, and I'm pretty sure both Johnsons are dead. Give me a minute here. I can visualize the face, but I can't quite recall the name. In fact, when I think about it, I'm not even sure the face is right. Just one question for you, doc. Am I dying?"

"I told you, no. Now, what's your name?"

"Can I see the chart?"

"Your name."

"Black. Thomas Black."

"What do you do for a living?"

"I'm a private investigator."

"Where did you go to school?"

"Wilson High School in Tacoma and then a short stint at the University of Washington before they threw me out. I worked some odd jobs and got hired on with the police department. From there I became a private investigator. Am I getting any of these right?"

"You're doing fine. And where are you now?"

"Here. With you."

"Where is that?"

"Don't *you* know?"

"Can you answer my question?"

"My hospital room."

"Which hospital?"

"I forget."

"What's my name?"

"F.A.O. Swartz?"

"Close. It's Miranda Swartz."

"That's not fair, doc. You've had your whole life to learn your name, and you only just told me a few minutes ago."

"What city are we in?"

"Seattle."

"And what happened to put you in the hospital?"

"I'm not sure."

"We'll keep working on it, Mr. Black."

"I'm better at multiple choice."

"You're amusing, Mr. Black, but you're not well. I'm scheduling another MRI for late tomorrow. Do you have any questions I can answer for you?"

"Has my wife been visiting?"

The doctor stares at me as if wondering whether to answer the question truthfully. More than anything, I am afraid she's going to tell me my wife is dead—because others have told me that, although I cannot remember quite when—but apparently news of my wife's death is not what she's deliberating. "I'm not on the floor all that much during the day, so I couldn't say for sure."

"But you haven't seen her?"

"No."

"Or spoken to her?"

"No."

"Not since I was brought in?"

"No."

"Has she called?"

"Not that I'm aware of. Mr. Black, I see benchmarks of progress every time I come here. It may not seem like it to you, but you will get well. Will you have all the mental acuity you had before? Nobody can say. Most likely you will. And most likely there will be some short-term memory loss you'll never recover. For instance, the events leading up to your admission here. We'll just have to wait and see."

After she leaves, I still can't name the president or the vice president. I begin to think about my wife. I've been thinking Kathy is visiting in the middle of the night, but now I'm not so certain those weren't hallucinations. If my doctor hasn't met her, maybe she hasn't been here. If I can get my brain to work, I'll ask one of the nurses if my wife has been in.

SEVEN

TONIGHT IT'S A TUXEDO—not rented, either—with black dress shoes and a starched shirt with a bow tie. The first time she saw me in the tie Kathy told me it would look best alone. So far, we hadn't gotten around to testing it. Neither of us had the time or energy for that sort of fooling around. Nor was she in the mood to say anything quite that flirtatious tonight, not after our squabble. I bought the tux for the plethora of black-tie functions I would be attending during the campaign, money-raising dinners having become the staple of political life these days. I purchased two new suits, too, though after the elections I would probably never wear either again. Now, standing in front of the mirror in our living room, I felt like a spiffed-up monkey. All I needed was a tin cup to collect nickels.

"You look pretty spectacular, big guy," Kathy said as she emerged from the bedroom. "Too bad you're working for the dark side."

"You look great, too." She was wearing a sinfully slinky dress that I thought was lavender until she informed me it was cornflower blue, the same color as her eyes. Just a little tinge of color blindness going on there. Either way, I told her she looked terrific, and she truly did.

"Thanks," she said as I helped her on with her coat. We got into her car without speaking. We'd had one of our rare disagreements and were both trying to cool off before confronting seven or eight hundred people who expected us to be relentlessly cheerful.

Kathy ran a one-woman law office and specialized in criminal law, not a specialty that brought in a lot of money. This autumn she'd put most of her cases on hold so she could work on Jane Sheffield's senatorial reelection bid, and in one of those ironies that collide with real life, I found myself working for Sheffield's opponent, James Maddox. It was going to be a bone of contention between us until after the elections, perhaps even longer.

Kathy and I didn't bicker often, and when we did it was more in jest than for blood, but she was incensed that I was working for Maddox. Early in our relationship we forged a pact not to go to bed angry, established it as a firm rule, a rule that had prompted more than one make-up session stretching into the wee hours, the two of us dragging ourselves to work the next day, exhausted from conversation, satiated with make-up sex, and friends forevermore. Practically from the day we met and long before we were ever intimate, Kathy and I had been best friends, and we were bent on keeping it that way.

As luck would have it, when we walked into Bellevue's Meydenbauer Center, under the colored banners and balloons, past the smiling greeters, past the coat-check room, the first person we ran into was a colleague of mine from the Maddox headquarters. Deborah Driscoll was almost as tall as my six one, urbane, sophisticated, chatty when she needed to be, and apparently in a hurry, because she was bumping her way through the crowd. Already it was a huge crowd, and we'd just that moment wandered through the entrance, skimming the outskirts of the throng, when Deborah appeared out of nowhere.

Kathy spotted her first. "Hello, Deborah."

"Oh, good to see you, Thomas. And . . . ?"

"Kathy. My name is Kathy."

"Of course. I don't know why I always forget. My apology. I'll see you later, Thomas. I have . . . you know . . ." She shrugged at how busy she was and sank into a sea of suits as if by osmosis. She was wearing a poured-on emerald green sheath that revealed an astonishing amount of décolletage, displaying her wares as if she was out to prove something. I was struck by how tall she was next to Kathy.

When I turned around, Kathy said, "Finished ogling your friend?"

"What?"

"What what?"

"I was just daydreaming about something."

"Yeah, her ass."

"No, really—"

"Or her phony breasts. She had enough cleavage showing to use as a canvas for a mural of the winning of the West."

"Really? I didn't notice."

"And why is it that every time I run into her she pretends to forget my name?"

"She doesn't pretend to forget your—"

"If she's actually forgotten it, that's even worse. You realize she's a professional name rememberer. Have you ever known her to come up lame on anybody else's name?"

"Well, now that you . . ."

"I don't like it when people try to play mind games with me."

"Come on now, she's not that bad."

"Oh, but she is. Deb-oooo-raaah is every woman's worst nightmare."

"How so?"

"Tall, skinny, with tits like medicine balls. And, oh yeah, interested in my husband."

I was rescued by a loud commotion twenty feet in front of us, as a trio of women who apparently hadn't assembled in years greeted one another with squeals and hugging. When the hubbub died, Kathy turned back to me and said, "Also, it's a fact that something like ninety percent of redheads dye their hair."

"So we're going to go with statistics, now?"

"In her case, yes, I'll go with statistics."

"I don't think she dyes her hair."

"Oh, come on."

What I was really thinking was that her tits weren't like medicine balls, though they were close enough. Earlier when she walked away, every man she passed, including the gay guys, had done a double take. Kathy mistakenly assumed I was caught up in the testosterone rush, but I wasn't. Deborah Driscoll had worked for the James Maddox campaign since before it was a campaign, had been on Maddox's payroll in his private company for years now, billed as a public relations expert, though her duties extended far beyond any single title. She was a genius at public relations, having single-handedly reeled in some of the largest contributions in Maddox's campaign chest. These days the engine of modern politics ran on filthy lucre. If you could raise enough money, you could win, and if you could win, you could raise more money. Of course, money didn't buy votes . . . not exactly. Money bought TV ads, which were horrendously expensive and all too influential with a voting populace that got most of its information from fifteen-second spot ads, headlines, and hunches. The most effective TV ads slandered your opponent so that people who didn't keep up on the issues—which was almost everyone—viewed the ads and got scared to vote for a candidate because of . . . whatever. Forget about the facts. And now, with four weeks to go before the election, and Kathy's candidate, Jane Sheffield, holding an almost insurmountable lead in the polls, Maddox's TV ads were getting uglier and uglier.

Kathy had been working for the Sheffield campaign longer than I'd been working for Maddox, and with all her heart Kathy believed in what Sheffield stood for. The latest Maddox ads had prompted a robust session of bickering between us. I didn't approve of the ads and said as much to Maddox, but I was only a cog in the machine and nobody was about to give me veto power over them.

"You're over there working with those nitwits," Kathy said. "You're as responsible for what they're doing as anyone. Anybody with a whit of self-respect would have turned in his resignation a long time ago."

"You know I'm paying back a debt."

"And how about if he asked you to burn down a church? Would you do that, too, and claim you were paying off a debt?"

"He hasn't asked me to burn down a church."

"You consort with people who are committing moral crimes. Those ads are nothing but vicious lies. You're all guilty over there."

"I don't know why you're worried. Maddox doesn't stand a chance."

"It's the principle of the thing."

I don't need to go into the particulars of the ads. You've seen the type. They distorted Sheffield's voting record and attacked her on a personal level, mostly by implication, so that she couldn't directly counter the attacks without appearing to be the one who was lowering the level of discourse. It was a nasty season, and there wasn't an incumbent in the country who wasn't up against the same smear campaign. I didn't like it. In fact I didn't much like Maddox or his politics, but I owed him, and knowing Sheffield was unbeatable anyway, I'd taken the position Maddox offered in order to fulfill my obligation and be done with it—and hopefully with him. At the time I made the decision I'd thought Kathy and I were mature adults and could put aside politics when we had to, but apparently I was wrong.

The evening was a celebration of the governor's engagement to one of the dot-com billionaires Washington State seemed to produce as easily as we produced timber, mushrooms, apples, and airplanes. The gala wasn't directly related to the elections, but we were sure to run into major players on both sides, since the governor was a Democrat and her fiancé, oddly enough, was a staunch and active Republican. I didn't like parties this large, or any parties for that matter. You had to be good at blathering about nothing for hours on end to survive them, and my bullshit tolerance was too low for that. Kathy, who loved people in any and all formats, would luxuriate in every moment of it . . . except perhaps those spent with Deb-oooo-raaah.

For a while we hovered at the periphery of the gathering like two kids waiting for the other to jump into the lake and give a report on how cold the water was. Deborah Driscoll popped into view one more time, chatting with Sheffield, Kathy's candidate, laughing and making Sheffield laugh, too. It was a tribute to Sheffield's equanimity that she was able to socialize so calmly with one of Maddox's staffers. "She's stately, isn't she?" Kathy said.

Tracing Kathy's gaze, I said, "Sheffield? I guess." Sheffield was middle-aged and had never been stately by anybody's standards. She wore her hair choppy and had a plump figure political cartoonists made hay with. Tonight, clad in her usual gray business suit, she looked like a comptroller who'd wandered out onto the floor to get some information before going back to her booth to work a calculator.

"You know who I mean."

"You mean Deborah?"

"Don't you think she's attractive?"

"I thought we were talking about stately."

"Now I know why you like going to work so much."

"She doesn't dress like that in the office."

"No. But I bet you wish she did."

A pair of women bustled past as if on a mission. After they were out of earshot, I said, "You could sell the jewelry off some of these people and have more money than we'll see in our lifetimes."

"You could always work full-time for Maddox after the election. Then we'd be in the chips."

"I'm not going to work for Maddox after the election. Besides, I like being poor."

"We're not poor."

"We're not rich." Together we made enough to get by, but not enough for either of us to retire early or to embarrass ourselves by purchasing gobs of status symbols. We didn't have vacation houses or stock options or second vehicles. We had what we needed, and so far we were happy with that.

"He keeps asking, though, doesn't he? For you to work full-time? Or is it Deborah who keeps asking?"

"Deborah's not interested in hiring me full-time. She's not interested in me at all."

"She's not interested in you the way Exxon Mobil is not interested in black stuff under the sand."

"Well, I'm not interested. You know that."

"Women like her have a way of changing the minds of men like you. She wants you working for Maddox. I know that from past conversations. You know, those conversations in which she can't remember my name. I know this sounds petty, but I don't like you working with her."

"Okay, I'll tell Maddox it's either her or me, that my wife doesn't like her."

"Don't get too funny. You have a habit of getting too funny."

"When have I ever been too funny?"

"How about that charity thing on Queen Anne Hill? The crab dip?"

"What crab dip?"

"I don't believe for a minute you don't remember it."

It had been the earliest days of the campaign, when the political contestants were still friendly and eager to show their support for the same charitable cause. Library funding? Cancer research? I no longer remembered. Kathy and I were clowning around in the kitchen of the large mansion where the benefit was being held. Correction: I was clowning around, and Kathy was trying to get me to settle down. I spilled some crab dip on the black dress Kathy was wearing, and when we tried to get it off, the stain only got worse. We did our best to clean her up but when we emerged from the kitchen, the first person we ran into was Maddox, who couldn't help staring at the chalky stain on Kathy's breast. Kathy saw him staring and told him I'd done it while fooling around with her in the back room. Maddox got a funny look on his face and scurried away before she realized what he was thinking and could explain further. "Oh, my God," Kathy had said. "You don't suppose he thinks we had a Monica Lewinsky moment, do you?"

"Oh, I remember now," I said, pretending it was all coming back to me. "The crab dip."

"One of the single most embarrassing moments of my life."

"He didn't think what you thought he thought. He was just—"

"He most certainly did think what I thought he thought. He thought exactly what I thought he thought. I just want to know what you said to him earlier that would make him think we might go into the kitchen and have sex."

"I didn't say anything."

"He must think I'm an idiot."

"Stop worrying about what he thinks. And stop worrying about Deborah. I'm not the least bit interested in her. Or working for Maddox full-time. I'm interested in you only.

Besides, I could never meet Deborah's qualifications. She goes after guys who own banks, not guys who can't get loans from them."

"You might not have money, but judging by the way I've seen her sizing you up, you have everything else."

I must have given Kathy an "I do?" look, because she added, "Put your tongue back in your mouth."

"Why? Was I attracting flies?"

"No more than your normal number."

EIGHT

IT HAD BEEN a tough autumn for Kathy and me, each of us putting in twelve- and fourteen-hour days. Lately we could count the waking hours we spent together on the fingers of one hand. I'd been put on the Maddox payroll and thus was able to drop most of my other work until after the election, whereas Kathy was volunteering and trying to keep up with her law practice as well. The Sheffield folks had offered to put her on salary until the election, but out of some misplaced sense of volunteerism, she refused, which only increased her resentment over the fact that I'd accepted wampum. "Resentment is like swallowing poison and hoping the other person dies," I said.

"Yeah, well, consider it swallowed."

"Kathy . . ."

"You're working against your own best interests. Everything he stands for means less for the little guy. And in case you haven't noticed, you're one of the little guys."

I couldn't have been less of a political thinker, and on a list of priorities, I generally relegated politics right below cleaning the lint out of my underwear drawer. I left the groupthink projects to people who didn't wither from boredom in meetings the way I did. "I'm just working off a personal debt."

"Wrong way to do it."

Jane Sheffield was a two-term incumbent senator with a solid record of championing progressive causes, a woman who'd gotten big business angry with her so many times that last spring the CEO of one of the country's largest oil companies publicly denounced her as the biggest traitor to this country since Ethel Rosenberg. As fatuous as it was, the accusation continued to garner news coverage, mostly in the national media, while the local media, as well as the local populace, supported Sheffield in the way they supported the local ball teams. She was one of us. She spoke for us. We loved her.

Sheffield began her working life as a grade school teacher. From there she moved on to become a high school Spanish teacher, librarian, principal, councilperson for the city of Tacoma, representative in the Washington State legislature, and currently U.S. senator. For weeks she had been running fifteen and twenty points ahead of Maddox in the polls in her reelection campaign.

James Maddox started out as a police officer on the streets of Seattle before working his way up to a deputy chief, and later the appointed head of the Washington State Patrol. After several years of running that agency, he entered politics and ran for congressman, serving two terms in D.C.

There were multiple differences between the candidates, but if I had to put it in a nutshell, I would say Maddox stood for economic growth and corporate freedom while Sheffield worked indefatigably for ordinary citizens. Maddox had big money backing him, as opposed to the thousands of small contributors who supported Sheffield. If prompted, Kathy would lay out a more elaborate catalog of differences, emphasizing Sheffield's championing of veterans' rights and the working and nonworking poor, as well as health care for all. She would contrast that with Maddox's emphasis on smaller government and lower taxes at the expense of social services.

It was interesting to watch the two candidates work the room: Maddox, silver-haired, immaculately coifed and dressed, shaking hands, making small talk, and patting people on the back. On the other side of the room, the much shorter Sheffield kept vanishing into the crowd like a swimmer disappearing in the whitecaps. She was her normal serious self, her gray mop of hair flopping as she spoke. Even in social settings she refused to relax for a minute and talked constantly about the issues the country was facing. Maddox avoided shoptalk when he worked crowds, but that was all Sheffield did. She'd been known to pull out her cellphone and call a federal department to rectify an injustice moments after somebody brought it to her attention. Some said about Maddox that you didn't have to worry about getting stabbed in the back, because he would gladly stab you in the chest. Others called him forthright.

Ten minutes later I was alone when a man in a white tuxedo approached: Kalpesh Gupta, a second-generation American of East Indian extraction who worked with Kathy on the Sheffield campaign. He was a remarkably handsome man, his dark skin set off by his flashing teeth, white tux, and regal blue bow tie. I shook his hand, remembering he liked to squeeze hard on the off chance that I might have a broken bone. I'd been caught off guard at previous meetings, but tonight I gave back more than I got and was pleased to see him wince.

"Hey, Thomas," Kalpesh said. "Kathy around?"

"She's here somewhere."

"I was just with Jane. She's not over there."

"I'm supposed to meet her at the south exit in two hours. I'm headed there now. You're welcome to wait with me."

Kalpesh knew I was joking and gave me an impish look. Kalpesh liked a good joke, or better yet, a bad one, and almost always recognized when I was joshing. There were already too many people who failed to discern what Kathy called my "dry wit." I'd learned a long time ago that when somebody said you had a dry wit, it meant they didn't think you were funny, and anyway I'm pretty sure Kathy actually meant "juvenile humor" and was trying to be kind. "Is that what you're doing? Waiting until it's time to go?"

"Yeah."

"You two just get here?" he asked.

"Basically. You?"

"I came early with Jane and some others. She wanted to have a chat with the governor before everything got rolling." It was hard to know if he'd thrown the tidbit about the governor out as some sort of bait that I would take back to the wolf den to poison the rest of the pups with. Since Jane Sheffield and the governor were both Democrats, the alliance was natural. But it would not please Maddox to think that the governor was conspiring with his opponent. Surely, Kalpesh knew I would spread the news. "Lotta beautiful women here tonight," he added.

"I've just seen the one."

"Kathy?"

"Right."

"You are a good husband. I'll have to take notes for when I get married."

"Like you need any help with women."

"I wonder what the governor is going to do with all the money she'll have after the wedding."

"They probably have a pre-nup."

"I heard they don't. Makes you wonder what it would be like to all of a sudden be worth a couple of billion dollars, doesn't it? You think he'd be interested in her if she wasn't the governor?"

"I don't know. You think she'd be interested in him if he wasn't worth a couple of billion?"

Kalpesh was too handsome, especially considering he worked so closely with my wife, but I couldn't help liking him. He did all the man-boy things that I did: watched old cowboy movies, told fart jokes, participated in endurance sports with varying degrees of success—triathlons in his case, having been a distance runner in college and a cyclist more recently. We kept talking about doing a bicycle ride together, but I noticed we both talked about it as if it was never going to happen. The only things I didn't like about him were the foul-smelling cigars he sometimes smoked and the fact that his name came up a little too frequently at home.

Kalpesh was single and had courted dozens of beautiful women over the years, breaking hearts wherever he went. He'd graduated from Harvard and, for the past five years, worked in Washington, D.C. Before that he'd traveled to South America and later toured Africa. He'd lived in Europe and spent a year in Asia. He spoke four languages and could get by in three others. Me? I spoke bad high school Spanish and didn't own a passport, but on the plus side, I could spit a cherry pit over twenty feet.

Before we could work ourselves into more manly discourse, we were joined by Deborah Driscoll. I noticed a blue-green jewel on a pendant that I hadn't seen before, bobbing in and out of her plunging neckline, as if to entice me to look in there. I resisted the best I could.

Deborah and Kalpesh had a routine and they fell into it immediately, she greeting him in French and he returning the greeting, both aware the exchange was completely incomprehensible to me. They laughed and flirted, and for a few moments it was as if I wasn't there. I made a move to slip away, but without taking her eyes off Kalpesh, Deborah took hold of my sleeve, saying, "Now, don't you be going anywhere, smarty pants. I want to talk to you." Then she addressed Kalpesh: "Why don't you come over and work for us? I don't know why you want to work for that BHL." Kalpesh laughed.

BHL meant "bleeding heart liberal," and was a phrase Maddox and his staff used every day. It irked me for many reasons, not the least of which was that the label applied to me and it certainly applied to Kathy. Deborah Driscoll asking Kalpesh Gupta to switch sides was funny to all three of us. In the latest ABC poll Maddox trailed Sheffield by nineteen and a half points, so switching to the losing side at this juncture would have been just short of political suicide. Unless something very odd took place in the interim, in five weeks Sheffield was going to annihilate Maddox in voting booths across this state, which was precisely what everybody had been predicting since before he filed. It was one of the reasons I'd felt safe in taking the job. Had joining the Maddox campaign been the tipping point, I would have thought long and hard about it, but I wasn't going to tip anything. Maddox was running a doomed campaign. Asking Kalpesh to switch sides was like asking General Grant to join the Confederacy during the final days of the Civil War.

"You people never give up, do you?" Kalpesh said, smiling at Deborah before turning to me for the first time since she popped out of the crowd. When she looked at me as well, I caught him taking advantage of her inattention to take a gander at her chest.

"I'm serious," Deborah said, pressing her point with Kalpesh. "If you come over now and we win, it'll look like a stroke of genius. Wait until after we've won and you'll just be another jobless politico looking for work."

"This all presupposes you people are going to win. You are *not* going to win."

"Nobody has counted a ballot yet, have they, Thomas?"

"The counting doesn't start until later," I conceded.

"In the unlikely event we lose, you can go back to Sheffield with some sob story and get your old job back."

"Jane asks for many things, but most of all she asks for loyalty. I assure you I would not get my old job back."

"Listen to you," said Deborah, "talking about getting your job back. You've already crossed out of the I-would-never-do-it category into the how-will-we-work-it category. Now you're talking tactics. You want to do it or you wouldn't be talking tactics."

"I am sorry," Kalpesh said. "But Maddox represents everything my convictions say is wrong with modern politics. Jane Sheffield represents everything right about them."

"Oh, come on now," Deborah said. "Nobody in this business could possibly be that idealistic."

"I am," Kalpesh said.

"I'm serious about the offer," Deborah said as he walked away. Turning to me, she smoothed one of my lapels with her palm and said, "He'd be great in our office."

"Sure, but he's not going to jump ship."

"Care to bet on it?"

I stood back and looked into Deborah's eyes. "You think you can accomplish anything, don't you?"

"Yes, I do."

"You really think Maddox is going to win?"

"You know I think he's going to win."

"But we're losing."

"Only if we think like losers."

"I'm glad you and Maddox are so confident. I'm not, but then I don't count much in the grand scheme of things."

"*Au contraire,* Thomas. You bring a refreshing voice to our discussions. We enjoy your take on things. But elections can turn on a dime. And one never knows when that dime is going to drop."

For weeks I'd had the feeling Deborah and Maddox and maybe one or two others knew something I didn't: that Jane Sheffield had had a torrid affair and it would be exposed, or they had film of her shoplifting skin-care products from

Nordstrom. Whenever I asked Maddox, he denied it. "Sure, we're confident," he said. "But it's about winning. Winners never let their guard down. You can learn from this, Thomas."

"What did you want to talk to me about?" I asked Deborah.

"I meant to catch you during the week, but we've all been busy. You worked with Maddox years ago in the Seattle Police Department. The thing is, we've been trying to get an endorsement from anybody in the department but so far haven't had any luck. He *was* popular as a policeman, wasn't he?"

"Maddox was a square peg in a round hole."

"That's not how he presents it."

"I'm not sure he ever knew."

NINE

"**IN THE NEXT FEW WEEKS** this campaign is going to heat up, and what we don't need is surprises. For whatever reasons, he's not willing to tell me much about his career in the police department, so maybe you'll tell me exactly how he was a square peg. You know him from that period, and you obviously had a good rapport or you wouldn't be here now."

"We didn't really cross paths until the end of my career when he did me a small favor."

"It must not have been too small."

"Small to him. Big to me. As far as I know he didn't have any friends in the department. When he was working for SPD, he went into the hospital for heart surgery. I had a friend who had to take him some official paperwork to sign, and at the time Maddox told him not one member from the department visited him during the five days he was there. He was a guy who was basically insulated from everyone around him. But here's the funny part. He loved to run for office. Union rep. Union secretary. Anything that was up for grabs. He repeatedly set himself up so people could vote against him."

"I like how your mind works," Deborah said, switching the conversation abruptly from Maddox to the two of us. Her look lasted just long enough to make me uncomfortable, and when I get uncomfortable I drop my eyes. Without realizing it, my glance dropped to her breasts, and when I looked up I could see she'd misinterpreted my gaze. "What was Maddox like on the job?" she asked, smiling.

"A lot like he is now. Cool. Efficient."

"He talks like he was a tough police officer."

"On the street there's two kinds of tough. There's the kind when you're running down a dark alley chasing a half-crazed wife beater you know has a weapon, and there's the other kind. I never saw it, but I heard stories about his bullying hand-cuffed suspects."

"What else? Bear in mind I would never repeat any of this." Deborah was probing for parts of Maddox's story she didn't need to know, but there was no harm in sharing it with her. Gossip cements a bond between people. Tonight I was becoming an insider.

"The worst thing I ever heard about Maddox involved a shoot-out he and a partner had in which they went into a sup-posedly vacant house in the Rainier Valley to do a welfare check. Maddox and his partner walked in on a burglary. Shots were exchanged. Maddox's partner got shot several times, superficial wounds, but was able to describe both burglars to a T; Maddox, on the other hand, wasn't hit and could not de-scribe the assailants. Afterward, his partner accused Maddox of cowering behind a door during the shoot-out. I don't know what actually happened, but Maddox claimed he'd fired mul-tiple times, that he'd been in the thick of it, and that his part-ner was simply too excitable and unprofessional to accurately remember what happened. But then the department did its investigation and discovered Maddox's service pistol hadn't been fired. In the police department, a story like that sticks like flypaper. I heard it dozens of times. Eventually, Maddox took a desk job and worked his way up through the ranks without going back on the street. Later, when he found him-self in charge of officers who *were* on patrol, he made a habit of refusing to cut malefactors any slack. As you might imag-ine, none of this earned him any friends."

"But you were his friend?"

"I knew him."

In the middle of my tale, we had each been given a small plate of hors d'oeuvres by a passing caterer. I must have spilled some of the dip on my chin, because Deborah stepped close and wiped my lower lip with her napkin, making an elaborate production of dabbing at my face. I laughed, and looking out at the crowd, caught a glimpse of Kathy watch-ing us through about six layers of people. I waved, but the crowd sealed itself before I could tell if she saw me. Drat. Ordinarily, it would have meant nothing, but tonight things between us were strained.

A moment later, a heavyset woman accompanied by a grumpy-looking man approached us, the woman smiling broadly.

"Letha," I said, holding my arms out. "Letha Fontaine." We hugged and then stood back and looked at each other. She smelled of lavender.

"Thomas Black. How have you been?"

"Terrific. Really terrific."

Letha had entered the Seattle Police Department in the same academy class I had, and for a time we'd carpooled to class. In her first year on the street, she had three serious automobile accidents in her patrol car, after which she worked in administration in clerical positions. People like Letha tended to find a niche and hide out in it. The last I'd heard, she was pushing paper in the dispatch center.

"I want to hear all about you," Letha said. "Don't leave anything out."

"You first."

"I'm doing the same thing I was doing when you left. Dispatch. Hey. I'm sorry about how things went down when you left. I never had a chance to talk to you about that."

"Water under the bridge."

"Seems like yesterday, though. You look terrific. Somebody told me you got married. Is this your wife?"

The comment was Deborah's signal to blush, but she didn't. Instead she gave me a look that I couldn't quite figure out. It was almost as if she was trying to see if I was embarrassed. "No. My wife is out there somewhere. This is Deborah Driscoll, a co-worker."

After they chatted a bit, Letha turned back to me. "I heard your wife was a defense attorney."

"Right now she's working on the Sheffield campaign as well."

"I think Sheffield's great."

"Isn't she?" I said, watching Deborah try on a smile.

"Tell me exactly what you've been doing. I want to hear everything."

"I don't want to bore these people."

"No," Deborah said. "I want to be bored."

"I don't mind," said Letha's companion.

"Sure. Okay. There's not much. I left the police department and for about a year I worked for a private investigator, also a former officer with Seattle. Then I opened a small office. Times were lean for a while, but lately I've been passing up more work than I accept. Unfortunately, a lot of it is just mining information through the Internet. I also do interviews for defense attorneys and for insurance companies, mostly fraud and theft, some accident investigations. I still do a lot of biking. Right now I'm working for the Maddox campaign."

"They have a problem? A break-in or something?"

"I'm on staff."

"But I thought you said your wife—"

"Is working for Sheffield. I'm working for Maddox. I'm glad you caught that."

"Gee, isn't that . . . ?"

"We hardly fight over it. When it gets real bad, after dinner sometimes we load pistols in the backyard and let fly until one of us draws blood."

Letha laughed so loudly people around us turned and stared. Years ago she'd had a crush on me and had always found me amusing. What I liked about Letha was that even in her darkest moments, she was relentlessly cheerful. "The last time I saw you, you were going out with that Russian."

It was my turn to laugh. "I forgot. That was a long time ago."

"So how'd you and your wife meet?"

"Kathy and I took a law class together back when I was still in the department. Criminal Justice. The professor had obsessive-compulsive disorder or something, so he seated us all in alphabetical order. Birchfield, Black. Over the course of the semester my renter moved out and Kathy started renting my basement apartment. Things went on from there."

"Darn. I should have snagged you when I had the chance."

"Should have."

"Still live in that same old place?"

"Right. The dump over on Roosevelt."

"It was never a dump. It was just—"

"I keep meaning to fix it up, but we're so busy. Besides, it gives the street character. Helps keep prices down so ordinary folk can move into the neighborhood."

"You still have that old couch on the front porch?"

"Uh, no."

"And that old truck? I remember you always drove the oldest, most beat-up truck around."

"It got wrecked."

We nattered for a few more minutes before Letha Fontaine and her date ambled off toward the refreshments.

Deborah turned to me and said, "You had a Russian girlfriend?"

"Uh, yeah."

"What was she like?"

"You know. The normal. She could tow a railroad car with her teeth. Used to kiss me and afterward my face would be all black and blue. Weighed about three hundred pounds."

Deborah laughed. "You're never serious, are you?"

"I was just trying to draw a picture for you."

"What was that she was saying about the way you left the department?"

At the best of times, I didn't like talking about this, but especially here, among all this jabbering. I told her the story quickly. How a fifteen-year-old kid in a stolen car had trapped me on foot in a Belltown alley and how I drew my service pistol and fired a round through the windshield when he tried to run me down. How he died.

"I'm assuming you were exonerated."

"I was, but it didn't make me feel any better. He'd be in his late twenties now. He probably would have gotten his life straightened out." We thought about it for a moment while the party began to boil up around us. More people crowded into the hall and the noise level became frightening. Off in one corner a band began testing sound equipment.

"I didn't know you rode a bike," she said.

"When I'm in shape and have time."

"I used to race. Back at Wellesley after I hurt my knee fencing. I have a carbon-fiber bike. Small world, isn't it?"

"We'll have to ride sometime. I didn't know you went to Wellesley. What else do I not know about you?"

"Want the whole résumé?"

I nodded.

"Take notes because I'm not going to repeat any of this. I was a straight-A student all through high school. I ran cross-country and played tennis. I took up fencing at Wellesley because I was having knee problems running. Unfortunately, the knee problems worsened in college. That's when I turned to biking. Early in my junior year of high school I discovered boys, or to be more specific, boys discovered me. Until then, I'd been a tall, gawky girl in thick glasses and braces, but contact lenses and straight teeth did wonders for my social life. Somewhere around Christmas, my mother leafed through my diary and decided I had become promiscuous. Just for the record, I was not by any stretch of the imagination what you would call promiscuous. Still, I suppose by my mother's standards . . . We lived in Vermont, and nearby there just happened to be an all-girls prep school. After Christmas, I was trucked off to the school like so much dirty laundry. I guess they were hoping I would come back a virgin. Am I making you uncomfortable?"

"Not at all." But of course, she was. Any time a married man stood around a party talking with a woman on a topic that needed to be discontinued the instant somebody else walked up, he was flirting with trouble. She was trying to make me uncomfortable.

"Ironically, there was a boys' school close by where, in the backseat of many a car, I in fact did experience everything my parents were trying to shield me from and probably a good deal more. My parents were both doctors, so money was not a problem and I knew my college tuition had been put aside long before I was born, but in my senior year our English teacher asked some of us to submit essays to *Seventeen*. First prize was a four-year scholarship. I wrote about presidential powers and won.

"I went to Wellesley, where, believe it or not, I started off as an archaeology major. I switched to art and then English before I found public relations. I had an affair with one of my professors, thinking it was something you were supposed to do. He got fired over it, which I still feel bad about, and ended up teaching community college somewhere in Arizona. My name stayed out of the headlines, but he left school in a blaze of infamy. God knows what sort of Freudian scenarios I was working through. I continued to distinguish myself in academics, which had always been easy for me, and graduated with a minor in psychology. I went to graduate school at Yale. After I got my master's, I went to New York, where I worked in an advertising agency and met my first husband, Frederick. Three years later our marriage unraveled when he had a series of affairs. After the divorce, in a friend's hot tub, I met the man who would become my second husband. Curiously, a year later, in that same hot tub, we had the argument that was the beginning of the unraveling of our marriage. Dan couldn't stand the fact that the water was too hot for me and that I had to keep standing up to cool off. After that divorce, I moved to Washington, D.C., and got a job in the State Department. A year later I was recruited by one of Maddox's people to work in the international security firm he started. I've been with him five years, and now I'm working on his campaign."

Out of nowhere, Kathy joined us in time to overhear the last part of Deborah's bio. "Gotta go," Deborah said, nodding to Kathy as she left. "Sorry we couldn't talk, Katie."

After she was gone, I said, "Why would her husband get in a fight with her because she was standing up in the hot tub?"

"Think about it."

"I already thought about it."

"They were nude, dear."

"Oh."

"She was standing nude in somebody's face, probably some drooling male who wasn't her husband."

Having Kathy solve the mystery made me feel even more stupid than normal. "I thought you had to circulate."

"I *did* circulate. I came back to save you. It's a woman's thing, honey. And I know what you're thinking. It *is* dyed and those aren't her real breasts."

"No, I wasn't thinking that at all. I was thinking she called you Katie."

"Don't worry. She can't get my goat. I'm willing to wager that the whole monologue she gave you was salted with sexual innuendo. Let me guess. Her first experience with a boy. Lesbian experiments with roommates. All the titillating details of her sexual past disguised as her life story? Tell me that's not what she did, because I wouldn't want to think that while I was over there working, she was over here turning your brain to mush. Tell me that didn't happen."

"Of course it didn't."

TEN

I HEARD SOMEBODY PICKING THE LOCK before I saw the shadow of a man in a cowboy hat crouching on my front porch, his steel picks gnawing at the brass locks. The thought of a home invasion frightened a lot of people, but my experience in the Seattle Police Department told me most bad guys broke into homes they knew were empty.

He'd been knocking for some time, at both the front and back doors, had even tapped at the side windows along the driveway like a drunk locked out of a party. Now, while he fiddled with the locks, the streetlight threw his shadow on the window next to the front door. He unlocked the doorknob lock with little trouble but had to slave away at the dead bolt for several minutes before sliding the bolt. Weaponless, I sat in the dark and watched him pick his way into my haven. I was in a stupor, drugged on my own feelings, or lack of same, too enervated, careworn, and just generally whipped to answer the door, to tell him to go away, or to fight him off. I'd been alone for days. Maybe I wanted the company. I was watching *Groundhog Day,* my fifth viewing in succession.

When the front door inched open, he had a gun in his hand. It was early evening, autumn, and the only light in the room was radiating out of the television like a small sun from behind a cloud. I froze the picture as Bill Murray and the groundhog drove the mayor's pickup truck off a bluff to their conjoined deaths. "Hurry up and get in here. I'm trying to watch Bill Murray kill himself."

The rim of his cowboy hat edged around the door. "It's me. Don't shoot. It's your old friend Snake Slezak."

"You're the one with the gun."

"You didn't answer, so I . . ."

"Broke in? You used to be faster working a lock."

"You got a new dead bolt. The new ones are hard."

"It's got six tumblers. They told me nobody could open it."

"How the hell do you expect any visitors if you keep getting new locks?"

"Most of my visitors don't pick the lock."

"I've been phoning for a couple of days. You never answer."

"That's right. I don't."

I pushed a button on the remote and watched Bill Murray and the groundhog crash their stolen pickup truck and burst into flame. I laughed a loud and wicked laugh.

"Thomas, are you okay?"

"Fit as a fiddle."

Same as me, Elmer Slezak made a living as a private investigator. We'd worked together before, but in the main, our business dealings did not intertwine. We'd been friends for years, and while I didn't subscribe to all of his tactics, he'd taught me valuable lessons about interview technique, and he kept up on the latest electronic gadgetry. I tried to live by a strict moral code and rarely violated my principles, yet there were two people on the planet who knew enough about my past that they could get me tried for murder. One of those was Kathy and the other was Elmer Slezak. While I didn't think I deserved a prison sentence and neither did either of them, going by the letter of the law, and given a strict judge, a bumbling defense attorney, and a typical jury addlepated from too much television, it was not unthinkable that I could receive a quick trial and a long sentence. I knew an equal number of secrets about Elmer, though none as dramatic, and had shared a few of what I considered to be the funnier ones with my wife, which was probably the reason Kathy regarded our friendship with distrust.

While I fed my indolence with the electronic ether, I was vaguely aware that Snake had begun touring the house like a strange dog who'd been let in by accident. He deposited a sheaf of papers next to my feet on the end of the couch and continued to clomp around in his high-heeled cowboy boots, sniffing through the house as if I'd hidden a ten-dollar hooker somewhere.

The home I'd shared with Kathy for the past several years was a one-story grandma-style house with two bedrooms, an overlarge old-fashioned kitchen with a bay window looking out onto our driveway, and a daylight basement that had been turned into a mother-in-law apartment we rented out to an engineering student from the University of Washington. Though remodeled and updated, it was the same basement Kathy had rented from me.

I was aware that the place was a mess and that I hadn't showered in days, that I was wearing pajama bottoms, grungy socks, and an old sweatshirt speckled with pinpoint holes and traces of my last meal. My hair was matted and my face felt as if I'd been eating greasy chicken wings for three days.

Snake caught me sniffing one of my armpits as he came back and stood in the doorway. "Mind if I disarm?"

"You planning to stay?"

"I'd like to sit down, but I can't do it with all this metal on me."

"Disarm."

"We were worried about you."

"Who's we?"

"Everybody. The pope. The vice president of the United States. Really. He called the Maddox headquarters to ask after you."

"The vice president is a moron."

"I see you're in a good mood." He laid three revolvers on the coffee table in front of the sofa. I knew he still had at least one weapon somewhere on his person, because Snake never disarmed completely, not if he could help it. He probably had a derringer behind the silver world championship bull-riding belt buckle he was never without.

Snake and I were a study in contrasts. He was small and wiry, what some would call scrawny, and as close to a true paranoid as you could get outside of a straitjacket, while I was optimistic and living a life that was, until recently, filled with sunshine. Where he looked for flaws, I saw the good in people. I was tall and angular, well muscled from pumping iron in my makeshift weight room in the garage. I had never seen Snake strip down to anything less than the long underwear he wore all year; when Kathy saw him in the underwear she said he looked like a dead chicken in a laundry sack. I had a history of amateur athletics and spent my spare time with friends or reading at home, while he had a history of bull riding, cigarettes, alcohol, wild women, and homegrown cannabis. I was a lifelong teetotaler, while he had been a drunk until a couple of years ago. He cursed like a longshoreman and believed in armament "in case he needed to shoot somebody on short notice." He carried as many guns as he could conceal on his person, while I no longer carried anything more lethal than a fountain pen. Despite our differences, we did a lot of laughing together, sometimes too much.

As he settled onto the sofa and propped his cowboy boots on the coffee table, he let out a couple of grunts that were more bovine than human. He knew Kathy didn't want his boots on the table. I said nothing. "You been home all week?" he asked.

"Far as I remember."

"Having trouble with your memory?"

"Not that I recall."

"Probably a lot of things you'd rather forget."

"A few."

"I *have* been calling."

"Lot of people been calling."

"You going to keep watching that damn movie all night?"

"It's on some sort of psychotropic loop. I can't seem to get away from it."

"Mind if I watch with you?"

I shrugged.

We hadn't been together very long when Snake spotted my collection of movies neatly cataloged in a bookcase, along with about four hundred books. "Hey. You've got *Last of the Mohicans*. Mind if we watch that?"

"Help yourself."

He inserted the Michael Mann flick. "You don't mind, do you?"

"I already know how this one turns out."

While he tinkered with my player, I glanced at the stack of newspaper clippings and computer-generated news reports he'd brought. For the first time in days I felt like reaching out

with a purpose. The top article had caught my eye: STILL NO
CLUES IN SHEFFIELD'S DEATH. EIGHT PIECES OF WRECKAGE RE-
TRIEVED. I didn't know whether it was my inertia or my un-
willingness to show somebody else how totally at sea I was
with regard to the news of the world, but I did not budge.

After the opening credits began, Snake said, "You been sitting here in the dark all week?"

"It hasn't been a week, has it?"

"Prett'n near. Been eating?"

"Dinner last night. Or the night before."

"I'll fix you something later. You don't mind if I stay the
night, do you?"

"You got an angry husband on your tail?"

"I haven't had anything like that happen in . . . and that
Heatherton woman don't count. She told me she was sepa-
rated."

"Wasn't she the one with the glass eye?"

"You got a memory for other people's infirmities. Thanks
for coming to pick me up that night."

"What's going on tonight?"

"They're fumigating my building. Cockroaches. They say
it's all right to stay there, but I'm thinking I need to be gone
for at least twenty-four hours."

"I don't mind, but I'm keeping pretty erratic hours."

"I'm just glad to have a roof over my head."

We watched the movie for a few minutes. I knew there was
no cockroach-spraying program at his apartment house. He'd
come to check on me and was going to hang around until he
was certain I wouldn't kill myself. It suddenly occurred to me
that I'd been hypnotized by a movie in which Bill Murray
killed himself dozens of times, that I'd been watching it for
days on end. Was I exploring the possibility of my own suicide? Or was I indulging in somebody else's misery to put my
own into perspective? Or was Bill Murray's conversion what
interested me? I'd never been in a blacker mood, had never had
so many things in my life go so wrong in such a short span.

"You been keeping up with the news?" Snake asked.

"Not really."

"I brought you some clippings from *The New York Times,*

The Wall Street Journal. There's a few from *The Seattle Times* and the *Post-Intelligencer,* too." When he realized I wasn't going to respond, he added, "So how are you doing? Really."

"Ducky."

"Don't bullshit me. You look like you been dragged through a pig farm behind a leaky rendering truck. That kitchen looks like there was a food fight. But hey, it's only natural. I mean, it might take a year just to assimilate what happened. And hell, it's been what? A week? You want the truth, if what happened to you happened to me, I'd go back to the baby."

"Heroin?"

"Or hard liquor. Probably both. I can't say I know how you feel, because I never had anybody like Kathy to lose. Nobody even close to her caliber. But I'm here for you, man. I'm here for you."

"Thanks."

"No, really. Anything you want, I'll do it." He picked up a .44 Magnum off the coffee table and waved it at the television. I wasn't sure if he was trying to be funny or if he actually meant he was prepared to shoot me in the event I wanted to die and didn't have the guts to pull the trigger myself. Given the right circumstances, I had no doubt Elmer would shoot almost anybody—nobody hauled around that many guns without a secret hankering to use them. But then, there were other ways to kill myself. The fact that I could think of three of them right off the top of my head told me suicide had been closer to the surface than I realized. Maybe it was a good thing Snake had showed up.

"You mind putting the gun down?"

"Kathy never did like me, did she?"

"She liked you."

"You don't have to be making excuses. It doesn't bother me that she thought I was a scoundrel. I *am* a scoundrel. And Kathy was sweet. It's only natural she would be repulsed by me."

"She was never re—"

"In a funny way, I believe what caused the whole issue between her and me was she thought if you hung around me long enough, I would corrupt your ethics. There was never any chance I would corrupt your ethics. If anything, it was the other way around. You make me a better person. You really do, Thomas."

We watched the movie. After a while, I nodded off. It had been some time since I'd slept more than a couple of hours at a stretch, and my nervous system was in a netherworld. When I woke up, Snake was still engrossed in the saga of Hawkeye. I tried not to stare at the pile of newspaper clippings.

══ ELEVEN ══

LYING IN THE HOSPITAL BED has become a form of torture. Tonight I'm feeling a dull pain where the metal spike pierced me.

The inability to remember is my personal inquisition, a thousand images teasing me over the agony of a fractured past and a future as blank as the sky. I struggle trying to recall what's happened in my life. I wrestle with disjointed images, some bloody, all confusing. I trap half-remembered scraps of conversation and then drift back to sleep. At times somebody is in the room with me when I awaken. More often I am alone. Rarely am I alert enough to engage in a conversation.

So far I'd seen a doctor, two nurses—maybe three—Elmer Slezak, Kathy, and a redhead whose name I cannot recall without putting more effort into it than I'm able to exert just now. What worries me most is Kathy's sporadic appearances. Something is wrong, but I don't know what. If our positions were reversed, I wouldn't leave her side for a minute.

Is she failing to visit because she's not able? Or is it possible her infrequent visits have all been in my fevered, drug-addled imagination and she hasn't been here at all? I'm beginning to suspect not everything I'm remembering is going to make sense when I come out of this. Once begun, my thoughts are incapable of shifting directions. I worry until I fall asleep, which is not long at all.

Over the past weeks I've been hard on Kathy. Sure, she was irritated with me, too, stumped by my participation in the Maddox campaign. I had my excuses, but excuses were like . . . well, we all know the end of that soliloquy.

The governor's engagement party had been the worst.

I'd behaved abominably.

*   *   *

"IT'S NOT LIKE you don't have your own Deborah in the Sheffield office," I said, fingering my bow tie.

Kathy and I had just broken off a conversation with two couples from the Tri-Cities, a pair of mayors and spouses, and now the foursome was wandering off to join a group that included Kalpesh Gupta. "Who?" Kathy asked, turning to me. "Who could we possibly have in our office who's anything like that succubus?"

"Oh. Now she's a succubus?"

"Look it up."

"I know what a succubus is. A female demon who has sex with sleeping men. Your counterpart would be Kalpesh Gupta."

Her look was incredulous.

"Come on now," I said. "You know he's the male equivalent of Deborah Driscoll."

"Kalpesh is not a femme fatale."

"No, he's a *male* fatale. He uses his masculinity and looks in the same way Deborah uses her feminine wiles. And what's with all the hugging every time you two meet?"

"You're not going to complain about that, are you?"

"He hugs way too long."

"Kalpesh is a very expressive individual."

"He didn't give *me* a hug."

"Did you want a hug from him?"

"I do, but he's not going to do it because I don't have breasts to feel up."

"No, you ogle breasts."

"My eyes accidentally strayed. It could have happened to anybody."

We chewed on that for a few minutes as we made our way through a sea of tuxedos and evening gowns. We spoke with several groups I'd met while on the campaign trail and then with some whom Kathy had met traveling with Sheffield. We ran into a group Kathy knew from the courthouse. Insider jokes were exchanged; I understood about half of them. Ordinarily, Kathy would have explained the rest, but not tonight.

When we were finally alone again, I said, "Kalpesh is from India, isn't he?"

"His parents are. He was born here, but he goes back occasionally."

"I read an article where they did a study and found over fifty percent of Indian men are too small for normal-sized condoms." I let that sit between us for a moment, hoping it would fester, but once again Kathy demonstrated her knack for allowing me just enough rope to hang myself. The cacophony in the room was growing more noticeable by the minute, so I had to speak louder. "Apparently, they have these little tiny dicks," I yelled. When Kathy still didn't respond, I added, "They must be losing rubbers like crazy. Be like a kid trying to run around in his dad's hip waders." I couldn't help bursting into laughter. The thought of condoms falling off half a billion undersized dicks did something to my funny bone. Not that there was anything wrong with people who were, on average, smaller than most American males in that department. Still, I couldn't stop laughing.

"Thomas," Kathy said, solemnly. "Be careful where you're going with this."

"Hey, I didn't make this up. It was an AP report. Half of Indian men don't fit a normal-sized prophylactic. No wonder they have a population problem. I'm thinking there's a business opportunity here. You have half a continent that needs a product nobody has had the foresight to produce: tiny little condoms. The company that markets these in an intelligent and nonoffensive way is going to make millions."

"I'm glad you're thinking about all this in a nonoffensive way."

"Right, because I'm not insensitive to the shortcomings of others. And I use the term *shortcomings* loosely. The main problem is what are we going to call them? They're going to be about half the size of a normal condom. I've got it. Why not 'Half Pints'?"

The thought propelled me into another round of laughter. The notion that Kalpesh might have a dick the size of a child's thumb somehow seemed the most hilarious thing I'd ever heard. I knew there was nothing romantic going on between him and Kathy, that there never would be, just as I knew he was incredibly handsome and devilishly charming and that as long as he was breathing he would continue to ply his wares on every female in his vicinity. My laughter continued for what I admit was probably too long, after which I dabbed at my tears with the back of one wrist. Kathy had not cracked a smile, but even if she thought something was funny, and I could see she thought this was, she could always maintain a straight face. "Or 'Runts.' We could call them Runts." More laughter. "How about 'Mini Mags'? They're not Magnums; they're mini magnums. 'Shrunken Heads.' I like that." I was out of control now. My stomach was starting to hurt with all the hee-hawing. "And here's how we'll market them. 'Shrunken Heads. They're not just for Junior. They're for Dad, too.' "

"Thomas, you better not do any of this where Kalpesh can hear you."

"I think he would find it amusing. In fact, I'm willing to bet this wouldn't be news to him. He might even have personal experience with this. Maybe I should go ask him to invest in my company, Tiny Dick, Inc."

"Watch out now. I don't want you doing anything to incite him. He's working very hard on this election, and he hasn't done anything to deserve your infantile jokes."

"Infantile jokes based on a continent-wide survey. Gee, I wonder how they took the poll." My laughter was beginning to attract attention. Some of that attention came from Jim Maddox and a couple of sycophants who'd been shadowing him all evening. Maddox had been making his way through the hordes, shaking hands, introducing himself, unable or unwilling to remain in one place for long. I'd learned recently he had restless-leg syndrome when he slept, too. When he saw me and Kathy, he walked over in his stiff-legged gait.

"What's so funny?" Maddox asked, putting on the mask that was half smile and half grimace, the one people used when they'd walked into the back end of a joke.

"Don't mind him," Kathy said. "He's having one of his girlish fits."

Maddox, who was as tall as I was, hovered over Kathy while he glanced from her to me and back again, trying to figure what was so amusing. I'd learned early on that Maddox was usually afraid the joke was on him, and that as soon as he confirmed otherwise, he was put at ease. "I was making fun of somebody in the Sheffield camp," I said. "One of Kathy's co-workers."

"You work for Sheffield?" Maddox asked, as if I hadn't already informed him of that fact.

"Don't mind my husband. He was just being his imbecilic self. How are things, Mr. Maddox? We keep wondering when you're going to take us up on that second debate." They'd already had the first of three promised meetings between the candidates, but the morning-after poll numbers for Maddox had dipped substantially, and now all talk of a second meeting had been nixed.

"What do you think about this shindig?" Maddox asked. "Pretty nice, huh?" Maddox was looking around, standing too close to Kathy, but looking around. It was as if he wanted to move in on her and thought I wouldn't notice if he did it without looking. Like a lot of male politicians, Maddox had an eye for women and, like others before him, seemed to believe he gave off some sort of natural aphrodisiac. I had no information to make me think he was a philanderer—he'd been married to the same woman for thirty years—but he sure liked to eyeball. James Maddox was fifty-five, a man with a broad and impassive face, pale, with a booming voice he spent a lot of time modulating. Around the office people called him Old Iron Pants because of the rigid way he stood, legs apart and anchored to the floor, unmoving from the waist down as if he had the legs of a statue. Maddox hated the appellation.

"It is a nice gathering," Kathy said. "I find it interesting the governor invited both parties."

"Well, she's a Democrat and her fiancé is a Republican, so I guess they decided to go nondenominational," Maddox said, smiling humorlessly at Kathy. Maybe I was getting touchy about guys slobbering over my wife. Or maybe I was still tweaked because Kathy thought Deborah had been making a fool of me. Maybe that was why I did what I did next.

The room was enormous, but even so it was beginning to bulge at the seams. The decibel level was rising, and Maddox and I found ourselves leaning down to talk to Kathy, while she was almost on tiptoes trying to hear us. It occurred to me that I was next to Maddox's bad ear. Everyone who worked with him knew he had a good ear and a bad one, that you needed to be on his good side when there was a lot of background noise.

Speaking loud enough for Kathy to hear but not so loudly that Maddox would distinguish anything but gibberish, I said, "You probably don't know this, but Kathy likes to call you Old Iron Pants. In fact, she may be the person who got it started."

"I *certainly* was not," Kathy blurted. She turned to Maddox. "That isn't true. It's not true at all. I don't even know why he said that."

Maddox looked at Kathy curiously, leaned over, gave her his good ear, and said, "What?"

Now Kathy was almost yelling. "I said I'm not the one calling you Old Iron Pants. I'm not the one who made it up. 'Iron Pants' came from somebody in our office, but it wasn't me. Honest." Maddox still didn't know what she was talking about, but she hadn't realized it yet. "I apologize for calling you Old Iron Pants," Kathy yelled into Maddox's good ear.

Taking it poorly, Maddox gave Kathy a caustic look, turned to one of the sycophants who'd been behind him, mumbled something I couldn't hear, and left.

"I can't believe you did that," Kathy said.

"Did what?"

"Why on earth would you want to embarrass me and him at the same time?"

For a few moments I found myself grasping at straws to explain. "I thought it would be funny. I mean, I was talking into his bad ear. I thought you would figure it out. At a party with this much background noise you can say almost anything on his bad side and he won't hear it."

"So why didn't you stop me?"

"It happened too fast."

"It wasn't *that* fast. You made me look like an idiot."

"I couldn't stop you. Besides—"

"You deliberately maneuvered me into saying I call him Old Iron Pants."

"I didn't think you'd repeat it to him. I just wanted to see the look on your face."

"Well, you've seen it." She turned and walked away.

It was a dim-witted stunt if ever there was one. Even I didn't know why I'd done it. I couldn't blame alcohol because I hadn't been drinking. When I thought about it, as I did off and on for the rest of the evening, while the speeches and toasts were being made, while the bands played, and while I had nobody to dance with, I realized that as much as Kathy had been peeved by my actions in the last few weeks, I'd been even more peeved by hers. By and large we did share the same politics, but I wasn't acting on it. But then, where was it written that I had to? I was helping Maddox for my own recently unearthed reasons, and if I chose to do so, she had no right to carp at me. Okay, so I had accidentally on purpose inveigled her into offending Maddox. When you thought about it, except for the fact that I'd gotten Kathy steamed, it had been a slick piece of chicanery.

As the evening wore on and Kathy failed to materialize beside me, I realized I didn't regret having embarrassed Maddox, but Kathy's mortification was something else entirely. What the hell had I been thinking?

TWELVE

"YOU'RE HERE ABOUT the position on the campaign staff?" asked the redhead.

"Right. I'm Thomas Black. Jim Maddox called me yesterday."

"He said you'd be coming by. If you don't mind waiting a moment?"

"No problem."

We were in a small office complex in Kirkland, the windows looking out over Lake Washington about a block away. The day was sunny and warm, considering it was the last week of September, and the building offered an impressive view: Soaring gulls littered the sky; a water-skier made graceful arcs on water that looked like blue molten glass.

The redhead, whose name was Deborah Driscoll, wore a conservative suit and a pair of plastic-rimmed glasses that looked as though they were just for the office. About once every two minutes somebody trotted in from the main room. Ms. Driscoll fielded their queries, complaints, and concerns in an adroit, businesslike manner. She was tall and moved with a Spartan efficiency one saw in ballerinas and other athletes. She was younger than I was, probably around thirty, and did not once glance in my direction while I hunkered on a sofa against a wall and thumbed through a golfing magazine. I didn't play golf, but the choices were golf or airplane magazines. I didn't fly, either. Maddox did both.

I'd met James Maddox early in my tenure in the police department, and while we'd never worked together, our paths had crossed a few times, always with polite words and deference on both sides. Maddox had ingratiated himself with the administration and was highly regarded in the mayor's office. Nobody wrote a better letter or performed favors for those outranking him more frequently or efficiently than James Maddox. And, as I was to learn later, nobody crapped on those below him with more casual disdain.

At first, people thought challenging Jane Sheffield for her Senate seat was a rash move, but Republicans were on a national tear to replace roadblock Democrats wherever they could, so even though he didn't have the voter support, he was attracting huge amounts of money both in and out of state. In the beginning he'd polled only a few points behind Sheffield, but in their debate he'd been unable to parry Sheffield's extensive utilization of facts and figures; at one point he even lost his temper and called the moderator a jackass. For many it was a snapshot of a personality for which they were not ready to vote.

Over the years I'd followed his politics and found him sincere in his beliefs but austere and judgmental in the way he regarded the man on the street. He went to church and wore the fact on his sleeve. His motto seemed to be "Let no good deed go untouted." As a representative in Congress, Maddox had been implicated in some shenanigans involving payoffs, and the word around the Hill, according to the blogs, was that he had escaped an indictment by the skin of his teeth. The federal prosecutor who was investigating was grievously injured in a car wreck, and the prosecutor who took over from her dropped the ball. It was odd how chance played out in certain careers.

I couldn't help thinking about my links to Maddox while I thumbed through *Golf Digest* and waited for him to return to the office. I had loved every aspect of being a police officer and would have been one still if it hadn't been for a young man named Charlie Rivers, a fifteen-year-old with a short history of antisocial behavior. Everything about Charlie was short: his height, his temper, his educational credits, even his life span. He'd served time in juvenile facilities for burglary, car theft, and glue sniffing. Me? I'd been top ranked on the department pistol team and practiced shooting for long hours each week. It must have been karma that our paths collided.

When Charlie Rivers spotted a Volvo station wagon idling outside a liquor store, he took it as an invitation to a joyride, a felony he'd committed before and no doubt would have committed again. My partner and I had been passing through downtown when another unit caught sight of the Volvo blowing a red light and gave chase. When the other SPD unit inexplicably lost him in the vicinity of Fourth and Bell, we were nearby and took up the hunt. At the same time our dispatcher called and told us the owner of a furniture store in Belltown was reporting suspicious activity in the alley behind his store, so we broke off our search to handle the call. After walking through the store with the owner, I located the stolen Volvo in the alley behind the building. The suspicious activity behind the store turned out to be our quarry, Charlie Rivers. My partner went back to get our car so he could blockade the alley while I remained at the rear entrance of the store.

When I saw activity inside the Volvo that indicated he might be getting ready to bolt, I stepped into the alley and approached the vehicle. The engine fired up and the Volvo rocketed toward me. Charlie steered directly at me in an attempt, I could only surmise, to crush me against the wall. I was on foot and had few options. As I drew my weapon, I found a niche where the brick walls of two buildings were not joined evenly and pressed up against it, realizing it wasn't going to protect me from a ton and a half of steel.

The vehicle thundered onward. I leveled my pistol and placed a single bullet through the windshield. Any other driver, it probably would have hit his chest, but Charlie was small for his age, so the bullet penetrated the windshield and entered his face, lodging in the back of his skull. Missing me by a mere ten feet, the Volvo nosed into the wall. The whole incident took less than eight seconds to play out, though oddly, it became a cancer that over the course of the next year finished off my law enforcement career.

I couldn't help thinking about Charlie Rivers as I sat on the sofa in Jim Maddox's office. Maddox's phone call the day before had resurrected the past in a way I hadn't thought possible. What destroyed my equanimity more than anything was the fact that I'd probably spent fifteen hundred hours on the pistol range practicing so that when the time came to do what I eventually did, I did it flawlessly. It was an impeccable shooting born of endless impeccable rehearsal. For years afterward they told my story in the academy. Your gun may be the only tool between you and hell. Practice, practice, practice. I had and it was. I'd drawn, flicked off the safety, aimed, and hit him just under the right eye, all so quickly that neither of us had time to register what was happening.

When I stepped over to the wrecked car, I found Charlie slumped across the gearshift, gasping for breath as if he'd been hit in the lungs instead of the head. I could smell the hot steam from the Volvo's broken radiator. I reached past him and shut off the motor. Quarters were tight because Charlie had short legs and had moved the seat forward. Except for the heavy breathing, he was motionless, conscious, and reasonably alert, even though his eyes weren't working. The eye on the side where the bullet entered was gone, and the other, still open, appeared to be sightless. While the two of us waited for the fire department medics to arrive, Charlie told me he was fifteen.

"I'm sorry, Officer," Charlie gasped. "Honest. I was just try-ing to scare you." During a thousand nights when I replayed it in my head, I never did decide whether he was telling the truth.

"Am I hurt?"

"Pretty bad."

"How bad?"

I tried not to respond, thinking the medics would arrive in time to bail me out, but I waited and nobody arrived except a few lookiloos from a nearby apartment building, a pair of gay men who, having witnessed the incident from their bed-room window, later testified on my behalf.

"Am I going to live?"

"Of course you're going to live. Just hang in there. We're going to do everything we can for you."

"I think I'm going to die."

"Don't say that."

"It's true, though. Shit. I'm going to die."

He was fifteen, and fifteen-year-olds are prone to a certain type of fatalism. They are also prone to stupid stunts. True, he'd stretched the limits further than most. If I hadn't found him in a blind alley and cornered him, if the alley hadn't been so tight, if I hadn't been so damn calm and steady when I fired, he probably would have driven away and ditched the car the way he'd ditched all the other cars he'd stolen. He might have grown up and at some point found a nice girl, or become religious, or trained in a profession; he might have turned his life around. At the time I was not a whole lot older than he was—he could have been my younger brother—and while this wasn't the first time I'd been around somebody dying from violence, it was the first time I'd been around somebody dying from *my* violence. From my perspective on Maddox's office sofa, it seemed as if it had happened in a different world, a different epoch, to a different me. The only part of it that hadn't changed was the victim, Charlie Rivers, who was still fifteen and would always remain fifteen. *That* was never going to change. I was officially exonerated, but my guilt was never going to be assuaged. I'd been doing my job, protecting my own life, but that didn't take the sting out of the fact that I'd airmailed a bullet into a fifteen-year-old boy's brain.

Before he died, he'd made me pledge to tell his mother he loved her and to explain how his death was his own fault, not mine, but I knew that no matter how I parsed it, I was going to sound self-serving and his mother was going to think I was lying. I didn't tell her that night and I didn't tell her the next day or the next week. I never stopped thinking about telling her, but I never did it, either.

It was one of those failures that, every time it crossed my mind, I wished I had the cojones to revisit and revise. From time to time over the years I would look her up in the phone directory, but to date I hadn't cooked up the nerve to follow up on my oath to a dying boy. Knowing they blamed me for his death and knowing how badly his mother had taken the tragedy at the hospital—they'd had to sedate her—I simply could not scrounge up the strength to do what I promised. I went through a complex set of mental gymnastics trying to justify my lack of action, but in the end it was nothing more or less than abject cowardice.

Without my realizing it, during the next months my career began unraveling like a two-dollar sweater. To put it in a nutshell, I found it hard to live with the fact that I'd killed a boy and might, somewhere in the course of my duties, be forced to kill another. My feelings about carrying a gun were transitory, I told myself; they would evaporate in time and I could go on and be a competent police officer again. If I let enough time pass, I could put it behind me. But eventually it became apparent that as long as I was still on patrol and carrying a 9 mm, the feelings were only going to worsen. My emotions had become a major encumbrance to the performance of my job. Within a year I was a private citizen again.

Somewhere between the time I shot Charlie Rivers and the day I decided to resign from the department, Jim Maddox showed up at my place unbidden on a Saturday afternoon. I'd been painting the side of my house, the side that faced south, that absorbed the broiling sun every summer. Maddox parked on the street and strode up the driveway, where I was perched on a ladder. He was off duty for the weekend and wore an old dress shirt and jeans. "Need help?" he asked, picking up an extra brush I'd been using on the trim.

I looked down at a man who was by then a chief, a man I barely knew. "Sure. If you want, you can finish the trim around that basement window. Rags are under the ladder."

He was so intent on painting the window without mistakes I almost forgot he was there. After we'd been working side-by-side for twenty minutes, he said, "Sometimes things don't go the way you think they're supposed to."

"No." I'd been feeling sorry for myself all week, but it had gotten particularly bad that day. I'd blown off a dinner date and a bike ride with cycling buddies. I'd dropped out of a course I was taking at the university. I'd resigned from the shooting team. Looking back on it, I now see that this particular day marked the nadir of my downswing. I'd never really gotten over Charlie Rivers, but that Saturday was by far the worst. I didn't want to paint the house, but I didn't want to sit inside it feeling sorry for myself, either. It was almost as if Maddox had sensed my doldrums and flown to my rescue. I didn't need a lot right then, just a few kind words, which he was thoughtful enough to provide.

"I was thinking about you," he said. "A couple of people said you mentioned resigning."

"It's been on my mind."

"I wanted to let you know a lot of us have had things happen on the job we weren't prepared for. You go into this believing you can handle whatever they throw at you, and then one day you realize you've hit a wall and you can't handle it after all. It's no disgrace. If you choose to resign, you'll make a success of something else. These experiences make you stronger."

Somehow, just knowing he was supportive, this man I barely knew, knowing he'd had the foresight to visit on that particular day and to say what he'd said felt like a phenomenal gift. "Look," I said. "It means a lot to me that you've come. I appreciate it more than you know."

"I had my own problems a few years ago. One of the old-timers came by the house and said a few words. I told him I owed him. He said to pass it on. I'm passing it on."

We painted for another hour, and then I told him I needed to stop and fix dinner. I invited him to stay, but he said he had to get home to his family. Maddox helped me put the ladder away. "Hey, Jim," I said, as he headed down the driveway toward his car. He turned around and stumbled but did not fall in my driveway, a perfect example of his infamous clumsiness.

"Yeah?"

"Thanks for coming."

"I should have been by sooner."

"I owe you. Anytime you need anything at all, call me. I mean that."

"I just might do that."

My sense was that either Maddox was an exceedingly considerate man or he'd faced so much scorn and ridicule in the department that he was able to empathize with a castoff. For years Maddox had been more or less ostracized from the mainstream, and he must have seen a kindred spirit in me. Never mind that the reasons for our exclusion were different: Over the years, Maddox's kindness had become inextricably linked in my mind with the shooting.

After he entered politics we lost touch, and then out of the blue Maddox called and asked me to take a job with his campaign. The moment I heard his voice I thought of my unfulfilled pledge to Charlie Rivers. Somehow, it seemed as if in keeping my pledge to Maddox I would be making up for my failure with Charlie. It wasn't completely logical, but emotionally it felt like the right thing to do.

When Maddox finally arrived, he extended his hand and said, "I'll only be a minute. I need to talk to Deborah."

He and Deborah Driscoll went into the inner office, where he sat down, loosened his tie, and clasped his hands behind his head. Through a window between the offices, I could see them talking. I knew they were talking about me. Five minutes later I was invited in.

THIRTEEN

THE SHADES WERE DRAWN, blotting out the view of the lake
and rendering Maddox's face a pale smudge in the dark afternoon. Deborah Driscoll had retreated to a shadowy corner
after seating me in one of the two cushioned chairs in front of
the desk. "Let me give it to you in a nutshell, Thomas," Maddox said, without getting up from the desk. The nutshell
speech was one he had been famous for back in the police department, and it meant you were about to be bombarded with
a diatribe of inestimable length.

"The thing I always liked about you, Thomas, was that you
seem to have this radar for shit. That's what I want you to do
here. Find what needs to be found and help us deal with it. If
we're being spied on, I want you to find out. I need somebody
who's not that integral to the campaign, who I can take aside
and say, 'Go fix that' and know it's going to get done. Somebody with allegiance only to me. We're taking on a lot of new
people, and it would be helpful to have somebody with a good
nose checking things out. You're also the kind of person who
can blend in. But, like I said, the one trait I've always admired
about you, Thomas, was your radar for shit."

I glanced at Driscoll in the corner. "Something's happened, hasn't it?"

"We had a blackmail attempt. It's history now, but something
like it could happen again." Some of the old self-importance
showed up in Maddox's irritable response. In his rise to fame—
state representative, U.S. representative, and now senatorial
candidate—he'd decided he was important. Hard to fault him.
He *was* important. With his silver hair, chiseled features, piercing gray eyes, and dignified Roman nose, he was recognized
everywhere he went. The word *blackmail* seemed to leave a

bad taste in his mouth, because as he said it he swabbed his tongue around the inside of his teeth. "We'll bring you aboard as a logistics expert. Nobody will know why you're really here. What do you think?"

"Before I say yes, I have to warn you I'm not one hundred percent behind your ideology."

"You're not here to write policy. You're here to make sure we don't get blindsided."

"You should also know that my wife, Kathy, is an active volunteer for Sheffield."

"We already know that, and we're confident we can count on you to not let it interfere with the work you do for us."

"Tell me what this blackmail attempt was all about."

When Maddox hesitated, Deborah Driscoll stepped into the light and spoke. "A woman threatened to set off a bomb if we didn't pay her forty thousand dollars. Jim fired her son a couple of years ago. A few weeks after he left, he put a gun in his mouth. Apparently she blamed us for his suicide and wanted his back pay and funeral costs. The man . . . all his life had been having mental problems. She didn't have the capability to make a bomb, so we weren't all that worried, but it did give us pause. Nutcases come out of the woodwork during an election."

"I didn't read about this incident in the newspapers."

"We tried to keep it under wraps. Besides, we don't want to give the next guy ideas, do we?"

"The suicide didn't make the headlines, either?"

"Uh, no," said Driscoll.

"Has there been another threat?"

"Not yet."

"Surely you have your own people in case there is?"

Once again, Deborah replied. "We want somebody who's not attached to the apparatus."

"You suspect somebody in the campaign is working against you?"

"Possibly," Maddox admitted.

"Not at all," said Driscoll, almost at the same time. They looked at each other, and I could see it wasn't so much a disagreement as the fact that Driscoll had decided to hand me a little white lie. I decided to keep that in mind with regard to our future dealings.

"Okay. I'm on board. I'll need to clean up some things this afternoon, but after that I'm yours."

"Going to be some long hours," said Maddox.

"I've worked long hours before."

"Good. Tomorrow morning. Six o'clock. I want you to start by going over the names of the people in the office, everyone except Deborah."

I already knew Deborah was the first person I was going to check out. "Sounds good."

As I left the office, I had a few seconds to watch the two of them in the reflection of the window that divided the office and the anteroom. Maddox was reaching for the telephone. Driscoll was watching me.

=== FOURTEEN ===

THE TROUBLE WITH MARRIAGE to a woman as attractive as my wife is that wherever you go guys are eyeballing her, some to the degree that you want to put a boot up their asses. It doesn't help that, as a criminal defense attorney, Kathy represents her share of impoverished, indigent, and sometimes mentally ill defendants. Her profession puts her into proximity with dirtbags who are lonely and easily swept up by her charms, men whose lives are circling the drain and who, when they get close to someone like Kathy, think they've met a creature from paradise.

The classic example is Bert Slezak, identical twin brother of my longtime friend and confidant Elmer, aka Snake. Two years ago, recommended by Elmer, Kathy defended Bert in a trespass and theft case after he was caught carting off a two-ton piece of statuary from the estate of a local judge.

Bert and Elmer were both named after their mother's favorite film star: Burt Lancaster, who starred in *Elmer Gantry*. Elmer and I are close, but Bert, whose name was misspelled by his father on the birth certificate, crossed way over a line that Elmer only straddled, and at times I found him close to despicable. Like Elmer, he had a long résumé: soldier, stump grinder, pressure washer, door-to-door salesman, drum maker, author (a book on UFO abductions), long-haul trucker. I didn't believe his claim to having once been a gigolo any more than I believed Snake's. Over the years, Bert's frequent contact with my wife had been an irritant. Once, I overheard Bert trying to convince her to leave me, supposedly to spend the rest of her days guzzling beer and munching Cheetos with him in his trailer while watching reruns of *Gilligan's Island*.

Two mornings after the governor's ball I made my way to Kathy's office in the Mutual Life Building, braving crowds of tourists queued for the underground tour in Pioneer Square. When I stepped into the office, Beulah rolled her eyes and gestured with her head toward the inner sanctum, where through the open door I could see Bert's arms constantly moving in time to his rapid-fire speech. His sentences came out like machine-gun bullets, lickety-split and often punctuated with the same nervous giggle Snake sometimes evidenced.

I stepped into the small cubicle I was using as an office. It contained two chairs, a desk with a computer, and a file cabinet. When I interviewed people, I did it over the phone or on their turf; if they came to the office, I borrowed Kathy's meeting room, which was generally empty because Kathy spent so much time up the hill at the King County Courthouse either consulting with clients or working deals with deputy prosecutors, or in court itself. Bert spent his share of time up there, too. Like a lot of habitual criminals, Bert was always suitably contrite and humble around the courthouse.

"What if my ex goes back to court and says she doesn't need the restraining order anymore?" I heard Bert asking Kathy.

"The point is," Kathy said, "you've already violated an existing order, and that's the charge we'll be responding to in court next week. The order was in place; you violated it. We're going to have a hard time getting around that."

"But she called and said she wanted me. *She* called *me*. What am I supposed to do? She's a good-looking woman." I'd seen Bert's ex. She'd been a swimsuit model in her youth and carried her good looks and healthy lifestyle into middle age. "She called me."

"That's not what her statement says."

"She said she missed me, and I knew what that meant."

"So you went over to visit even though she has a restraining order forbidding you to be within one hundred feet of her residence. Then what happened?"

"Her boyfriend showed up."

"And?"

"He was supposed to be at work. He works the night shift down at Nucor Steel in West Seattle. You think somebody tipped him off? Maybe the government? I've been seeing more undercover federal agents in town. Did I tell you that?

I'm being followed by government agents. I ditched one this morning on the way here." Bert's paranoia showed up in almost every conversation, though it was usually under some degree of control by the time he headed to court, as if the sweat factor snapped him out of it.

"Okay. What can you tell me about the car?"

"They can't prove a thing."

"They have a witness who ID'd you. And it is quite a coincidence that the boyfriend throws you out of the house and three hours later his car burns down to the rims."

"Coincidences happen all the time."

"We drew Anderson and she's tough on domestic cases. It would help if you could show some remorse in court."

"Sure. I can fake remorse."

"Genuine remorse would be better."

"No problem. I can fake that, too." He must have made a comical face, which he was prone to, because Kathy laughed.

"You're laughing. They say that's the key to a woman's heart: Make her laugh. Check out how many comedians have married beautiful women. What do you say? Costa Rica? Just you and me and a thatched roof under the stars. We could be there in two days. We'd never have another care in this world. I would read Emily Dickinson out loud and massage your feet after long walks on the beach. Haven't you ever wanted to have a man who made you laugh, worshipped your every move, and knew how to skin a rabbit?"

"The man I have makes me laugh and worships my every move, and what's more I believe he's sitting outside that door."

"Can he skin a rabbit?"

"Probably not, but I wouldn't be surprised if he was about to tan your hide." Tuning them out, I lost myself in some work on the computer. By the time I looked up, Kathy was alone in her office, on the phone but alone. I was due across the lake at Maddox's headquarters, but I needed to talk to her. Bert was long gone and Beulah was missing, too.

I got up and wandered into Kathy's office. Neither of us had spoken on the drive home from the governor's ball. Sunday we'd been polite but distant, and this morning Kathy left the house before I rolled out of bed. She spoke on the phone for another minute.

"So who's chartering the plane now?" Kathy asked. "She still thinks that's a good idea?" She watched me while she finished the conversation, then hung up the phone.

"I'm sorry for the other night," I said. "I was out of line. I set you up, and I'm ashamed of myself. Can you forgive me?"

"I knew he was hard of hearing, but I forgot. I'm sure I'll tell the story at a party someday and everybody will get a big kick out of it, including me."

"You forgive me?"

"Of course, I forgive you."

"I think we need to take a couple of days just for ourselves."

"But we've got—"

"Commitments? Our first commitment is to each other. And we're beginning to get a little off track. I really think we need to carve out the time."

"We *have* been at each other's throats."

"I was thinking a trip to the ocean. How about that rust-bucket motel on the beach where we stayed last fall during the storm?"

"You sure it's not too plush for you?"

"Long walks on the sand. Nothing to think about for two days. Just you and me. Cinnamon rolls for breakfast, ham and eggs for lunch at that dumpy little diner, popcorn and a video for dinner. Build a fire on the beach and roast hot dogs till midnight. Maybe buy a kite and fly it over the waves. I can't quote Emily Dickinson, but I might be able to remember a couple of booger jokes."

Kathy got up, walked around the desk, and sat in my lap, draping her arms around my shoulders. "You do know how to sweet-talk a girl."

"What do you call an anorexic booger?" I said.

"What?"

"Slim Pickens."

"Oh, you are a charmer."

I buried my face in her chest, nuzzling her, an activity I'm sure Bert would have handed over his life savings to perform. Not that he had any life savings. She stroked the back of my neck.

"I'll try to find a replacement for this trip I'm supposed to take with Jane."

"So we can scram out of town tonight?"

"I'll make a reservation. At this time of year they're bound to have openings in the middle of the week, but I'll call anyway. I'm glad you thought of this. See you tonight. We can have dinner on the road."

"Sounds good." When I reached the doorway, I turned around and said, "Don't you think Mr. Slezak was a little out of line?"

"He's harmless. Do you know what they've got him on now? The latest?"

"Lithium?"

"No. His brother bailed him out this morning. Friday night and Saturday morning he held off a sheriff's SWAT team. They went out to arrest him because he was back on his grandmother's property again. He was in the trailer watching TV when they asked his grandmother if he had any weapons. She admitted he had three shotguns, a couple of semiautomatic rifles, at least eight pistols, and five thousand rounds of ammunition. So the SWAT team surrounded the trailer and ordered him out. He looked out the window, sized up the situation, and told them to get lost. They ended up waiting eight hours until he drank himself to sleep. God only knows how I talked the judge into bail."

"He fire any shots?"

"He didn't even talk to them. He just wouldn't come out. I wish there was some good mental health facility we could get him into, something that didn't cost an arm and a leg. And to answer your question, no. He claims he didn't touch any of the weapons. I'll have to wait for discovery and see what they're actually alleging."

"Ought to be good."

"Don't be gleeful about somebody else's misfortunes."

"Me?"

"You're the one who always says we're all just one banana peel on the sidewalk away from being in the shoes of one of these crackpots."

"That was a wise man, said that."

"Yes, it was. And I love him, too."

FIFTEEN

I WAS SLIDING BEHIND the wheel of my Ford sedan in a quiet little parking spot under the Alaskan Way Viaduct near the ferry terminal when a man appeared at the side of the car, opened the door, and skidded into the passenger seat as if stealing third base. For a second I thought he was a panhandler hopped up on speed, but it was Bert Slezak, smirking as if we were best friends, his pale blue eyes entombed in his perpetually sunburned face.

As always, his features were capable of contorting through an infinite range of expressions. Snake was the same. I'd never figured out if the brothers did it in a calculated manner, or if it was some Marlon Brando acting gene they were born with. They both also wore a façade of toughness like a Kevlar vest, though underneath they were uncommonly brittle.

"Hey, man," he said.

"What do you want?"

"I would never have propositioned your old lady if I'd known you were in the other room."

"Of course not. You might get your neck broken. Best to do it while I'm out of town, or laid up with a bad gall bladder."

"The government's still after me for things I did years ago. They'll frame me any time they get the chance." He let the non sequitur hang in the air, as if he were well-known for thumbing his nose at the highest echelons of power, world famous for his imbroglios with the U.S. government, spats with congressional leaders, and the president—instead of just being a common drunk who ended up in court for punching out waiters or cutting parking meters down with a Sawzall. "You want to knock my head off?" Bert continued. "Go ahead. Take your best shot. I won't do nothing. One free shot, right there." His smile was disarming. His brother could smile disarmingly, too, though on a normal day neither smiled much. When they did, their contagious enthusiasm vacuumed you in. I knew they came from a family where their alcoholic father had beaten them regularly, where their mother was blotto most days, and that one day when they were fourteen their father vanished in the desert near their New Mexico home never to be seen again.

"What do you want, Bert?"

"This isn't a regular Taurus, is it? It's the sleeper with the big motor and the race-tuned suspension."

"Spit it out, Bert. I've got someplace I need to be."

"It's just Kathy is still working for Sheffield. I warned her, but she won't listen."

"What's wrong with working for Sheffield?"

"Seriously, can you get her out of there?"

"Tell me why."

"Can't you just trust me on this?"

"No."

"Sheffield's got a black cloud hanging over her."

"What does that mean?"

"Just tell Kathy she needs to be someplace else for the next few weeks."

"Are you making a threat against Sheffield?"

"Don't put words in my mouth. I wouldn't hurt a flea on my dog's ass. This isn't about politics. They're all the same to me, politicians. They all come out of the same barrel. But Kathy's special, she can make shit smell like pineapple, and I don't want to see her hurt. Get her out of there."

"Give me a reason." I was fishing now, trying to see if I could get him to incriminate himself, for this sounded vaguely—or perhaps not so vaguely—like a threat against Senator Sheffield. Despite his protest to the contrary, from some of the things his brother had said about him over the past months, I had a feeling Bert was a political nutcase, though the cast of his politics was unclear. His life had been lived in a blur of mismanagement and screwups: five marriages, an erratic employment record, and a sequence of petty crimes that never seemed to let up. I'd looked up his record when he first came to Kathy and learned that, although nearing fifty and having been exhibit A in more courtrooms than any of us could count, he had only one major conviction.

Most people had established some sort of order in their lives by the time they reached their fifties, yet Bert's life continued to soar out of control. People of his ilk camped under bridges or slept inside a cardboard box in three pairs of pants and four coats, and I had a notion he was only a few steps from that ignominy himself. That or the nuthouse. He knew it, too, and it must have terrified him.

"A reason? You need a reason? I can't give a reason. Can't you just get her out of there on my say-so?"

"No."

He stared at the dashboard for a minute. "Okay. I get premonitions."

"You have a premonition about Sheffield?"

"Right."

"What does your premonition say?"

"She's not going to make it."

"You talking about Sheffield falling down the stairs or—?"

"I'm not predicting . . . Maybe it'll be more like an asteroid hurtling through the skies and obliterating her building. Think along the lines of an asteroid. Would you want Kathy standing next to Sheffield if you knew an asteroid was going to squash Sheffield next week?"

"You got a hot tip on an asteroid?"

"You're making fun of me. Okay. I can buy that. I've been made fun of. But . . ."

"You can see into the future?"

"Sometimes, yeah."

"Why didn't you see that you were going to get arrested last week?"

"I know you don't think much of me, but Kathy needs to quit Sheffield."

"Tell her yourself."

"I did. She told me to get lost."

"You want my honest opinion?"

"Yes. Yes, I do."

"Get lost."

He gave me a sheepish look. "She says I need mental health counseling."

"Something to think about."

He gave me a bashful grin. "I was hoping you would see the light."

Like his brother, Elmer, Bert was considerably more lethal than he appeared to be, like a horsefly with a stinger. Out of curiosity, I'd read his book on UFOs—proud of his brother's literary legacy, Snake kept a box of the books at his place. Reading *After the Abduction*, one had to admit Bert was an imaginative storyteller and that he believed in his product, which was undoubtedly why the book sold, and also why he was only a couple of ticks off walking around in a canvas sweater with the sleeves sewn behind his back.

Over the years I had collected some stories about Bert, including the one from his brother claiming Elmer was the most dangerous man he had ever known. Bert had once resisted arrest so violently it had taken twelve police officers to get him into cuffs. Soaking wet he didn't weigh a hundred and thirty-five pounds so, if true, the story was remarkable. Another tale had Bert getting pulled over for public drunkenness by a bullying deputy in some small town in the southern part of the state. Thinking Bert was drunk and defenseless, the deputy began pushing him around. The next morning a paper delivery woman found the deputy cuffed to a telephone pole with his own handcuffs. Bert had removed the deputy's trousers and hoisted them to the top of the flagpole over the town post office, his boxer shorts flying below them like a state flag.

"Why do you really want Kathy out of the Sheffield campaign?" I asked. "So she'll be around to babysit you?"

In exasperation, he threw his head into his hands and combed his fingers through his slicked-back hair. "There's a pattern. Don't you see it? Things have to be squeezed to fit into the pattern, and when they don't fit, there is a machine that does the squeezing. I've known some of the agents for that machine, and I know how they think."

"So it's not an asteroid, it's some agents you know?"

"She's a defense attorney. Don't you think she should

support the law-and-order candidate? Kathy should be backing Maddox."

"Get out of the car."

"You don't believe anything I've said, do you?"

"No."

"Okay. Here are the facts. I'll lay them out so there's no mistake and you won't think I'm some fruitcake who shinnied over the fence at the funny farm. But you have to promise never to repeat a word to anyone, not even Kathy. I'm serious. You repeat any of this, I'll call you a liar. Sheffield is not going to make it through the campaign. She's not going to make it to the election. I don't know how or when or by whom, but she's not coming out of this alive."

"And this is by design?"

"Oh yeah."

"How do you know?"

"Careful analysis."

"I thought you said it was a premonition."

"I'm not sure exactly how they're going to do it, but I have a few ideas I'd rather keep to myself. It will be somebody from the government, though. I mean, they might not be working for the feds in any way you can trace, but it will lead to D.C. At least to Virginia."

"CIA headquarters?"

"They have a whole repertoire when it comes to dirty tricks. Could be anything. A heart attack. Stroke. Car accident. I'm not sure how it's going to come down, but I know she's not going to make it through this campaign, and when she does go down there's a chance she'll take people with her. I don't want one of them to be Kathy. Trust me."

"That's just it, Bert. I trust you about as far as horses can fly."

"Remember when that senator had the brain problem? That brain problem was caused by a machine. They aim it at your head. You could be sitting in a movie theater and the guy with the machine is sitting behind you. You'd never even know."

"Open the door and step out."

"You think I'm crazy, don't you?"

"Yeah."

As he climbed out, he said, "You're her old man. Put your foot down. Grow some hair on your ass."

"Close the door."

"Look," he said, holding on to my car roof while leaning back inside the space he'd just vacated. "You saw building number seven go down, didn't you?"

"What?"

"At the World Trade Center on 9/11. Did you not see building number seven go down? Think back on what you saw. That was a controlled demolition. Just like the first two buildings. If they can do that right in front of your eyes and make it so you don't even know what you saw, they can do anything. Compared to bringing down a forty-seven-story building and convincing you it came down by itself, eliminating one pesky senator will be child's play."

"Goodbye, Bert."

"Promise you won't tell Kathy we had this conversation?"

"I'm not going to promise anything."

WE WERE SITTING across from each other in a Thai restaurant in Olympia. Maddox had been okay with the idea of my taking leave for two days. Kathy, on the other hand, had run into some choppy water with Sheffield. There was a flu bug making the rounds and Sheffield was shorthanded, so Kathy promised she'd check her cell messages every four hours. Kathy didn't have any problem with that. I did, but she didn't.

We were planning to stay on the Washington coast at a little motel north of Ocean Shores, a joint that had special memories for us. Assuming we didn't encounter the same tumultuous weather and traffic we'd plowed through tonight, we'd be only about a three-hour drive from Seattle.

Outside it was dark and the streets were wet from a continuous downpour we'd been fighting since leaving Seattle. Kathy's dark hair was pulled into one of those thick plaits that ran down the center of her back past her shoulder blades. I loved the look. I was in love with just about everything about Kathy. That was how it worked. I fell in love again every six months or so. Not that I ever fell out of love with her; it was just that the brain chemistry between us seemed to slacken from time to time and then, out of the blue, whether it was a look or a touch or something she said, it refreshed itself.

We had officiated our differences in the rainy stop-and-go traffic between Seattle and Olympia, the state capital. For my part I did a long riff on why I felt the need to fulfill my pledge to Maddox, even though I was planning to vote for Sheffield. Kathy pretended the discussion mollified her, although I could tell it hadn't. She spent fifteen minutes outlining her irritation with the way I'd been fending off her pleas to jettison Maddox, and I dutifully apologized. I didn't like to be pushed and it had shown. She acknowledged she'd been pushing, and I acknowledged I'd been recalcitrant and, worse, sarcastic. We both promised to be more thoughtful in the future.

We both agreed to turn off our cellphones for the rest of the night, even though Kathy would have to regularly check for messages as promised. The room had no radio or TV, no computer hookup, and we weren't carrying any newspapers, so local and national news would be out of our purview. I'd packed a thick historical novel I'd been wading through, and Kathy had brought a draft of her first solo attempt at ghost-writing a speech for Senator Sheffield. I'd read part of it and it was pretty damn good.

"Did he mention the asteroid?" I asked after we'd ordered our meals.

"Of course he mentioned it. It's one of his favorite metaphors."

"I'm not sure it was a metaphor. I think he may actually believe an asteroid will come screeching out of the sky and land on Jane Sheffield just like that house landed on the Wicked Witch of the East."

"He's really very sweet and a lot more sensitive than you give him credit for."

"Sweet? Bert could go into a library to check out a copy of *Vegetarian Times*, and the next thing you know the Army Rangers would have the place surrounded."

"He does have an uncanny knack for irritating authority figures. It's part of his southwestern cockeyed charm."

"I didn't think he had any charm, cockeyed or otherwise."

"I worry about him."

"You should. All your clients . . . well, most of them . . . are screwballs, but he's the worst."

"I'm worried that one of these days he's going to get into real trouble and never see daylight again."

"Maybe daylight should be reserved for people who are sane."

"He can't keep himself on track long enough to make anything good happen in his life. I've often thought Snake had bipolar disorder. Do you think if one twin had it the other would, too?"

"I'm not sure either has it. Bert's a drunk, is what he is."

"There's more to it. He has issues that go way back. Serious issues. And it's not just his childhood. I'm convinced something happened in the army, or around the time he was in the army, that he hasn't recovered from. I want to try to get an appointment for him with Cindy."

"Who's going to pay for it?"

"I might be able to talk her into doing it pro bono."

Cynthia Darwell was a friend of Kathy's from college who did grief and marriage counseling in a chic clinic on the east side of the lake, treating broken marriages and emotionally wounded children of the fabulously wealthy, mostly dot-com millionaires.

Our meal arrived: pad thai, pad ga pow with basil, sesame beef with broccoli, and a side dish of steaming jasmine rice. After we'd traveled the rainy highway through Aberdeen, a small city that had once been sustained by logging and was now struggling, I said, "We're almost there. Going to be too tired to fool around?"

Kathy looked at me, and for a split second an oncoming truck's headlights made her eyes seem like gems. It was one of those moments driving in the rain late at night on a two-lane highway when you thought the truck was headed right for you, except it wasn't. "Have I ever been too tired, big fella?"

═══ SIXTEEN ═══

WE'D ARRIVED AN HOUR EARLIER, checked in, unpacked, and, lacking any plans more virtuous, made love while basking in the artificial light filtering through the blinds on our patio slider from a spotlight over the beach. The light had beguiled hordes of moths, which in turn had drawn a congregation of wildly zigzagging bats in a feeding frenzy. Remaining in a stuporous, postcoital haze, I watched the bats from the bed, what I could see of them through the blinds, wondering at their ability to navigate in the darkness, as well as their uncanny knack for changing directions with alarming dispatch and unerring accuracy. Funny. All they were doing was eating dinner.

So far on the junket we'd been disciplined about not answering our cellphones, though Kathy had left hers beside us on the nightstand, and several times it had made music, a mildly distracting counterpoint, I thought, to our own music making. Before heading for the shower she glanced at a short list of messages, giving the list enough of a look to identify who had called but not staying with it long enough to return calls. The mere fact that she'd checked her messages nettled me, but I wasn't going to make a point of it, especially in light of how well things were going.

The next morning the idea had been to sleep in, maybe lie around for a few hours planning for the time when our lives wouldn't be absorbed with the minutiae of phone calls, conferences, poll results, co-worker squabbles, and a billion little concerns that had absolutely no relevance to our actual existence. The plan had been to make love again in the morning, or to play at it, depending on whim, urgency, and mutual inclination—at least that was my plan—but when I woke up at seven-thirty, Kathy was sitting up in bed sorting through cellphone messages, scanning the list for the one message that would call her back to Seattle. It was almost as if she *wanted* to cut our holiday short. Pretending I didn't know what she was doing, I reached over and pulled her close. The silky skin of her stomach was hot to my touch. Outside, we could hear the steady rattling of the halyard from a wind sock against an aluminum pole. We made love one more time and then, sheets gnarled around our limbs, dozed off, entwined in each other's arms; I thought it wouldn't be too bad if the nuclear war started now and this became my last memory. It was that perfect.

Two hours later we took a stroll on the sand, forty-five minutes out and forty-five back. The beach was deserted except for an old couple with an Irish setter chasing sandpipers in front of us. The tide was out and the sky was darkened with a high, hoary overcast. By the time we got back to the room, we'd worked up an appetite. While she sipped fresh-brewed tea, Kathy leaned to one side of the small kitchen table, enabling her to sneak a glance at her cellphone. I was determined not to be peeved, but it was getting tougher every minute. I had also been determined not to mention the fact that I wasn't sure where my cellphone was.

"Gee. Did you get a call? I'm not sure I even know where my phone is."

"It's in the car, buster. You made a big production of locking it in."

"I did?"

"You know you did."

"Maybe I should go out and check. I think the president may have been calling. Maybe Angelina Jolie needs a bodyguard."

"If Angelina calls, let me talk to her. I'll warn her."

"Who's been phoning you?"

"I'm just checking to make sure Jane or Kalpesh haven't called. They promised not to call unless it was critical."

"Go ahead. Check. I'll be reading my book. Maybe after lunch we'll take a nap." I bobbled my eyebrows and smirked like an imbecile. Really—like an imbecile. If you practiced, you could get good at it.

"I'm game for a little nap after lunch."

"As long as you're begging, okay. Maybe I'll go jogging first. Want to come?"

"I didn't bring my Adidas. Did you mean it about checking my messages? You won't pout?"

"Be my guest."

Kathy did not return any calls. Instead, she worked on Sheffield's speech while I lost myself in a historical novel about the Civil War; a couple of blissful hours passed like that. At one o'clock I went for a jog, promising myself a shower and a nice long nap with mama afterward. Kathy elected to remain in the room. Forty-five minutes later when I returned to the room and saw the look on Kathy's face, I knew something was wrong.

"I'm sorry, Thomas. I'm so sorry. I've been having such a good time and I'm so relaxed, and this has just been the best day of my life. I'm sorry to ruin it for us."

"I had a feeling something was going to happen."

"Don't be upset. Kalpesh is driving down from Seattle to meet Jane at some little airstrip near the Oregon border. He wanted to swing by here and pick me up, but I convinced him we would drive ourselves. I'm sorry. They want me on the flight with Jane."

"I thought you had permission to take a few days off. What's so urgent?"

"Kalpesh is sick. Everyone else is out of position, so I have to replace him."

"Crap."

"You don't mind, do you?"

"No, I guess not."

"The drawback is, after you drop me off, you'll have to drive back to Seattle by yourself."

"Double crap."

"Jane's hired a plane to fly up the coast to Sequim, then to Port Townsend, Bellingham, and eastern Washington. There's a landing strip not far from Cape Disappointment. It was supposed to be Kalpesh, but he's come down with food poisoning and he gets queasy in a small plane at the best of times. I'm so sorry. We did have one day together. Well, almost a full day. And we're okay now, right, sweetie?"

"We always were. I know this isn't your fault. I do have one question."

"What's that?"

"If Mr. Kalpesh has food poisoning and can't fly, why is he driving three hours to meet you guys at the airstrip?"

"It's not Mr. Kalpesh. You know that. It's Kalpesh Gupta. So if you're going to 'mister' him, it would be Mr. Gupta."

"Or, I could just call him Short Stuff. Mr. Short. No, wait. It would be Mr. Stuff."

"You're right. He is ill. If he's in a rented car maybe he could drop it off and you two could drive back together in our car?"

"No way am I letting Mr. Stuff toss his cookies in our car."

"Now that I'm thinking about it, his parents live in Portland. I bet he's staying with them."

"It's still a long drive if he's sick."

"Kalpesh likes to suffer. Driving all that way to deliver me and drop off papers for Jane is just the sort of martyrdom he likes."

"You'd think a tiny little penis would be enough to satisfy anybody's martyr complex."

Kathy gave me what she thought was a withering look, but instead of shaming me it made me laugh. "You be nice when we see him at the airport."

"I'm nice to everybody."

"In November after the elections, maybe, if we can scrape up a bankroll, we'll fly to Hawaii. This is so crappy. We were both so relaxed."

"I know. We relaxed three times."

"At least we'll have the drive together. If Kalpesh had swung by, we wouldn't have that."

While Kathy watched, I packed hurriedly, which was fine because I always packed hurriedly. "You going to have enough clothes for a two-day flight around the state?" I asked.

"Actually, I knew this was a remote possibility when we left yesterday."

"So you brought enough for a plane trip?"

"Right."

"Ms. Efficiency."

She hoisted one of her bags off the end of the bed and began dragging it toward the door. I grabbed it and loaded up the car while she tidied the room and left a tip on the pillow.

The roads near Ocean Shores were wet from an overnight mist, but most of the drive was dry and overcast. If everything went according to schedule, Kathy and the others would be in the air around sunset, perhaps sooner. My plan was to drop her at the airstrip and skedaddle with a minimum of fuss and introductions. There was a chance I could be at Cape Disappointment by the time the plane got out over the ocean, and with luck I might see Kathy and the others cruising north over the Pacific. It wouldn't be on a par with the nap we were missing, but it would be fun.

We'd been meaning to take in the Cape on our drive home. Kathy had never seen it, while I'd visited it once with my sister when I was small. Tucked into the southwest corner of the state, it was easy to bypass. It included a lighthouse, some World War II fortifications, and a Lewis and Clark interpretive center. As we drove, Kathy fumbled in her purse and pulled out her cellphone, peered at the caller's ID, and answered. "Bert, what's going on?" She listened for a few moments. "I can't be in Seattle in an hour. I'm on my way to hook up with Sheffield." Kathy gave me a long, pensive look. "I can't just turn around and drop everything for you. What? Okay. So tell me what's happening." She listened for a while and then hung up.

"What's going on?"

"He wants me to call him back. He's convinced people are listening in."

"Who would be listening?"

"Hey. This is Bert, remember?"

"The government?"

She dialed. "Bert? I'm back."

We were on Highway 101, which wound through a sparsely

populated area of western Washington along the coast, mostly two lanes, a twisting road with lots of coastal hills covered in underbrush and fir, rare glimpses of the ocean to the west. The road passed through tiny towns such as Raymond, South Bend, Naselle, towns you only read about in the papers once every ten years or so when they experience a one-hundred-year flood, or when a murderer or a world-class violinist turns out to be the unlikely denizen of one of them.

All in all, Kathy hung up and dialed Bert four times. During the last part of their conversation Bert insisted that Kathy tell him where she was, precisely, to the milepost, and what her vehicle looked like, as if the information was of any use to him in Seattle. "No, Bert. We *were* at the ocean. Just my husband and me. No, we didn't build a fire on the beach. We thought about it, but we didn't get around to it. Listen, Bert. I have to go now. Whatever is going on, we'll handle it at the end of the week." Kathy heaved a sigh and tilted her seat back, closing her eyes.

"Go ahead, grab some shut-eye," I said. "You're going to have a couple of busy days."

"I'm beginning to think whatever is wrong with him is getting worse."

"You mean he's . . . let's see . . . what would be the technical term for it . . . going nutso?"

"It's nice to hear a clinician put it into medical terms. You know what I think, Thomas? I have this weird feeling he's killed somebody."

"Did he say that?"

"He's hinting around at something."

"Let's hope not."

The landing strip wasn't far from Ilwaco, a tiny town on the peninsula. The strip was a couple of hundred yards long, with a wind sock and six or eight small planes parked near a shack that served as an office and repository for a raft of Coke and candy machines. Looking green around the gills, Kalpesh was there, as was Jane Sheffield and her cadre of campaign workers. A twin-engine plane sat on the end of the runway, one pilot inside the cockpit prepping the plane. It would hold ten or maybe twelve passengers.

"You want to come?" Kathy asked as we pulled up next to the burgundy Lexus that Kalpesh had driven from Seattle. "They said there's room."

"I'd have to leave the car. Besides, you'll be working and I'll be bored. I might start fondling you."

"Yeah, well, there is that."

"Thanks, but I'll stay with the car."

Kalpesh and the rest of the gang were standing next to the shack laughing about something. Kalpesh looked terrible, ashen. Apparently he *was* sick. He was deep in conversation with a man who appeared to be the second pilot.

I walked to the rear of the Prius and pulled out Kathy's bag. When I got back around the car, she was on the phone. "Bert, I said—" She rolled her eyes at me, and I leaned over and kissed her forehead. "No, Bert. I said I'm going to be gone for two days, and that's what's going to happen. Yes. We're at the landing strip now. What? I don't know. A few minutes. Inside half an hour for sure. Okay. Okay. Just don't do anything rash. I mean that. I'm serious. You do anything crazy and I am no longer your attorney. You understand?"

When we approached the group, Kathy and I fell into a long hug. As she always did, Kathy felt small and firm against my lanky frame. "I wish it could have been at least two days," I said. "That would have given us a few more naps."

"I'll ask the pilot to tip his wings as we pass the Cape. I think we'll be going past the lighthouse. Love you. See you at the end of the week. I'll call."

On the way back to the car I crossed paths with Kalpesh Gupta and the man he'd been talking to, Freddy Mitz, who was one of the pilots. "Why is this flight originating here, in the middle of nowhere?" I asked. "Why not Seattle?"

"That was my doing," admitted Kalpesh. "The plane and pilots were in California until late last night, brought a rock band up to Portland for a couple of sold-out shows. And Jane was in the Tri-Cities, so I thought it would be easier for everybody to meet here. Kathy and you were nearby. It worked out best this way."

I turned to Freddy. "Pretty good band?"

"I never actually heard them play."

"Nice to meet you, Freddy. Take care of these people. The pretty one's my wife."

"We always take care of our people."

I took the single-lane road out to the highway. The overcast was beginning to break up, so I had high hopes for a splendid sunset at the Cape.

=== SEVENTEEN ===

I WAS STANDING in front of the lighthouse at Cape Disappointment amid a congregation of senior citizens who had arrived by bus. I hadn't spotted any planes in the cloudy skies yet, nor did I have the place to myself the way I'd hoped. The clouds were foreshadowing a watercolor sunset. I'd located the black and white Cape Disappointment lighthouse and found a spot where some good citizen might snap a photograph of me that would include the lighthouse, the ocean, and perhaps Kathy's flight, maybe even with a touch of sunshine blasting through the blanket of clouds.

"Hi, baby," I said.

"Hey, big boy."

"You got people around?"

"Well, sort of."

"Can you talk?"

"I can talk."

For reasons I could not define, we both knew our goodbye was not going to be complete until the plane had passed the Cape. As we talked I spotted a twin-engine plane cruising out over the water. It was traveling north and had to be Sheffield's charter. I handed my digital camera to one of the tourists in front of the lighthouse and asked him to snap a picture of me, positioning myself so the plane would be framed over my shoulder. It was going to make a terrific joke photo, our vacation together, Kathy in the plane, me in front of the lighthouse, the two of us on the phone.

The old man snapped a picture and I motioned for him to do it a second time as an insurance shot. He did so and then with trembling hands returned the camera. I thanked him, turned around, and used my field glasses to bring the plane up close. "Kathy, I see you. You're . . . maybe a mile out. Are you all right?"

As I spoke the plane tipped its wings, first right, then left. In the beginning I thought the cutoff in our phone conversation was due to Kathy holding on to her seat because the pilot was overdoing it. For a second or two, watching through the 8x50 binoculars, I thought he was losing control of the plane and was taking it into a spin, but then he got the wings level. They were three thousand feet over the waves, maybe four, just under the scudding clouds. Then I realized that our connection had been cut off. I dialed again, but her phone did not ring. I dialed one more time before realizing my phone was dead. No signal strength at all, even though it had been at its maximum a moment earlier. I hated this new cellphone company.

A man from the tour bus with a hearing aid in each ear began shouting into his phone. "Marshall, are you there? Marshall? I can't hear you. Marshall?"

Astonishingly, the plane dipped its wings again and did some sort of flip spiral, turning toward us, but on its side. To my amazement and horror, the plane began a sputtering descent toward the ocean in a slow, seemingly uncontrolled corkscrewing motion.

Cursing loudly enough that all of the old folks from the tour bus stopped what they were doing and followed my line of sight out over the ocean, I watched helplessly. Like a kite with a tangled tail, the plane was going down, flipping and fluttering and finally taking the final part of the dive toward the waves in what was more or less a straight line. The last thousand feet or so it went down like a lawn dart, straight and undeviating.

As the plane struck the ocean, a gout of water shot up from the ocean swells, and then the spot was lost in the rolling of the waves, a mile or a mile and a half out. There were no boats in sight, and as far as I could see, no other planes. I had two immediate thoughts. The first was that the plane wasn't Kathy's. It couldn't be Kathy's. Kathy couldn't be dead. None of them could be dead. The second thought was that I was hallucinating. Neither speculation was based in reality.

A woman was weeping while a man with a camera around his neck tried to console her. Two nearby figures had cell-phones pressed to their ears, calling the authorities, no doubt. For some inexplicable reason, I called Kathy back. Or tried to. It was a reflexive act. The phone was dead, her phone, my phone, everything was dead. None of the others around me seemed to be getting their calls through, either, but they were all old and doddering and their nerves had taken over. The plane had plummeted into the ocean in a classic vertical dive, but I was hoping for survivors. I was an idiot. There would be no survivors. Kathy's body was sinking to the bottom of the ocean. A plane hitting the water from that height would impact with roughly the same force as if smacking a concrete field. Anybody who'd ever gone off a high board at a local swimming pool and muffed the dive knew how unyielding a body of water was. There would be no survivors.

Two women and a man made a beeline for the lighthouse so they could importune the attendant to get help. As the trio scurried past, I heard one of the women say, "We have to get a boat out there before they drown. They're going to drown. We have to act fast."

It was a fiction to think passengers from the plane were alive and awaiting rescue—or at least, that was what I told myself. Kathy was dead. She was most certainly dead. They were *all* dead. There had been some sort of malfunction and the plane went down and by now they were at least a hundred feet underwater. The irony was that after promising myself I wouldn't live through her death twice, over the course of the next week I found myself replaying it hundreds of times.

More people began clustering around us, and as they did so, those who'd witnessed the crash or had been standing next to someone who'd witnessed it explained to the newcomers what the commotion was about, displaying the pride people first on the scene of a catastrophe seem to adopt. Two of the elderly women wept. In a strange way, I was grateful for their compassion. Already I could feel myself withdrawing inward, as if becoming autistic. My brain felt like a shattered mirror.

"What happened?" asked one of the newcomers.

The man who'd taken my photo replied. "There was a

plane out there, and it just all of a sudden went down. It didn't even look like they were trying to save it."

"It was like a maple seed or something," said his spouse, her voice shaky.

"I don't see any crash," said the newcomer.

"You look close, you'll see plane parts floating on the waves."

He was right. When I got the binoculars focused and the swells allowed it, I saw what appeared to be two sections of a wing in the water. "See any people out there?" somebody asked.

"No. No people." My voice sounded as if it were coming from somebody else.

"But they might be alive," said a woman. "They might be waiting for the rescue boats. I mean . . . what if there are sharks?"

I walked away and kept walking until the discussion was a buzz in the breeze. It was hard to believe our idyllic vacation had turned into this nightmare. My legs felt shaky. I felt like vomiting. Not knowing what else to do, I stood in the breeze. I couldn't stand next to the lighthouse for the rest of my life. Surely there were actions I should be taking, but I couldn't think of what they might be.

It was all so wrong. If Kalpesh hadn't phoned Kathy this morning and told her he was sick, Kathy would have been in the rustic little motel room on the beach with me. We would have heard about this on the radio or from a phone call. It was Kalpesh's fault. If Kalpesh hadn't gotten sick, Kathy would be alive. Kalpesh was the reason Kathy was gone. She'd taken his seat on the plane. He was the one who should have been dead. The others were all going to be on the flight anyway, including Sheffield, but Kathy had been placed there by a man I would hold a grudge against for the rest of my life. Even as my brain churned, I knew I wasn't thinking straight. I knew, but I didn't care. Strange how tragedies beg you for somebody to blame.

Kalpesh.

═══ EIGHTEEN ═══

I FOUND HIM along the Columbia River between Ilwaco and the small town of Chinook. Ironically, the kid's name was Noah and he had at his disposal a twenty-foot fiberglass launch stocked with a searchlight, sonar, GPS, and depth finder. He also had half a case of beer and had already generated at least two empties that I could see. It was his dad's fishing boat, but Noah was on a three-week sabbatical at his parents' vacation home at the gorge with his girlfriend and had full use of his parents' play toys, including Jet Skis, sailboards, motorcycles, and the boat. Noah was twenty-two, I think, or twenty-three.

The mighty Columbia River drained into the Pacific Ocean here, forming the Oregon-Washington border. Because the winds howling down the gorge could be pretty spectacular and the river was as wide as many lakes, the area was a mecca for sailboarding enthusiasts on the water and mountain bikers on land. Vacation homes lined both sides of the river.

He'd been docking the launch up against an ancient, broken-down quay when I pulled up in Kathy's car. He said his girlfriend was holed up in the family vacation cabin with the flu and he'd been gadding about all afternoon looking for something to do. An expedition onto the open ocean with me seemed like the ticket. It didn't hurt that I handed him four hundred dollars cash. With Noah piloting, we sped out past the bar and onto the open ocean, bashing through the waves, heading north as rapidly as the launch would carry us, which was pretty fast.

During the next twelve hours Noah did his best to flesh out the silences and ended up telling me almost everything about his life, including how he'd lost his virginity, though I forgot most of it as soon as he finished telling it. I could have shut him up, but his silly self-involvement, along with my sea-sickness, took some of the edge off my anguish. He'd graduated from Pepperdine over a year ago and still hadn't received any job offers. His father was a prominent Kirkland cosmetic surgeon—faces, butts, boobs—and was having a difficult time adjusting to Noah's inactivity and joblessness, though Noah confessed he personally regarded it as a much-deserved vacation. Life was good. He had a vacation home, free use of a boat, and his girlfriend was on the premises.

By the time we arrived at the scene, a helicopter was hovering three hundred feet over the water. Below the chopper a small Coast Guard boat trolled the choppy waters looking for wreckage and, presumably, corpses. When we got close enough, the Coast Guard hailed us with warnings to steer clear of their search grid. I shouted back, "My wife was on that plane. You want me to go away? Shoot me!" That was Noah's first clue as to what was really going on. The Coasties pretended we hadn't heard them and they hadn't heard us and turned back to their work without hailing us again, probably because night was dropping fast and they figured darkness would send us home.

More small craft arrived in the vicinity: two more Coast Guard boats, some fishing boats, a couple of pleasure craft, and even a bearded man in a twelve-foot aluminum dinghy. For the first hour all we found was a section of a wing and a gas slick that seemed to wrap around our hull like beautiful rainbow spiderwebs, but then as evening dropped and more watercraft joined the search, somebody on the Coast Guard boat hoisted a pilot's cap up on an aluminum pole. For some reason, seeing the drenched cap nauseated me as much as if they'd pulled the pilot's head out of the waves. It was the first personal item anybody found and the first material proof that we were dealing with dead people and not just a downed piece of machinery.

A bit farther north two half-submerged pieces of luggage were lifted out of the drink by the crew of a pleasure boat. A briefcase was retrieved. Women's shoes were found floating here and there like flotsam drifting in from the Orient. I eyeballed each and tried desperately to recall what shoes Kathy had been wearing. I had the insane thought that because I couldn't remember I hadn't loved her enough. But I had loved her enough. As far as I could tell, none of it, including a loose bra, had belonged to Kathy. At least I could identify her lingerie. There was that. At eight-thirty Noah and I found our first items: a bag and a woman's sandal. I didn't recognize the sandal, but the bottom dropped out of my guts when I examined the bag. It was Kathy's.

I fished it out of the ocean with a net and opened it, even as somebody on the nearby Coast Guard boat told me not to. Actually, what I desperately wanted was a note in the bag that said, "Thomas, sorry I couldn't make this flight. Meet you at home." The bag contained no note, just Kathy's clothes and bath kit, all still packed neatly despite having fallen almost a mile out of the sky. The meticulousness with which she had ordered the items in the bag watered my eyes. It was the first time I'd cried since watching the plane slam into the Pacific.

I had a habit of getting seasick every time I got on the open ocean, and that night, true to form, I was as sick as an old dog after gobbling a quart of motor oil. I didn't want to view any of the corpses, and I certainly didn't want to view Kathy's body getting jerked out of the brine on a hook. Particularly not out here with a gaggle of pleasure boaters gawking and in all likelihood taking souvenir photos they would post on the Internet or try to sell to the press. This was going to be big news. A United States senator had died in a plane crash. News outlets all over the country would be clamoring for information and photos.

I was growing colder and wetter from the spray flying out of the dark every time the wind hit a cresting wave, and it wasn't long before, in addition to the nausea, I felt myself beginning to get hypothermic. Noah saw me shivering and loaned me one of his father's old rain capes. His thoughtfulness meant more to me than it should have, and I suddenly wanted to put him in my will in the same irrational way I wanted to shoot the boisterous men in a nearby pleasure boat who kept talking about what the bodies were going to look like when they were finally pulled out. Everything out here was heightened: my anguish, my animosity, my seasickness, my sudden indefinable aloneness. In losing Kathy I'd lost everything, and I was acutely aware that nothing in my life would ever be the same. It couldn't have been worse if a nuclear strike had taken out everyone in the country except those of us out here in boats. Hell, there was no way it could have been worse.

At just after nine o'clock one of the fishing boats that had been closer to the lighthouse brought a body to the surface. They motored toward the Coast Guard boat, towing the corpse on a long aluminum arm that was probably designed to gaff fish, the corpse vanishing in the dark waves and then bobbing back to the surface in an odd dance that changed with the shifting spotlights. After Noah maneuvered us into a position where we could see the half-submerged corpse alongside the Coast Guard boat, I saw that it was a woman. She wore a dark blazer very much like the one Kathy had worn in the car.

In the darkness and with the water and the spotlights, it was hard to know if it was Kathy's blazer. I strained desperately to recall if any of the other women at the airport had been in similar jackets. As they struggled to bring the body around to the stern of the Coast Guard boat, I could not look away even though I feared for my sanity should the corpse turn out to be the one I thought it might be. It didn't seem to me as if there should be *any* bodies. They should have all sunk to the bottom in the plane's cabin or been carried away in the current. It had been close to six hours since the crash. On the other hand, I craved resolution and for some flaky reason believed it would come when I finally saw Kathy's broken body.

They brought the corpse around with the aluminum pole and delicately transferred the payload to the Coast Guard people, who had their own gaffs. What a horrible feeling it must have been to be tossed around in that cabin as the plane fluttered toward the ocean. Had they been belted in or had they cartwheeled around the cabin? Had they been momentarily weightless? Had the luggage popped out of the overhead so that the suitcases ricocheted around the cabin like cannonballs through an infantry line? Had Kathy reacted with disbelief? Had she been petrified? Had she ridden the plane into the water calmly, thinking the pilots were going to fly them out of trouble? Or had she squandered any of her last seconds trying to call me? Was that the reason I hadn't been able to reach her after we'd been cut off, because she'd been on the line attempting to reach me? It was a measure of my despair that no matter how hard I tried, I was completely stumped as to how she might have occupied herself during those last moments. Not only that, but I couldn't stop thinking about it.

Word had gotten out, and the plane crash was the leading news item all over the country. In the last two hours on the ocean with Noah and the Coast Guard, I'd used my phone several times and had fielded calls from Beulah, Kathy's mother, various attorneys who worked with Kathy in the courthouse, one of our neighbors in the University District, and others. The conversation with Kathy's mother had been the worst. I wasn't sure if she was blaming me or if I was imagining it, but I had the definite feeling she somehow considered this my fault.

When Kalpesh called, it was obvious he thought he was going to have to break the news to me. "Thomas? Have you heard?"

"I'm out with the Coast Guard now. I saw it happen."

"You saw the Coast Guard start the search?"

"I saw the plane go down."

"What?"

"One minute it was flying out over the ocean, and the next it was diving into the ocean like a stunt plane at an air show."

"How could you have seen it?"

"I was at the lighthouse at Cape Disappointment. I went there after I dropped Kathy off at the airport."

Following a long silence, Kalpesh said, "That must have been awful for you."

"It's not up there on my list of favorite moments."

"I'm so sorry this happened. But what exactly did happen? Can you tell me? No. I guess you . . . I called because I wanted to make sure you didn't hear it on the radio or TV like I did. Maybe I should leave you in peace. You say you're with the Coast Guard?"

"Out on the water."

"Maybe, if you're up to it, you could give me a few more details."

"What do you want to know?"

"The TV news is saying the plane didn't radio for help, that it just vanished off the radar. There's speculation they tangled with another plane. Did you see another plane?"

"I didn't see another plane."

"Either that or a freak storm blew through. A localized squall, perhaps?"

"We had a good view, and there was no storm. It's kicking up now, but not then. I didn't see lightning or anything else that might have brought it down."

"Have they found anybody? Sheffield or . . . ? Have they recovered any of the wreckage?"

"They found one female. They're pulling her out now." Even as I spoke, two Coast Guardsmen hoisted the corpse out of the water, doing their best to be delicate about it. The impact of the crash had ripped off the dead woman's clothing below the waist. Her face and head were oversized and misshapen from the impact. Her skin had a puffy look, the way skin did after it had been in the water awhile. All of her bones seemed to be broken, and she'd come out of the water like an oddly malformed statue, elbows pointing in awkward directions, one leg askew. I knew rigor mortis usually began two to four hours after death and could be accelerated by cold temperatures, so she was broken and then frozen into position like a human pretzel.

Even though I had expected something like this, I was stunned at the condition of the body, at the seminudity, and most of all at the injustice of this woman's random debasement. One of the Coast Guard people turned to me and shouted across the waves. "You know this woman?"

I knew it wasn't Kathy. Nor Jane Sheffield. I believed it was a woman I'd seen at the airport but had not been introduced to, a woman whose name I'd heard from Kathy but couldn't recall. I shook my head.

"Have they found anybody else? Or any parts of the plane?" Kalpesh asked. He'd been asking questions on the phone all along, but I'd been hypnotized by the body. Now they laid the cadaver out on the fantail and stood in a semicircle as if they'd just landed a trophy marlin.

I explained to Kalpesh what was going on, sounding, I thought, particularly cogent and calm, considering the circumstances and my role in them. Perhaps I was only imagining I was calm and was actually coming across as a blithering fruitcake. Even as I wondered how I'd shucked the depression and shock, I began to remember how much I despised Kalpesh for being the instigator of Kathy's death. My awakening had something to do with his failure to ask the identity of the corpse. After all, there was a possibility I was staring at the body of my dead wife as we spoke, yet he kept blathering on as if we were arranging a golfing date.

I knew he was an irrepressible womanizer and had flirted outrageously with Kathy, but I despised him most of all for making her take his seat on the plane. Fury began to course through me like a dose of rat poison.

For the third or fourth time I vomited over the gunwale of the boat. I was puking onto the grave site of a dead senator. And of my wife.

"Thomas? You still there?"

I sat numbly in the stern of the boat as it rose and fell with the waves, staring into the lights that reflected off the roiling water. It was dark now, and I was looking for the shark somebody had spotted a half hour earlier. "I'm here."

"I caught you at a bad time."

"Let's see. Kathy just died in a plane crash, and I'm out here in the rain getting seasick while we search for bodies. And, oh, wait. Kathy was in the seat you were supposed to be in, so you should be dead instead of her. Yeah, I'd say this is a bad time."

"Thomas, I feel dreadful about it. I hesitated even to call, but I couldn't bear the thought that you might find out from the news. I wish it was me instead of Kathy. I don't even know what to say. I don't know why they had to be on the plane, really. It was a stupid idea. I'm sorry I ever thought of it."

"That makes two of us."

"But I am sorry."

"Sorry doesn't bring any of them back."

"No, but—"

"You're a shithead, Kalpesh."

"Go ahead, blame me. I blame myself. I should have been on that plane. I should be dead. I am the worst of the worst."

I hung up on him rather than continue. I wanted to tear him limb from limb, but he had rolled over like a dog who knew he deserved a beating and there was no satisfaction for me in that.

We were on the water for twelve hours total, Noah and myself in his father's fiberglass twenty-footer. The Coast Guard was out for considerably longer, rotating teams and bringing in four more boats for a total of five, along with a series of helicopter flyovers once dawn came. To my astonishment, we continued to bring up bits and scraps from the wreck, including more shoes and two more bodies. The first of the next two bodies was one of the pilots, who was almost unrecognizable, and the second was another man from the Sheffield team. Three corpses in all, along with papers, seat cushions, a Thermos bottle, shampoo bottles, and an electric shaver in a watertight case. By morning only Noah and I remained with the Coast Guard, though we saw a fishing smack loaded with news photographers heading out as we were heading in. Noah had been a good soldier and, once he realized we were looking for my wife's body, had not complained about any of it.

He dropped me off near Chinook, where Kathy's Prius was parked, and said, "Geez, man, I'm sorry. That was just . . ."

"Yeah." Feeling leg weary and unsteady on shore, I clambered up the embankment toward the car, stumbling like a child who'd been thrown off a merry-go-round. The unsteadiness would linger for another five or six hours, but I knew I'd be way off-kilter for far longer than that.

Noah said, "I hope they find her, man. I really do."

"What difference does it make?" I said, although we both knew finding her would be like closing a book.

Later as I was trying to work my way to the Coast Guard station at Cape Disappointment, I saw her.

It took almost an hour and a half to locate the station, and during the drive I passed a rickety old pickup truck hurtling along the highway in the other direction. For a split second I thought Kathy was in the passenger seat. An old man with whiskers was driving. I saw *him* clearly, but the woman I saw less clearly. Still, I was almost certain it was Kathy. Pulling into a turnout where I could turn around, bucking a barrage of honking motorists, I followed.

It was impossible to know how she could have come to be passing me in a strange truck. I was thinking all kinds of screwy thoughts: that Kathy had escaped the plane via parachute, that she'd survived the crash and washed up on shore, or that she'd missed the flight entirely and had been hitchhiking around the peninsula all night looking for me. None of the scenarios made any sense, but I chased the pickup truck anyway.

Driving like a madman, I tooted the tinny Prius horn— doing the whole pursuit in the oncoming lane as if I had a date with death myself. As I pulled even, both individuals in the truck peered out the driver's window at me. No doubt thinking I was indulging a bad case of road rage, the old man with the whiskers gave me the bird. The woman was fifteen feet away, and I could plainly see she did not look anything like Kathy. She was a crone in a black hooded sweatshirt that—given my sixty-mile-per-hour glimpse—had mimicked Kathy's hair. Crap. The adrenaline boost had revived me almost to normalcy, but as I turned around and headed toward the Coast Guard station I found myself overcome by exhaustion. The disappointment of discovering my wife was alive and then being forced to realize she was still dead had wiped out my last reserves.

Eventually I found the Coast Guard facilities at Cape Disappointment, parked, and went inside, where I waded through the cacophony and introduced myself. The place was a beehive of civilians on cellphones and others clamoring for attention from officials. It took half an hour, but in the end a young guardsman named Hutchins was assigned to look after me, partially because the station was already packed with reporters—the parking lot was rife with TV vans—and partly because I'd had a run-in with a cameraman. I don't remember what either of us said, but some of the bystanders felt we were about to come to blows and stepped between us. Seeing all these people who were only going to make my day more miserable had put me over the edge. I was ready for a fist-fight over any little thing, and the cameraman bumped into me and then tried to push his way past when I didn't move. He was a big guy, undoubtedly used to getting his way, but I wasn't impressed.

Periodically for the rest of the day, Coast Guardsman Hutchins brought me doughnuts, bottled water, and ongoing news of the search, which went even more slowly during daylight hours than it had during the night. That second night I slept in the parking lot in the car—or more accurately, I dozed, listening to local radio stations. Actual sleep was for the guiltless. I'd decided on all sorts of ways in which Kathy's death was my fault. I never should have allowed her to break up our tête-à-tête with a plane trip. I should have insisted we spend two days at the ocean. I should have been more curious about the condition of the plane and the expertise of the pilots. What had caused the tailspin? Had it been the action of dipping their wings for me over Cape Disappointment? That was a possibility I couldn't bear to consider. Even though the scene of the crash was continually and mercilessly being re-run in my brain, it kept altering so that I could no longer trust my own memory of what I had witnessed.

By four in the afternoon of the third day, they'd located the fuselage where it had settled on a sandy bottom eight hundred feet below the waves. The government was going to bring in remote-controlled machinery to recover the wreckage and, with luck, the remainder of the bodies. Around noon a fishing boat had found the second pilot's body on the beach near Ocean Shores.

Near sunset of the third day, hope for finding more bodies began to dwindle. My cellphone battery had long ago given out, and I didn't bother to charge it in the car charger. I knew when I finally got it running again it would disgorge dozens, if not hundreds, of messages, none of which I wanted to field. I'd already received more than my share of commiserating calls from assorted friends, family, and from myriad political hacks who hadn't known either Kathy or me eight weeks ago. Also, there would be more calls from Kalpesh, the shithead.

What galled me about Kalpesh's apology was that I believed his sincerity. I wanted to detest him for deceitfulness, but he'd been genuinely remorseful, and because of that I couldn't detest him with half the vigor I wanted to, which only made me despise him all the more.

═══ NINETEEN ═══

DEBORAH DRISCOLL WAS ALMOST more infuriating than Kalpesh Gupta, although she did nothing more than try to be my friend. My urge to find fault with her was like the inclination a lunatic might have to slam his fist into a wall, except it wasn't as satisfying to indulge. Kathy hadn't liked Deborah and, in fact, had been a little jealous of her, which I'd found somewhat amusing while Kathy was alive, but now that things had changed, everything about Deborah irritated me. What galled me the most was that she was still breathing and Kathy was not.

Eight days had passed since the crash, and by my estimate I'd slept less than twenty hours during that span. The biggest problem with trying to sleep was every time I woke up I would once again have to tell myself it was true, that Kathy had died in a plane crash and was missing—dead. Sometimes, as I slept, when I slept, I would wake up in the middle of a crying jag. I didn't like it. None of it. The neolithic part of my brain solved the problem by refusing me sleep. Because of my grief and lack of sleep, I was alternately despairing, unbelieving, spiteful, and once or twice hallucinatory. I was also afraid I might be turning lethal.

I'd never particularly thought of myself as dangerous. I got into trouble, sure, but I usually did it pursuing legitimate ends, and while it was true that over the years I had been responsible for at least two deaths, both were justifiable and could be placed in the sphere of things unavoidable. Both could have been classified as self-defense. I did not consider myself a murderer, and as far as I knew, thugs and felons did not tremble when I tromped through the halls of the King County Courthouse. It was hard to explain even to myself why I might be dangerous now or what I might do, but I was beginning to get the feeling that sane people and people of delicate sensibilities had best steer clear.

Deborah Driscoll seemed unable to comprehend this. She had telephoned twice between the time of the crash and the fourth memorial service eight days later. The services, the funerals, the memorials, had all been delayed because of the retrieval efforts and because of the fact that some of the bodies had not been recovered. Kathy's hadn't been. Deborah's first call was "just to see how you're doing," though I believed there might have been darker undercurrents. She hinted she might be able to put some time aside to come over and visit, possibly late after she left the office. It was likely there was nothing suggestive about her offer, but it was hard to tell. My antenna for that sort of thing was broken.

The next time she called she invited me to drive with her to the Sheffield memorial service at the convention center in Bellevue. I had been dreading the Sheffield memorial, the largest and most formal of the services. Kathy's was slated to be among the last, but I had been unable to bring myself to think about it or to help her family with details.

I drove with Driscoll to the Sheffield service, but only because she sounded down in the mouth on the phone and made noises to the effect that funerals were difficult for her and I would be doing her a favor by accompanying her. She picked me up in her silver Lexus, which still smelled new. "How are you doing?" she asked, and as soon as she asked I could tell by her tone she thought she was doing me the favor.

"Fine," I lied. "I'm doing fine." It was my fourth memorial service in three days. She had not shown her face at any of the others, nor had any other Maddox campaigners. The Maddox machine plunged ahead undiminished, in fact very much enlivened by the unexpected demise of their opponent. Maddox and a few of the others in his campaign seemed, if anything, invigorated by the Sheffield tragedy. That's what the media was calling it now: the Sheffield tragedy or, alternately, the Sheffield crash, or the Sheffield accident. As if there hadn't been ten other people on board, as if the pilots and the staff and the cameraman and producer doing the commercial had never existed, as if Kathy had never existed, as if nobody was dead but Jane Sheffield. It was a natural posture for the media to assume, but it pissed me off. These days everything pissed me off.

"You don't have to talk if you don't want to," Deborah said, as she drove east toward Lake Washington and ultimately across the water on the 520 bridge and into downtown Bellevue. Apparently she'd been trying to engage me in conversation for some minutes, but I hadn't noticed.

"Good. We won't talk."

As much as I hated to acknowledge it, Deborah looked particularly fine in her black suit, the black contrasting with her red hair and pale skin. I wore the same dark suit Kathy had helped me pick out for official campaign dinners and whatnot. When we bought it, I'd made a batch of tasteless jokes to the effect that now that I was outfitted with a spiffy dark funereal suit, all my friends and relatives could start kicking the bucket, and the sooner the better, before my suit didn't fit anymore. The jokes seemed eerily prescient now and made me seem like a horrid man.

Traffic was heavy, and Deborah, as always, drove aggressively. Kathy hadn't been especially adept as a driver, while Deborah had taken race-car lessons three summers in a row and had even steered a Formula 1 car around a track somewhere in Maryland. Her parents had paid for it. Wealthy family, I thought, from that and other things she'd said over the weeks.

"I know you said we weren't going to talk," Deborah said, "and I respect that, but we were wondering how long you were planning to stay away from the office."

"What?"

"Things are ramping up at the office, and there are some items Maddox needs you to look into. No pressure, or anything. There's still over a month until the election, but the ballots have already been printed and Sheffield will still be on it."

"She shouldn't be hard to beat. She's dead. Or haven't you guys noticed?"

"Don't mock me, please. This is turning into a real battle."

"It always *was* a real battle. Maddox never got close to her in the polls. But like I said, it should be easy now."

"John Ashcroft lost to a dead man in Missouri in 2000. After he was elected, the then governor appointed the dead man's wife to take his seat. All perfectly legal."

"Is that what you're afraid is going to happen here?"

"It's not over until it's over. This state has a Democratic governor, and the word is that if Sheffield gets reelected, she'll appoint Sheffield's husband. That plus the sympathy factor, and we've got a fight on our hands."

"Shucky darn."

"I'm beginning to wonder where your sympathies lie."

"I've never made it a secret."

But she didn't pursue it, so it was between us for the rest of the day, along with a few other things. Later, after she'd had some time to come at it from another angle, she said, "I know you have some life changes you're trying to cope with, but sometimes it helps to keep busy. You might be surprised how getting back into the harness keeps your mind off your troubles. We'd love to have you back. What do you say, Thomas?"

"I haven't buried Kathy yet." Besides Kathy's, there were still five other bodies missing, though they'd brought up the fuselage two days before. One of the pilots, Sheffield, two aides, and the producer for the commercial were unaccounted for. And Kathy.

"Well, sure, I understand. Give it some thought, Thomas. You can come back part-time or full. Whatever makes you feel comfortable. We miss you." When she said that, she took her right hand off the steering wheel and reached over for my hand, but I moved it and she accidentally laid her hand across my thigh. "You're sweet, Thomas."

We didn't say another word on the drive. We didn't say much at the service, either. There were thousands of people in attendance, crowds in the street outside, bagpipers, a bugler, more U.S. flags than I'd seen anywhere in a long time, and a special seating section for VIPs. We sat up high to the left of the stage, where we had a fair view of the room.

There were preliminary comments by the other senator from Washington state, from the governor, who had cut short her honeymoon to attend, and from Kalpesh Gupta. They were all short, emotional, and to the point. Gupta's comments were particularly poignant and his thoughtfulness surprised me. The reverence surrounding Jane Sheffield was almost palpable. Each time a new speaker took the platform, the room grew hushed. Deborah and I were seated on bleachers, packed in alongside hundreds of others, squashed so tightly our thighs were warm from the contact.

The low point might have been the confused and jarring, mostly political speech by Sheffield's distraught and sometimes foulmouthed twenty-seven-year-old son, who had been slated for the fatal flight but had missed it.

It was clear from the thickening tones in his voice that he was sobbing as he spoke. For a while all was well, but then he began making political comments against the Republican Party, a couple of former presidents, and some of the right-wing radio and television pundits who he claimed had been spewing venom onto his mother's corpse. To say the least, it was ill advised, and as he got more and more wound up, we could see his father trying to decide whether to escort him off the stage. In the end, his father and one of the Sheffield aides gently removed him while the bagpipe band began playing a version of the "Skye Boat Song."

By the time we got to my house, the national radio newscasters were already jumping on the Sheffield people. It was deemed a shame that family members and Sheffield campaign organizers had thought it appropriate to talk trash against the opposing party at a funeral. The talking heads accused the Democratic Party of bad form. Kalpesh Gupta was cited as the spark plug in a "dying" campaign, who had turned the funeral into a public pyre upon which had been thrown the last vestiges of good taste. All the right-wing noisemakers took up the gauntlet, and by late evening pundits were reporting things that hadn't even happened. It was said that the audience had cheered when Sheffield's son told the crowd he wished Maddox and his staff had gone down in the plane instead of his mother, though Sheffield's son had said nothing of the sort, and that the audience had been aghast throughout his remarks. It pissed me off the way Maddox's side refused to cut any slack for the young man, who was so clearly overcome with grief.

"Thomas?" Deborah had said as we drove up to my house. "How are you doing? How are you really doing?"

"Pretty shitty."

"Is there anyone here to help out?"

"My sister was here, but I sent her away."

"How long was she there?"

"Half an hour. I need to be alone."

"There are a million little things that have to be done at a time like this. I've been through similar situations before. I know your head is in no shape to be handling the guff people are going to be asking you to handle. Are the funeral arrangements completed?"

"I think her family is taking care of that."

"When was the last time you ate?"

"A day or two. I'm not hungry."

"I'm not leaving until I'm sure everything's okay."

═══ TWENTY ═══

AFTER WATCHING THREE talking heads reviewing the Senate career of Jane Sheffield for fifteen minutes, I channel-surfed until I found an old Alain Delon movie. Deborah couldn't take it and went out to the kitchen to listen to more Sheffield news on NPR. I could hear her clearing dirty dishes off the table, chairs, and presumably the floor, but I wasn't going to apologize for the mess. Feeling ashamed meant you could feel, and feeling wasn't in my repertoire just yet.

Our single-story house had been built in 1929 and added on to several times. The basement apartment Kathy had once rented now housed an engineering student from the U whom Kathy had branded the "mole" because of his proclivity for working all night on school projects and sleeping most of the day. I'd run into him only once since Kathy's death, by accident when he came out to get the mail off the front porch. Neither of us said anything. He'd been harboring a not-so-secret crush on Kathy since the day he moved in.

It was a simple house and needed work. The gutter out back by the crab apple tree leaked. The garage door needed to be rehung. It wasn't a shabby house, not exactly, nor was it a match for Horace's spick-and-span showplace next door. My humble home had a tiny backyard next to a detached garage, a long driveway that ran between my house and Horace's, and, because it was situated close to the sidewalk, no front lawn to speak of. The living room collected a fair amount of traffic noise from the street. I didn't groom and curry what lawn we had, and you probably couldn't eat off the floor the way you could at Horace's place; but I had a nice collection of roses, and in the summer I grew tomatoes outside beneath the kitchen window, where the afternoon sun beat against the house.

Most of my neighbors had left notes of condolence or come over to talk to me since the accident. Horace hadn't shown his face, but his wife had delivered inedible casseroles every two days, which I would have fed to the dog if he hadn't run away during my delirium at the Coast Guard station. So far I hadn't found the pluck to go looking for Spider. Originally we'd found him on the street, so I knew he could take care of himself if he had to.

When I wandered into the kitchen, my eyes quickly scanned the room for familiar items of Kathy's I'd been staring at all week, but they were missing: a pair of earrings on the windowsill over the sink; her handwritten recipe card for ginger coin cookies, which she'd left on the counter, hoping to find time to make them; the saucer still holding the tea bag she'd used just before we left for the ocean. It was all put away.

As much as I resented the meddling, I was too stupefied with grief and indecision to say anything about it. I resented the hell out of Deborah, but she meant well, and God knows, I'd been needing somebody to come and do this.

Deborah noticed me looking around and said, "I know it doesn't seem like it and it probably will be heresy coming from me, because I know Kathy didn't like me, but you'll love again, Thomas, and it'll be almost as wonderful as what you had. I'm not telling you to drop everything and go searching for another wife. I'm just saying I know it seems like the end of the world, but I felt the same way when my brother died."

"When did your brother die?" I asked.

"When I was seventeen he went away to college and got mixed up in one of those stupid fraternity stunts that went wrong. I'm not saying I don't miss him still, because I do, as I'm sure you'll always have a special place in your heart for Kathy, but you have to realize there is a future waiting for you out there. There *is* a life waiting. And you know what? Kathy would be the first to tell you that. So do your grieving, but at some point start pulling out of this funk."

It was solid advice, but I resented the fact that it was coming from a woman Kathy had viewed more or less as a potential rival. It didn't help that Deborah worked in the wrong camp and that Kathy felt the upcoming election was as vital as anything she'd ever taken part in. Nor did it help that I believed everyone in the Maddox camp was jubilant over recent events, that they were all secretly gloating because Sheffield and her top aides were permanently out of the picture.

I even resented the fact that she was sitting in Kathy's favorite chair without knowing it, just as earlier she'd managed to find Kathy's favorite spot on the couch. Hell, there wasn't anything about this woman I didn't resent. I tried not to wolf down the meal she had made for us, but that didn't last more than a few bites, because I was starving, and then when I went to the sink to drink a glass of water and fill a second glass, I realized my stomach hurt from the sudden influx of food and liquid.

"I might have fixed something other than scrambled eggs and toast, but there isn't much in the house," Deborah said. "I *can* cook other things."

"I need to go shopping."

"Would you like me to go for you?"

"No, thanks."

I needed to send Deborah packing, but I couldn't drum up the energy and I apparently craved human companionship, because after we finished eating I let her blather on and on about the week's political news. "I know you realize how important this election is, not just here in this state but nationally. The Washington Senate race has been named as one of the two most important races in the country. Our party is two seats away from taking the majority from the Democrats, and if we can do that, we can get some things done for this country."

"I don't care about this. You might as well be talking about the Tibetan high school basketball championships."

"We've got a whole raft of television and radio pundits working the point that it's outrageous that the governor will appoint Sheffield's husband if she wins the election. We're hoping the public pressure will force the governor to change her mind. Anyway, some of the talking heads are refusing to discuss much of anything besides the fact that the polls haven't changed since the accident. Sheffield's still in the lead. What they don't take into account is the sympathy factor. I mean, if Maddox had gone down in a plane crash, he'd be ahead in the polls, don't you think?"

"Actually, I don't."

"We're thinking after this service for Sheffield maybe the sympathy factor will taper off. At least we're hoping it will. You know what we found out this morning? *60 Minutes* will be taping a piece on the election. In addition, money is coming in from all over. It would just be such a shame to lose by a nose and then have the governor appoint the husband. Thomas. I'm running on and on, and what I should be saying is, I thought you and Kathy were just the sweetest couple. I always thought you had the relationship I was looking for and have never been able to pull together. You were devoted to each other but also independent in your own right. You were both just a treat to be around. It's a tragedy. I'll be sick about it for a long time."

"Thanks, Deborah. And thanks for coming. But I think I should be alone now."

"Yes. Of course you need time by yourself." Instead of leaving, she tipped forward in her chair, crossed her legs at the ankles, and said, "The president called yesterday. Did I tell you? He said the whole nation was watching our race and it was vital we not let up."

"Funny he should call you guys, seeing as the other camp lost their candidate and six staff members."

"Of course he's talked to the Sheffield people, too. Just a week earlier Maddox and all of us were in a small plane together. It could have been us. It was terrible, but we still have a job to do and we're going to do it the best we know how. That's what *they* would have done if we'd been in that plane."

"Sure."

"Look, kiddo. Would you like me to come around later in the week and spend a day going through Kathy's things? I could sort them and help you decide which should go to the Goodwill and which—"

"Can you leave now?"

"Sure." But instead of grabbing her coat, she began clearing the table, one last favor for the widower. Widower. Jesus. I was a widower.

"Just leave!" I yelled, whereupon she picked up her coat, slipped into her shoes, and stepped out the back door.

TWENTY-ONE

SNAKE HAD PICKED THE LOCK on the front door, let himself into my house, and was now ensconced in an easy chair with his cowboy boots propped on the coffee table. He'd come to comfort me, but he wouldn't do it by pouring me vodka and looking me in the eye, partially because neither of us drank— he was a reformed alcoholic, while I'd never touched a drop in my life—and partially because looking me in the eye with words of consolation was not his style. Parking his boots on our coffee table *was* his style. He'd asked to stay the night, handing out the excuse that Emerald City Pest Control was bug-bombing his apartment house again.

Groundhog Day had been my security blanket for most of the day, but now we were watching Michael Mann's *Last of the Mohicans*. We'd been at it awhile, and I was finding this new flick a distraction from watching Bill Murray stumble through one suicide after another. I'd been housebound most of the week, still feeling as if I was living somebody else's life and doing it in a borrowed body. Until now, catastrophes were events I investigated for other people, not incidents I lived through myself. Late this afternoon, despite the fact that I had attended two more funerals after throwing Deborah Driscoll out of the house, I was beginning to sense the first vague stirring of normalcy since the accident. I'd actually walked to the store and returned with a bag of groceries, though afterward I left a container of ice cream on the counter until it melted.

I'd had an elderly uncle who committed suicide a year after his wife died, and now for the first time I was beginning to understand his frame of mind. I had never thought it possible for a human being to feel this bad and still be alive. I was lonely but I didn't want to be around people. I was sad but I didn't want to be jollied along. The one person I pined for was dead.

Over the course of the past days my mind had run through the gamut of methods to kill yourself. Poison was icky, jumping was scary, and I didn't like sharp instruments. For philosophical reasons, I was not going to use a gun. All the really smart ways to die eluded me. But then, I wasn't going to kill myself; I only wanted to mull it over. I was like an impoverished kid test-driving sports cars—all bluff.

I must have dozed through the movie, because I woke to a dark screen. Minutes later, Snake came back into the room with a stack of freshly printed photos he tossed onto the coffee table. Apparently he'd downloaded everything in my camera, which I'd placed on the coffee table a week ago, and run it through our printer in the spare bedroom. "You okay?" Snake asked.

"Just ducky."

"Thought you might want to look through those."

"Why don't you just strangle me with one of Kathy's stockings?"

"I just thought . . ."

"Okay. Sure. Thanks."

He started the movie again while I surprised myself by pulling the stack of still-warm photos into my lap. Kathy had taken snapshots of me while I was driving between Seattle and Olympia in the rain. Later, she'd taken some of us unpacking at the little motel we liked to stay at, and then I'd playfully snapped a couple of her as she started to get undressed, my efforts interrupted when she confiscated the camera, which was about the time we ended up tussling on the bed. I didn't see the camera again until the next morning when she carried it down to the beach to click her standard string of ocean shots as we walked, the nothing foreground made worse by the nothing background, a hodgepodge of blue-gray water and gray-blue sky. If she'd lived, she would have thrown all those shots out, saying, "I thought they were going to turn out better."

There were even two shots of me jumping in front of the camera as she tried to take pictures of the ocean. One garbled picture as I picked her up and ran down the beach with her slung over my shoulder while she screamed bloody murder.

There was one snapshot of her in the car after we arrived at the landing strip. "So I can have something to remember you by when I'm old and lonely," I said as I took it. It was the last photograph anybody ever took of her, and at the time I thought it a grand joke. I stared at it for a long while. Kathy had been gazing out through the windshield wistfully, a perfect profile shot of a perfect face. I'd like to think the look in her glistening eyes indicated she was sorry to be leaving me, but it was probably in anticipation of the flight.

The penultimate photos were taken by the old man I'd given my camera to in front of the Cape Disappointment lighthouse: myself in the foreground, the lighthouse behind, and in the distance a speck of an airplane carrying my beloved. I'd meant it as a gag, but now it was evidence. There were two such pictures of me and the plane, one blurry and useless, plus a third shot of what must have been the old man's knee he'd probably snapped when he was passing the camera back to me. What I hadn't expected were the last two shots, photos of the plane plummeting out of the sky. I had no memory of taking them, but the old man had already given the camera back by then, so I must have.

In the first shot the plane had already accomplished about a third of its descent. There was no other plane in the photo and no debris in the sky, just the falling plane, which appeared to be intact. In the second, the turboprop had hit the water and was creating a white spout in the ocean, the tail and part of a wing above the surface, everything else under. It was hard to tell if the wing was already broken at that point.

I'd captured the instant of Kathy's death, of all eleven deaths. I knew the other families had a right to know about it, even if they couldn't stand to view it, though I dreaded the newspaper editors getting their hands on it. "Snake?"

"Yeah?"

"You look at these?"

"You talking about the plane going into the drink? Hell of a shot."

"They know what caused the crash?"

"Nope."

"You heard any theories?"

"There's a rumor circulating that one of the pilots may have committed suicide. Decided to take a bunch of people with him and get some headlines. That one keeps cropping up."

"You think there's any basis to it?"

"I wouldn't know. They haven't found a note or anything, but they're still looking. Then there's the hypothesis that they ran into a localized electrical storm and it disabled their instrumentation. Some people think there may have been another plane. They've launched a search for any other aircraft in the area that may have sustained damage."

"If there was another aircraft, why didn't the other pilot report it?"

"Could be they didn't realize what they hit."

"I didn't see another plane, and none shows up in these pictures."

Snake hadn't taken his eyes off the movie. "You know you're going to have to hand them over to the authorities."

"Think there's any way to keep them from the media?"

"I doubt it. I was thinking maybe you should sell them."

"You've got your head up your ass if you think I'm going to sell Rupert Murdoch photos of my wife's plane at the moment of her death."

"Yeah. Right. Sorry. The thing is, they'll probably get leaked anyway."

Getting off the sofa was like dragging myself out of a hole. Once on my feet, I scooped up the newspaper clippings Snake had brought and carried them into the kitchen. It took a while to organize them and a while longer to organize my thoughts. It seemed as if it had been months since I'd done anything purposeful. I'd dragged myself to the funerals, but I'd done that in a partial fugue state, believing I had no choice, believing the best way to pay tribute to the dead was to honor the survivors.

Sitting at the kitchen table, I prepared to think about the specifics of an event I'd been avoiding all week. I'd replayed the plane falling out of the sky maybe forty thousand times, but I hadn't put any constructive thought into why or how it happened. Nine and a half days had elapsed since the crash, and on each of those days I'd pulled further from reality.

I skimmed the headlines and the photo captions. The local interest stories and general background pieces I placed to my right. The national press pieces I cached an arm's length away in the center of the table. Anything with Kathy's name highlighted—somebody, presumably Snake, had used a yellow grease pen to color her name wherever it appeared—I placed in front. The conspiracy articles from the Internet, of which there were a surprising number, I pushed off to my left. It was just like Snake to give me a collection of clippings that included headlines like WAS SHEFFIELD ASSASSINATED? DID THE CIA KILL JANE? WHY IS THE WHITE HOUSE TERRIFIED OF AN INVESTIGATION? COULD A FOREIGN GOVERNMENT HAVE BEEN INVOLVED? Snake was almost as bad as his brother when it came to getting snookered by conspiracy theories.

The *Seattle Post-Intelligencer* had done a feature article on Kathy, quoting half a dozen people from the courthouse. They'd called me requesting a comment for the article, but I never called back. Even Bert Slezak had been quoted. "Ms. Birchfield was more than my attorney. She was my friend. She was the best person I ever knew."

"Nice piece on your bride," Snake said from the other room.

"They call her effervescent."

"She was that, my man. And a lot more."

A defense attorney who'd been in the business thirty years was quoted as saying, "Birchfield had the capability to become one of the best trial attorneys ever. You could see that right away. She was smart, methodical, knew the law, and cared about clients." Another attorney from our building at First and Yesler said, "You could tell she was headed for bigger things." Kalpesh Gupta said, "I wouldn't have been surprised if, at some point, she'd entered politics. Everybody loved her. She was like a sister to so many people."

One of the notices was clipped out of *The Seattle Times* and announced the service Kathy's sister and mother had planned for the previous day. I hadn't been looking forward to it, and the actuality proved even worse than I'd imagined. Except for the day the plane went down, it had been the single worst day of my life. To my mind, holding a service for Kathy was tantamount to giving up, although when I thought it through, I had no idea what exactly I would be giving up that I hadn't already lost.

I found article after article recounting the crash. The most complete article was from *The New York Times,* and along with interviews from eyewitnesses—mostly old gummers from the tour bus at Cape Disappointment—it sported statements from a Coast Guard spokesperson, a quote from the man who'd been manning the lighthouse, and liberal quotes from the special agent-in-charge of the Seattle FBI office. "We're investigating this and will continue to investigate until we determine the cause of the crash," said Winston Seagram. "No stone will be left unturned. As far as we can tell at this point, this was a regrettable accident. We will, however, continue to look into it along with the FAA and the NTSB team."

A statement from the head of the National Transportation Safety Board investigating team, Timothy Hoagland, who reportedly flew to Washington State from the District of Columbia the morning after the crash, said simply, "We're focusing on the possibility that there was some freezing weather at the eight-thousand-foot level. They dropped to four thousand feet just prior to the crash, and we're trying to figure out why. There's a possibility they dropped down because they were icing up. Any number of small planes have gone down over the years because of icing problems. It can come on suddenly at this time of year."

A long article from *The Oregonian* explained how a typical plane crash was investigated, complete with a photo layout of the Cape Disappointment Coast Guard Station and a hangar at Boeing Field in Seattle where they were collecting recovered pieces of the Beechcraft King Air. Judging from the photos, they had most of the large pieces assembled into the shape of an airplane. The plane was not required to carry a cockpit voice recorder, and one had not been installed.

The New York Times had done a series of small pieces on the crash and then two days ago printed a feature article laying out the information investigators had gleaned so far. I studied the section about the airplane. "Beechcraft King Air," I said aloud.

"One of the most reliable aircraft in the world," Snake barked from the other room. "Tons of 'em out there and only two fatal crashes in the last ten years."

The Beechcraft King Air had been in continuous production in one form or another since it was introduced in 1964. The King Air came out in a number of different models, and the cabin configurations could be switched to suit the customer. Behind the cockpit, there were seven small passenger windows. The aircraft Kathy and Sheffield and the others had flown in contained seats for twelve passengers. The plane could be piloted by one person, but Northwest Apple Flight, which owned and operated the aircraft, preferred two pilots for groups and high-profile passengers like the senator. The plane had a range of just over 2,000 miles, a service ceiling of 32,800 feet, and a maximum speed of 289 knots. According to the story, Northwest Apple Flight had serviced the plane two weeks before the crash.

Both pilots were experienced, knowledgeable, and considered "top hands." One had worked for Northwest Apple for fourteen years, while the other had been an air force pilot for ten years prior to coming to Northwest three years ago. The day before the flight both pilots had completed a long trip down the East Coast and back up the West Coast with a rock band and the night before the crash had flown to Portland, where they stayed with the married sister of one of the pilots. After dinner and several hands of poker with the sister, her husband, and friends, both pilots slept overnight at the sister's house. According to the family, neither had imbibed alcohol, though there were Internet rumors to the contrary.

When I dropped Kathy off at the airfield I'd spoken to Freddy Mitz, the pilot who'd flown for the air force, and he'd appeared neither drunk nor hungover. But I'd only been with him a minute. Mitz was forty-two and had a grown son from a previous marriage. He lived in the Seattle area with his second wife, who acted in local theatrical productions when she wasn't working as a substitute schoolteacher. After his time in the air force, Mitz worked in a real estate firm for several years before returning to his first love, flying.

Charles Hilditch, forty-nine, had flown for Northwest

Apple since its founding. Before joining Apple he learned to
fly at Central Washington University and then collected most
of his early hours ferrying Microsoft millionaires around the
country on business junkets. When he wasn't flying, Hilditch
liked to golf and take long, solitary motorcycle trips. One
anonymous source claimed there were rumors that his marriage was breaking up and that he'd been despondent.

The article that surprised me concerned Bert Slezak.

The title of the article was "On the Bizarre Side."

On Thursday National Transportation Safety Board investigators were surprised when a man identifying himself as
the husband of one of the victims in the Sheffield crash began interfering with the investigation at the Coast Guard
station near Cape Disappointment. Bert Nelson Slezak was
arrested by the FBI and twelve hours later turned over to local authorities after he broke through barriers and handled
parts of the wreckage. Witnesses said he was "raving and
acted oddly." Some Coast Guard officials speculated pri-
vately that he may have been under the influence of drugs.

Slezak conned his way onto the site by falsely claiming
his wife had been a passenger on the downed plane. Despite warnings from officials that picture-taking was pro-
hibited, he began snapping photographs with a disposable
camera. When NTSB investigators ordered him to stop, he
allegedly bit one of them. It was later determined that
Slezak was not married and that he had no close ties to
anybody on the flight, although the FBI is looking into the
possibility that Slezak may at one time have been represented by an attorney who died in the crash. No motive
was given for his actions. He is being held for obstruction
of justice, trespass, and battery.

The FBI held him for twelve hours and *then* turned him
over to local authorities? What was that all about?

"You know where your brother is?" I yelled to Snake in the
other room.

Turning the sound down, he said, "What?"

"Where is your brother?"

"I don't know. He called yesterday. He didn't say where he was hangin'."

"He call from jail?"

"It didn't sound like it."

"You bail him out a few days ago?"

"Nope."

"What'd he call you about?"

"*You,* actually. He thought you might be in trouble. Wanted me to come over and guard you."

"Guard me? Is that what he said?"

"That's what he said."

"Why would I need protection?"

"He thinks you're taking this pretty hard. Which you are."

"Did you know he warned me not to let Kathy travel with Sheffield?"

"When was this?"

"A few days before it happened. He said he had a premonition. Now that I think about the meeting, I remember getting the feeling that there was more on his mind than he was admitting."

"Jesus."

"Snake? Why don't you fill me in on your brother."

Snake froze the picture on the movie and stepped into the dining room. "Jesus H., I hope Bert's not messed up in this."

"You have any reason to think he might be? I mean, besides his arrest?" When Snake didn't reply, I said, "Snake?"

"He could be mixed up in *anything.*"

"Mind telling me about him?"

"Where do you want me to start?"

"Let's try the beginning. Start with him in diapers."

Snake gave me a lugubrious look and turned a chair around so he could straddle it backward. "At least you're not moping anymore."

"Cut to the chase, would you?"

═══ TWENTY-TWO ═══

"YOU REALIZE YOU'RE ASKING me to rat out my brother."

"Only if he's involved."

"But he's still my brother."

"And my wife is dead."

"I didn't say I wasn't going to do it. I just wanted you to know I'm making a sacrifice here."

"Yeah, well, I made a sacrifice, too."

Snake and I stared at each other. "He told me something once . . ." he trailed off. "I want this to remain confidential."

"Like hell."

"Five years ago, right before I went on the wagon, he told me about something he'd been involved with in South America ten or fifteen years earlier. He said it was so ugly he couldn't tell people without worrying about their mental health afterward."

"What about *his* mental health?"

"Right."

"No, I mean it. I've just known him the last year or two, but from the start I thought he was a couple of pickles short of a full jar. Was he always like that?"

"He may seem like a nut job, but I wouldn't underestimate him."

"Is there a possibility he might have had something to do with that plane going down?"

"Listen, Thomas. It was an accident. The sooner you get a grip on that, the better off you'll be."

"But what if it wasn't?"

"It was."

"They haven't found the cause yet. And Bert warned me to keep Kathy from traveling with Sheffield."

"They never find the cause of an airplane accident quickly.

As for your second point, he told me about the original World Trade Center bombing a couple of days before it happened."

"You're kidding, right?"

"I wish I was. Same with Oklahoma City. A month before 9/11 he told me not to fly for a while. But, hell, even the attorney general was telling people he wasn't going to fly. That whole event stinks."

"So he's got what . . . ? Ties with terrorist groups?"

"With the government."

"You saying the government knew about Oklahoma City before it happened? About 9/11?"

"I'm just telling you what Bert told me. Bert knew something. And he didn't get it from terrorists."

"So tell me about this business he was involved with in South America."

"He worked for a place called Green Farms, which was a CIA front company. Or maybe it was called Green Produce. Something like that."

"You know for a fact it was CIA?"

"With my brother, you never know anything for a fact. But yeah, even though he'll deny it if you ask, I'm pretty sure. He told me he was eventually sold out by the Company. They set him up and sent him up for selling drugs. Came out of the slammer with a real hostile attitude."

"He ever have a good attitude?"

"Well, no. Our father was a steelworker, a big sloppy guy, but strong, with these massive forearms. If he grabbed you, you'd feel it for a week. I learned my lesson pretty quick, but Bert never got tired of taking him on. He was in the hospital once with a concussion when we were ten. Oh, our father could be a charmer. He had these electric-blue eyes so you thought he was looking into your soul. Women melted. Mom loved to tell the story about how they met. She was seventeen and he was maybe thirty-five, serving him dinner in a small restaurant where she worked in Louisiana. Against her parents' advice, they were married a month later.

"He was raised to believe the wife did what the husband said and the man did whatever he damn well pleased. It broke our mother's heart, but he took that in stride, too. He took everything in stride except back talk. Give him anything except 'yes sir, no sir,' and wham, you were bouncing across the room on your butt. He hung me by the heels off a bridge over the Mississippi River when I was eleven. When I was stupid enough to say he wouldn't dare let go, he dropped me into the river. Then he jumped in and saved me. It was in the papers. FATHER RISKS LIFE TO SAVE SON. Hell, they were going to give him a medal, but we moved away before he could collect it. He thought that was funnier than shit. After that, he used to threaten us by saying, 'Don't make me collect another medal.'"

"They should have given him the medal for bad fathering."

"When we were in our teens we were living in New Mexico in a trailer. That was when he started giving most of his attention to Bert. Sometimes he'd use a belt, sometimes his fists. Sometimes he'd just slap him around and ask why he was such a pussy. That was the worst, actually, the humiliation. I can't say Bert didn't ask for it, always lipping off.

"One day when we were fourteen Bert was home from school faking sick, and our dad left work at noon and came home to catch him banging his sister."

"Your sister?"

"Hell, no. We didn't have no sister. Besides, that would be incest. It was our dad's sister. Aunt Arianna."

"And that *wasn't* incest?"

"Well, not like if it'd been our own sister, no."

"Sheesh. Okay. So what happened?"

"I got different stories on that over the years. When I got home from school Bert looked like hell. The whole side of his face—Dad was a lefty—looked like hamburger. Blood everywhere, all over the house. Bert said Dad slammed him around, then got drunk and walked out into the desert with a bottle. Took the Luger he kept under his pillow. That was his pattern, slam us around, get a bottle, and walk out into the desert. There was a lot of places you could get lost out there, little arroyos, even some mountains nearby. This time he didn't come back the next morning the way he generally did. After a week went by we figured he either walked too far out and got lost or fell in a hole."

"And?"

"We never saw him again. His truck sat untouched in the driveway for months. Our mother was afraid to drive it without his permission. Mom eventually sold it when we moved a year later."

"Your mother alive?"

"Living in Tulsa with a really sweet guy she met ten years ago. Retired and still bowling once a week. Still a live wire. She's got all my rodeo trophies."

"You ever find out what really happened to your father?"

"I don't know if I'll ever get the whole story, but five years ago Bert told me most of it and I've cobbled enough together to sense the gist of the rest. Arianna's like eighty-something now, but back in those days she was the blue-plate special. It's tough to watch what thirty-five years can do to someone. When Bert banged her we were fourteen, almost fifteen, and she must have been . . . early forties. With a husband and three kids. Lived just across town. The way Bert told it, one day our mother mentioned to Arianna that Bert was home sick from school and she needed to be at work herself. So Arianna, who was a stay-at-home mother and kind of a goody-goody, or at least that's what I always thought, made some chicken soup and took it on over. The long and the short of it was, they ended up sharing the soup she brought while he poured his heart out about how bad our father was treating us. Bert started crying and Arianna hugged him, at first to comfort him I guess, but then it turned into sort of a clinch and they fell onto the sofa and things progressed from there. Arianna kept trying to break it off but Bert would play hooky and then get her out to the place on a pretext and the next thing she knew they'd be at it again."

"What happened when your father found them?"

"He went ballistic, whipped off his belt, and began beating whichever one of them was closer. On his own, Bert would have taken a beating, but he couldn't stand to see this woman he adored being beaten and humiliated. Bert hit our dad with a two-by-four, stunned him long enough for Arianna to escape, then kept hitting him until he was lifeless. After that, he dragged him to the truck and took him out into the desert.

We both knew how to drive by then. Out in the desert, he shot him in the head with his own Luger and buried the body in a wash."

"Your brother admitted killing your father?"

"He was drunk out of his skull when he told me, but that *is* what he said. Not that our father didn't ask for it."

"And he lived through his high school years without ever telling you about it?"

"Not me or anybody else."

"That's what I call a rough childhood."

TWENTY-THREE

"**MOM ENDED UP** moving us to Las Cruces to work for a former boss of hers. I got an executive starter position mucking out stalls at a dude ranch. Bert worked there, too, until he got kicked in the head by a mare and decided to even the score with a shovel. He did enough damage to the horse that they fired him. Bert ended up hanging out with a bunch of greasers all through the rest of high school. Most all of them ended up in prison."

"But not your brother?"

"He went into the army. By that time I was rodeoing pretty strong and getting a few wins, so I didn't see where a hitch in the army was going to do me any good. He did a four-year hitch, and signed up for a second tour. We hardly ever saw him after that. I worked on ranches and kept on with the rodeo. Once in a blue moon he'd send Mother a postcard."

"Bert got busted up pretty good, too, judging by the way he moves."

"He had a bad parachute drop in the army and spent five months in the hospital. The army was good for Bert, though. He liked to travel and it instilled some discipline. He was still a Ranger when the army recruited him into some outfit I never did know the name of. It was all very hush-hush. I know he used to get flown to foreign countries to teach guerrillas how to use weaponry. He was an expert with anything that fired a projectile, from slingshots to rockets. Did that for another eight years. Sometimes he'd be out of the country for six days, sometimes for six months. After the army, he signed up with some company that did contract work for the U.S. Department of Agriculture.

"I think the first one was called Tidewater Stone. He worked a couple of years for them out of Maryland. Then he switched to some other company. After a while, I couldn't keep them straight. Always traveling. I didn't see him hardly until he did time at Walla Walla. At least there I could see him on visiting days. I *can* tell you this: He was a sniper for the army. I don't know what the hell he was doing for the U.S. Department of Agriculture, because he doesn't know anything about growing food or farming, but I visited him in Bolivia, and one day when I was alone in his apartment, I found a Dragunov in the closet."

"What's that?"

"Russian sniper rifle. It had been modified but was in perfect working order and had a noise suppressor. He had a couple of boxes of ammunition with Russian writing on them. I took a picture of it and had somebody translate when I got home. It said the ammunition was for sniper use only and it wasn't supposed to leave the Soviet bloc under any circumstances."

"You ask him about the rifle?"

"You don't admit you've been snooping through my brother's closet."

"Are you saying your brother was some sort of government hit man?"

"I don't know what he was."

"What else do you know about South America?"

"He was drunk when he told me this as well, and so was I, so I don't remember as well as I might. He said there were gangs of street kids in Rio de Janeiro. Death squads were taking them out. These death squads were mostly made up of police. In the middle of the night they'd round up a group of kids, drive them somewhere, shoot them, and leave them for the buzzards. Other times they'd just shoot them in the makeshift shelters where they slept. Drive by in a Suburban and riddle their shacks with gunfire. Homeless kids posed quite a problem down there. Stealing. Begging. Prostituting. The goon squad retaliations began after a German tourist was apparently killed by a gang of kids. The cops wore masks, but there was no doubt among the local populace that they were cops. Same guns as the cops. Same boots. They even used some of the same commands. But this is the worst part: They weren't observers, this CIA—or whatever—group Bert was sent down there with. I don't know how or why, but they were involved in the killings. And not just in Brazil."

"Killing kids? Are you kidding me?"

"I ever tell you he once had a dog chain around his neck and was actually swinging from a doorway when a neighbor walked by a window and pulled him down? It was about that time he burned his passport and quit the feds. Except they set him up for the drug thing, and before he knew it, he was doing time."

"The CIA set him up?"

"So he said. I'm not sure why. I'm sure it's complicated."

"He working for the CIA now?"

"I don't think so."

"Where's he staying?"

"With our grandmother on some undeveloped property out past Kent. It's acreage full of blackberries with a couple of trailers on it. Grandma lives in one of the trailers. Out in the back near the old barns, Bert has his own broken-down trailer. Grandma has a restraining order against him to stay off the property, but he still hangs there. She just ignores him unless he pisses her off, and then she calls the cops. That's how that SWAT team incident started."

"How many times has he been in prison?"

"Just the once. But he's been in and out of the county jail more times than he was in and out of Aunt Arianna. Of course, you know all about his recent history. Kathy was defending him on most of it."

Snake went back to the living room and turned the movie back on while I returned to the news clippings. I was back in tune with my instincts, or so I thought. I laid out the crash clippings and perused them in chronological sequence. The more I read, the more unanswered questions I had.

It wasn't until I began looking through the stack of unread newspapers I'd been collecting myself that I began to see an emerging pattern, though it didn't concern the crash, just the way the public relations for the investigation was being conducted. Glancing back through the papers, it seemed as if a new theory was proposed each day. One anomaly that struck me was that Timothy Hoagland, chief investigator for the NTSB, stated early on that finding the cockpit voice recorder was their number one priority. He made the statement in at least three separate interviews over the first two days, but then an unnamed spokesperson for the NTSB announced that they were not looking for the cockpit voice recorder because there hadn't been one on the plane. Hoagland did not retract his previous statements. The head investigator should have known whether the plane had a cockpit voice recorder.

On the third day of the investigation, Hoagland announced, "We're looking into all possibilities. Pilot error, icing problems, mechanical failure, freak weather abnormalities, electrical irregularities, and the possibility that another aircraft collided with the Beechcraft King Air." *Was* he looking at all the possibilities? Conspicuously missing from his list were several that had been on my mind. He hadn't mentioned sabotage. Nor had he mentioned terrorism, as alleged by at least one of the elderly witnesses in an interview with Portland television station KGW. I happened to believe she was mistaken, because I hadn't seen the missile trail she claimed she saw, nor had anybody else. So while they asserted they were looking into all possibilities, they had eliminated at least two at the outset. It was possible a mechanic had done something to the plane prior to takeoff. It was possible one of the passengers had gone berserk and jumped into the cockpit with a box cutter or a nail file or even a bottle of water, any of the contraband the homeland security people were worried about at airports. There were a lot of possibilities not being addressed, at least not publicly, but when I mentioned as much to Snake, he said, "They don't want to start a panic."

"Like we're all going to run into the streets and get killed in traffic?" Snake ignored my sarcasm. He'd long contended the government was withholding information about UFOs to stave off a panic. In fact a good portion of his pet theories revolved around the idea of staving off public panic.

I didn't know whether Bert's warning a week prior to the crash was the source of my paranoia or if I was just bent on uncovering some sort of crime. I knew this: I needed somebody besides myself to blame for Kathy's death. All week I'd been thinking I should have been working on the Sheffield campaign and not Maddox's, thinking (quite illogically) that had I been by Kathy's side for all those weeks I would have seen the crash coming. I should have insisted Kathy keep her promise to me and remain at the ocean instead of rejoining Sheffield. I should have heeded Bert Slezak's warning. I should have asked more questions the day he stopped at my car. I cursed myself for things left undone, words left unspoken.

Scrutinizing eight days' worth of the *Post-Intelligencer* and *The Seattle Times,* I couldn't help but uncover a pattern: First, there would be a specific theory posited in print, usually offered by someone from the FAA, FBI, or the NTSB investigating committee, touted as the direction the investigation was now headed. Always with a big headline; always on the front page. Then a couple of days later, buried in a tiny article in the depths of the paper, that theory would be discounted. After a barrage of loud theories and nearly mute retractions the air was filled with various possibilities for why the plane had gone down. It was almost as if somebody was purposely muddying the waters.

The first such accusation and subsequent retraction was that the pilot might have been inebriated or hungover. This was attributed to "an unnamed NTSB investigator" who credited an anonymous tipster from Portland. *Unnamed* and *anonymous* came up a lot. I noticed they talked about *the* pilot, singular, as if there was only one. There had been two. It occurred to me that it was easier to believe the tragedy had been precipitated by pilot error if you were laboring under the notion there had been only one pilot. Two pilots made the case for pilot error or drunkenness less likely. The next day Hoagland said, "We're closing in on the possibility that it was a weather disturbance." Two days later at the back of the second section next to the obituaries and in front of the comics, *The Seattle Times* printed this: "Early reports saying the pilots of the Beechcraft King Air carrying Senator Sheffield and party were drinking the night before the flight have now been discredited. Today witnesses who spent the evening with the pilots in Portland denied either pilot drank any alcohol the evening prior to the flight."

Big accusation; small retraction. It was a staple of political manipulation and had been for years. The Maddox campaign had done it several times this fall. The accusation tends to stick in the collective mind. The retraction gets overlooked.

Also not mentioned in most of the articles was the information that the Sheffield plane had two separate deicing systems. Now, eight days after the crash, they'd recovered most of the plane, and yet another early theory—that one or both of the engines had cut out—was being discarded. The damage that both props sustained on impact indicated they'd both been turning. One investigator said there was no evidence of a midair collision, yet the next day Timothy Hoagland proposed it as a possibility. One day he said they had pretty much ruled out pilot error. The next day they were looking into it again. It seemed almost as if the investigators wanted people thinking it was a near miracle the plane had been in the air in the first place.

"Snake?"

"Yeah." The sound on the movie went down.

"Where was your brother the day of the crash?"

"Maryland, I think. Looking for a job. And seeing old friends."

"The day of the crash he called Kathy. He wanted to meet her in Seattle. I don't think he was in Maryland. Not then, not now. He got arrested at the Cape. When was your last contact with him?"

"I talked to him on the phone."

"When he asked you to come and check on me?"

"Right."

"Cellphone?"

"Yeah."

"And you're supposed to report back about me?"

"He wanted me to call him sometime tonight."

"Why don't you call him now?" Snake froze the movie, pushed a couple of buttons on his cellphone, put it to his ear, and waited.

"He's not answering."

"He called us when we were on the way to the landing strip."

"He likes to make phone calls, don't he?" The possibility

that Bert had something to do with the crash had been nagging me all week. How else would he have known in advance?

I drank two tall glasses of water at the sink and went into the bathroom, where I showered, toweled off, pulled on a pair of jeans, my Montrail trail-running shoes, a T-shirt, and a fleece jacket. I picked up a camera, a pair of binoculars, and my car keys.

"Let's go," I said.

"Where to?"

"I need to ask some questions."

"You want a babysitter?"

"More like a witness."

"I'm watching a movie here."

"With your boots on Kathy's coffee table. Besides, the movie's on disc. You can start where you left off. One of the joys of the modern age. None of us ever have to miss anything trivial."

Snake grew even more disgruntled when I asked him to move his vehicle so I could drive the Taurus. He holstered his two largest revolvers, concealed a third semiautomatic handgun in his coat, and followed me out the back door. In all the years I'd known and worked with him, I had only once seen him pull one of those weapons, and it had been to shoot out a stoplight that was getting on his nerves.

On N.E. Forty-fifth I pulled into a gas station. As I pumped gas under the fluorescent lights of the service station, I felt as if I were Rip van Winkle waking from a twenty-year snooze, looking around at anything and everything as if encountering it for the first time. A man and a woman walked down the sidewalk, and just seeing the normalcy of their lives, she carrying a packsack full of books, he a single bicycle wheel with a bent rim, made me realize how my cocoon of grief had insulated me from the world. A man and a woman in a minivan with three small children in car seats pulled up next to the pumps. One child's blue eyes twinkled with delight when I waved. He was almost as cute as the children Kathy would have borne.

"Who are you going to see?" Snake asked when I got back

into the car. He'd been dozing, straw cowboy hat tilted rak-
ishly over his face.

"I want to find out what caused the crash."

"You got the NTSB on it. You got the FBI out there. You
got—"

"You trust the FBI?"

"Well, no, but—"

"Between your brother's prognostication and the news stories, I'm beginning to get suspicious."

"What's a prognostication?"

"A really big word."

"Suspicious of what?"

"That maybe the NTSB has its own agenda, and maybe it
doesn't include telling us what really brought that plane
down."

"I wouldn't read too much into newspaper articles. You
and I both know they never get all the facts straight. What
you're doing here is hoping there's some nefarious conspiracy under way and that you're the man to uncover it."

"A guy who knows the word *nefarious* should know *prognostication*."

"You're hoping to be the hero. Thomas, don't go down the
conspiracy rabbit hole. People go down, and they never come
back up. I'm serious. That kind of thinking is what drove my
brother nuts. Don't get your dander up. I'm just telling you
what I think."

"You want me to drop you off back at the house?"

"I'm going with you. In your frame of mind, you're going
to need some backup."

"Stay awake, then."

"Just resting my eyes."

═══ TWENTY-FOUR ═══

IT WAS ALMOST EIGHT O'CLOCK when we set out for downtown Seattle, the sky crowded with black clouds that set off the lights of the city brilliantly. In the distance, a bolt of lightning split the sky. Eschewing the freeway, I motored along Eastlake Avenue to Fairview and then Broad Street, cruising alongside Lake Union, where oceangoing ships berthed in the heart of the city. Six hundred feet above the street, the Space Needle restaurant was lit up like a flying saucer.

I'd been leaving my warren only to visit the dead and commiserate with grieving relatives. Kathy's funeral had been the low spot of my life, and I was doing everything I could to put it out of my mind. It would probably take longer even than I supposed, but I had turned a corner. I was a different man now. Instead of the happy-go-lucky wisecracking guy next door I'd been eight days ago, instead of the neighbor who worked out too much, rode a racing bicycle all summer, and was addicted to movies produced before color film became the norm, instead of the private investigator who let complex cases and anxious clients put his life on hold, I'd morphed into a somber, introspective, and pessimistic study of my former self. I hadn't worked out in over a week, had only infrequently rolled off the sofa, and got light-headed just doing that.

In many ways I felt like a comic-book character who'd met his doppelgänger in Bizarro World and was confronting a version of himself that could pass for the real one in a crowd but lacked the positive characteristics that had formerly defined him.

Kathy once told me the first trait she noticed about me was the attitude I carried that no matter how badly things seemed to be going, everything would come up roses. I'd always exhibited an underlying sense of goodwill and optimism. I mourned for the man I'd been almost as much as I mourned Kathy, because the truth was, in the past eight days I had become infused with hate.

I pulled the rearview mirror around and looked at my face; I'd forgotten to brush my hair after my shower, but my brown eyes were flinty and penetrating. When I tried on a smile, the mirror revealed a face that might be considered handsome in an outdoorsy West Coast kind of way; tanned, pale circles around my eyes from sunglasses; yet it was a face I barely recognized.

We were headed for Belltown, where historically the sidewalks were littered with homeless men and drunkards. That hadn't changed much even though in the past twenty years developers had threaded the area with expensive condominiums in an effort to make it the hub of hip uptown living.

I parked on Bell and we walked west toward Elliott Bay. The neighborhood was populated with well-off, childless couples, heterosexual and otherwise, who flocked to the city to snap up the high-priced condominiums and apartment conversions. When it started to rain, Snake said, "How far are we going? I don't want to get my hat wet."

"I thought hats were supposed to protect you."

"Not this one. I protect it. By the way, it's good to see you up and about. You've always had testicular fortitude, Thomas. I ever lost a woman like Kathy, I'd go back to drinking. I'd take dope. I'd kill myself."

"Thanks for the pep talk."

On the next block we edged into the security lobby of a fourteen-story building as a trio of young people left, too self-involved to realize we were interlopers. On the fourteenth floor, Kalpesh Gupta seemed surprised to see me. "Thomas, my good man. Thomas . . ." he said, as he swung the door wide.

"Kalpesh Gupta, this is my friend Elmer Slezak."

"Call me Snake."

Kalpesh gave me a startled look, as if I'd brought a bum or a pickpocket into his private haven. "Well, yes, of course. Why don't you come in, Thomas? You too, Snake. What brings you this way? Just in the area, or . . ."

"Just passing by," I lied.

Kalpesh led us into the foyer. I pulled off my shoes and contributed them to the neat row of footwear along the wall by the front door. All the shoes were Kalpesh's except a pair of patent pumps that looked to be about a women's size nine.

It was a nice layout, a minimalist black-and-white theme, with about half a ton of chrome in the kitchen, splashes of colorful modern art on the walls, to the right a living room with a small deck and a stupefying overlook of the bay, to the left a hallway with a series of closed doors, probably two or three bedrooms and a den. In the living room an expensive Persian rug had been laid over bamboo flooring. It was the kind of place that could be featured in the Sunday supplement of the local paper.

"Nice digs," said Snake, striding to the living room window, where he checked out the thunderstorm over Puget Sound. Snake had not removed his cowboy boots, which sank into the plush rug as if into warm chocolate.

"Something to drink, gentlemen?" Kalpesh asked, switching on a light in the kitchen and opening the refrigerator. "I can offer whiskey, white wine, or beer."

When we both declined, he stepped into the living room and sat primly on the edge of a black leather and chrome sectional. I plopped onto the uncomfortable angular chair across from him. Snake remained at the window. "So, Thomas? What can I do for you? I know you came for a reason."

"How did you book that airplane?"

"The Sheffield flight?"

"No, the Birchfield flight."

"I'm sorry. The way people are looking at this must irritate you."

"A lot of things irritate me."

We looked at each other for a few moments, Kalpesh trying to evaluate the depth and intensity of my feelings. He was well aware that my fuse was short. At Kathy's funeral the previous day, I'd snapped at a couple of people, maybe even at him. I remained furious that it was his seat Kathy had been occupying when she died. My love was dead, and here sat this bozo in his silk socks and spotless linen shirt.

"You politicos must make a fortune," Snake said, peering around the rooms. "On what I earn, you'd have to steal till the cows came home to afford this joint. How about you, Thomas? How much would you have to steal?"

I shrugged. It didn't bother me that Snake wanted to play good guy/bad guy, or that he'd placed Kalpesh on the defensive by essentially accusing him of being a corrupt political operative. Sheffield and her staff were among the cleanest operations to hit Washington, D.C., in ages and everybody knew it. Kalpesh especially knew it. It was a major reason Kathy had been such an enthusiastic supporter.

"Fourteenth floor?" Snake continued. "Pricey. You get a deal or did you buy it with coupons?"

"I'm glad you like it," Kalpesh said, trying on a genteel smile, "but I'm a houseguest. It belongs to a friend who's out of the country for a few months."

"Good to have friends."

Kalpesh turned his attention to me. "You want to know about the flight?"

"You arranged it?"

"With Northwest Apple Flights."

"Why Apple?"

"It's a company we've used before."

"Who planned the trip?"

"I did. The original program was to fly up the coast, get some footage for the TV commercials, then hit Port Angeles, Port Townsend, Bellingham, cross over the Cascades, and touch down in all the northern rural towns in eastern Washington nobody else was doing."

"But Kathy wasn't originally scheduled to go?"

"A couple of staffers caught the flu. And then I got sick. We were shorthanded."

"You had the flu?" Snake asked from the window.

"Whatever it was, it lasted forty-eight hours and then was gone."

"You didn't see a doctor?"

"No. Thomas? I want you to know Kathy meant the world to me. Listen, Thomas. You know Jane didn't like to fly.

Whenever I set up something like this, I did everything humanly possible to reassure her. I made certain there were two pilots with sterling credentials. Booked a plane with an impeccable safety record. I had them double-check the weather reports. In spite of being sick, I even drove there myself to make sure everything went smoothly. I can't think of anything I might have done differently."

"You almost could have predicted it," said Snake, from the window.

"How is that?" Kalpesh asked.

"Northwest Apple? I mean, the apple is how Sir Isaac Newton discovered gravity. Right?"

Kalpesh ignored him.

"Did Sheffield have any enemies—I mean, besides the normal political rivalries?"

"These days every politician gets angry calls and letters. And emails. When it's bad enough, we pass it along to the FBI. Listen, you're not suggesting somebody brought that plane down on purpose, are you?"

"I'm not suggesting anything. They keeping you people apprised of developments?"

"We've been in contact with the NTSB. The FBI, also."

"And?"

"They're at Boeing Field now, will be there for a while, as I understand it."

"I thought the NTSB was out at Cape Disappointment."

"That's where they're staging the plane parts, but they've got a hangar at Boeing Field where they're putting it all together. If you want, I'll make a phone call in the morning and advise them you want to meet."

"Don't bother."

"Okay. But listen, Thomas. The FBI's working with the NTSB, and they're not going to take kindly to a local private investigator getting involved. Not even if your wife was on the plane. In a week or two, a month at most, they'll announce the cause, and you'll realize how silly your concerns are. They'll find a frayed wire in a rudder controller or a bad engine or whatever. Why not just go back home?"

"I guess I want to be silly."

"Forgive me. I didn't mean you're being silly. But, Thomas? I beg you not to do this."

"Good night, Kalpesh," I said, rising.

Snake and Kalpesh followed me to the front door and waited while I put on my shoes. After we were out in the corridor, I eyeballed Kalpesh. "By the way, do you happen to have any runts in there?"

"Pardon me?"

"Runts."

"I don't know what you're talking about."

"Later, then."

We were in the elevator, almost to the lobby, when Snake said, "What's a runt?"

"Like a Trojan, only smaller."

"You mean miniature condoms?"

"Right."

"Somebody whittle down his dick?"

"I read an article that said more than fifty percent of Indian men are too small for standard-issue condoms. I was wondering what one of the little ones looked like." Snake was still laughing a minute later when we ran through the rain to my car. His laughter made me feel almost as shallow as the puddles we were jumping over.

TWENTY-FIVE

WHEN I CLOSED my bedroom door at eleven, I could hear Snake in the other room watching *The Last of the Mohicans*. A little before two I woke up soaked in perspiration. The TV was still running in the other room and Snake was asleep, stacked on my sofa like a car wreck. Although the house was cold, I kicked off a blanket and spent the next forty-five minutes trying to get back to sleep. All I could think about, when I wasn't thinking about the empty spot beside me in bed and the miserable funeral service for Kathy, was how the news media had failed to point out certain inconsistencies in the statements from the NTSB investigators. Why didn't the lead investigator know there had been no voice box recorder? And why hadn't the reporters noticed? Why did they seem confused about the number of pilots? I tossed and turned, and when it became apparent sleep wasn't coming, I crawled out of bed and fired up the computer. At the other end of the house Snake was snoring in a miasma of bad breath and farts. Outside it was pouring, as evidenced by the flurry of water in the downspout beside the back door. I checked to see if Spider had returned, but he hadn't. I should have been more concerned, but I knew he could take care of himself and I had more important things missing than a dog—my wife and my sanity, to name two.

My starting point was the pilots. The first, Charles Hilditch, had a personal space on one of the national websites that catered to such things, informing us he was fond of jazz, purebred cocker spaniels, fly-fishing, and downhill skiing; that he had a wife and three grown kids and had accepted Jesus as his personal savior after his youngest child died of leukemia. There was nothing to indicate incompetence. I had met the other pilot at the airport and liked him. According to articles I'd read earlier in the day, Freddy Mitz had learned to fly in the air force and then had retired and moved into commercial aviation. Both pilots had airline transport certifications, the highest industry rating. As far as I could tell, Mitz had not been drunk or hungover when I met him. It hardly seemed possible either of these men had caused the deaths of eleven people.

I still couldn't get used to Kathy being gone. Even after dragging myself home from Kathy's memorial service two days ago, I felt as if I'd been part of a charade, that she wasn't really dead, as if it hadn't been a funeral service but rather a very bad play about a funeral, and that I'd tell Kathy about it when she returned from wherever she was. I'd gone through the ceremony in a trance, wasn't even sure who else had been in attendance.

Coincidentally, another senator had died in the crash of a Beechcraft King Air 100. I read about Minnesota senator Paul Wellstone's fatal crash on October 25, 2002, when a Beechcraft King Air went down in the Iron Range, killing Wellstone and seven others. The Internet was full of conspiracy theorists writing about the Wellstone crash, and many of those commentators were among the gang now blogging about the Sheffield crash—speculating it was not an accident but would be whitewashed by the authorities to resemble one. Several of the Wellstone articles sported links to other conspiracy sites, some dealing with 9/11 and the subsequent, largely forgotten anthrax attacks that had been headline news at the time. I couldn't help recalling Snake's caution about descending down the rabbit hole.

It was astonishing how many bloggers thought our government was being corrupted and run by a cutthroat cabal of power brokers and fat-cat billionaires. This was the same contingent who contended our elections were frauds and the true vote hadn't been counted in a national election in over a decade. We all knew the two-party system pumped out eerily similar candidates in a mysterious and complex manner, but according to these conspiracy theorists, even with only two candidates, the reigning powers found it necessary to engage in massive electronic election fraud. Other websites claimed a silent coup had already taken over the government. It was enough to make my head swim. Two weeks ago it would have taken a cattle prod to force me to read this kind of conjecture, but now I gobbled it down whole. Strange how losing your wife in a plane crash stretches the boundaries of what you are willing to entertain as reality.

I knew there were only a few indicators that my suspicions had any basis in reality, and those indicators might have been attributable to poor reporting and sloppy statements. But then, there had been Bert Slezak's exhortation that I bar Kathy from traveling with Jane Sheffield. He must have known *something*. Any of these items taken singly could be brushed off, but together they raised my antenna.

Snake said I would feel better after I found somebody to blame. He was right. Having it attributed to a burned-out wire or a seagull flying into a prop wasn't going to give me the satisfaction that finding a living culprit would. As I continued to read, the wackiness factor began to fade and I found myself open to theories that would have sounded perfectly preposterous two days ago. I began to believe the Paul Wellstone crash in 2002 had been sloppily and/or fraudulently investigated. What made it worse were the parallels between the Wellstone and Sheffield crashes.

Wellstone had been highly critical of the administration at a time when it was being accused of dirty tricks, at a time when every senatorial vote was crucial, at a time when key administration critics were being silenced by various means. Sheffield had been in much the same position, having been a radical and constant critic of the current administration. What could silence a critic more completely or permanently than a plane crash? During the current elections, national commentators had repeatedly opined that the course of the nation and of world affairs would hinge on one or two key elections around the country, and one of those elections was Maddox versus Sheffield. It had been disturbing to the conservatives who were backing Maddox to realize the polls placed him so far behind Sheffield. Party insiders were frustrated that his campaign hadn't gained traction despite the millions of dollars poured into TV ads. The vice president himself singled out the Maddox race as a grave disappointment.

The hue and cry over the election was one of the reasons Kathy and I had been at odds. The stakes were enormous: control of the U.S. Senate and thus the country for the next few years. Ideologically, I'd been on Sheffield's side, but personally I'd thrown in with Maddox. I'd taken it as a matter of faith that any aid I gave him would be futile, but now that Sheffield was out of the picture and national pundits were attacking our governor for promising Sheffield's position to her husband should she be elected, I wondered if there wasn't something too convenient for the current White House in these events. It was fine to have good luck, but sometimes a dealer rolled sevens so many times in a row you had to suspect the dice.

Because I had so consistently dismissed 9/11 conspiracy theories in the past, I was reluctant to align myself with their sponsors now, but most of the people who were suspicious about the Sheffield tragedy were also distraught with the 9/11 Commission report.

My thought was that in the morning I could begin corralling the facts and correct my false impressions, if any; I would discard the batshit theories and adhere to the known, but tonight, just for the hell of it, I read on. It was interesting stuff in a kind of sci-fi way. Strangely, energized by wildcat hypotheses here in the middle of the night, I had more vigor than I'd had all week. It was amazing how much adrenaline a good conspiracy can inject into your bloodstream. I don't remember falling asleep or even going to bed, but I must have, because it was after eight o'clock when I woke up under the covers.

I went into the spare bedroom, where I kept my weights when it was too cold to use them in the garage, and pumped iron for twenty minutes, just enough to get my blood circulating, then took a shower. I shaved, combed my hair, dressed in slacks, put on one of the two ties I owned and a dark blazer.

After preparing a breakfast of eggs, toast, and grapefruit juice, I called Snake, who, without a word, made his way to the bathroom to wash up and then a minute later began inhaling food as if he'd been stranded in the outback for a month. He'd spent the night in his hat and boots. "You got anything to do today?" I asked.

"Yeah. I'm going to follow you around and make sure you don't step in any cowpies. You in a hurry?"

"I'll wait for you to finish."

"Better give me time to drop a deuce, too. Man, you hate that guy from last night, don't you?"

"Kalpesh? Just for the part where he got my wife killed."

"He couldn't have known the plane was going down."

"Your brother did."

"Yeah, but—"

"You're not going to talk me out of it."

"Okay. Want me to whack him?"

"Maybe later."

Once again we took my SHO. The streets were slick with an overnight rain, and clouds to the south were scudding along in front of a strong southwesterly wind, puddles of blue sky over Lake Washington to the east of us. It was good to be out of the house and traversing the planet. Over the years Snake and I had been through a lot. I valued his friendship, his quiet nature, even his eccentricities. Most of all, right now I valued his presence.

We slogged through traffic on I-5 for forty minutes before the Albro exit took us to surface streets and then Boeing Field, which was visible at the south end of the city just off the interstate. Northwest Apple was based in a hangar on the east side of the field off Perimeter Road. On the tarmac I saw another Beechcraft King Air 100 with a Northwest Apple Flight logo on the side of the fuselage. The parking lot was filled with TV vans. Because it was beginning to sprinkle again, ten or twelve reporters were huddled under an awning outside the front door.

We elbowed our way into the Apple office, where we were told Hoagland was in a meeting and wouldn't be available to answer questions for at least an hour. Hardly larger than a dentist's waiting room, the Apple office was crowded and stuffy, the windows fogged over. Snake and I joined the gang under the awning outside. Near the corner of the building, one man talked too loudly on a cellphone, as if putting on a performance for the rest of us. That inspired two women to take out their phones and compete with him. Snake exhaled loudly through his nostrils and looked around for something or someone to occupy his time. He chose a tall, gawky woman with huge feet and teeth that looked too big for her face. Her pretty blue eyes were desperate with eyeliner.

She was almost as tall as I was, which put her at eight inches taller than Snake, but neither that nor the wedding ring on her finger deterred him. He joked with her about the weather, the wait, the man on the cellphone. I recognized her name from *Seattle Times* articles: Ruth Ponzi.

"I've been reading your stuff," I said.

"Oh, thank you. I appreciate that. I really do." She turned to Snake and said, "Do you by any chance have a brother or a cousin who lives in the state?"

"My brother, Bert. You're not dating him, are you?"

"No. I'm married."

"That wouldn't stop Bert."

"Yes. Well, it would stop *me,*" she said. "Can you tell me anything about his arrest at Cape Disappointment a couple of days after the airplane crash? I saw him get hauled away in handcuffs. When I tried to get a short interview, they told me he was being held incommunicado."

Snake and I exchanged a glance. "We knew he'd been arrested, but we don't have any of the details," Snake said. "Which agency arrested him?"

"I'm not sure."

I made a mental note to call Beulah and ask if Bert had phoned.

Beulah was still working half days, collecting phone messages left by people who didn't realize Kathy was dead, and messages for me left by people who didn't realize I was out of commission. Periodically Beulah would stack up the messages on my answering machine, but I'd been ignoring them. At the funeral I hugged her and sat by myself. If I saw her afterward, I had no memory of it.

"You've been doing most of the reporting on the crash investigation for the *Times,* haven't you?" I asked Ponzi.

"I don't know that I've been doing *most,* but certainly a lot. I'm glad you like it."

"I never said I liked it."

"I'm sorry. Is there something wrong with my reporting?"

"Just the inaccuracies."

Taking umbrage, she stretched to her full height, something she'd been avoiding in the way that tall girls tried to avoid but tall women didn't. "In what regard have I been inaccurate about the accident?"

"There's your first inaccuracy. Was it an accident?"

Her face turned pink, and she was doing something with her mouth, covering her teeth with her lips. Snake was giving me a dour look. If he'd had any chance of bedding this woman, I'd blown it for him. "I suppose you were there?" she said, finally.

"I watched the plane go down. Yes."

"Even the Coast Guardsman manning the lighthouse didn't see the plane go down."

"I did. So did half a dozen old gummers off a tour bus."

We stared at each other for a moment, and then, in an effort perhaps to buttress his chances with this woman, Snake said, "Thomas's wife was on the plane."

She regarded me for a long time. "I'm sorry," Ponzi said, blushing again. Snake had been trying to make her feel better about my onslaught, but his declaration had the opposite effect. "I had no idea. In fact . . . I tried to talk to you. We did a piece on each of the victims . . . I called you. Maybe you didn't get my messages."

"I got them."

"I don't understand."

"You don't understand why I wouldn't talk to the news two days after watching my wife's plane go into the ocean?"

"Thomas," Snake said. "Be nice."

"Everyone else talked to us," she added.

"I guess I'm just a sissy, then."

"My editor was all over me for not getting quotes from you, but I guess I wasn't taking your feelings into account. I sincerely apologize." Tears filled her eyes as she stepped closer. But then, incredibly, she flipped her notebook open while at the same time crabbing her left hand around in her purse for a pen, never once taking her eyes off mine. "You mind if I ask a few questions now?"

"Not until you answer mine."

"Sure."

"For starters, why do you keep writing that there was only one pilot?"

"Well, that's how the NTSB people are saying it. There was a pilot and a copilot. So there really was only *one* pilot. Isn't that right?"

"You're framing the tragedy so that it can be explained away more easily. People think of a small plane going down with only one pilot on board and they can come up with a thousand scenarios for a crash. One guy could make a mistake. Misread the instruments. Have a heart attack. But it doesn't get so easy if there are two."

"Point taken. From now on I'll write 'pilots,' plural."

"Also, you keep hinting the weather might have been a component by saying it was less than ideal that day. Anything other than clear blue skies and no wind is less than ideal. You know the weather wasn't a factor, but by repeating that it was less than ideal, you create a climate in which it's easy for your readers to dismiss the crash as weather-related when you and I both know it wasn't. And as for the iced-wing theory you keep proposing, local pilots who were up that day have already discounted the possibility. Also, the plane had two separate deicing systems on board. You didn't bother to mention it."

"I thought I'd put that in."

"No."

"You reported that the NTSB was looking for the voice cockpit recorders, but there were none. Why didn't they know that?"

"Listen. Some of these things are editorial decisions."

"Then there was that crap about it being a close race. There was *nothing* close about the race."

"Now that *was* an editorial decision."

"Right up until the time the plane went down, Sheffield was way ahead and you know it."

"If you disagree with something I've written," said Ponzi, "you can email me. I *do* want to get this right, you know."

"Is anybody looking into the possibility that the plane might have been brought down on purpose?"

"You mean a tinfoil-hat conspiracy?"

"The very fact that you call it that tells me you don't have an open mind."

"On the contrary, I have an extremely open mind. But there are conspiracy nuts coming out of the woodwork, and that's one of their accusations, that the plane was brought down on purpose. A missile or something."

"Is that why nobody in the mainstream press brought it up? Because they don't want to be seen as crackpots?"

"It's the sort of thinking we're trying to avoid. That it was shot down."

"Why?"

"Well, because . . ."

"Because why?"

"I guess . . . I don't know, really."

"Something bad happens," I said, "an accident or a crime occurs without an explanation, you list the possibilities and then eliminate them one by one, and you make sure people know when a theory has been discarded and why. You list those who might benefit from the event and eliminate *them* one by one. When somebody makes a list and leaves off a possibility— even if it's being touted by a bunch of twits—I have to wonder why."

Ponzi was about to respond when something occurred inside the office that sent reporters funneling through the front door.

═══ TWENTY-SIX ═══

THE ROOM WAS A COMMERCIAL HANGAR, complete with high ceilings, workbenches, and oil stains on the concrete floor. Up front was a microphone and a meeting table where eight or ten suits were pushing their chairs out from the table. Two of them were preparing to speak to the journalists. Oversized electric heaters were mounted on brackets hung from the ceiling, each throwing off a dry heat that several damp reporters made a point to stand near. There were fifty or sixty folding chairs, half already filled by reporters, cameramen, and others. Just as the news conference started, Snake left his seat and squeezed into a chair beside Ruth Ponzi.

Timothy Hoagland, the man heading the NTSB investigation, was a tall, ponderous-looking man whose face was mostly forehead, his thinning, light brown hair cropped so close he may as well have been bald. He was overweight but carried it in a way guaranteed to have a lot of people telling him he wore it well. The line of his chin went straight down into his collar as if he'd been stuffed into the shirt and tie. He wore stylish black-rimmed glasses and an expensive dark suit. His arms floated out to the sides as if they were too muscular to remain flat against his torso. For some minutes he talked about the plane, about how many pieces they'd brought up—more than a hundred and twenty—about the four remaining bodies they had yet to recover—one of them was Kathy's—about finding the second pilot's corpse yesterday, and about the reduced odds of recovering more.

"Accident investigations are a painstaking process," Hoagland concluded. "Every item has to be sifted and examined individually and put together with the other pieces. It's the largest jigsaw puzzle you'll ever see. I know people are anxious for a speedy resolution here, but with an airplane crash, especially one that goes down over a body of water, things don't happen quickly. I'm asking you to be patient."

As he spoke, I found it hard to think of anything but the fact that Kathy's body was still in the ocean, possibly being gnawed on by crabs or sharks. At the memorial service we'd had for her two days ago there had been no coffin. It was hard for me not to think about what might be happening to her body. Was she trapped under wreckage eight hundred feet down? Or, having washed out to sea, was she headed for Asia? Had she been cast up on some local beach waiting to be found by clam diggers? When I was finally able to focus on the events around me, I heard Hoagland say, "Finally, in one of those ironies that sometimes happens when you're delving into an accident scene, we were told just this morning that the Maddox people had recently planned to use the same plane the Sheffield party flew, but canceled."

"Are you saying it might have been Maddox and his people who went down instead of Sheffield?" asked Ruth Ponzi, jumping to her feet while continuing to scrawl frantically on her notepad. "That it was a matter of happenstance we lost one candidate instead of the other?"

"You could look at it that way," said Hoagland.

Hoagland was a confident speaker, at ease with his position and the public trust, much more at ease than I would have been in front of a group. He glanced at a subordinate who had been biding his time during his spiel and said, "I believe that's all I have in terms of prepared remarks. If you have questions . . ."

A flurry of hands shot up, and several people in the front blurted questions without raising their hands. A television reporter asked, "Did the Maddox people cancel their lease of the plane because they received a warning about the plane or the pilot?"

"No one received any kind of warning that I know of," Hoagland said.

"Will the investigation be completed before the election, and if so, will you issue your conclusions before the election?"

"We can't be certain when the investigation or the report

will be finished. If we've concluded our work and come to a satisfactory determination by the election, I can assure you we will not hold back our report. But we're not running this on a timetable."

At the initiation of the Q and A, a young man in jeans and a wrinkled Windbreaker had walked toward the front of the room, waiting for his turn. After several more routine questions and replies, the young man in the aisle found his opening and spoke loudly. "My name is Joey Hilditch." It took a few seconds, but the background buzz died down until we could all hear the fan, in the heater, high on the wall. The young man was tall, thin, and in need of a haircut. "I'm wondering when you're going to clear my father's name."

"Pardon?" It was the first time I'd seen anything close to discomfort on Hoagland's face.

"The papers have made references to the pilots being drunk the night before the flight. They get their information from you. The letters section of both local papers are full of comments wondering why the pilots were even allowed to fly. It's like you're deliberately trying to discredit my father and Mr. Mitz." He stopped to gather his resources, thinking through what he had planned to say. "If you've taken back any of those statements about the pilots drinking the night before the flight, I haven't seen it in any of the local papers. I'm asking you to present evidence my father was drinking, otherwise stop implying it. My father was an awesome pilot. So was Mr. Mitz. In twenty years my father never even had a close call."

"I beg your pardon," Hoagland said. "It remains to be seen exactly how and why the plane went down. If you'd been listening, you would have heard me say our investigation would involve a long and painstaking process."

"Meanwhile you're spreading rumors about my father and Freddy Mitz. Look at your own quotes from the news two days ago."

Hoagland looked around and then made one of those astonishing and provocative statements officials sometimes deliver, which are then overlooked by his audience. "I thought nobody was supposed to be here without press credentials."

"Just answer the question," I said, rising to my feet. "What purpose does it serve to malign the pilots when there is no evidence? *The Oregonian* has done a series of personal interviews with the people who were with Mitz and Hilditch the night before, and they all swear the pilots had not been drinking. Why hasn't this information been circulated to the major media?"

Hoagland spent almost half a minute shuffling through some notes he took out of a briefcase, then conferred with an aide. When he finally replied, he looked at just about everyone in the room except me and Joey Hilditch. "As far as we know at this time, neither of the men in the cockpit had been drinking prior to the accident."

"What do the toxicology reports say?" I asked.

"I'm not . . ." Hoagland looked around for help. "I don't have that information at my fingertips, and if I did I'm not sure I would be at liberty to disclose it. Now, for the rest of today we'll be assembling plane parts, talking with the technical team, and conducting background interviews. There is still an ongoing retrieval process out at the Cape. Parts will be trucked here from the Cape as they are found. That is all."

As people began to disperse, I edged through the crowd and caught Joey Hilditch's eye as he was being braced by a couple of print reporters, one from *The Stranger,* an alternative weekly newspaper in Seattle that catered to hip young adults and the gay crowd. I waited, watching the crowd getting shooed out of the garage by NTSB personnel and employees of Northwest Apple. It seemed strange that the NTSB was conducting a good part of their investigation on the Apple premises. It smacked of something, though I couldn't put my finger on what.

When Joey Hilditch was finally alone, I said, "I'm sorry about your father. I was at the landing strip right before they took off."

"Did you see him?" Joey seemed younger and more disingenuous than he had from a distance.

"Your father was already in the plane. I spoke to the other pilot, Mitz. He seemed squared away."

"They both were. That's why all this makes me so angry."

A man in a brown Northwest Apple shirt came over and

said, "Joey?" They shook hands while I stood aside. "Jase Larson," he said, introducing himself. "I'm sorry about your father. It's got us all pretty broken up around here. Your father and Freddy were among our mainstays. And your father was such a gentle guy. We're all going to miss him."

"Thanks," said Joey.

"We got your email. I'll try to hit your points one by one." Larson looked at me and, when I didn't say anything, turned back to Hilditch. "Would you like to go somewhere or . . . ?"

"Here's fine." Despite the NTSB's attempts to clear the building, clusters of people were still standing around, including Hoagland, who was conferring with two of his co-workers in coveralls.

"The plane had major servicing right before the flight to the East Coast. They flew just over seven thousand miles without incident."

"Is it possible the plane was tampered with?" Joey asked.

"Your father and Freddy did a thorough preflight check."

"What if a skilled mechanic had done something?" I asked.

Joey said, "This is . . ."

"Thomas Black," I said.

"Sure. Sure," said Jase. "A competent mechanic? I suppose that could have happened. But if it did, these people will find it."

"The way I understand it," I said, "they flew into Portland the night before without any problems. Is it possible something happened in Portland and it didn't take effect until they had a full load and were out over the water?"

"The FBI has been all over that airport, and they say no," said Hoagland, approaching us.

"Is anybody entertaining the possibility a missile was fired from the ground or from a boat?"

"If that was the case, we'd have found evidence of it in the wreckage by now," Hoagland said.

As we talked, we were joined by Ruth Ponzi, Snake, and two other NTSB officials in coveralls, or at least I assumed they were NTSB. Led by Jase Larson, the Apple employee, the eight of us slowly gravitated to a side door and filed outside into a light drizzle. A flatbed truck with its load carefully concealed under a tarpaulin sat on the tarmac, the driver presumably waiting for the hangar to empty and the big doors to be raised. I glimpsed a piece of an airplane under the tarp.

No sooner were we clear of the building than Hoagland looked at Snake and said, "Don't I know you, sir?"

"My brother. I have a twin brother."

"Ah, yes."

"We read you guys arrested him," I said.

"Slezak?"

"That's him."

"We held him and questioned him for interfering with our investigation. He was saying some pretty crazy things. I hope you're not here to cause trouble, too." Hoagland looked Snake up and down. "Just why are you here? You with the press?"

"No," Snake answered and pointed to me. "I'm with him."

Hoagland turned my way. "I don't believe I've had the pleasure."

"Thomas Black. I work for James Maddox." It was clear from the look he gave one of his subordinates they'd heard my name before. Last night Kalpesh had offered to pass my name ahead, but I'd declined the gesture. Apparently, he'd gone ahead anyway, paving my way or warning them, one or the other. Or maybe they just recognized my name because it was on their witness list. "What's the likelihood of finding the rest of the bodies?"

"I'm told by the experts we've consulted that if we don't find the rest in the next day or two, it's not likely we'll find them at all."

"You been doing this long?" I asked.

"My résumé is public record. As far as my team goes, I've got some of the same people who worked the crash down in Florida last year with the ballplayers. They did tremendous work on that."

Ponzi spoke up. "Is there any possibility one of the pilots was trying to commit suicide?"

"Of course there isn't!" said Joey Hilditch.

"I heard one of the national reporters talking about it over coffee this morning," Ponzi said, "and I was thinking we should quell rumors before they get started. I'm trying to help you out here, kid. I'm on your side."

"We'll know more when we begin reassembling the plane," Hoagland said. "As far as we can tell, the plane was flying normally and didn't perform any heroic avoidance maneuvers. A handful of senior citizens saw it from the Cape Disappointment lighthouse, but they haven't been much help. There were no radio communications during the crash and certainly no warning that they were in trouble. No voice cockpit recorders. They simply dropped off the radar."

Hoagland didn't ask me any questions about what I saw that day, so apparently he wasn't aware that I'd witnessed the crash. In spite of that, I couldn't help thinking Hoagland had a handle on the investigation and knew what he was doing. He looked and spoke with the confidence of a man who was skilled at what he did. He wasn't the most personable guy in the world, but it was clear he wanted you to like him and that when it came to investigations, he was all business.

I handed him the disc with the photographs on it. "I took a couple of photos while the plane was going down. My name and phone number are on the disc."

"You saw the plane go down?"

"I'm on your list."

"Thank you. We'll look into it, and we'll be in touch with you," he said, handling the disc as if it were of little consequence. He would feel differently once he saw the photos.

TWENTY-SEVEN

THE DRIZZLE INTENSIFIED as the last groups on the tarmac broke up. On my way to the car I lost track of Snake and then was waylaid by Ruth Ponzi, who asked if she could have a few minutes of my time. "I don't think so," I replied rather uncharitably.

"But . . . that's not fair," she sputtered. "We had a deal. I was going to answer your questions and you were going to answer mine."

Reluctant to welsh on a bargain, at least not openly, I let her ask questions for five minutes, giving replies that were either shrugs, expletives, or "I don't recall." In a sadistic way it was actually kind of fun teasing her, something I would regret later. She fished for personal tidbits about Kathy and me being on opposite sides during the campaign. She wanted all the details of my watching helplessly as the plane went down. Ponzi wanted a story with human dimensions, but I wasn't about to offer up my life or Kathy's for the gum-chewing masses. In the end, I answered her questions, but didn't give a single credible detail to scribble down. "If you decide you want to talk, give me a call. I would really like to write this."

"I know you would."

Not far from my Ford, in the parking lot by the fence, I found Snake chatting with Joey Hilditch, who was standing next to a Honda with side panels of different colors. They were talking about the stock market, Joey happily and rather shyly explaining how he'd bought a bundle of penny stock in a company that purported to be researching the biggest AIDS medication breakthrough in history. He'd invested everything he could scrape together, had even borrowed from his girlfriend and his girlfriend's parents. "The odds of it hitting big are one in a thousand," he said. "But when it hits, I'll be set for life."

Snake said, "I've dumped every cent into a new Internet idea. It's going to be the hottest thing since sliced bread."

Everybody had money in a secret stock.

"Joey," I said. "Anything in your family history that might give these suicide theories room to breathe?"

"My dad's father killed himself. But that was a long time ago, before I was even born. And I guess, now that you bring it up, I had an uncle who killed himself, too."

"Your father's brother?"

"Yeah."

"How long ago?"

"My uncle shot himself when I was about two. You don't think my father killed all those people? He would never do that." Joey looked desperate. I hadn't meant to alarm him, but the question had come up, and it would come up again.

"No, I don't," I said, though I had no idea if he had. "How was your father's marriage?"

"Twenty-six years and going strong."

Once we were in the car, I turned to Snake. "There's no way he committed suicide, except his father did and his brother did?"

"Give the kid a break. He loved his pop, and he doesn't want it to be a murder-slash-suicide. Even *you* don't want that. What we want is for it to be an accident."

"Yeah? What does your brother want it to be?"

"With Bert, anything bad happens, it's a government setup. But don't *you* go down that path."

"No way."

"I'm warning you."

Less than twenty minutes later we were on Mercer Island searching for an address off West Mercer Way, a twisty road famous in the cycling community. On a summer evening, you might see sixty or eighty cyclists pass by in an hour. It was drizzling when we found Freddy Mitz's property, which sloped steeply down to the beach. Across the lake we could see the verdant hills of Seward Park and beyond that housing clusters in Seattle. As we hiked the steep driveway, Snake observed, "This would be the place to watch the hydro races from."

The house was sprawling, two stories over the garages, but one story everywhere else, extensive landscaped shrubbery in front and a small wrought-iron gate through which we passed to descend a set of staggered concrete stairs to the front door. I'd called earlier, so Claire Mitz was expecting me. She opened the front door and was startled to see Snake. In this neighborhood he looked more like some mountebank selling phony magazine subscriptions than anything else.

"Mr. Black?" she said, turning to me with something akin to distress.

"That's right, but call me Thomas."

"At Freddy's funeral somebody pointed you out. I was told you'd lost your wife on the plane."

"And you made it to Kathy's service. I hope I wasn't rude. I think I was rude to everybody. I was in shock."

"I was the same at Freddy's."

"Maybe so, but you were very gracious. I was rude."

We were members of an exclusive club, the membership select, the dues painful. For me, the endless chain of black-clad grieving widows, brothers, sisters, fathers, mothers, children, friends, and associates had made life during the past week almost unbearable. At night, when I wasn't thinking about riding a plane into the ocean, I got lost amid a sea of grieving faces. The truth was, I'd attended so many funerals by the time Kathy's came along, I had all the favorite Bible passages memorized; I could recite the Robert Frost poem by heart. Partially because of that numbing effect, Kathy's services had barely scratched my consciousness. I'd passed the day in a fog.

"Come in," Claire Mitz said.

"This is Elmer Slezak. Claire Mitz." Snake took off his hat. His cowboy boots made a racket on the slate entranceway. She walked us through an airy atrium to a large living room overlooking the water and the hills of Seward Park across the lake. "Beautiful home," I said.

"Thank you. The property was in Freddy's family for forty years before we put a house on it. I just hope we can keep it in the family. The taxes are going to kill us."

We sat on tall, firm sofas in the living room while Claire bustled into the kitchen and came back with a silver tray bearing coffee and cookies. No matter what she claimed, she still had that deer-in-the-headlights look over the loss of her husband, though she did her best to play the hostess role. Everything in her life had been turned upside down. All of her thinking about what she was going to do next week and next year would have to be recalculated. She was probably still wrestling with the problem of what to do with her husband's personal effects. I sure didn't know how to handle Kathy's.

Claire Mitz was in her early forties, young-looking with a shock of short-cropped hair a stylist had frosted. I noticed she wore makeup and earrings, along with a smart little ensemble in pink: trousers, a white blouse, and tiny pink shoes. It made me wonder if, unlike me, she was able to attend to her personal hygiene in spite of her grief, or if she'd been wandering around her empty house in the same pair of food-stained sweatpants for the past ten days, as I had. She was thick through the middle and large-breasted in the way some women become when they take on weight. She had pretty blue eyes framed by bangs cut straight across. You could see she'd been a heartthrob in high school and college.

When we were all seated, she said, "It was nice of you to come."

"You're getting along all right?"

"Fine." I'm sure my face betrayed the fact that I knew she was doing poorly. Misery recognizes misery.

"I'm here to pick your brain, Claire. If you don't mind. Anything you can tell me about Freddy or Chuck Hilditch. Does anything you've been reading in the papers strike you as not making sense?"

"I haven't been reading the papers."

"Thomas is investigating the crash," Snake said. "He's a private investigator."

"I'm trying to stay out of the way of the official investigation," I said, in response to her look.

"He's given them a couple of pictures of the crash as it happened," Snake added. "So it's not like he hasn't helped."

"Pictures? You mean photographs?"

"I was at the lighthouse on the coast when the plane went down. I got two photos of the plane going into the water."

Claire looked as if she were strangling. It was more or less the reaction I'd expected, which was why I hadn't brought it up myself.

"Does . . . ?"

"They don't show much. It's so far away it almost looks like a toy plane."

When Claire had composed herself, she said, "Do you have any reason to think the official investigations aren't going to uncover the truth?"

"I'm not sure. I only know I have to do this myself." Outside the window a floatplane flew low over Lake Washington, then headed up into the drizzle. Every time I saw a small plane now I expected it to crash. "Is there anything about the accident itself that strikes you as odd?"

"It was all odd."

"They stayed the night in Portland?"

"Chuck had a sister he wanted to visit. He hadn't seen her in a while, and she'd had a baby."

"Which meant you weren't going to see your husband for at least three more days?"

"Right. He'd been gone over two weeks. In some ways, it almost feels like he's still on a trip."

"They were close? Chuck and Freddy?"

"Very."

"And Freddy thought Chuck was a good pilot?"

"Freddy thought Chuck was as good as anything the air force had ever produced, including himself. Chuck lived to fly. So did Freddy, for that matter. I guess they died doing something they loved."

"You've heard the suicide rumors? That one of the pilots might have been trying to . . ."

"That's absurd."

"What about the plane? Had your husband mentioned any problems with it?"

"He didn't usually talk to me about the plane, but if he'd been worried about it, I'm sure he would have told me, and he didn't say anything."

It was beginning to look like a waste of time: my trip here, Boeing Field, all of it. And then, as so often happens during an investigation, something we'd said or done toggled a series of synapses in her brain and she said, "There was one odd thing, but I'm sure it isn't relevant."

"Everything is relevant."

"That last night on the phone Freddy mentioned he'd seen a man he thought he recognized from the airfield in Seattle on a street in Portland. Freddy told me he went over and said hello to the guy. That's the sort of person Freddy was. If he knew you, he'd go over and say hi. But the man claimed he'd never seen Freddy before and hadn't been to Seattle in years. Freddy could have sworn he'd seen him at the airport in Seattle the day they left."

"At Boeing Field?"

"Yes. And then ten days later on the street in Portland."

"Probably somebody who looked like somebody else," said Snake, the twin.

"That's what I told him," Claire said. "But Freddy was sure he recognized him, even though he didn't know who the man was."

I said, "But he was certain enough to walk up to the guy and say hello?"

"Yes. Freddy would never call anybody a liar, but he thought this man was lying. Knowing he was going to be flying a senator in a day, Freddy thought maybe it was a Secret Service agent who was embarrassed about getting spotted. You think?"

The Secret Service didn't make a habit of following pilots on the street, not unless they were considered a threat. And if he had been Secret Service, what had he been doing at Boeing Field two weeks prior to the flight?

"Did he happen to tell you what this man looked like?"

"No. He only mentioned it to me because he thought it was kind of strange."

We spoke for another ten minutes. They'd been married young, back when Freddy was still in the air force, and had raised two children, a boy and a girl. The girl was at Mount Holyoke. The boy had an engineering degree from the University of Washington and was working for a software firm five miles away in Bellevue. As we left, I said, "The man Freddy recognized in Portland? You tell the other investigators?"

"I didn't think of it until today. Should I?"

"Maybe. Yeah."

"What do you make of it?"

"I don't know."

TWENTY-EIGHT

WE WERE STILL ON MERCER ISLAND when I rolled my car window down to let one of Snake's farts clear out. "Let's find Bert," I said.

"Now don't be dragging my brother into this. And close the window, would you? It's cold."

"Where is he?"

"I thought he was back in Maryland looking for work until I read he got himself arrested at the Cape."

"Why don't you call him now?"

"I will if you close that window. What do you want me to say?"

"Find out where he is, but play it coy. Set up a meeting."

"Have you ever seen me not play it coy?"

"About a million times."

"Are you going to close that window?"

"As soon as my eyes stop watering. Just be subtle. See if you can find out where he is. And don't let on you're with me. I don't want to spook him."

"Listen, Thomas. I'm your friend. I can guarantee there's nothing bogus about this plane crash."

"You can't possibly know that."

"Sure I can. The preponderance of the evidence suggests it."

"The preponderance of the evidence isn't in."

"Your wife and some other people got onto a plane and it crashed into the Pacific Ocean, and now there are government agencies handling it. That's all there is. Anything else is just quackery. The feds investigate plane crashes for a living. When was the last time you investigated a plane crash? What you need to do is butt out. I know you don't want to hear this, but you tell me the truth when I need it, so I'm telling you. Just look what you've found out so far. Zilch."

"You're kidding, right? Freddy Mitz—"

"Saw some jackass on the street he thought he recognized. So what? I bet the joker was having an affair and didn't want his wife to find out he'd been in Seattle."

"Four days before the flight your brother warned me to keep Kathy away from Sheffield. You told me he warned you before Oklahoma City. And before 9/11. He's got some sort of conduit."

"You don't want to mess with my brother. He's the baddest thing you've ever met."

"Oh, come on."

"I told you he was a government-trained killer. I know you think he's a flake, but he's also dangerous."

"I'm supposed to back off because I'm afraid of your brother? Try again."

"I know he presents like a second-rate thief or some pencil dick with anger management problems, a drunk and all of that, and he is those things, but only in the last couple of years. I can only liken it to a sleeping cobra. You don't want to be petting it. That stuff I told you with the dead kids in South America? It broke his spirit and turned him into what he is now. I didn't tell you this last night, but he once told me his personal kill count in the army was a hundred and seven. God knows what it was by the time he retired. You need to stay away from him."

"If he's as bad as you say, it makes it more likely he had something to do with the accident. Or knows who did."

"Why would he be involved?"

"That's what I want to find out."

Snake flipped open his cellphone. "Bert? Gee, I didn't think you'd be there so quick . . . Yeah, yeah. I spoke to him. Uh, huh. Well, if you want my take on it, he's not doing so well." Snake glanced at me. "Tell you the truth, bro, I think he's going paranoid on us." Snake listened for a while. "Can't say, really. Just . . . weird. Wanders around all night. Yeah. I spent the night there. Now? Right now? He's going . . . somewhere . . . I don't know where. Listen, Bert, if we're going to keep talking I think we should do it in person. When are you going to be back in town?" Snake listened for a few moments and said, "Because I don't want to do this over the phone."

I hadn't had much of a chance to review what Snake told me about his brother the night before. I'd known Snake and his brother had a tumultuous upbringing, but the details of Bert's early life had come as a shock. The more Snake told me, the more I knew he was leaving out. I'd thought of Bert as a lightweight, and now Snake claimed that when his brother was in the military he had killed more than a hundred people, combatants—at least I hoped they were combatants—and that there was a high probability that at the tender age of fourteen he may have murdered his own father.

After some brotherly banter, most of it not repeatable, Snake flipped his phone shut and said, "He's at the trailer." When I gave him a questioning look, he added, "In Enumclaw. With Grams. She's ninety-six. Part Cherokee. Her grandfather actually had some white scalps in the house. We found them in her attic. Maybe that's where Bert gets it."

"Don't tell me Bert's scalped people."

"I wouldn't put it past him."

"He tell you he was in Enumclaw?"

"He didn't tell me diddly, but in the background I could hear the crummy old radio he keeps in his trailer. He's forty miles southeast of here in his sardine-can mansion in Enumscratch."

"I thought he was forbidden to go back because of a restraining order."

"I don't know that Grams even knows he's there. Or cares. She's got her soap operas. Besides, her trailer's a couple hundred yards away. She can't see his place."

"He still have all those guns?"

"He may not have five thousand rounds of ammo, but he'll have something. When we get there, we're going to talk to him nice, right?"

"Maybe."

"That's exactly the attitude I was afraid of."

≡ TWENTY-NINE ≡

ENUMCLAW WAS SITUATED in the shadow of Mount Rainier, but today the low clouds formed a gray blanket that obscured even the nearby rolling hills. We'd driven south on 405, where the traffic had been gridlocked as usual, then traced Highway 169 down through the valley to Enumclaw.

Though the region's developers were working like ants, the town itself retained a distinct rural character, and there were still a few one-man farms dotted with six or eight head of beef grazing behind fences, rural farmhouses surrounded by fields, and milk cows and horses staring at us from paddocks. We drove past brick storefronts on one of the main streets in town, and as we were stopped at a red light, I caught a glimpse of a woman getting out of a parked car and entering a nearby bookstore. I'd been confused before, but this time I was certain. Or certain enough.

"Thomas! What the hell are you doing?" Snake yelled.

Without being aware of how it happened, or where my brain was in time and space, I leaped out of the car. A delivery truck behind us honked. A second truck traveling from the other direction almost clipped me. Snake barked from the passenger window, but I ignored him and followed the woman into the Lindon Bookstore. Inside I saw three or four customers, including a woman with a baby in a stroller and a woman working an espresso machine.

"I'm sorry," I said to the employee at the espresso machine, "but somebody just walked in here. Young woman. Jeans and a blue ski coat?" She gave me a peevish look, probably because in addressing her I'd interrupted her conversation with a customer.

"Are you a friend?" the woman asked warily.

"She dropped a wallet in the street," I said, pulling out my own wallet and displaying it as if I'd just found it.

Holding her hand palm out, she said, "We'll see she gets it."

"Is she in the back?"

"Listen. If you don't identify yourself . . ."

"I found a wallet. Geez." I slipped the wallet back into my pocket. Maybe it was my eyes—they'd been bloodshot for days—or my short-tempered and imperious manner, but both women at the espresso machine were on alert. I might have pulled off this stunt ten days ago without incurring a shred of suspicion, but something in my deportment had altered. When the door to a small restroom in the back of the store opened, I thought my heart was going to jump into my mouth. Carrying a yellow watch cap, a short Asian woman with her hair in a long plait stepped through the doorway. When I approached, she jumped backward and gave me the startled look of someone who'd just missed tangling with a freight train. I didn't see how I could have inspired that much alarm, but I had. Intensity can sometimes be mistaken for mental illness, and I knew in the last week or so my demeanor had been mistaken for that by any number of individuals. I peered past her into the darkened, empty bathroom, then fled the store.

"Aren't you going to give her the wallet?" somebody yelled.

When I got back into the car, Snake was uncharacteristically silent. The detour had befuddled me but had shaken him. I had no idea what was going through his mind, but he had to be wishing he'd brought along a tranquilizer gun and maybe a couple of burly assistants. For a minute or two I actually believed the woman in the store was Kathy. It had seemed so plausible when it was happening and so *Twilight Zone* now. It made even less sense than dying in a plane crash. The incident had spiked adrenaline through the top of my brain like a Roman candle. It was the sort of momentary deflection from sanity that made you question everything about yourself.

Snake, who had earlier been giving a nonstop running monologue about his brother and the five wives he'd ditched, some of which I'd already heard and most of which I'd been ignoring, now spoke only when he needed to post an addendum to the driving directions. I couldn't tell how much of the acreage belonged to his grandmother, but as we pulled off the highway, it appeared to be a large piece of property, perhaps fifteen or twenty acres, some of it treed, some just knolls and weeds. The entranceway was an unmarked driveway, the kind of place you would never locate without a guide.

We parked under a tree heavy with aging crab apples and got out, inhaling the aroma of rotten fruit in the cold, moist noon air. There were no trailers in sight. Throughout the funerals, including Kathy's, I'd been as dull as a rock, but now as we walked to meet Bert I was hyped to the point it almost scared me.

Snake led me along a barely discernable path over a nearby hillock. It was closing in on noon as we paraded past a ramshackle trailer surrounded by fifteen or twenty car hulks in various states of degradation, a chronicle of one family's economic fortunes, the wrecks ranging from the most recent, a twenty-year-old Chevy Impala, down to the six or eight vintage Ford pickups. All of the windows in the trailer were obscured by curtains or objects inside. "That belongs to Grams," Snake said. "Bert's place is over yonder."

We hiked past the trailer without incident and followed the faint car path over another hillock. "This the only way in?" I asked.

"There's a dozen ways in and out. That's why Bert likes it here."

On the other side of the small rise we found five small outbuildings, two of them falling-down barns that stood like old men leaning into a storm. All the wire fencing on the property was either missing or sagging. Judging by the age of the barns and the state of disrepair, it had been at least thirty years since anybody had worked this land.

Bert was staying in one of those tiny camping trailers that reminded me of the trailer in the old Mickey Mouse cartoon when Minnie and Mickey take a vacation. I had a vision of ten or fifteen SWAT team members surrounding it while Bert sat inside watching TV and drinking beer.

The sounds of "Bad Moon Rising" were so loud one of the windows rattled to the heavy bass beat. The small wooden makeshift porch vibrated beneath our feet. Snake tried shouting and, when that didn't attract his brother's attention, began banging on the aluminum door with his fists. For a while even that didn't work.

When he finally pulled the door open, Bert Slezak was dancing like a drugged-out rooster. "Hey, bro," he said to Snake. When he recognized me he lost the beat to the music, turned around, and disappeared into the darkness. Snake followed him inside, and I followed Snake, ducking so as not to strike my head on the doorway. The moment I closed the door behind me the dim lights were extinguished.

Later, we figured it was some sort of stun grenade or maybe a gas canister without the gas. If it had been a military-issue grenade, we would have all three been dead, but as it was, Snake and I turned into a ball of panicked arms and legs as we battled our way back out the front door and rolled off the porch into the wet weeds. The explosion had come close to blowing out both my eardrums. I was on my hands and knees trying to clear my head when Snake landed on top of me, poking a bony knee into my shoulder. One of the guns he was carrying clonked me on the back of my skull. When I looked up through the snarl of limbs, I spotted Bert hightailing it past one of the old barns.

I scrambled to my feet and started jogging unsteadily after him. When he saw me giving chase, he produced a pistol and fired two rounds. Knowing I wasn't going to be discouraged by gunfire, he tucked the gun into the folds of his clothing, put his head down, and began running in earnest. Why had he attacked us and why was he now running? Guilty conscience? Or had he, like the women in the bookstore, sensed something malignant, even monstrous, in my deportment?

He darted through a copse of fir trees, ran along a small creek, and found his way under a wire fence. I'd been gaining rapidly, but each time he scaled, eluded, or hurdled an obstacle, I had to make my way around it, too, and I didn't have all the shortcuts memorized the way he obviously did. By the time I got to the highway, there was a stream of fast-moving traffic between me and Bert, who was already on the other side.

The area on the far side of the highway was cluttered with new housing. Bert sprinted through a backyard with two portable basketball hoops, into a cul-de-sac, through another yard, and over a wooden fence. A dog nipped my trouser leg as I followed him over the fence. Who would have guessed spindly little Bert Slezak, who more often than not had trouble walking a straight line, could remain in front for so long? To be frank, I was out of shape and amazed at how much damage eight days on a sofa and the loss of a spouse could do to the human physique. I was breathing so hard it felt as if the insides of my lungs were sloughing off. I kept spitting up phlegm that seemed as if it had blood and maybe gravel in it. I was light-headed. My knees hurt. My left calf was beginning to cramp.

As I began to edge closer, we found ourselves on the skirt of a country road, speeding along like two men in a footrace. When he felt me converging on him, he began to duck and weave, but I grabbed his collar and, still running, slung him around and slammed him into the ground. As it happened there were no motorists to observe my shenanigans. He hadn't been hurt too badly, so as he began to get back up, I slammed him into the embankment alongside the road. This time he came up fumbling for the pistol in his belt. I knocked it out of his hands and hit him across the jaw with my left fist. He went down like a sack of sand while I picked up the gun.

Somewhere along the way, probably at the beginning, we'd outrun Snake.

"Why'd you bail out like that?" I asked.

"Why'd you chase me?" Bert was still trying to catch his breath.

"You're the one who set off the bomb."

"Because you were chasing me."

"All I did was step into the trailer."

When he stood up, I pushed him a couple of feet backward, watched him stumble and fall. After putting the cartridges into my trousers pocket, I slipped the empty pistol into my waistband. Bert was bleeding from the nose. His cheek had a laceration.

"Why did you warn me not to let Kathy travel with Sheffield?"

"I didn't." When I started toward him, he added, "I just wanted to stop you two from squabbling, you know? You were working for one candidate, and she was working for the other. I was trying to put things right."

"You knew something was going to happen."

"Maybe I had a *feeling*."

"Tell me about it."

"It's going to sound certifiable."

I stepped closer.

"I know six ways to kill you without moving from this spot," he added, forming his upper limbs into a martial arts pose I didn't recognize. Before he could finish the pose, I knocked him on his ass with a right cross. He was light, and the blow lifted him off his feet. From the ground, he tried to do a leg sweep, but all he did was kick me in the knee. He might have been a martial artist at one time, but years of bad living had eroded his skills. A pickup truck down the road screeched to a halt and reversed until both the passenger and the driver were looking me in the eyes, the passenger leaning out with his bulging biceps on the truck windowsill.

"You okay, buddy?" the passenger said, addressing Bert. They were good old boys, tattooed and beefy and, despite the weather, in sleeveless shirts and straw cowboy hats.

"I'm fine, yeah," Bert said, bounding to his feet and dancing like a fighter coming up to beat the count. "I bet him he couldn't knock me off my feet, and now would you look at this? I owe him ten bucks." Bert smirked, his teeth outlined with blood. "Okay, Thomas. Your turn. I get a free whack at you."

They must have known from the look in my eyes I wasn't going to let Bert swing. As they drove away, I had a feeling they were planning to call the cops.

"What do you know about the plane crash?"

"Listen, we gotta get outa here. I don't need to see the cops right now."

"What about jail? I thought you were in jail."

"That didn't last but a few hours. They were just harassing me."

Taking a different route than the circuitous zigzagging trail we'd used earlier, Bert led me back to his grandmother's property. "I would have talked to you," Bert said. "You didn't have to go Arnold Schwarzenegger on me."

"You're the one who set off the ordnance."

THIRTY

WHEN WE REACHED THE TRAILER, Bert tried to step inside the half-open door. "We'll just talk out here away from the ammunition dump," I said, grabbing his arm. The music was still playing, though not as loud as it had been. I could smell the odor of gunpowder lingering inside the small space.

"I'm cold. Besides, it was only a percussion cap. Nothing to get jacked up about. And it was an accident."

"I suppose running was an accident? And taking shots at me was an accident?"

"You may have noticed, I didn't hit you. I'm not likely to miss if I want to kill someone. You're welcome. Can I go in now?"

"No."

Snake appeared at the door with a titty magazine in his hands and, without looking at either of us, sat on the stoop thumbing through it, addressing me as if I hadn't been gone, and as if we hadn't both been blown out of the trailer ten minutes earlier. "I told you not to turn wild man on me," Snake said.

"You're bleeding from your ear."

"Hey, you found yourself a gun. I thought you didn't carry."

"It was a gift."

"Okay," Bert said, settling on the stoop below his brother. "I'll just sit here and freeze my balls off." Again, I was amazed at how identical twins could present so dissimilarly, the feat accounted for mostly in their disparate grooming and body language. In his cowboy hat, boots, and jeans, Snake sat with his shoulders hunched and his posture sloppy. Bert, clad in baggy old suit trousers, suspenders, and a dingy, food-spattered V-neck T-shirt, made a habit of sitting, standing, and walking in the manner of a guard at Buckingham Palace, even though he dressed like a homeless man from Bulgaria. I had a fleeting thought of how unfair it was that these two semidegenerate brothers were still walking the planet while Kathy was not.

"Your brother told me you predicted 9/11," I said.

"The attorney general of the United States was publicly saying he wasn't going to fly on a commercial airliner. Cheney was running military air exercises. When was the last time a vice president personally ran war games? Of *course* something was going to happen. Any idiot could have foreseen it."

"This idiot didn't."

"All of this stuff is related. You need to get with the new paradigm."

"I've been reading about 9/11. I'll agree the official explanation has plenty of holes in it."

"Thinking it stinks and knowing what really went on are worlds apart. Do you know anything about all the microbiologists who went dead or missing since then? You know what they were working on? Do you know why there was so much dust when those towers went down? Why there was no furniture and so few bodies? Why the rubble pile was not higher? Do you know about the death ray from space theory and how it might have brought those towers down? Did you know the military told their planes to land just before the first tower crumbled?"

"Why would they do that?"

"Did you know Bush's brother and cousin were on the board of directors of the company running the security for the trade towers? Also, when was the last time a U.S. airliner went off course and was *not* intercepted by an air force fighter within minutes? Remember when Payne Stewart's Learjet went off course? They were on that like stink on shit. On 9/11 we had four airliners go off course, and over an hour later not one had been intercepted. Did you know the Pentagon was protected by a missile defense system? Or that none of the bodies from the flight that hit the Pentagon were ever returned to the relatives?

Or seen by anyone? Do you know what an EMI weapon is? Do you know what caused TWA flight eight hundred to go down in ninety-six?"

"You're jabbering. Tell me why you thought Sheffield was under a black cloud."

"Hey," Bert said, turning to Snake. "There's a brunette in there who looks kind of like Gina. Get to her yet?" Somehow, Bert thought because his brother was sitting next to us pawing through a dirty magazine and that I had arrived with his brother, that we were all buddies. Turning to me, he said, "Gina was my third wife. Temper like a firecracker."

Without knowing I was going to do it, I doubled up my left fist and knocked him off the stoop. He landed in the weeds and lay staring up at me, nursing his jaw. As he got up, he said, "You're not going to hit me again, are you?"

"I didn't know I was going to hit you that time."

"What's wrong with you?" Snake asked.

"He's jacking me around."

"I'm not jacking you around," Bert said. "You have to understand the new paradigm, or none of it will make sense. Addition and subtraction before algebra."

"You sure hit him hard," Snake said.

"Not as hard as I wanted to."

Without getting off the stoop, Snake examined his brother's face. "Jesus, Thomas. Leave him alone, would you? We're twins. Every time you hit him, I feel it."

I felt bad for losing my temper. It wasn't anything I would have done a week ago, but then, I wasn't the man I'd been a week ago. "Saturday before the crash you told me something was going to happen. How did you know?"

"If you're thinking I knew that plane was going down, I didn't."

"You warned me not to let Kathy travel with Sheffield."

"I didn't have any specific information. I just knew she was due. Sheffield was. I mean, look at her career. If you woulda let me go through the facts with you, you could have figured it out on your own. Since day one Sheffield's been a thorn in the administration's side. The powers that be had justification to off her long ago."

"Are you saying the plane crash was planned by our government?"

"All I'm saying is, if you've got your head screwed on straight, it's the first thing you suspect when something like a small plane crash happens to a major political rival of the administration." Bert looked at me as if *he* thought *I* was the crazy one, as if reasonable people always blamed major catastrophes involving political foes on political operatives, as if we were living in some third-world country where secret backdoor vendettas were taken for granted.

"Let me provide you with a little background," he said. He was back on the stoop now, and on the soapbox. I'd stepped away so he could know I wouldn't hit him again. "Right after the towers collapsed, the White House wanted to expand their powers. They declared war on terrorists, who of course could be anybody they didn't like, and asked for more power to track down and punish them. They came up with some shaky legislation that was debatably unconstitutional. There were two Democratic senators in a position to put the kibosh on it, Patrick Leahy of Vermont and Tom Daschle of South Dakota. In the middle of all that, somebody decides to use germ warfare; letters are sent through the U.S. Postal Service with anthrax spores in them. Guess who got the anthrax? Of all the senators and judges and so forth in Washington, two guys are singled out, the two guys who together formed the biggest stumbling block to passage of the Patriot Act. Go look it up. Now, who stood to benefit if those men got killed or, even better, scared out of their wits? That's what you want to look at with a crime. Who stands to benefit."

"What did you know about the plane?"

"Absolutely nothing. When I found out Kathy was working for Sheffield, I started digging. Sheffield has been antagonizing this administration for as long as she was in the Senate. And everybody knew she has a solid base here in Washington State, so she wasn't going to be easy to remove. There was an attempt a year or so ago to implicate her in a scheme involving cash for votes. Remember?"

"Vaguely."

"The FBI didn't spend more than four hours on it before

they told the papers it was a frame-up. Then the machine coughed up a ton of money to get rid of her by democratic process, except that wasn't panning out, either. Turns out a democracy doesn't always do what you tell it. Every time Sheffield turns around she's laying down a nail strip in the path of the machine."

"So they replace her with Maddox?"

"It didn't matter who. They get somebody they can work with, and they make an example. Whether that example comes because they crush her in the elections or because she's dead, it makes no difference."

"It makes a difference to me. One's an election. The other's murder."

"You and I know that, but these folks only care about coming out on top."

"You're saying the crash was done on purpose for political motivations?"

"Hey, I'm not the only one thinking along these lines. D.C. is rife with jokes about not flying in small planes until after the elections. Of course, you'd never in a million years hear any of those guys say anything in public. But don't listen to the jokes. And don't listen to me. There's a team of investigators working on it. They'll file a tidy little report. They'll come up with a crossed wire. Pilot error. Ice on the flight attendant's ass. Whatever. Back East they'll still be making jokes. Are you listening? You get on the wrong side of the machine and have enough clout to make a difference, and eventually you're toast. Not always, but enough times for the majority to keep their heads down.

"You think the CIA and the DIA and the other alphabet agencies are there to protect you? They exist to do the bidding of the machine. Why have so many directors of the Agency been multimillionaires and one was even the head of the Securities and Exchange Commission? Because the CIA's job is protecting big business. Take William Casey. Remember when he was about to testify before Congress in the Iran-contra hearings, and there were hints he might be planning to talk out of school—in fact, afterward his attorney said he'd been planning to spill it all, Reagan and the contras. Suddenly he has brain cancer? What happened during the surgery? Is any of this ringing a bell? The part of his brain that controls speech was damaged so he could no longer talk. That's as close to the Mafia cutting out your tongue as you can get. I've talked to specialists about the surgery and they can't understand it. They could have killed him, but what they did was so much scarier. He died a little later anyway."

"You're not telling me they got a doctor to—"

"In this world you can get anybody to do anything. And how about Sheffield going down in that plane? Don't you think critics of the administration might not pull back just a little bit now, even if they're not sure Sheffield was assassinated? Even if they only think it somewhere in the deepest recesses of their brains? Think the naysayers in D.C. aren't already muted? Or maybe it's only slowed their reaction time. That might be enough. A lot of politics involves slowing down the opposition's reaction time."

"If even half of what you're saying is true, the media would be all over this."

"You obviously haven't been taking notes. These days a handful of corporations own the media. It's the same machine that's doing all this. Look at the controlled demolitions on 9/11. What does the mainstream media have to say about them? They say you're crazy if you think they were demolitions. Look at the polls in Europe and Canada. Those people all agree they were demolitions. Are all those people nuts, or maybe our machine doesn't have the same control over their media that it does over our own? All you have to do is watch the videos to see it, a massive case of the emperor having no clothes. Of course those buildings were brought down by insiders. And what about building number seven? Towers one and two supposedly went down because they were thumped by airplanes—which is, in itself, ridiculous—but number seven wasn't hit by anything. It went flat anyway. Do you know it wasn't even mentioned in the official commission report? A forty-seven-story building falls to the ground in its own footprint for no visible reason, and not a word in the official report? FEMA's report said it went down because of internal fires. In the history of the earth, no tall steel building has ever collapsed from fire, or a combination of fire and other damage. It's never happened before, so there are no experts who can explain how it happened three times in one day. But apparently you're a fruit loop if you're suspicious."

"You're way off topic. Talk to me about Sheffield."

"God, you're a hard man. This *is* about Sheffield. Ten years ago I was thinking about getting out of the business. I had a friend named Connelly. Connelly wanted out, too. Only he thought he might talk to a reporter beforehand, spout off about a few of the stunts we'd pulled. Mind you, we had all signed confidentiality agreements, so what he was planning was a breach of etiquette.

"He's in a small village in Mexico where he's supposed to meet a reporter from *The Washington Post*. On his way to the meeting, he gets into a minor fender bender with a Mexican military vehicle. Almost no damage to his car, but the military vehicle has him blocked in. He says he's all right, but he's hustled off to a nearby clinic to be treated for what bystanders said were minor injuries. He fails to show up for the meeting with the reporter. He fails to show up back at his hotel room. He fails to call home. A week later when she still hasn't heard from him, his wife sends his best friend down to Cuernevaca to find out what happened. The best friend is me. I find him in a small clinic. He's strapped into a wheelchair with bandages wrapped around his head. He doesn't recognize me. He's got an IQ of sixty. All he does is eat, sleep, play with his own poop, and make halfhearted attempts to grab the nurses. We got him back to the States, where a doctor told his wife he'd had a large piece of his brain removed and replaced with a Neuticle."

"A Neuticle?"

"It's a fake testicle they put into a dog's nut sack after they neuter him."

"Jesus."

"That's what I said. He died four years later. I think somebody on the staff of the nursing home where they'd parked him suffocated him, maybe at his own request. His wife didn't want me to pursue it, so I let it go. By the way, I was at the funeral. Kathy had a lot of friends."

"I didn't see you."

"You didn't see anybody. You looked like you got hit with a wrecking ball. She meant a lot to me. I hope you know that."

"I know it."

"I couldn't . . ." He was beginning to choke up, and I was afraid if he choked up I would, too, and pretty soon we'd all be weeping like a bunch of kids standing over a dead dog. I didn't like the way Bert was controlling the conversation, and I didn't like the fact that some of what he was saying made more sense to me than it should have.

One of my knees was wet where it had touched the ground, but virtually all of Bert's clothing was damp and soiled from rolling on the wet earth. I'd hit him with everything I had, but he'd bounced back each time like a blow-up clown. In that respect he was a lot like his brother, the ex–bull rider: able to take punishment without a quibble, fearless, and nearly bulletproof. Having a Neanderthal of a father who beat you weekly could do that. "Bert? Tell me what's really going on here."

"Okay. The plane goes down at what . . . three? Four p.m.?"

"Three thirty-seven."

"Okay. Right." He seemed taken aback by my command of the details. "Then a car full of FBI agents arrives in Ilwaco at four-thirty and begins their investigation, having driven from Seattle."

"It takes three hours to drive from Seattle."

"Right. Were they going someplace else and got detoured to the plane crash site? Or did they have advance notice that a plane with a senator on board was going down? Why don't you see if they can answer that? There's also a guy named Timmy Hoagland."

"We met him this morning."

"Nice guy, right?"

"He seemed squared away."

"He worked for the Agency. I knew him about fifteen years ago, and back then even people inside the Agency were afraid of him. Dollars to doughnuts he's cut human throats more times than you've missed your Sunday paper. He was a wheeler-dealer with connections that went higher than most of us in the Agency aspired to. He's also the one who was in charge of the Wellstone crash investigation. The Carnahan investigation. TWA flight eight hundred. He's the go-to guy for cover-ups."

"You can't know those were all cover-ups."

"No, you're right. But on the basis of a whole hell of a lot of insider information, I can sure suspect it. You want to know about the crash? I can tell you this. There was an inside man. He may not have known what was going to happen and he may still have no inkling he was part of it, but he knows he's a traitor to the cause. He knows that. Sometimes it's cash, women, a better position. You play into people's dreams. Or you blackmail them. In our unit, we found greed worked better than guilt."

"Are you saying we're looking for somebody in the Sheffield campaign who was feeding information to the enemy?"

"Find them and you find a buried cord that's going to lead you directly into the heart of darkness. Just keep pulling on the cord."

"So you'd—"

"*Me*? If this was me, I wouldn't stop running until I was in Greenland, or Tahiti, someplace where they wouldn't find me and cut my throat. If we're even halfway close to the truth, just standing here talking about it makes our lives worth about a nickel. Come inside. I want to show you something."

Bert set me up in front of his computer, hooked it up to the Internet, and found a website he apparently knew well. There were multiple videos on the website, each showing a different building collapse. The first two were controlled demolitions, one in Las Vegas and one in Seattle. Then he played the videos of the three buildings that went down in New York City in 2001. I'd seen them before, but we played them again.

"Bet you never heard how all the tenants were locked out of the towers the weekend before it happened?" said Bert. "It wasn't something they slapped on the front page of *The New York Times*, but it's true. People who tried to go in to work were told the buildings had electrical problems and the towers would be closed all weekend. Seems like a weekend might be long enough to set up a bunch of demolition charges, doesn't it?"

"You realize, I'm going to check this out?"

"I'd be disappointed if you didn't."

THIRTY-ONE

IT WAS AN HOUR before Snake was able to drag me away from the computer, Bert sitting at my shoulder kibitzing, Snake complaining all the while that he was hungry. As we left, Bert apologized for taking potshots at me earlier, and once again told me how terrible he felt about Kathy's demise. That was what he called it: Kathy's demise. There was something uncertain and choked in his voice when he spoke about Kathy, something elusive about the way he locked onto my look as if he were trying to sell me a used car. I didn't know whether he was exhibiting complicity in her death or merely the kind of longing that die-hard fans felt over something like Elvis's death. I didn't know him well enough to read his signals, and Snake wasn't any help, having spent the past half hour thumbing through a stack of Bert's magazines.

I hadn't gotten the answers I wanted from Bert, but he'd managed to intrigue me with his theory that whatever happened to Sheffield's plane, if it *had* been a covert op, was related to all this other mumbo-jumbo he was having me look up on the Web. As we walked back across the dewy landscape to the car, it occurred to me that I had come here with only a vague idea of how I needed to proceed but was leaving with two plans of attack. On the one hand, if Bert was right, I could enlist Kalpesh's help in looking for a possible stool pigeon in the Sheffield campaign and trace the line of complicity to the killers if they existed. As unlikely as it seemed, at least it was a plan, albeit one given to me by a petty criminal with a record of thievery, urinating in public, gun hoarding, and paranoia. On the other hand, maybe Bert wasn't the nutcase he seemed and was purposely leading me around in circles to throw me off track. After all, he was the one with the uncanny prescience and the nefarious connections. As things now stood, determining

Bert Slezak's real role in all of this seemed like the most promising plan of attack.

"We get into an accident with all that smut in the car," I said to Elmer as he deposited two bags of magazines at his feet, "I'm going to be pissed."

"Then you better drive careful, pilgrim."

"Why don't you leave the eighth-grade research materials here?"

"You're doing *your* research. I'm doing mine."

"I just don't want anybody to—"

"'Recently Widowed PI's Car Full of Porn,'" Snake said. "That's not a bad headline. If we get into an accident, I'll be sure to tell everybody it was yours."

"Thanks. But I don't belong to CMA."

"What's that?"

"Chronic Masturbators Anonymous."

"Is that a real group?"

Once we were rolling down the highway, Snake said, "If your suspicions are right and you get close to the people who did it, you're going to end up holding a wolf by the ears."

"You don't have to stick around."

"Sure I do. They're fumigating my place."

We stopped at a greasy spoon, part of an international chain, where Snake flirted with the apparently pregnant teenage attendant after ordering what appeared to be one of nearly everything on the menu. "I hope you don't think I'm paying for all that," I said.

"You *should* pay. There's nothing to eat at your house. I've been starving since I got there."

"I don't remember inviting you."

"I don't remember being turned away."

"I fed you breakfast."

"Eggs from anorexic chickens."

"Tomorrow morning I'll tie a bag of oats around your neck."

I sulked in a corner nursing a milk shake and a bag of salty fries. Even that meager repast made my stomach hurt. As Snake started to spoon up his second dessert, I gazed out the window. It took almost ten minutes before I realized I

was inspecting passing cars for Kathy. It was beginning to
seem as if I was going to spend the rest of my life looking for
her. It would have been so much simpler for me if they'd
pulled her body out of the Pacific.

I snapped out of my reveries and used my cellphone to contact Deborah Driscoll. "Thomas? It's good to hear your voice.
Are you ready to come back to work?" She was as chipper and
high-energy as ever, in stark contrast, I noted, to the dismal
moron I'd become.

"Not just yet. I would like to come in and touch base,
though. You folks going to be around this afternoon?"

"I don't think so. James and I and a few others are on our
way to Tacoma. Everybody else is off doing something. Why
don't you come in tomorrow? We do miss you, Thomas."

"Tomorrow it is."

"I'm in by seven."

"Right."

Next, I called Kalpesh Gupta. I hated talking to him, but
he was the one Sheffield worker still alive whose number I
had.

"Thomas, my man. It was good to see you last night. You
should drop in more often. We could have dinner."

"Sounds great."

"Tomorrow night?"

"I have plans."

"How about the night after?"

"Listen, Kalpesh. I was wondering if I could come over
and maybe clear out Kathy's desk?"

"Her desk has been cleaned out. We gave everything to her
secretary."

I hadn't been taking calls from Beulah, but it didn't much
matter, because the bid to empty Kathy's desk had been a
bluff. I could no more have sorted through her personal effects than I could have performed an autopsy on my mother.
"Could I come over anyway?"

"We're having meetings for the next couple of days. In
fact, I'm in one now. So much has changed around here, as
I'm sure you can imagine. Drop by tomorrow, though. Any
time. We'll make room for you."

"I'll be there."

I closed the connection, and after Snake and I policed the plastic tabletop, we went out to the car. Back on the highway, Snake said, "Thomas? When we were passing through Enumclaw the first time? You chased somebody into the bookstore." After it became obvious I wasn't going to reply, he turned and looked out the side window for the rest of the trip. I appreciated his presence and I wanted him to stay, but I didn't need stooges in the peanut gallery thinking I'd gone bonkers, at least not if they were going to remind me of it.

It was after one o'clock when we got back to my house. The dog hadn't returned. I put out another bowl of food, hoping the raccoons wouldn't raid it before nightfall, and then went inside, where I was greeted by a pair of Kathy's shoes on the closed-in portion of the back porch under the shelf where we kept the extra flowerpots. They were her gardening clogs and still had dirt on them. There was something insufferably sad about their toe-in placement, about the fact that she had been the last to handle them, about the fact that I didn't know what to do with them and probably never would. There was nothing lonelier than the shoes of a dead person, nothing quite so personal, so concrete, and useless.

Snake clomped through the house and threw himself onto the living room sofa, where he began thumbing through one of his brother's magazines.

Trying to get over the minor hurdle of Kathy's shoes in the same way that I had been forced to get over a hundred other little reminders of her every day, I sat at the computer and discovered that Bert had already sent me two dozen website addresses for study. I read for a while and then wandered around the house aimlessly mulling over a new—to me—and less virtuous view of the universe and the United States in particular than I was used to imagining. In the other room Snake was snoring. Eventually I found myself slipping into my winter cycling tights and a weatherproof jacket and heading to the garage, where I pumped up the tires on my winter bike, a single-speed converted track bike with a fixed gear.

It was chilly in the afternoon gloom, but the Doppler on the Internet hadn't detected any rain showers, so I rode up the hill to Seventeenth, then took it south through the fraternities and sororities, weaving through the University of Washington, and exiting campus near the Montlake Cut. I rode through the arboretum, then down to Lake Washington and along the lake to Seward Park and back. Claire Mitz's place was just on the other side of the water. Because of the chill, I saw only five or six other serious riders. The trip took an hour, a short ride for me, but when I got back I was spent. I'd been unable to think of anything but Kathy. Somehow the exercise loosened me up, and unexpectedly I started crying, consumed by how much I missed her and would continue to miss her, by how unfair her death was, by the anger welling up inside me over the possibility she and the others may have been murdered as part of a political plot.

As unlikely and even irrational as Bert's theory of the plane crash was, he had left me with a host of questions to mull over. Had the FBI been alerted *before* the crash, and if so, by whom? Was Timothy Hoagland's real job to whitewash the murders and make them appear accidental? If so, did Hoagland know what actually happened or was he simply following orders? Was anybody else on the NTSB investigation team involved, and if not, how was that possible? And last but most important, who would murder eleven people just to achieve what would be a hollow and likely temporary political advantage?

Back home, I took a shower and then, shoeless and sockless, sat down once more at the computer in the hallway. Minutes dissolved into hours, and before I knew it, the sky outside was dark and Snake was stomping around in the kitchen banging pots and pans and chopping carrots and potatoes on my cutting board.

"New Mexico lizard goulash," he said when he caught my eye. "Gonna make you feel like a right new man."

It would take weeks to thoroughly examine every topic Bert had brought up, but in the space of a few hours, I managed to touch on most of them. I wanted to see, in each case, whether he was alone in his conclusions, or if there were others who believed what he did. I wanted to fact-check. I wanted to inspect his reasoning for fallacious arguments.

Although I already knew that a sizeable contingent in this country believed the 9/11 report was a cover-up, I was surprised at the strength and depth of their support around the world, hundreds, if not tens of thousands of doubters, many of them experts in their fields, bestselling books written in Germany and France on the topic.

If our government was conspiring to cover up the true dimensions, bungling of, or the real reasons for 9/11, I could believe almost anything. In fact, belief that the events of 9/11 were covered up was a springboard for buying into all kinds of horrors involving our government's dark side, which was probably the reason most people refused to even entertain the possibility of anything but the official story.

The event Bert wanted me to read about that most correlated with our plane crash off the Washington coast was Paul Wellstone's death. When I looked up the Wellstone plane disaster in 2002, I found plenty of chatter on the Net, much of it critical of the official investigation, which had, indeed, included Timothy Hoagland. On a lark I Googled Hoagland's name, then spent two hours sorting through one inconsequential and inappropriate webpage after another until I stumbled upon a ten-year-old item in *The Charlotte Observer:*

A two-car accident last night on Davis Lake Parkway resulted in injuries to two men and one woman. Bert Slezak and Timothy Hoagland sustained injuries that were thought to be minor. The woman was taken to a nearby hospital, where she was treated and released. Her name and the extent of her injuries were not available at press time. The accident, thought to be caused by a tractor-trailer rig crossing the center line, is being investigated by police.

Bert didn't tell me he'd worked closely enough with Timothy Hoagland that they would have been together in the same vehicle ten years ago in North Carolina. And when Hoagland spoke of Bert's arrest at Cape Disappointment, he gave no indication he knew Bert from the past. Did the two have a current connection they both had a reason to keep hidden?

At dinner Snake interrupted my brooding and said, "You realize there's nothing worse than losing someone you love and knowing there was no reason for it. The most painful thing in the world is a senseless death. Human beings don't do well with senseless stuff. They want a cause for everything that happens, and better yet, they want to be able to blame someone. You know that's the only reason you're giving Bert's conspiracy bullshit any consideration. You want to think Kathy didn't die for nothing."

"Because I need it doesn't mean it isn't true."

"You should see yourself. You look like a mad scientist."

"You look pretty good yourself with that stack of jack-off magazines."

After dinner I went back to the computer and found more information on Hoagland. He was forty-seven, and astonishingly enough, I found a source saying he'd worked in the CIA for twenty years. His other credits included several years with the Department of Agriculture, the same as Bert Slezak. As had Bert, he'd spent time in Argentina and Brazil. According to an article I found in *The Washington Post,* he once owned his own company, which did contract work for the FBI. One article claimed he had a near-genius IQ and had whipped through all the course work at the FBI academy on the Marine Corps base at Quantico in record time.

When I looked up the NTSB report on the Carnahan airplane crash, I found that Bert was right about Hoagland's association with the investigation. He hadn't been the lead investigator, as Bert claimed, but he'd been on the team. He was also on the investigation team after Paul Wellstone's plane went down. I stayed at the computer for hours, printing out relevant material and adding it to my stash. When I needed to stretch, I walked out to the backyard to see if the dog had returned from his sabbatical, but he hadn't.

Just before going to bed I discovered an article by a prominent psychiatrist claiming people who were confronted with stories of massive government misbehavior tended in overwhelming numbers to line up in the camp they started in, that is, those who already had a mistrust of government institutions tended to readily believe stories of conspiracy and malfeasance, while those who routinely trusted government entities and believed most politicians had our best interests at heart tended to disbelieve stories of government corruption, even after being confronted with overwhelming evidence of same. For my part, I'd never been completely trusting of those in power. But then, neither had the founding fathers. That's what all the checks and balances were about.

═══ THIRTY-TWO ═══

THAT NIGHT I SLEPT TWELVE HOURS, which was amazing in itself, and woke feeling refreshed for the first time in weeks. I felt calm. I picked up my cellphone and realized I'd received a call during the night. Instantly my calm vanished. It was from Kathy's number—Kathy's cellphone calling mine. I sat on the edge of the bed to let the cold morning air wake me and stared at the familiar number. Kathy's phone was at the bottom of the sea. There wasn't any way it would be operable, yet my cell had logged a call from her number. It was impossible to know what it meant. I would like to say I let the implications slowly rumble through my brain, but nothing passed through my mind except disbelief. No message had been left. God only knows what I thought would be on a voice message from Kathy's phone, as if she could carry it into the afterlife and some ethereal cell tower would connect us.

I was shaking. *Somebody* had called me from Kathy's phone. I could only wonder what might have happened if I'd answered. This was worse than anything that had happened since the accident, worse than going off half-cocked and chasing Kathy doubles. It flummoxed me to the point of paralysis. I sat on the edge of the bed for twenty-five minutes.

It was almost eleven o'clock when I padded into the kitchen, where Snake was reading the morning newspaper at the table. I handed him the phone and said, "What do you make of this?"

"Looks like Kathy's number."

"Yeah."

"Kathy called you?"

"Her phone did. I was asleep."

"They got her phone."

"Who? Who has her phone?"

"The recovery people at the Cape. They probably found it when they emptied out the fuselage. Why? You didn't think it was Kathy calling, did you?"

"I just . . ."

"You thought it was Kathy?"

"No."

"You did. Jesus, Thomas. You've got to realize where you are with this. She's gone."

"I know that!"

"Do you?"

Turning back to the paper, Snake gave me a look no sane person wants to be on the receiving end of. He tried to conceal it when he realized how I was reacting, but it was precisely the sort of overly sensitive, semifaked sympathetic grimace you might give to someone who'd just, through a complicated series of tragic misunderstandings, lost a kitten in a trash compactor.

"The phone went down with the plane," I said. "I know because I was talking to her when it went down."

"Isn't that what I said? They pulled up the plane."

"That phone's been in eight hundred feet of water for more than a week. You think it would still work?"

"Apparently it does."

"But what are the odds?"

"Call one of your techie friends and ask him. Or better yet, put your own phone in a bucket of water and see what happens. Maybe it was in an air pocket. It *is* kind of spooky. I'll grant you that. You *did* watch Kathy get on that plane, didn't you?"

"I left before it took off, but she was on the plane."

"Jesus, I didn't realize you were talking to her. That must have been . . ."

"Don't say anything else."

In the car Snake got on his own cellphone, calling the numbers we'd collected for the FAA, the NTSB, and for Timothy Hoagland, but all he got were recorded messages. On each he left a synopsis detailing the middle-of-the-night phone call I'd received, then left our names but *his* number. I recognized it as a clever way of binding himself to me, because as long as we were expecting calls on *his* cell, I wasn't going to wander off. Snake, I could see, was determined to watch over me the way a dog owner watched over a Rottweiler he thought might be going bad. When we couldn't raise any official government response, he called a couple of friends in the electronics industry who told us what we'd already guessed: If Kathy's phone had been submerged hundreds of feet below the surface, the likelihood that it was still in working order was slim to none.

Beyond the south end of Lake Washington, Mount Rainier loomed in the distance. Sunshine glittered off the whitecaps on the lake. It should have been enough, in the middle of this cloud-drenched season, to brighten my mood, but it wasn't.

After we parked at Maddox headquarters in Kirkland and entered the offices, we were confronted with a heavyset, crew-cut security guard in a tan uniform with a portable metal detector. The guard and the detector were both new. I waltzed through while Snake was asked to remove four pistols—two of them .44 Magnums with eight-inch barrels—a pair of handcuffs, a sap, and some brass knuckles. I knew he had at least one more weapon on his person, though it wouldn't show up on the detector. Snake also kept a standard handcuff key secreted in his clothing. When Armageddon came, he was determined to be ready.

"When we're out in the boat I use him for my emergency backup anchor," I joked to the guard. Snake flashed his private investigator's license and concealed weapons permit for the city of Seattle, but it didn't stop the guard from getting on his walkie-talkie and summoning reinforcements. The first to arrive was one of Maddox's regular security people, Glenn Boddington, whom I'd worked with until ten days ago. I nodded at Boddington and said, "He's with me."

"Just the same, we can't let all those weapons in."

"No. That would be nuts."

"He's going to have to check them with Neil," Boddington said. "How've you been, Thomas?"

"Weathering it."

"Good to see you. Coming back to work?"

"Not just yet."

Leaving Snake at the door with the security guard, I wandered through the rooms until I found Deborah Driscoll near Maddox's dark office, Deborah looking not as bright or as attractive as I remembered, though just as tall, her hair just as red. She looked wan and tired. "Jesus, that's one hot dish," Snake whispered into my ear after catching up with me. I had to look around to see who he was talking about, because there were probably twenty people within spitting distance and most were women, but of course he was referring to Deborah.

"Thomas, Thomas." Deborah seemed particularly enthusiastic to see me. I introduced Snake, who did his best to fade into the background. "You coming to work with us today?" Deborah asked.

"Not today."

"I wish you'd change your mind. It would do you good to keep busy."

"I am keeping busy."

"Really? Doing what?"

"We're investigating the Lincoln assassination."

Deborah smiled and sat on the edge of her desk, nodded to somebody peeking through the window in her office door, the nod signifying she would take care of whatever the problem was later. Snake flopped on the sofa and picked up the same golfing magazine I'd read the day they hired me. It was easy to see why Deborah Driscoll had managed to convince so many CEOs to dump money into the Maddox coffers. Even from across the room she had a way of making you feel as if it were just you and her in a phone booth. Crossing her arms under her breasts, she trained her green eyes on me and said, "Tea?"

"Sure."

She brought out cups and a teapot. The office was bustling with campaign activity, but she was going to fix tea for me. It was a sign that she cared and that I was valuable. I liked her for it. Snake declined.

"What can I do for you, Thomas?"

"Deborah, it occurs to me that our office occasionally has had information we shouldn't have had."

"What do you mean?"

"Information only the Sheffield people should have been privy to."

"Like what, for instance?"

"The fact that she was getting an endorsement from a former president. A lot of little stuff."

Deborah gave me a smile she probably reserved for retarded children and said, "It's a small community, Thomas. Telephone, telegraph, tell a campaign worker. I'm sure they knew plenty of what was going on here, too."

"Just the same, I'm wondering if somebody with the Sheffield group wasn't leaking campaign information to this office."

"We don't do spy networks. You should know that. In fact, that's why we hired you, isn't it? To keep an eye out for that sort of thing."

James Maddox came bustling through the offices, surging across the room to shake hands. "Thomas! Great to see you! We're feeling your pain. I mean that. All of us. You losing your wife like that, well . . . it's hard to know what to say."

"Thank you."

"But here you are. Ready to roll up your sleeves and go to work."

"Not exactly. I'm poking into the events surrounding the accident."

"You don't mean the plane crash?"

"That's what I mean."

"I know you're a private eye, but don't you . . . ? The government will handle it. You need to stay out of it, don't you think? I wasn't going to mention this, but I had a conversation with the National Transportation Safety Board people this morning. Your name was mentioned. They don't want to hear from you again, Thomas."

"They told you that?"

"I guess you represented yourself as a voice of this office."

"I told them I worked for you. I do, don't I?"

"Of course. But—"

"Listen, Jim. There was something wrong with that plane going down and I'm not sure I have any faith in the way it's being investigated. I'm going to look into it."

"I've had talks with the man in charge over at NTSB, Thomas, and I can assure you they're going to find out what happened."

"Are you saying you know they're going to get to the cause of the crash because you have information the rest of us don't, or are you saying you have a generalized faith that our government can sort this out?"

The question befuddled Maddox. His normally impassive face ranged through a panoply of emotions, so that I couldn't tell what he was thinking. In the end, my guess was he knew nothing about the probe. "They're going to handle it, Thomas. They're going to find out what happened. I know they are."

Maddox proceeded into his own office and closed the door. Deborah looked at me and said, "I don't blame you for wanting to know why your wife is dead."

"Thanks, Deborah. How's the election looking?"

"The numbers are leaning the wrong way. But Sheffield's husband has never even served on a school board. We're going to run ads about it that will hurt them."

Deborah gave me a lingering look and cast a glance over her shoulder at the closed door to Maddox's office. "Look at it in this light, if you can," she said. "If there were such an individual as you were asking about earlier and they had made some kind of deal with us, don't you think part of that deal would include a promise to keep their name confidential?"

"So there is a spy?"

"There's always somebody."

"But you're not going to tell me who?"

"Thomas, the information they give is never important. Just morsels they send along. You know nothing in politics is secret for long. The thing is, it makes the staff feel better if they think they're being fed inside dope. It never amounts to anything, and it works both ways."

"They might have been giving information to somebody else, and if they were, I need to know about it. Who was it? Tell me."

"Listen to me, Thomas. After Maddox gets elected, he'll have the clout to make this plane crash investigation get done properly. He can set up an independent panel. Whatever you want."

"Sweep it under the rug until then? Is that what you're asking? Sweep my wife's death under the rug?"

"You know I'm not saying that. It's just—I want to help. I like you, Thomas, and I want to see you get through this."

"If you wanted to help, you'd give me the name."

Outside in the parking lot, Snake turned to me. "That is one hot mama. Think she's a natural redhead?"

"Don't even go there."

$\equiv$ **THIRTY-THREE** $\equiv$

I WAS SPRAWLED OUT on the saggy motel bed, gazing toward the shower. I couldn't help smiling as I watched her moving behind the glass panel. After she stepped out and finished toweling herself off, she noticed me watching and gave me a grin. Still smiling, she strolled across the room, climbed onto the bed, and lay down beside me. After a moment she propped herself on one elbow and gave the tip of my nose a kiss.

Kathy rested her wet head in the crook of my elbow and rolled over so we were both facing the ceiling. "This is exactly what we needed. To spend some quality time together."

"Would you like some more quality time right now, sister?"

"*This* is quality time."

"Even more quality."

"I'm all qualitied out for a while."

"I guess I am, too."

"I guess. So, to change the subject, what are you planning for after the election?"

"More quality time?"

"Be serious."

"What am I planning? I'll go back to the office and chase down philandering husbands. Or wives. Check out the computer geek some nervous woman found on the Internet, then give her the sad news he's not marriage material and he's not the CEO of his own investment firm like he said he was, but drives a rendering truck three days a week and goes to the dogfights on the weekends. Snake has a warehouse theft ring he wants me to help out with. How about you?"

"Jane has asked me to go back to D.C. with her."

It took a few moments to figure out if I'd heard correctly. "That's quite a bombshell."

"I know."

"How long has this been on the back burner?"

"Not long. Besides, it's not a signed and sealed offer. She has to win first."

"In order not to win she'd have to be videotaped engaged in sex with . . ."

"Don't say it."

"Say what?"

"A band of Hungarian circus acrobats, or something similar. Don't you want to know what I said to Jane?"

"Of course I do."

"I said I'd talk it over with you."

"And that's what you're doing now."

"Right."

"Is it what you want? To go to D.C.?"

"It never entered my mind. What would you think?"

"I don't want to live back east. Besides, we've got that little house where we met. We'd never find anything nearly so charming or so dumpy."

"I would be asked for a three-year commitment."

"I don't know if I want you hanging around a woman who has sex with acrobatic dwarfs."

"Who said they were dwarfs?"

"I just assumed they were."

"Really. Be serious. I can't go unless you come with me."

"It would sure be lonely around here without a wife."

"Glad to hear that."

"I'd miss all the quality time."

"Good, because our quality time is about the only reason I keep you around—" I cut her off with a kiss. Then we did some more kissing. And then we were both asleep. Sometime in the night I woke up mulling over Jane Sheffield's offer and Kathy's reluctance to tell me about it when it was first proffered, which I knew hadn't been yesterday or even the day before. I could only guess how long she'd been keeping it to herself. She should have been able to predict my feelings on the matter. I'd lived in the Pacific Northwest my whole life and loved everything about it. She had to know I had the mountains and the water in my blood. She had to know there wasn't anyplace I would rather live than where I was.

In the middle of the night, I woke up and realized by the pattern of her breathing that Kathy was awake, too. "You sleeping?" I whispered.

"I couldn't help thinking what a seedy motel this is."

"And?"

"I was thinking about all the people who've been in this room. What they must have been escaping from to come here. About all the people who couldn't afford anything more than this. We're kind of slumming, but this is the best some people ever get."

"You're right."

"It's all I want. It's on the beach. All those bats flying around outside the light. It's perfect."

"So are you," I said, giving her a hug. It was the last thing I remembered until morning.

I'M STRUGGLING TO COME AWAKE. It's not unlike trying to swim to the surface of a huge bowl of pudding. I'm in a hospital bed. I'm groggy, trying to figure out where I am. I feel like I'm drowning. I've had the feeling before. I've been in this room before. There's a patch of night sky showing at the dark window. Slowly, I roll out of bed and walk to the window, where I sit on the sill. I'm aware I've been up before. I'm also aware the doctors don't want me moving around. I'm dizzy. I have bandages on my skull. My ribs are taped. My stomach hurts when I move.

Outside, the city is quiet. The streets are empty. I believe I'm in Swedish Hospital, the Cherry Hill campus, but I'm not certain. I'm here because of the bomb. It all starts coming back. It doesn't seem fair that each time I awaken I am again forced to the realization that Kathy is dead. It's like getting the news for the first time—over and over. For a few moments I actually think I'm back in the motel room with her. I limp back across the cold floor and struggle to get between the sheets. A nurse checks on me, mistakenly assumes I'm asleep, then leaves the room.

THIRTY-FOUR

MY RENEWED VITALITY lasted about a day and a half. I could feel the energy draining out of me as we exited the Maddox campaign headquarters. I'd worked up my gumption, invested in a good night's sleep, come up with new ideas, and now on the second day of my quest to discover whether my wife had been murdered and by whom, I was stricken with a depression that came on like a dose of strychnine.

I was a few blocks from my house, sitting alone at a table in a Thai restaurant called Araya's, one of Kathy's favorites. Snake had been pestering me to stop for lunch ever since we ate breakfast. The place was packed, and we had a table near the giant Buddha in the corner. Snake had gone to the washroom to clean up and was now making calls on his cellphone on the sidewalk in front of the restaurant.

"What's wrong?" he asked when he came back inside.

"Nothing."

"Like hell. You look like warmed-over death."

"My wife died. Maybe was murdered."

"Not that. What happened today?"

"I don't know. It just came over me."

"Christ, you look like you're about to stick your head in a meat grinder. Want to go home? I can go another few minutes without food in my belly."

"I'll make it."

It was the longest lunch of my life. Snake took me at my word and ate at a leisurely pace, failing to note I didn't touch a morsel of my order. It was good to have a friend nearby, even if that friend was pushing food into his mouth like he was shoveling coal into *Titanic*'s boiler. He insisted on driving the car to my house, and for that small gallantry I was grateful, collapsing into the passenger seat like an invalid.

Once home, he gave me an aspirin, as if aspirin might cure the black mood I'd fallen into. Aimlessly, I stumbled around the house while Snake made phone calls, most having to do with various investigations he was working on. I couldn't help wondering how much money it was costing him to babysit me.

By rights, I should have been on my way to Sheffield head-quarters, but I knew I wasn't going to leave the house again today.

I had a hunch that going through two weeks' worth of stacked-up mail might alleviate my misery, or at least take my mind off it, so I sat in an overstuffed chair near the front door and pulled over a small table piled high with envelopes. Sun-shine slanted through the windows on the south side of the house, dappling the Oriental rug Kathy had bought for the din-ing room last spring. After separating the junk mail from the bills, I got down to the envelopes with personal handwriting on the front. Most were condolence cards printed with drug-store salutations like "My deepest sympathy" or "A prayer for you." "May warm memories of your loved one soothe you in this time of travail." There were cards from people I knew, from people I used to know, from people I never wanted to know. There were a substantial number from folks who'd seen the crash coverage on television but didn't know either Kathy or me personally. There were cards from people I'd known in high school but had lost contact with. There was a note from the employees in the toy store on the first floor of our building at First and Yesler. I put their note under the window with the last of the now-dying flowers. One by one, I opened and read the cards.

Somewhere toward the end of the condolences I opened a fat card with an embossed drawing of lilies on the front. In shaky longhand somebody had penned:

Dear Mr. Black,

At the time you asked me to take those pictures of you, I had no idea who you were. Since we got back from the tour, Louise saw you on the news refusing to answer questions. Good for you. I don't like those news people

either. You may or may not remember us. We met briefly
at the Cape Disappointment lighthouse on the day
Senator Sheffield's plane fell into the ocean. I still find it
hard to believe we were standing in plain sight when it
went down.

Anyhow, if you don't remember me, I was the one
trying to call the authorities when everyone else was
running around hollering. My cellphone wasn't working
so we went to the lighthouse but I guess the attendant
had already made the call. You acted calm and
determined throughout a complex ordeal. It is hard to
believe your wife was on that plane.

Once again, Louise and I extend our deepest sympathy.

Burl A. & Louise Reid

P.S. In February, Louise and I will celebrate our 59th
wedding anniversary.

I wondered stupidly if, after fifty-nine years together,
Kathy and I would have looked as haggard and stooped as
the couple I remembered from Cape Disappointment. I
opened two more cards before it struck me. *My cellphone*
wasn't working. At the time of the crash, during those few
moments when we'd all stared dumfounded at the ocean, my
cell had given up the ghost, too. I wondered if Burl Reid's
cellphone had lost its signal, or if he'd forgotten to charge the
battery. Or if he'd been so nervous at seeing the plane go
down that it had been operator error. I wondered if his cell
company used the same transmitting towers as mine.

It took less than a minute to retrieve his phone number on
the Internet. Reid resided in Tacoma, not far from Wilson
High School, where I'd been a student about a million years
ago. When he answered, Reid sounded the same as I remembered, old and crotchety. "To whom do I have the pleasure of
speaking?"

"This is Thomas Black. We met a couple of weeks back at
Cape Disappointment. You took a picture for me."

"Black?" I heard him cover the mouthpiece and shout, "Louise! It's that private investigator. From the plane crash."

"Mr. Reid, if you don't mind, I'd like to ask some questions."

"Fire away, boy. What is it? You know, Louise couldn't record it that first time they did the piece about your wife on the TV, but she stayed up and got it on the late news. It's in the middle of our *Sound of Music* tape. We can make a copy and mail it to you."

"That's very thoughtful of you, but I recorded it myself. Do you remember taking a picture of me?"

"You wanted to get you, the plane, *and* the lighthouse all in the picture. I remember that."

"After it went down, did you make a cellphone call?"

"As I recall, there was a period when the phone didn't work. But later, I made calls till I about wore out my hearing aid."

"How much later?"

"Only time it didn't work was when I tried to notify the state patrol."

"What cellphone company do you use?"

It wasn't the company I was with. I thanked Burl Reid for his time and went to the other room, where I thumbed through the stack of printouts I'd made the previous night. I found one about the Paul Wellstone crash. I read it twice. Then I phoned Bert Slezak, who answered on the first ring. "Thomas?"

"After the Wellstone incident several people in the vicinity complained that their cell service went out around the time the plane went down. My phone went out at the Cape. I've found another man who said the same thing happened to his phone."

"Can I get back to you?"

"No."

"I'll call you right back."

"Don't hang up, you—" But he was gone.

While I waited, Snake received a call on his cell. Despite his recent meal, he'd been in the kitchen ransacking the fridge and cabinets for edibles, had finally opened three cans of chili, and was mixing them in a saucepan on the stove with some of his own ingredients. "Here, Thomas. It's for you."

When I answered, a male voice said, "Mr. Black?"

"This is Thomas Black."

"Timothy Hoagland. I've been in meetings all morning. This was my first chance to catch up on my messages. You said something about a phone call."

"In the middle of the night I got a call from my wife's cellphone. I was wondering if you folks had recovered it."

"You received a . . . ?"

"I got a call from my wife's cellphone. I didn't answer, and there was no message. I was wondering if you'd recovered it, and if so, was it in working order?"

"We're not going to be able to return any personal effects for months."

"But did you find her phone?"

"As far as I know, no functional electronic equipment has been recovered."

"And you've brought up most of the large pieces?"

The line was silent for a few moments. "Mr. Black? I spoke to your boss. Has he gotten back to you?"

"My boss?"

"Jim Maddox."

"And?"

"With this type of investigation, amateurs have a way of gumming up the works. We've got twelve professional investigators working here in the state. Lab technicians back at Quantico. The local law enforcement community has supplied a number of people. We don't need help."

"My wife died in that crash."

"You have my sympathies. It's affected a lot of people around here. But if everybody who lost a loved one initiated their own investigation . . . well, you can you imagine what a mess it would be."

"But everybody isn't initiating their own investigation. Only me."

"Surely, you see my point?"

"Do you or do you not have her phone?"

"You're not listening."

"Have you recovered any more bodies?"

"I want you to tend to your own business and leave this to the professionals."

"You're not going to tell me whether you have my wife's body?"

"The site where the fuselage came to rest off the coast has been pretty much picked clean now. We're going to scan the bottom today and then call off the search. I don't know that your wife's body . . . It may wash up on one of the beaches. I have to warn you . . . bodies left in the open ocean for long periods . . ."

"I was wondering on the day of the crash what time the FBI arrived out at the coast."

The connection was quiet for a time. Finally, Hoagland said, "I'm going to reiterate. I do not want you horning in on our work. Don't contact any of my people, and don't get caught interfering in our investigation."

"Is that an order?"

"I'm afraid it is."

"Is it legal?"

"You bet your ass it is."

"You going to arrest me?"

"Don't turn this into a clash of wills."

"You better send somebody over right now. I might not be home later. The media should love it."

"If I have to arrest you, it'll be under the antiterrorism statutes, and I can guarantee you the media won't know anything about it."

"What are you afraid of, Hoagland?"

The line went dead. Anybody in his position would have wanted me out of the picture: a private investigator retracing their case? Hell, *I* would have wanted me out of the picture. Using Snake's phone, I called the FBI and was eventually and surprisingly put through to the special agent-in-charge of the Seattle office, a man named Winston Seagram. "Mr. Seagram, my name is Thomas Black. I work for James Maddox. I've got a couple of questions, if you don't mind."

"I just saw Jim Maddox this morning."

"I'm wondering if you still have agents out at Cape Disappointment?"

"Uh, the Cape? I don't believe so. Not today, anyway. Our time out there was limited."

"So you were there a few days?"

"Right."

"And you got there the day of the crash?"

"Correct."

"That would have been Tuesday afternoon? What time did your people arrive on scene?"

The line went quiet. "What are you up to, Mr. Black?"

"Just checking facts."

"Mr. Black, you're going to have to get your information somewhere else. And tell Jim Maddox he better get on the same page with the rest of us."

From across the room, Snake spoke after I'd hung up. "Didn't Hoagland just tell you to keep your nose out of it?"

"Yeah."

"You don't listen, do you?"

"One of many weaknesses."

I phoned the Coast Guard station at Cape Disappointment and asked for a guardsman named Hutchins. By a lucky accident he was on duty. When he came to the phone, he recalled who I was without prompting. He'd been my guardian angel during my days at the Cape, supplying me with hot soup and bottled water and staving off reporters.

"Hutchins? I wonder if you could do me a favor."

"Anything, sir."

"Could you get me the official time for the plane crash, as well as the official time the FBI showed up?"

"We have a logbook. Can you wait a minute?"

"I'll stay on the line."

When he came back, he said, "Fifteen thirty-seven for the crash. Sixteen thirty-five was when the FBI checked in."

"Three thirty-seven and four thirty-five p.m."

"Yes, sir."

"Hutchins?"

"Yes, sir?"

"How long does it take to drive there from Seattle?"

"Well, sir . . . gee . . . I see what you mean."

I was watching Snake gobble his chili concoction when my cell rang. It was the first time I'd gotten an incoming call since the one from Kathy's phone, and my heart skipped a beat. "Bert?"

"EMI devices."

"What?"

"Electromagnetic interference. It's long been suspected in the Wellstone crash. It's why when you fly commercial they don't want you using a cellphone or your laptop during take-off or landing. Your personal devices probably won't interfere with any crucial signals, but if they do, there's not much time to recover."

"Would an EMI device take out my cellphone?"

"Depends on how close you were and what sort of device they were using. You said somebody else's phone went out?"

"Yes."

"EMI."

"Is there such a device? Does somebody really have a contraption that could knock a plane out of the sky without a trace?"

"If your phone shut itself off, they didn't do it without a trace, did they? But to answer your question, yes. We've long thought the Agency had a way to knock planes out of the sky with EMI. Look, buddy. I think we gotta get back together."

"I was thinking the same."

THIRTY-FIVE

"YOU MEAN THERE'S *no* meat on the menu? None?" Bert was incensed, the veins in his neck standing up with his outrage. It was as if this culinary lapse had been perpetuated solely to ruin his day. "You said it was a vegetarian restaurant, but I didn't think that meant there wouldn't be *any* meat. Can't you see how wrong this is? Is there a steakhouse in America that doesn't serve salad? So why can these clowns get away without serving me a lamb chop? Hell, lamb is practically a vegetable."

"Tell you what. After we leave, I'll help you kill a buffalo in the arboretum, and you can roast it over a campfire."

"Funny guy." Like his brother, Bert was always hungry. He was also preoccupied with the impending arrival of our guest. Over the phone he had managed to convince me that good press relations were of paramount importance if we were to find the assassins who brought down the Sheffield plane. That's what it had devolved into, at least in his mind: a joint quest. It had been his idea to contact Ponzi, but once we were seated, he displayed enough anxiety that I began to think there was something he wasn't telling me. We were at Cafe Flora on Madison, on the garden side with all the plants and the waterfall: another one of Kathy's haunts.

We'd managed to grab a window table from which Bert soon spotted Ruth Ponzi trotting up the sidewalk in a tan trench coat. She looked as if she had three or four things on her mind and maybe had already forgotten to pick up one of the kids from ballet class. "Now, when she comes in," said Bert, "let me work on her. I know how to do this."

Ponzi stood in the entrance for a few moments, then spotted us and came over. She was as disheveled as she had been the other morning at Boeing Field, if not more so. She nodded at Bert and then looked at me. "Mr. Black, have you changed your mind about our interview?"

"Let's talk."

"Certainly. Hello, Bert. I tried to talk with you when you got arrested out at the Cape, but they wouldn't let me." She doffed her coat, pulled her bag into her lap, and withdrew a pen and small notebook, eyeing me and Bert purposefully while she laid down an indecipherable scrawl. In no particular order, Bert and I started throwing curveballs. It was fascinating to watch the way she wrote without looking at the page.

Bert said, "Have you ever heard of a company called Green Titles? It's CIA owned."

"I can't say that I have."

"Timothy Hoagland used to run it for the CIA."

"Timothy Hoagland, as in the man who's running the NTSB investigation," I said.

"Which makes the NTSB investigation highly suspect," said Bert. "Also, check out the time of the plane crash and the time the FBI arrived at the Cape."

"Less than an hour between," I said.

"We've all driven out to Cape Disappointment," Bert added, "and we know it takes more than an hour. Check out the Coast Guard logs if you don't believe us." Bert reached over and touched her knee. "Ever heard of an EMI device? Electromagnetic interference? At the same time the senator's plane started going out of control, Black's cellphone went cowshit."

"I found at least one other person in the vicinity whose phone went bad at the same time," I said. "There may be more."

"Same thing happened when the Paul Wellstone flight went down," said Bert. "An electromagnetic interference device, besides being able to take a plane down by interfering with the controls, would screw up anything electrical in the vicinity. Especially something like a cellphone."

"Timothy Hoagland was also on the Wellstone NTSB inquiry board," I said.

"Of course he was," Ponzi said. "That's what he does."

"Also, Black here got a call from his wife's phone last night. Except his wife's cellphone went down in the wreck."

"Who was it?" Ponzi asked, looking wide-eyed.

"I don't know."

"Okay. You've piqued my interest. I might be able to do a curiosity piece about the inconsistencies. Why don't you lay it all out step-by-step?"

"This isn't about inconsistencies," Bert said. "This is a major conspiracy."

"My editor is going to think it's a wild-goose chase."

"We have your attention, though?" asked Bert.

"You have my attention, all right. If even only half of these things check out, they need explaining. On the other hand, coincidences often turn out to be nothing."

"It could be the biggest story of your life," I said. "A Pulitzer Prize waiting to drop into your lap."

She thought about my statement while she regarded the two of us. I could tell the thought of uncovering something was hard to resist. "My editor doesn't live far. Let me call him."

After her call, Ponzi told us her boss would be there in ten minutes. While we waited, Ruth contacted a researcher at the paper and repeated some of what we'd told her, securing a promise to have the fact-checking done right away. While we waited for her editor and the fact-checker, Bert and Ponzi sipped coffee and chatted.

The editor was a short, stout, pleasant-looking man in a sport coat and gray slacks. He had gray eyes imbedded in a tight, fleshy face and meaty hands. Ruth met him at the doorway, where they conferred out of earshot, the dubious editor glancing at us from time to time with undisguised misgivings. While they were talking, Ruth received a phone call, presumably from the researcher at the paper, and stepped outside into the cold to take it. It was late afternoon, just getting dark, the cars on Madison shining their lights on the roadway. The editor jangled his keys in his pocket, glanced at us, then gave Bert that cockeyed look you sometimes get from relatives who know you well enough to dislike you but not well enough to avoid you, before following Ruth outside. From what I could glean, Ruth was importuning the editor and he was dragging his heels, but that was just a guess from their body language. In the end, the editor stalked down the sidewalk past our window without glancing in.

Ponzi raced back into the restaurant and sat heavily in her chair, draping her coat over her shoulders. "Hoo, it's freezing out there. Is it ever going to snow?"

"What'd he say?" Bert asked.

"He thinks it's a bum theory."

Bert's face registered the same disappointment and shock as a child's would if he'd just poured coal out of his Christmas stocking.

"The facts we gave you?" I asked. "They check out?"

"They did," Ponzi said, looking intently at Bert. "A lot of his attitude has to do with our prior relationship."

"What relationship?"

"I gave her a couple of stories in the past," said Bert.

"Which my editor didn't buy."

"Like what?" I asked.

Ponzi and Bert looked at each other, but neither spoke. After the waitress asked if we were ready to order and we put her off, Ponzi said, "A conspiracy of the world's leading geneticists to construct a disease that affects only black people."

"And all those dead geneticists," Bert added. "Don't forget there are dead geneticists all over the planet. Your editor is a typical corporate stooge."

"Never mind that," Ponzi said. "I'm going to use my own time to look into this. If I can dig up more of what you've got here, I can get the paper to go along with a feature article."

"It could grow from there," Bert said, optimistically. "Into a series."

"Thanks," I said.

"Don't get your hopes up. And you? Are you ever going to give me that interview? No, of course you're not. You're in no condition to be giving interviews. Go home and have some hot cocoa and get into bed. You look horrible."

"Thanks."

"I didn't mean it like that."

"I know I look like hell."

Not unexpectedly, Ponzi said she didn't have time to eat

with us and excused herself. When Bert and I were alone, I said, "I've never been this depressed."

"It come on sudden like?" Bert asked.

"Wham."

"You been drugged."

"Oh, come on."

"They can do that."

"Who?"

"You know who."

"You're telling me somebody put a drug in my system that makes me more depressed than I already am? What's the point?"

"To hamper our work. You've riled up a hornet's nest here. You think they don't know you're asking questions? Think they're not going to fight back? Slipping you a potion is just the tip of the iceberg. People doing what we're doing end up committing suicide more often than you would ever guess. Think about what you're doing. You're tracking down a government killing and cover-up. Imagine four guys, each the size of a small house, showing up at your place, putting a gun in your hand, and pulling the trigger for you. Think you could stop them? Think anybody in this town would be surprised to hear you'd put a gun in your mouth?"

"That's not—"

"How much evidence do you think they're going to leave?"

"There would be an investigation."

"There's an ongoing investigation into this plane crash, too. Didn't the CIA try to send poisoned cigars to Castro? Weren't there umbrellas tipped with poison darts in the U.K.? Some things we know. In a world of chemical miracles and secret prisons run by U.S. personnel, anything is possible. Don't be taking anything anybody gives you to eat or drink. A restaurant is probably okay, but even here they could go in the back and pay somebody off and you'd be in la-la land. LSD is one of their favorites."

"You're a raving lunatic." I pushed my chair out and stood up. "I'm getting out of here before I end up as paranoid as you."

"Too late, partner."

I left enough cash to pay for both our meals and abandoned Bert, who was rhapsodizing to the waitress over the sweet corn pizza he'd ordered. Despite their age difference, he was doing his best to pick her up. Like Snake, his motto seemed to be any woman . . . any time.

I went home, gathered some of the equipment I was going to need, and shouted to Snake, who was in front of my TV, that I was leaving again.

THIRTY-SIX

PARKING A BLOCK AWAY, I waited outside the Maddox offices in Kirkland, having stashed a car-wash flyer I'd found under my own wiper under Deborah's wiper, so she would have to walk around to the front of her little red sports car and show herself under the streetlight when she removed it. She didn't quit work until a little past seven-thirty. Out on the road I found myself running yellow lights to keep up with her. She was ruthless, cutting off other drivers, slipping into holes nobody else could see, and zipping in front of tractor-trailer rigs with impunity.

As I drove, I listened to the car radio, switching from one news channel to another, hoping for fresh news about the Sheffield investigation, but all I heard was the rehash they'd been dishing up all week. The plane was being reassembled at Boeing Field. Tests were being run. Autopsies were being performed. Sheffield's husband was running her campaign, and although pundits across the country were calling his leadership weak, Sheffield was still leading in the polls.

Driscoll drove straight to a market on Capitol Hill. When she came out, she drove three blocks and parked on the street, gathering up a small bundle of groceries and work-related materials and disappearing inside the three-story brick building where she was staying. For the next ten minutes I trolled for a parking space and eventually lucked into a spot within eyesight of her first-floor rooms. I'd brought a shotgun microphone I'd had made a couple of years earlier, which, all things being equal, should allow me to hear conversations in her condo. When I turned it on, she was listening to Norah Jones.

As the motor grew colder, I sat in the dark and waited. After she'd showered, I heard her eating and making phone calls, all related to work. The TV came on, one of those reality TV shows that had captivated the country. Her phone rang a couple of times, but she let it ring.

He must have parked around the block, but when he showed up, Kalpesh Gupta disappeared into the building so quickly I had to assume he had a key. A minute later I heard the front door to her unit open and close, also without any knocking. "Hey, babe." "I thought you were going to be here earlier." "Got held up." The TV show was still droning in the background, but my mike picked up their voices easily. It took a few moments to realize I was listening to the sound of a kiss.

Nobody in either campaign had any idea Kalpesh and Deborah spent their evenings together. It was obvious who was feeding information about Jane Sheffield's campaign to the Maddox group and whose shoes we'd seen the other night at Kalpesh's condominium.

"You love this show, don't you?" he said.

"Come here. Sit down."

"In a minute. You want a drink?"

"I'll have a glass of wine."

About then a car drove past on the street and the noise limiter on my shotgun mike activated. It was a police car, traveling slowly. I didn't duck, but I lowered the mike, knowing it resembled a rifle. The cop drove on.

"I missed you, baby," he said.

"I saw you on the news."

"It's not the way I like to get on TV."

"I like you in those white collars."

They were quiet for a few moments, in each other's arms, I guessed. The TV clicked off. I was beginning to be embarrassed. There were times when spying on people was fascinating and times when it was informative, but every once in a while the immorality of it made me feel like dirt. At heart we were all voyeurs, but few legitimately indulged in it more often or more shamefully than private investigators. I was thinking about folding up for the night when my car blazed with a bright light from behind. Pulling the headphones off, I pushed the mike and the rest of my paraphernalia under a blanket on the passenger seat, then placed my hands in plain sight on the steering wheel, my wallet and loose driver's license in the hand closest to the window.

I lowered the window just as the police loudspeaker announced, "You in there. Stay where you are. Don't move!" Approaching from the opposite direction, a second police car came ripping up the narrow street. Police radios squawked in the night. I hoped Kalpesh and Deborah didn't look out their window, because I was less than forty-five feet away from where they were making love.

"Driver's license, registration, and proof of insurance?" asked one of the officers at my window.

"What are you doing? You living in your car?"

There were two cops: a pretty African American female with a Taser strapped to her leg in addition to the Glock they all carried, and a large Caucasian guy who kept looking at the blanket on the passenger seat. I kept my hands in plain sight while the female cop shined her flashlight in my eyes and the male, first on the scene, went back to his cruiser and tapped into the computer. "We heard you do this every night," said the pretty cop when we were alone.

"I don't."

"We heard you were snooping in windows."

"That's not true."

"What *have* you been doing?"

"I'm a private investigator. I'm working for James Maddox. With his security."

"*The* James Maddox?"

"Yes. He worked for SPD once. So did I."

"As a civilian?"

"In uniform."

The two of us waited while she digested what I'd told her. When her partner came back with my driver's license, he said, "You live around here, Black?"

"In the University District."

"So you don't live around here."

The woman spoke without taking her eyes or light off me. "Claims he works for James Maddox. Used to be in the department."

"Is that right, Black?"

"East Precinct. I was on the pistol team with Phil Sherman."

"We heard you were peeping in windows."

"I haven't left my car."

"What are you doing in your car?"

"I'm on a case."

"He's a private investigator," said the woman.

"He's got a concealed weapons permit. Black, are you carrying a weapon now or do you have one in the car?"

"No, sir."

"If we searched your car, we wouldn't find a weapon?"

"That's right."

"What's under that blanket?"

"A shotgun microphone."

"And what do you use that for?"

"Recording bird calls."

"Would you care to show it to us?"

"They're not illegal."

"I asked if you'd be willing to show it to. us."

I reached over and flipped the blanket onto the floor, revealing the shotgun mike and the headphones I'd been wearing. The woman angled her flashlight until the beam illuminated the passenger seat. "A caller said there was a pervert spying in the windows of that building over there."

"I haven't seen anybody."

"You haven't left your car?"

"No."

"Would it surprise you to find out we've heard your name before?"

"No."

After a long pause, the male said, "All right, Black. You can go. I would advise you not to hang around this neighborhood again."

"Thank you."

I fired up my Ford. Now that the officers were no longer blocking the building, I angled my sun visor off to the side so that anybody in the condos would have a hard time identifying my face.

When I got home I sat in the car in the dark, ostensibly to listen to the end of a segment on National Public Radio about AIDS in Africa. I was so depressed I could hardly move. Rubbernecking outside the condo while Kalpesh and Deborah were making love only reminded me how much I missed Kathy. All I could think of was all the times I'd failed her. How I'd forgotten her birthday once. How I'd neglected to explain my attachment to the Maddox campaign to her satisfaction. How I'd embarrassed her in front of Maddox.

Snake had been worried about me, but not so worried he was going to roll off the couch when I came back into the house. "What's going on, buddy?" he asked.

"I think I was tailed tonight."

He sat up and went to the window. "They still out there?"

"I don't know. I got questioned by two cops. Somebody called me in."

"You didn't see anybody?"

"Nope."

Snake flopped back onto the couch. I sat down at the computer. In a few moments I had her work phone number. Letha Fontaine. I knew she would remember me from the governor's engagement party two weeks earlier.

"Letha? This is Thomas Black."

"Thomas? Gosh, it was good to see you the other night at that shindig. I'm so sorry about your wife."

"Thanks. Letha, could you do me a favor?"

"You name it."

"A call came in about an hour ago for an address near Eighteenth and East Howell. Probably came in as a one-sixty or a two-eighty."

"You still remember the codes?"

"Oh, yeah. I'm wondering if you could tell me who called it in."

"I suppose I could mosey over and look through the logs."

"Will you do that for me?"

"This isn't going to come back on me, is it?"

"Not if I can help it."

"Let me call you right back."

She called ten minutes later. "Thomas? It came in as a

stranger-in-the-neighborhood call. On Eighteenth on the block north of Madison heading toward Howell. It was a cellphone routed through the state patrol."

"Yeah."

"The phone is registered to a man named Dean Huffington."

"Is that all you have?"

"He said there was a man parked on that block and he was looking into people's bedroom windows."

"Thanks, Letha."

I looked up Dean Huffington on the Net, and while I was going through the various possibilities, I remembered that Huffington was a fictitious name the Maddox security people used for some of their extra equipment, including at least one cellphone that I knew Jim Maddox carried. I was still trying to absorb this development when Snake said, "Hey. You mind if I sleep in the spare bedroom tonight? This sofa's kinda getting to my neck."

The spare bedroom was where I kept my weights in the winter and where Kathy stored her clothes year-round, so it was basically Kathy's dressing room. I hadn't cleaned it out yet. In fact, I had only been in there twice since she died. "Yeah. Sure."

"What's wrong?"

"Maddox turned me in to the cops."

"You see him on the street?"

"Nope."

I wasn't even sure how I'd been tailed. I didn't like it, but then, I'd been doing the same thing, so I guess you could say I more or less deserved it. The pity was I didn't dare confront Maddox with the fact that he or one of his people had been following me, because to do so would imply I'd gotten confidential information from SPD, which could trigger an internal investigation, which could cost Letha Fontaine a lot of grief. The only reason Letha had done me the favor at all was because she'd had a crush on me practically forever.

THIRTY-SEVEN

SWEAT TRICKLED down my scalp and stung my eyes, but I was helpless to stop it. I was in the school gymnasium standing against the bleachers. It seemed as if every time I took my hands off the rod that had pinned me to the wall, the pain became even more excruciating. Initially I hadn't felt much of anything. I'd been walking across the gym with my cellphone in hand, and the next thing I knew I was against the bleachers.

I hadn't heard an explosion. Instead, it felt as if I'd been gang-tackled by six huge linemen. Now all I could do was grip the rod with both hands and hold on for dear life. I'd noticed something in the past few minutes. The end of the rod had a small American flag on it. Dust motes wafted through the air. Most of the walking wounded were gone now, having been urged to leave the building by a fire chief with a megaphone.

There were no rescue teams coming in to fetch the rest of us. As they had explained earlier, there were suspicions of a secondary explosive device.

In the far doorway I could see fire department officials, police officers, and from time to time James Maddox. A couple of times I caught a glimpse of red hair and a green blouse, which meant Deborah Driscoll was there, too. They were less than a hundred feet away, but it wasn't doing me a bit of good. I was bleeding to death. I could feel it. A jagged piece of glass was imbedded in my arm, torrents of blood snaking down my sleeve, oozing into my pants, dripping into my left shoe. Oddly, the shoe filling with blood seemed to be what bothered me most. My other fear was that I would faint and end up hanging limp on the rod.

Maddox should have been near death, not me. But he was

safe and sound, gawking from the doorway alongside Deborah like a visitor at the zoo. The others in the doorway had fled. Or were getting organized. Whatever safety personnel did when they were supposed to be rescuing and weren't. I'd read about the hazard they were trying to avoid. When terrorists planted a bomb, they were likely to plant two, the first to take out their primary target, and the second a well-concealed device to go off later and catch rescue workers at the scene. The second bomb would create even more havoc than the first and slow rescue efforts, thus making the likelihood of fatalities and chaos even greater. It was a one-two shot that had been employed successfully all around the world: Ireland, Baghdad, the Philippines.

Maddox took in the carnage, the dead bodies that lay in plain sight, the wounded, but most of all, the obliterated wooden stage where he'd been standing only minutes earlier. Deborah was crying. Twice I'd seen her start into the gym, only to be dragged back by Maddox or one of the firefighters. After a while I realized she was crying for me. She had good reason to believe she was witnessing my last minutes. The notion was a cute one, I thought, until it occurred to me that she was probably right, that I would soon be dead.

The gym looked as if an airplane had dropped a load of laundry through the roof and detonated a bomb in the center of it. Most of the laundry had dead people in it, three that I could see. An older woman had been patiently crawling across the floor in my general direction. I hadn't been paying her much mind, but now that she was inching closer, I said, "Why don't you head over to the doorway? You get close enough, they'll pull you out."

She said something I couldn't understand over the ringing in my ears and continued toward me, pushing herself through the detritus like a wounded crab. She wore a drab yellow dress under a woolen sweater. The side of her head had taken an impact from flying debris, and she was bleeding even more heavily than I was. I strained to understand her, but the explosion had compromised most of my hearing, my ears ringing like high-pitched chimes. She seemed to think what she had to tell me was important. From her vantage point on the floor, it must have appeared she and I were the only two people left alive.

Earlier in the day there were speaker introductions, and then while Maddox speechified, Deborah and I listened from behind the stage, a driver and two more security people waiting outside the hall. Five SPD plainclothes cops were helping out. Over the past week there had been threats received at the Maddox headquarters, phone calls that were being checked out by the FBI. The calls, Maddox's incessant importuning, and a desire to investigate Deborah Driscoll had propelled me into coming back to work for the campaign. After the speech numerous people from the audience wanted to shake Maddox's hand or chat with him, all of which he indulged.

As I slowly regained my reasoning powers, I wondered why the bomb had gone off after Maddox was out of the hall and not while he was giving the speech. Had somebody been clever enough to build a bomb but not clever enough to tell time? If they'd been meaning to take out a lot of people, or even to take out Maddox, they'd screwed up. As near as I could tell, the device had been directly under the podium, close to where the janitor had been. Had it gone off with our candidate on the podium, it would have sent him through the roof like a rocket.

Surrounded by a knot of people, he had made his way out of the Garfield High School gymnasium while Deborah and I followed, each keeping a wary eye out for suspicious-looking persons, even though I'd suspected Maddox was grandstanding when he talked about bomb threats.

The gabfest continued as the gym slowly emptied, Maddox and his followers standing out in the foyer in front of the trophy cases, starry-eyed women making up a good portion of the crowd. It was easy to see why some politicians came to think of themselves as irresistible to the opposite sex.

Somewhere along the line, I'd been asked to help locate the small leather satchel in which Maddox carried his speeches and other paperwork. I was headed back toward the podium to search when I got a call and detoured away from my planned route in an effort to improve the crappy cellphone reception inside the building. It was while I was on the far side of the gym near the bleachers that the bomb went off. Now I was impaled by Old Glory.

The woman crawling toward me was close enough to grab hold of my trousers at the knee, which she did with surprising strength. I wanted to lean down and comfort her, to stanch the bleeding in her scalp, but I couldn't move. "Mister," she gasped.

"Yes?"

"Nobody's coming to help."

"Not for a while."

"We need help. Can't they see that?"

"They think there's a second bomb."

"That was a bomb? I thought we had an earthquake."

"A bomb."

"It doesn't matter. I'm not going to make it."

"Of course you are. We'll make sure—"

"No, no, no. I *know* it's not my time, just like it wasn't *his* time," she said, gesturing at a piece of the janitor, "but that's not going to stop it from happening. Just listen."

"Go ahead," I said, softly, knowing she was probably right, that she was dying.

"I want you to tell my husband, Peter, I love him and I'm sorry. He'll know what I mean. Tell my son, Steve, to live his life on his own terms and never let anybody tell him otherwise, not even his father. My daughter, Jane . . . tell her I love her and I'm so proud of her. Can you remember?"

"I think so." I was getting woozy and light-headed and wasn't entirely sure I wouldn't be dead before this woman, but right now reassuring her was the thing to do, so I did it.

"And tell Peter the key to the safety deposit box is in my jewelry drawer. I already paid the cable bill. Don't let him pay it again. They've been double-billing us."

"Got it."

"I should reward you for this. Would you like to take one of our dogs?"

"I need a dog, but no thanks."

She pushed one bony hand toward me. I reached down with my own hand and clasped it, and she gripped me as if I were going to haul her into a boat, her hand cold and as stiff as a branch from a dead tree. As she clutched my hand, I thought for a few moments the woman at my feet had passed out, but then I realized she was dead. I held her cold, bony hand for a good while longer. I'm not sure how much longer, because somewhere in there I began to black out.

═══ THIRTY-EIGHT ═══

TWO DAYS AFTER MY MEETING with Bert at Cafe Flora, Snake and I headed to Cape Disappointment. During the drive it began raining with the determination you only saw in the Pacific Northwest, and even here, only near the coast. The radio had been predicting foul weather, but this was beastly. Everywhere we looked the landscape was gray and puddled. Plumes of water shot up behind vehicles on the road. An eighteen-wheeler covered us in road spray as if we were inside a car wash. Snake, who was driving, popped in one of his Willie Nelson CDs and began singing off-key.

I wanted to check out the Coast Guard logbooks at Cape Disappointment for myself and then poke around to see if we couldn't find other electrical devices that had lost power around the time of the crash. Perhaps I could find others who'd lost their cellphone service. Bert had speculated that some automobiles might even have lost electricity. It seemed like we were squandering time, but I had to get out of the house and, more than that, out of the city. Everywhere I went I was reminded of Kathy.

"Total waste of gasoline," said Snake when I told him my plan.

"You can go home. I'm doing fine on my own."

"Like hell you're doing fine. You're bluer than a Labrador with a dog cone on during bird season. No way I'm leaving you alone. Especially not in those regions."

"Afraid I'll do myself in?"

"Bert said to watch for it."

"Bert thinks a secret government cabal will fake my suicide. He thinks people have been slipping me pills to make me more depressed."

"Don't worry. I been on the lookout for government cabals all morning."

"I don't need any of your sarcasm."

"I know you don't. You got enough for both of us."

I'd awakened that morning to discover my picture on the front page of both Seattle papers, the color photo of the Cape Disappointment lighthouse, myself in the foreground, the Beechcraft King Air, a tiny dot in the distance but still airborne. I hadn't been expecting them to print the photo with *me* in it. There had been two good shots of the plane alone as it spiraled into the ocean. Dumbfounded, I stared and then sat down at the kitchen table and stared awhile longer. Not until the fifth page of the *Post-Intelligencer* had they published the photo of the plane actually striking the water. What made the photo of me on page 1 so odious was that at the time it was taken I hadn't realized the plane was about to go down. It had been a joke photo, my face molded into a lopsided smirk that some people might—and many later did—call moronic. I was joking around while eleven people were about to die. I looked like a total ass. The accompanying article was penned by Ruth Ponzi, which didn't make me any happier. I had the feeling she was punishing me for refusing to grant the interview she wanted.

Around eight-thirty that morning the phone calls began to trickle in, each confirming in one way or another that the papers had made me look like a champion jerk-off. Most of the callers seemed to have forgotten I'd recently lost my wife. Everybody had an opinion about the photo and about me. "It kind of makes you look like a dork, doesn't it?" asked my father. "How could you?" asked Kathy's sister, a question for which there was no reply. You only had to think for a moment to know I couldn't have known the plane was beginning its descent behind me, but everyone wanted to blame me for clowning while people were about to die. Eventually, I got sick of being chastised and let the answering machine collect the rest of the insults. Of course I'd shown poor taste. Anybody who knew me knew poor taste was my middle name. But I didn't know the plane was going down!

When we went to buy Snake breakfast at the local Safeway,

the checkout clerk hailed me. "Dude. I saw you in the paper. Famous. Yo." I received what seemed like false pity from the woman who cut my hair and was grilled extensively when we visited Sheffield headquarters. It turned into a pretty lousy day. People either unthinkingly treated my appearance in the photo as a positive accomplishment or as a venal act.

When I spoke with Kalpesh at the Sheffield headquarters I didn't bring up my knowledge of his ongoing affair with Deborah. Bert conjectured that the alleged inside man in the Sheffield camp had ties, concealed or otherwise, to whoever had taken the plane down, and it might well be Kalpesh. Still, I had no proof.

The heavy rain was beating against the car windows when my cellphone chimed. "Bert?"

"Thomas, where are you?"

We were maybe thirty minutes out from the Cape, but I didn't necessarily want him to know that. Lately he'd been a little too curious about my whereabouts. "I'm with your brother."

"And where the hell is that?"

"Someplace where it's raining cats and dogs."

"It's raining everywhere. Have you heard the news?"

"I've had my fill of news for a while."

"About Ruth Ponzi?"

"What about her?"

"Her husband's dead."

"What?"

"She's in the hospital. I tried to see her, but they're only letting in relatives and close friends."

"What happened?"

"Last night while they were going to dinner, some butthole crossed the center line and smashed into their car head-on. It was one of those dual-axle pickup trucks jacked up to about four feet off the ground. Ran all the way up and over the driver's side of the car. Her husband didn't have a chance. They had to pry her out. Witnesses said the other driver kept gunning it even after he was on top of them. Then he got out and ran into the woods. Caucasian. Medium height. Dark glasses. Ponytail. Turned out the truck had been stolen from a Krispy

Kreme Doughnuts parking lot in Puyallup the day before. It was just luck Ponzi's kids weren't with them."

"Jesus, Bert."

"This has all the trademarks of a hit set up to look like an accident. Right down to the baseball cap with the built-in ponytail. The machine got to her."

"What do you mean, right down to the built-in ponytail?"

"We *all* used to wear those. A baseball cap with a ponytail hanging down the back. Perfect disguise. You see a guy in a ponytail, you don't look at much else. Happened in the arboretum not far from that café where you tried to starve me to death. And it don't matter that they didn't kill her. They nailed her husband. When she comes to her senses, she'll be afraid. She'll stop looking into the plane crash. And so will anybody else. It's called messaging."

"Bert, I'm feeling pretty paranoid myself, but let's not go overboard."

"They count on you not wanting to go overboard. That's why they can be this bold and get away with it. Ruth was asking questions. They said she gave Hoagland hell at the press conference yesterday morning. Asked out loud if he had worked for the CIA."

"You're serious? You think somebody tried to kill her? Why not us? We're the ones instigating it."

"For starters, she was going to be a soft target, which wouldn't necessarily be the case for you or me. And she wasn't so far into her investigation that it was going to look suspicious the way it would if you or I were taken out. Besides, with her nobody's really sure it was murder."

"It has to be a coincidence."

"Keep thinking that. That way your friends won't think you're completely insane the way everyone, including you, thinks I'm completely insane. That way the fragile egg you've been calling reality doesn't crack open."

"I still don't—"

"They won't catch the guy."

"Is Ponzi going to live?"

"I don't know. Nobody at the hospital will tell me for sure."

*   *   *

IT WAS STILL RAINING. We were beside the lighthouse. I was
sitting on top of a fence facing the ocean, Snake begging me
to get off because he thought I might fall or get blown into
the water, which was a few stories below. We could see the
squalls blowing in from the south, the waves dancing in front
of them, and even in all this, California gulls cruised non-
chalantly up and down the bluffs. There were no boats, no
fishermen, and no recovery craft. They'd concluded their sal-
vage work. It was time to reassemble the pieces and see the
picture they presented. It all seemed reasonable, a task performed by meticulous men who were proud and careful in
their profession. It didn't seem possible any of them would
purposely botch the process.

Ruth Ponzi's husband was dead. Ruth was in the hospital.
Somebody had tailed me two nights ago. The Maddox campaign had been in possession of information it could only
have obtained from an informer in the Sheffield camp. Deborah and Kalpesh were sleeping together. My cellphone had
been on the blink at the moment the plane began its descent.
Timothy Hoagland was heading up the inquiry. He'd been on
the Wellstone crash team, another tragedy that ended up ben-
efiting a key Republican candidate for the Senate. I'd been
called in the middle of the night from a cellphone that may or
may not have been Kathy's, an incident I still wasn't sure
hadn't been the result of a weird electronic glitch.

Bert had me half convinced the accident was actually murder, but another part of me shrank from that conclusion. I
liked feeling sane, and believing Sheffield had had a secret
government group conspiring against her was a theory that
put me on the wrong side of the sanity equation. If somebody
had tried to murder Ponzi, then likely everything Bert had
been saying was true. There *was* a cabal. We *were* living in a
nightmare where government agents murdered U.S. senators
and their friends and later followed, discredited, or destroyed
inquisitive citizens who asked questions. I couldn't tell if I
was disbelieving, frightened, or mad, or a little of each.

Perched atop the fence on the bluff, buffeted by a driving
rain, I thought about what a tempting target I would make for

a rifleman. With all the wind, nobody would even hear the shot. I would simply collect the lead and fall into the sea. Above me the rotating beam from the lighthouse brightened the afternoon periodically. My jeans were soaked from the blowing rain, and my legs were freezing, but everything above my waist was dry under a hooded rain cape. Peering down at the beach, I could see the tide flowing out, a flock of plover chasing it. Not far up the coast on this same beach, they'd found two of the bodies. The thought brought to life the possibility of Kathy's corpse washing ashore in front of me. I kept seeing dark spots in the waves that might be her long hair. I could almost see her.

"Come on, man," Snake said. "Let's get out of here."

"Just a few minutes."

"You been saying that all afternoon. It's getting dark. We're going to catch pneumonia."

We'd already accomplished our mission. We'd talked to the guardsman on duty in the lighthouse and learned that none of the lighthouse electronics had gone out on the day of the crash, and that the question had already been asked by both the FBI and the NTSB people, which I found curious. We'd located my friend at the Coast Guard station, Hutchins, the lanky twentysomething guardsman, who was able to show me the logs of the FBI checking in on the afternoon of the crash. They had arrived a mere fifty-eight minutes after the plane went down. Hutchins said he'd asked around after my first phone call, and nobody had an explanation for their sudden arrival. He also said a memo had been distributed admonishing guardsmen not to talk to the press or anybody else not related to the official investigation.

"You're talking," I said.

"This is different," Hutchins said, glancing around to make sure we weren't being observed. "I consider you a friend."

"Thanks, pal." I slapped him on the shoulder, touched that my personal dilemma had affected him so deeply.

When I finally hopped off the fence, I could barely walk, my quadriceps cramping from cold and inactivity. Snake was gone, probably in the car harmonizing with Willie Nelson. This was turning into an ordeal for him, but still he refused to leave my side. The Coast Guard personnel in the lighthouse had been watching me, a suicide watch, no doubt, for they knew who I was but not exactly what I was hoping to accomplish out here. All I knew was that this was the last place I'd seen Kathy, even if she'd been a mile away; the last place I'd heard her voice. And it was the spot, give or take a few paces, where I'd watched her fall four thousand feet to her death. Whenever I thought about it, the shock ran through me like an electric current.

When I reached the parking lot, there were only four or five cars, mostly tourists whose timetables had been upset by the weather. A vehicle was turning around in the rain. The elderly woman at the wheel had short-cropped white hair and a large, blunt nose. Her passenger sat unmoving, as stiff as a mannequin, her head bound tightly in a scarf. It was only when the driver switched on the car's headlights and the interior panel lights lit up that I was able to glimpse, for just a fraction of a second, the passenger's profile. The nose. The chin. The position of her head, that slight cant to one side. As they drove away, I screamed, "Kathy!" The car didn't slow, and neither the driver nor the passenger gave any indication they'd heard me as I slopped through the puddles in the parking lot, running after them.

It was a faded red Subaru wagon, early eighties, the rear bumper dented, the plates so muddy I couldn't read the digits in the dusk. Who the driver was or why Kathy would be riding around beside her like a zombie was something I couldn't fathom.

My wet jeans pulled against my knees as I sprinted across the lot to my Taurus. The car doors were locked. I checked my pockets, but I didn't have the keys. "Snake? Snake, where are you? God damn it! Snake?"

I was racing toward the trail that led to the World War II bunkers when Snake emerged from the narrow path leading to them. "What d'ya want?"

"Give me the goddamned keys!"

When he flipped me the keys, I turned and ran to the car. "What the heck? What's going on?"

"I saw Kathy."

"In the ocean?"

I was scrambling into the car now, pushing the seat back so I could get my long legs in. I fired up the engine. "Come on, man," Snake said, climbing in. "Slow down. You trying to kill me?"

"Close your door." We were already moving.

"Close my door? I'm not even in yet."

We tore through the lot, spewing gravel and water behind the tires, then slewed onto the roadway, where I stopped and looked in both directions. There was no traffic in sight. On a hunch, I jumped out of the car and examined the road, hoping I could track the Subaru in the puddles the way an expert tracker would track a deer. It was a demented idea, and I found nothing except water and macadam. "Crap!" I said, climbing back in. Snake was fooling with the stereo, trying to get Willie Nelson to sing again. I grabbed the disc out of his hands, rolled down my window, and flicked it out into the afternoon rain squall.

"Christ, Thomas! Have you gone mad?"

Right or left? These were long country roads, and if I guessed the Subaru's direction and drove fast enough, I could be on them in minutes. I went left. "Thomas? Are you okay?"

"I told you. I saw Kathy."

"Kathy's dead. You know that. You know you do."

"It was her."

"You've seen her before. She was dead then, and she's still dead."

"Those were mistakes."

"Did you get a clear look?"

"She was in a car. The windows were steamed up."

"And it was dark in the car, right, 'cause it's dark in cars at this time of day. Look, Thomas. You only think you saw Kathy. You're out here at the Cape, and you and I both know this is the last place you spoke to her. This area will always bring back memories. It will always—"

"It was her."

"Okay. You saw her. Did she see you?"

"I don't know."

"If she saw you, why didn't she stop?"

"Some woman was driving."

"Kathy was the passenger?"

"Right."

"What were they doing out here?"

"I don't know."

"Kathy's alive? Okay. I can accept that. After all, they haven't recovered a body. Explain it. Did she parachute out of the plane?"

"I didn't see any chutes."

"She survived the impact and swam to shore?"

"I don't know."

"Think about it, Thomas. If she was alive, don't you think she would go home? Or at least call you to tell you she was okay?"

"She called the other night."

"How many times have you seen Kathy since the crash? How many?"

"Eight. Ten. I'm not sure."

"And none of them were her, were they?"

"No."

"I rest my case." A few moments later he added, "You're not going to stop, are you?"

"No."

By the time we'd driven a few miles down the road, careening at breakneck speeds, it became clear I'd chosen the wrong direction. I whipped the Taurus around in the middle of the road and headed south. Although his knuckles were white on the door grip, Snake didn't say anything. I had to give him credit for gumption. If I'd been in his place, I would have opened the door and bailed out.

THIRTY-NINE

FOR THE NEXT TWENTY-FIVE MINUTES I drove like a meth freak looking for his next hit, but during the lunacy, all Snake did was fasten his seat belt and push himself back into the seat. We drove down 101 and across the Columbia River into Oregon, and we still had not caught sight of the Subaru. "You going to pursue this to the end?" Snake asked, when I finally came to a stop at a red light and put my head on the steering wheel.

"What's the end?"

"You tell me. You actually *believe* that was your wife in the Subaru?"

"Yes. I don't know. Maybe. It looked like her."

"That was four different answers."

"All I know is I have to find out."

"You're beginning to worry me, Thomas."

"I'm beginning to worry myself."

"Tell you what. You want to find Kathy? Get a grappling hook and eight hundred feet of line. Go drag the ocean floor."

"I'm going to find that car. If it wasn't Kathy, I won't chase anybody else."

"Is that a promise?"

"Yes."

"I'm going to hold you to it. But we've got to get organized. We know they left Cape Disappointment and headed south, because we went north first, and if they'd been anywhere on the road we would have flattened them like a two-cent pancake. I suggest we go back and start at the Cape. We'll traverse every road south of there. We'll go into Naselle and Chinook, and we'll take 401 and we'll even . . ."

"The problem is, they could be anywhere. They might be on their way to Seattle."

"Don't get your panties in a twist. We'll get organized and make this work."

We searched until midnight, talking to anybody we could find, gradually widening our search pattern. I called my house in Seattle every half hour, saddened anew each time I heard Kathy's voice on our answering machine—the old recording, not a new one. I'd vowed never to erase it, but eventually I knew I would have to. It made me sick to think about replacing the message, even sicker to realize I'd lapsed into some sort of Alice in Wonderland parallel universe. But I had. I would play through this last obsession and regroup. I wanted to stop, but I couldn't help myself. Snake was right. I was becoming delusional.

It wasn't until after midnight that Snake insisted we find dinner and a place to sleep. We found both in Astoria, on the Oregon side of the Columbia River. The next morning, after sleeping maybe a total of two hours, I got up at six-thirty and called home from our small motel room, listened to Kathy on the answering machine, and got us back on the trail, Snake in the car beside me wolfing down a bag of maple bars and doughnuts we'd procured. My clothes were finally dry, though my shoes remained damp. By eight Snake had a pretty good sugar buzz going and a half hour later dropped off to sleep against the passenger door. Passing Naselle for about the fifth time since I'd begun the odyssey, I pulled into a gas station and bait shop where we'd gassed up the night before. The attendant was new. "I'm looking for a dark red Subaru wagon. Nineteen-eighties. Older woman driver. Short white hair. Know anybody like that?"

"Just about every woman who comes in."

"They all driving Subarus?"

The man wore a baseball cap and had a wad of chewing tobacco bulging one cheek. He was about twenty-five, fresh-faced, and I hoped destined for better things. "Why are you looking for her?"

"I saw her at a flea market and she said she had a boat to

sell, but then I went and lost the slip of paper with her number on it."

"She comes in for beer and chips and stuff. Always pays cash. She don't live far."

"How do you know?"

"She don't ever turn off her engine. Says if it ain't running longer than five minutes, she can't get it started back up."

"I guess that puts her less than five minutes away."

"I would say so."

On my way out the door, I turned back. "Anyone come in with her?"

"She's by herself. Seems to like it that way."

"Ever say anything?"

"Just about the weather and so on. I know she follows the Seahawks. God, they're having a great year, aren't they?"

"Sterling."

"What's going on?" Snake asked, coming out of his coma with a start when I slammed the car door.

While I explained, I took the first local road that branched off the highway. We examined every property, disturbing noisy dogs and in one case a curious goat. It took an hour and a half to locate the car on a serpentine farm road north of Naselle parked in front of a two-story ramshackle house with moss on the roof. The weed crop in the yard had gone to seed. A fifty-year-old rusted logging truck and a partially disassembled logging trailer hunkered in the trees on the side of the property. Parked haphazardly next to the Subaru was an older Toyota Corolla.

As we approached the house, I began having misgivings. True, it was a Subaru and it was old, but the rear license plate was clean and readable, not obscured by mud. It occurred to me that there was probably more than one red Subaru wagon in the area. "I bet these are old people," Snake said. "Don't go scaring the shit out of them."

"All I want to do is talk."

"Remember, they live out in the boonies. They won't be like city people."

"What the hell does that mean?" I asked, climbing the high front porch.

"People out here pack weapons."

"Just don't you be pulling yours."

"I'm trying to warn you so you won't get your fool head blowed off."

"Just stay out of my way."

"That'll be the day," Snake said, keeping close behind. Inside the house somebody was playing a Hank Williams record. Loud.

I knocked and waited. The porch was barren of everything except an empty flowerpot. I knocked again. It was impossible to see through the windows.

"Thomas, I swear to God, you're going to regret this. These are ordinary folk, and you're going to feel like a jackass."

"I feel like a jackass every day. Always have."

I had to knock three more times before he opened the door and blocked the narrow space with his body. He was medium-height, brown and brown, short hair, unshaven, with spindly arms and the beginnings of a paunch that was going to overpower his slender frame. Hard to tell how old he was. Around thirty, maybe. He had something in his right hand, because when he raised his arm I heard it clunk against the inside of the wooden door. A woman behind him turned the music down and said something I couldn't hear. He replied over his shoulder. "I got it. Probably some damned Jehovah's Witnesses." Looking at me, he said, "Yeah?"

"I'm wondering if I could talk to the owner of that red wagon."

"Why?"

"I clipped it in a parking lot yesterday, and I need to make things right."

He thought it over a few moments, then a wary look crept into his eyes. "She never said nothing to me about getting crunched."

"It wasn't bad. She probably didn't even see it."

"How did you know where to find us?"

"I just—"

"Get the fuck outa here, asshole." He tried to slam the door, but I had my foot in it. I could feel the pressure against my shoulder as he tried to close the door from one side while I pushed from the other.

"Jesus, Thomas," said Snake. "Get out of there."

Suddenly the weight on the other side stopped and his face reappeared in the opening, then the door opened wide. Still huffing from our fray, the disheveled man stood in front of us with a pistol dangling at the end of his limp right arm. He seemed flummoxed when he saw Snake, whose appearance took all the fight out of him.

In the back of the house a white-haired woman returned from what I assumed was the kitchen area and proceeded along a corridor toward us, then headed up the stairs to the second floor via a staircase at the back of the living room. The house was humid and smelled of pot roast. In the light under a window I could see she was carrying a hypodermic syringe.

"What's with the cowboy getup?" the man at the door asked.

"This is what I wear," said Snake.

Several things happened in the next moments. The man realized his mistake in letting me open the door, while at the same time the worst panic of my life slammed me. I couldn't have been more alarmed if somebody had pushed me off an ocean liner with an anchor chained to my waist. I could tell by the way she was carrying it that the white-haired woman was familiar with hypos and that the dose she was carrying upstairs was not meant for her own use.

"No!" I shouted. I flattened the man and hurtled toward the stairs. Behind me, I could hear Snake step into the house in my wake. The woman was almost at the top of the stairs when she saw me. A moment later I heard her heavy, thumping footsteps on the floor above us.

I half expected to hear a gunshot behind me, but all I heard were the sounds of a struggle as Snake and the homeowner tussled. I turned back briefly and saw Snake trying to wrestle the gun away from the man in the doorway. Neither of them was gaining the upper hand. By rights I should have gone back to make sure Snake wasn't killed, but I didn't.

And then I had a demented thought that the government cabal Bert was always talking about—the one that may or may

not exist, the one that may or may not have been a figment of
his imagination—that they had set this up, that this was part
of an elaborate plot to murder me and get away with it. They
dangle a fake Kathy in front of me, make it just hard enough
to find her that it's realistic, then cajole me into breaking into
the house, where they can legally blow me full of holes. My
thoughts were flooded with the idea that I'd been tricked.
Spotting Kathy everywhere I went. The whole thing was a
fantasy. I knew that now that it was too late. A shot rang out
downstairs and the fracas ceased, then slow footsteps crossed
the living room toward the foot of the stairs.

The second-floor hallway was in shadows, the white-
haired woman nowhere in sight. She was probably scrambling to find her own gun. In America everybody had a
gun. It occurred to me that if Snake was dead, I would be
next, and that nobody was ever going to know why we'd come
here. The papers would print some simple account: HOME IN-
VADERS SHOT BY FRIGHTENED RESIDENT. I opened one door, but
the room contained only an unmade bed. The second bedroom was empty. There was a partially open bathroom door,
but she hadn't gone in there. At the end of the hallway I found
the third bedroom locked. I stepped back and knocked the
door off its hinges.

The room contained a bed, a dresser, and a single straight-
backed chair. On the bed was a mound of blankets I assumed
had a human being buried underneath. The white-haired
woman was bending over the bed with the hypodermic
syringe. Behind me, somebody was coming up the stairs with
leaden footsteps. The woman nervously tried to inject the
individual in the bed.

Before she could complete the task, I vaulted over the end
of the bed and grasped her fleshy arm. "Who are you?" she
yelled. "Jimmy. Get this maniac off me! Jimmy? Help! Call
the police. Jimmy?"

Although she was probably twice my age, she was amaz-
ingly nimble and whipped her arms out of my grip. Then, with
a flash of inspiration, she came at me wielding the hypodermic
like a knife, ready to inject me with whatever medication was
in it. Up close, I could see she had blue eyes and rough-looking

skin. I grabbed her arm, but she struggled ferociously. I put an ankle behind her leg and pushed her onto the floor, wresting the hypo away from her as I did so. Elementary school judo. It was a trick I'd learned in fourth grade. Now that I had the needle, she scooted into the corner on her rump like a frightened cat.

I turned and looked at the bed, stalling. It was one thing to chase a figure I believed to be Kathy, quite another to unmask that figure and once again be forced to realize Kathy was drifting somewhere in the wild blue Pacific Ocean with the sharks. I didn't know if I could stand it again.

Behind me, the squeaky door to the bedroom swung open. I heard a large revolver being cocked. The woman got to her feet in the corner. Hoping I wouldn't get shot before I could talk my way out of this, I turned and faced him.

"Jesus, Thomas. What are you doing?"

"Snake? Where's the other guy?"

"Downstairs. I had to take his gun away from him after he fired it into the wall."

"Well, don't be pointing your forty-four at me."

Snake lowered the Smith & Wesson. "Is it her?"

"I don't know."

"You going to check, or are you going to stand here all morning?"

"My patient?" said the woman. "Leave my patient alone. Jimmy's downstairs calling the police right now."

When I glanced at Snake, he shook his head. "Is your patient's name Kathy Birchfield?" Snake asked.

"Her name is Marla, and she's quite ill. Don't touch her."

Despite the commotion and chatter, the lump in the bed had barely stirred. When I peeled the covers partially back, it was easy to see why. Her head was swathed in bandages, her left arm in a cast and sling. Her eyelids fluttered, but she did not awaken. I continued to peel the covers back. She was wearing a long cotton nightgown. Her left leg had a cast that extended above her knee.

"Christ," said Snake. "It's not her."

I knelt and touched the patient's hot forehead. It was hard to tell what was going on here. On the nightstand were several bottles of pills and a paperback mystery. The pill bottles had been prescribed for a patient named Marla Anderson. "Kathy?"

"Jesus, Thomas," Snake bellowed. "Give it up, will you? We broke into this house, terrorized these people, and now we need to get the fuck out of Dodge. Give it up!"

The patient opened her eyes, looked at the white-haired woman, who had by now stepped out of the corner, and then swung her gaze toward me. It took her a long time to say anything. "Thomas?"

≡ FORTY ≡

THE WHITE-HAIRED WOMAN'S NAME was Dorothy MacDonald. She claimed she was a nurse, had been hired by the day,
was being paid cash, and lived in Gresham, Oregon, but had
been here since the day after "that senator died in the plane
crash." She said this was a rented house, that none of them actually lived here, that she learned of the job through a friend of
a friend, that she was an RN but hadn't been working the past
few years because she'd been taking care of her husband, who'd
recently died of dementia. According to her, the patient's name
was Marla Anderson and she had been here for almost two
weeks. Also, according to MacDonald, the man downstairs was
an MD who'd recently graduated from medical school but had
run up against personal problems at the hospital where he'd
done his residency.

"Thomas?"

I sat on the bed.

"Thomas? Is that really you?"

"Kathy. Oh, my God."

"Am I dreaming? I thought you were dead."

"I thought *you* were dead." It was hard to believe, after all
of my near-psychotic disbelief, that she truly hadn't gone
down with the Sheffield flight and had been barely fifteen
miles from the spot where the world thought she died. Hundreds of people had attended her funeral. Her mother and
sister had been stricken. I'd lost about half my brain cells trying to come to grips with the fact that I was going to suffer
the next forty years without her. And now here she was, good
as new. Or almost. I touched her shoulder and kissed her
cheek. She smiled grimly and drifted back to sleep. With
her head swathed in bandages, she was barely recognizable,
and worse, barely recognized me. "What happened?" I asked,

turning to the nurse. "Her name is Kathy Birchfield. And she is my wife."

"Her husband died in the car wreck."

"Is that how she got hurt? A car wreck?"

"Two weeks ago. Her husband was killed. She's had a severe head injury and, because of that, needs to be kept sedated. I need to give her that injection."

"Why isn't she in a hospital?"

"There are . . . extenuating circumstances. We were warned about you. You're the ex."

"Kathy never had an ex. This is a first marriage for both of us."

I was still having a hard time believing this. The house. The nurse. The doctor downstairs. The fact that Kathy was alive. For days I'd been envisioning her last weightless moments as the plane hurtled toward the ocean, but she hadn't even been on the plane. Was it possible the patient in front of me was only someone who resembled Kathy, that she'd uttered my name as part of an elaborately rehearsed scam? Maybe the cops were on their way. Or a team of assassins. On her left-hand ring finger she was wearing a simple gold wedding band. I slipped it off and, without looking, handed it to the nurse. "Read inside. It says, 'From Thomas, all my love.'" I gave her the date of our wedding.

The old woman leaned down next to the lamp, squinted at the ring and said, "Typical male."

I grabbed the ring from her and read it. *Love Forever, Thomas.* Crap. I slipped the ring back on her finger. "At least I got the date right."

"Fifty percent is flunking."

"Who's paying for this?"

"Her brother. Out of his own pocket."

"She doesn't have a brother."

"Sure she does. I've seen him." Dorothy MacDonald was staring at Snake.

"Is that supposed to be her brother?"

"Looks like him, but it's not."

Snake and I exchanged a glance and spoke at the same time. "Bert."

"His twin hired you," I said.

"In case you ever get confused," Snake said, "I'm the handsome one. It's been a burden for Bert all along."

"That bastard," I said.

"Just don't kill him when you finally get your hands on him," said Snake.

"Who's going to stop me?"

"Just don't kill him."

I turned to the woman. "What are her injuries?"

"I'm not at liberty to disclose medical information."

"Don't piss me off, lady." My threat only made her more determined to stick to her guns. I had to admire her for that. She was scared, but she was going to continue to act in her patient's best interest if she could. I tried to look at things from her point of view. For almost two weeks she'd been camped out in this lonely house taking care of an injured stranger, probably hadn't had a single visitor, and all of a sudden two madmen burst in making allegations and pointing guns. Her world had gone topsy-turvy almost as fast as mine had.

Snake and I looked at each other. "Don't let her touch her," I said, as I left the room and went back downstairs. The living room was empty, a chair tipped over, the front door open. A cold wind blew into the house. "Doctor?"

In the yard the Subaru and my Ford were still there, but the Toyota was missing. A quick check of the rooms on the first floor revealed the bedroom where he'd been camping out had been ransacked, most of his personal possessions gone. There couldn't have been much or he wouldn't have been able to scram so quickly. It wasn't until I looked under a couple of old suitcases in the back of the closet that I found Kathy's purse, the luggage that hadn't gone down with the plane, clothing, and ID. Except for her cellphone sitting on top of it all, none of it appeared to have been touched since the afternoon I last saw her. I placed her belongings in the living room near the front door.

The house had been owner-occupied not too long ago. A collection of knickknacks adorned the mantel, mostly glass elephants. I walked back up and found Snake and MacDonald staring at each other like a couple of worn-out boxers waiting for the decision.

"I want you to tell me everything," I said, gently. When she didn't reply right away, I added, "Nobody's called the police. Your friend took off."

Hurriedly, MacDonald walked around the end of the bed and peered through the drapes at the front yard. "He's gone."

"That's what I said."

She thought about it for half a minute. "I knew there was something wrong with this setup, but according to Jimmy—"

"Jimmy? Is that his name?"

"Jimmy Crocker. All I know is, I was following orders. I thought it was odd we were keeping her out here instead of in a hospital. But her brother said there was an ex-husband running around loose who wanted to kill her and he had all kinds of resources and if she wasn't kept incognito she would end up dead. That's why Jimmy had the gun. This whole setup was to keep her hidden from her ex."

"When was the last time you saw the supposed brother?"

"A couple of days ago."

"And Jimmy's really a doctor?"

"That's what he said. He seemed to know his stuff."

Snake looked at me. "That's why he wants to know where you are every time he calls. He's been keeping tabs, making sure you weren't out here uncovering any of this."

"When is she going to wake up?" I asked.

"Jimmy's let her come out of it in the afternoons for a little while. You mean fully conscious? It could be hours."

I went into the other room and called a cycling pal I'd known for years. "Bill? Thomas here."

"Thomas. It's good to hear your voice. How are you doing? Sorry I couldn't make it to the funeral. Had a surgery scheduled that day. Did you get my card?"

"Yeah. Look. If I brought a patient around, do you think you could treat that patient without telling anybody?"

"Unless it's a gunshot wound. You know I have to report those."

"It's not a gunshot."

"I'll make room in the schedule."

"Be there in about three hours."

"No problem." Bill was a GP in a small clinic in Ballard, a Seattle neighborhood. I was still trying to figure out how Kathy had missed the plane. When and where she might have been involved in an automobile accident. And why Bert felt the need to hide her, even from me. Had the car accident been his fault? Had he felt I might take it out on him if she died? Or had he just gone batshit crazy and decided to drug her and keep her for himself? None of the likely scenarios made much sense.

Back in the sick room, I held up the hypo. "What's in this?"

"It's a sedative." Her eyes drifted back to the window.

"Don't worry about Jimmy. You're not going to see him again unless it's in court."

"We took the very best care of her. I was with her night and day. The best care."

"I ever find out different, I'll hunt you down. Both of you." She took a step back. "I took care of her."

"We'll see. Snake, get her information. There's a camera in my car. Take pictures of her and this place. The car registration. Her driver's license. Everything."

"We going to let her leave?"

"Just take the pictures."

"Who's going to pay what's owed?" she asked.

"We'll get back to you on that," Snake said.

It took fifteen minutes to bundle Kathy up and get her into the backseat of the Taurus, where she lay like an animal that had been hit by a car; another ten minutes to search the house for incriminating evidence concerning the doctor. The house didn't have a phone, and he'd left little except fingerprints, but we bagged a drinking glass and an empty beer bottle we knew he'd handled and stashed them in the trunk for future reference. As we were driving off the property, I flipped open my cellphone and tried to call Bert, but he didn't answer. Snake said, "Why would Bert let you believe she was dead?"

"I'm sure he'll pull some explanation out of the ether involving conspiracies and nine-foot-tall men from another planet."

We took Highway 4 east, and just before we got to I-5 a caravan of law enforcement vehicles passed us heading due west, blue lights twirling, sirens singing. I examined the other cars carefully as they passed. I said, "Wasn't Winston Seagram in that unmarked car?"

"Who's that?"

"Head of the Seattle branch of the FBI."

"I didn't get a look. Think they're headed to the house?"

"That's exactly what I think."

"Who tipped them off? Had to have been hours ago. Seagram works in Seattle. And don't be thinking it was my brother, because it wasn't."

Even though Bert would have been calling the authorities on himself, I didn't put it past him to sic the FBI on us. As long as we were going to find Kathy anyway, the resulting confusion might have worked to Bert's advantage. In the face of this lie, I was no longer sure Bert had told me the truth about anything.

In the backseat, Kathy continued to lapse in and out of consciousness. When we pulled into an official rest stop, I climbed into the backseat with her while Snake unexpectedly got out of the car and slid under the Taurus on his back. When he rolled out he had a small black rectangular object in his hand. "Is that what I think it is?" I asked.

"GPS locator. Probably been there awhile. No wonder they knew you was tailin' Deborah. Somebody knew exactly where you were and they know where you are now. To within a meter."

"Government, you think?"

"It wasn't the FBI, because they were going the other way. And I don't know why the government would be tailing you."

"Maybe Bert is working for the feds."

"This is a pretty expensive piece of gadgetry. And I don't think my brother's working for the feds anymore. And why would he keep asking where you were if he knew?"

"Maddox was the one who called the cops on me when I was at Deborah's. Maybe it was planted by the Maddox team."

"But you were working for them."

"And asking too many questions."

"He owns a security company. They're bound to have access to this kind of equipment. This model here is about five hundred dollars retail." Snake walked across the lot and affixed the device to the underside of an eighteen-wheeler.

For the duration of the trip, I sat in the back with Kathy, who was like a surgery patient coming out of anesthesia. She didn't seem to be in pain but was increasingly agitated. I was beginning to wonder if anybody else from the plane was alive. Sheffield's body had not been recovered. Was she alive? I'd seen the plane go into the ocean. It had been a near-vertical dive. Nobody could have survived the impact. Kathy couldn't have been on the plane. But had she been in a car wreck? Only one person knew the answers.

As we passed through Tacoma, Kathy looked up at me and smiled. "I thought you were dead," she said.

"How did I die?"

"Car accident."

"They're quite popular these days."

"Bert told me you were in a wreck. He was sad."

"I bet he was. Were you sad, too?"

"I was so sad they had to sedate me."

There *had* been a conspiracy; a conspiracy of one. Bert was the conspirator, not the United States government. Bert had been leading me around by the nose in an effort to conceal the fact that he was holding my wife captive. What his long-range plans were, I could only guess.

=== FORTY-ONE ===

BILL, WHO WAS BETWEEN PATIENTS just then, had me place her on an examining table in one of the small rooms, and then, after I told him everything I knew about her condition, sent me out of the room. He knew who the patient was, even if nobody else in the building did, and the recognition left him shocked and pale.

The afternoon sun had come out and was warming the wooden bench in the enclosed grotto, where I chose to wait. From time to time through the open doorway I could see Bill or the nurse bustling back and forth in the corridor. By the time one of the assistants wheeled Kathy into the grotto in a wheelchair, I was cold despite the sunshine. Wrapped in a blanket, Kathy was wearing hospital greens and a pair of wool socks to keep her feet warm. She smiled and reached out to hug me. I leaned down and kissed the side of her cheek until she turned and made it lip to lip.

The bandages were gone, her hair compressed and misshapen. The cast on her arm had been removed, as had the one on her leg. A moment later, Bill came out clutching a sheaf of paperwork and looking more confused than concerned. "We X-rayed the arm and the leg. We took off the cast on the arm first. As far as I can tell, there wasn't any reason to cast it. Same with the leg. I've never seen anything like it. We ran her through the usual blood tests, and her sugar was a little low but otherwise everything seems normal. Nothing wrong with her head, either."

"Those bandages were—"

"Strictly for show. It's my guess somebody's been pumping a fair amount of diazepam into her system at regular intervals."

"Dia—?"

"Valium."

"Jesus."

"She has close to no memory of the last ten days." Bill and I stared at each other for a few moments. "Thomas? What's going on?"

"She's okay to leave, then?"

"It'll take a while for the diazepam to get out of her system, but other than that, she's fine."

"You don't think she was in a car accident two weeks ago?"

"Not a serious one. There aren't any signs of it. You're not going to tell me what happened, are you?"

"I don't know what happened."

"Okey doke. We'll keep this on the QT until you say otherwise."

"You're the man."

Outside, Kathy managed to walk to the car, but it had been so long since she'd used her muscles she was like a baby. We sat down next to each other and I kissed her. Snake was snoring in the backseat. "Thomas? I don't remember all of it, but I remember somebody calling me at the landing strip and saying he was in trouble."

"Bert?"

"Yes. I guess it was Bert. He said he thought he'd killed somebody. That the police were after him and he wanted to turn himself in, but only if I came with him. He said he needed to show me some evidence before the police saw it."

"When was this?"

"A few minutes after you left, but before the plane took off. First he called my cell, and then he showed up in person and convinced me he'd shot somebody. I believed him. He was in a panic. I went with him in his truck. I didn't even get one of my bags off the plane. From there it gets hazy. The last thing I remember is opening a bottle of water he gave me. When you showed up, I thought a day or two had passed. At one point I woke up in a strange room and Bert was there with some doctor. My arm was in a cast. I couldn't move my leg. I believed them when they told me I was hurt."

"And your nurse, Dorothy?"

"She took me out to Cape Disappointment. I had to go

there after they told me you were dead. I assumed you and I had both been in the same car accident, but you weren't in an accident, were you?"

"No."

"Was I?"

"Doesn't look that way."

"So what happened?"

"I'd say Bert drugged you and hired that phony doctor to keep drugging you. I'm guessing the casts on your arm and leg were to convince you and the nurse you really were hurt and to keep you from trying to escape."

"Why would Bert . . . ?"

"That's one of the first things I'm going to ask him after I knock all his teeth out."

"Thomas, it's not worth going to jail over."

"I think it is. My biggest question is, how did he know the plane was going to crash? And if he knew, why not figure out a way to ground the flight and save everybody?"

"Tell me about the plane crash again." I'd given her the story during the drive to Seattle, but her short-term memory was like a sieve, so I rendered it once more.

When I finished, she said, "You thought *I* was dead?"

"I thought you were dead."

"It's kind of Shakespearean, isn't it?"

"You could say so."

"Good thing neither of us committed suicide."

"Good thing."

The knowledge that Bert had saved Kathy's life was the only thing that kept me from calling the police.

FORTY-TWO

THE REST OF THE AFTERNOON passed in the blink of an eye, beginning with a phone call from Bert Slezak before we were even out of the clinic driveway. The timing was so spot-on I looked around to see if he was following us. "Thomas?"

"Where are you, you little bastard?"

"Listen, I know you got Kathy back, and I'm happy for you both. It was killing me that you were in so much pain."

"Killing you so badly you told her I was dead?"

"Now, that's a complicated little evolution to try to expand on over the phone."

"I bet."

"Malcolm called. He thought you were going to kill him."

"Who's Malcolm? Your fake doctor?"

"You scared the hell out of him."

"You're the one who should be scared."

"I was protecting her. Don't worry. We're going to have a face-to-face, and I'll catch you up on all of it as soon as you calm down."

"You mean as soon as I catch you."

"Now, don't be angry, old chum. Remember, I saved your wife's life."

"You kept her drugged for almost two weeks."

"If she'd been running around free she'd be dead now— she'd be peripheral damage—just like Ponzi's husband. We've got a job to do, you and I. They're still out there, and they're still going to whitewash that plane crash unless we do something about it. I was hiding her for a reason. And now that you have her, you have to hide her, too. Trust me, the last thing on earth these people want is for your wife to turn up on national TV explaining how it came to be that she wasn't on that plane. She'd be dead inside of two days. Swear to God."

"I don't believe you."

"No. That's been your trouble all along. And it almost got her killed last time."

"Kathy said you killed somebody and the cops were after you."

"That was just some hooey to get her off the plane. Look, if she even mentions me, they'll have to shut her up."

"Why? Because you were part of the plot?"

"Because I'm on record, both with Ponzi and others, as to that crash being part of a conspiracy. Anybody finds out I was certain enough to kidnap your wife and save her life by doing it, they'll want to know what I knew and how I knew it. My yanking her off that flight is the strongest piece of evidence in favor of a conspiracy, and it's one we don't dare reveal. They may be tracking you right now. I wouldn't be surprised if the FBI shows up on your doorstep."

"The FBI's going to kill us?"

"No, they're going to turn you over to Homeland Security or the NSA or some other alphabet agency, and then you are going to disappear . . . you, Kathy, Snake, and anybody else dumb enough to be tagging along."

"You're full of shit."

"You willing to bet your life on it? Better yet, are you willing to bet Kathy's life on it?"

"Bastard."

Two Saturdays ago I had been willing to bet Kathy's life he was wrong about the advisability of her traveling with Sheffield, but now Sheffield and the others were dead. I was thinking, too, about how fast Winston Seagram and the local gendarmes had closed in on us in the southern part of the state after I freed Kathy, if indeed that was where they were headed. It was possible they'd been going out to Cape Disappointment to explore a major discovery on the beach, but I doubted they would be using emergency lights for that. "Bert? Let me ask you this. Who knew where Kathy was being held? Besides you and the two caretakers?"

"Nobody. That's what bothers me. How did *you* find her?"

"Was she in an accident?"

"You know she wasn't."

"You were part of it, weren't you? That's the only way you could know all this."

"I wasn't. I swear to God. Listen and listen good. Stash her somewhere where they can't find her. Then write out what happened and leave a note with your attorney or whatever. Keep her whereabouts secret. Make her safe."

"Why didn't you tell me Kathy was alive?"

"I sent my brother over to keep an eye on you, didn't I?"

"That's like offering to paint my house after you've set fire to it."

"Ten people were murdered. Eleven with Ponzi's husband. The most important thing now is to work on the links between the Sheffield camp and this outside cabal. If you've found a link, start tracing it."

"Fuck you."

The connection went dead.

The more I thought about Kathy being drugged and held in that musty old house while her mother and sister and I all went through hell, the angrier I became. There was a little part of me that said I was still being manipulated by Bert, that the plane had been brought down by design and that he'd had a part in it, that the reason he'd needed to conceal Kathy was because if his own co-conspirators ever found out he'd rescued one of the passengers, they would put *him* to death. Assuming that was true, I was tempted to reveal the fact that Kathy was still alive to the world and wait for Bert to get whacked.

As tempting as it was to upset Bert's applecart, I couldn't take the chance of endangering Kathy's life. I'd already put her at risk once by disregarding Bert's advice.

"All I want is my bathrobe and a hot mug of tea," Kathy said. "I just want to curl up in that big chair in the living room and look at you all night."

I wanted that, too, but a couple of blocks from our house I pulled into a side street. I got out and left Snake and Kathy in the car, making the rest of the trip on foot. It didn't take long to spot a government car on the other side of the street four doors up, two agents waiting in it. The house was being watched. I hated this. I was being sucked into something I didn't completely understand, my only guide a lunatic conspiracy theorist.

By the time I'd walked back to the car, I'd figured out where to go. Our receptionist, Beulah, had an unmarried sister who worked for the Seattle Police Department. The four of us went out to dinner together every couple of months. She lived alone in north Seattle, not far from the Northgate Mall, in a tiny house on a hill. Besides working for the SPD, Delilah taught martial arts, liked guns, fishing, and sex with women, all the same things Snake liked. It was midafternoon when I rapped on her door.

"Thomas? It's nice to see you. What's going on?"

"I wasn't sure you'd be home."

"Yeah. Yeah. My first class isn't until six."

"I need the biggest favor you'll ever do for me."

Delilah had long drab brown hair and smoker's lines etched around her eyes and lips. She had the beginning of a smoker's rough voice, too. She was thin and muscular, a vein popping in the tiny biceps in her arm as she held the door. "You know me. I'll do anything for you."

"Good."

I knew Delilah cherished secrets above all else, knowing, keeping, and savoring them. Knowing Kathy was alive while the rest of the world believed she was dead would be her cup of tea. What I didn't expect was the little yelp of surprise when we walked Kathy into the house. "Oh, my God! Oh, my God!" She said it five or six more times before she was able to settle down.

"It's kind of like I was resurrected from the dead," said Kathy, smiling slowly. Because of the sedative, everything she did seemed to be in slow motion. There was a palpable grace to it. I brought her bag in, got her settled, made an agreement with Snake that he would stay here when Delilah went to work, and took Kathy aside. "I've got some things to do."

Kathy gazed up at me, her blue eyes pale in the autumn light from a nearby window. "I'm glad you're not dead."

"I'm glad *you're* not dead, too."

"Well, I'm gladder."

We ended with a long kiss that was salty from the tears

streaming down her face. We talked for a while longer, and then when I saw she was getting drowsy again, I said good-bye.

"Don't die this time," she said, as I walked out the door.

"Don't you, either."

"That's always been one of my main goals. Not to die."

FORTY-THREE

I WASN'T GOING TO BAG Bert without turning the entire Northwest inside out, so I decided to go after easier quarry.

When I called the Sheffield headquarters they told me Kalpesh was out of the building and probably wouldn't return before tomorrow morning. The Maddox people said Deborah Driscoll had signed out to go to a meeting with some campaign donors. I was pretty sure Kalpesh had been feeding information to the Maddox campaign through Deborah, but was suspicious of Bert's claim that an insider in the Sheffield camp had helped cause the airplane crash. I simply did not believe it. There was no way Kalpesh had leaked information that helped get his candidate killed.

When I drove to Deborah's condo on Capitol Hill, the lights were on in her unit. The streets were dry and the sky was gray, scudding clouds pushed along by a cold wind. In the west, the dying sunset had become a scratch of orange on the horizon. The streetlights were just beginning to come on. It had been my impression that Kathy and I had spent only a few minutes at Delilah's getting reacquainted, but somehow two hours were missing from my afternoon.

I parked on the street and walked to Deborah's building. She buzzed me in. Remembering that Deborah must have been the woman in the other room when Snake and I visited Kalpesh's fourteenth-floor digs, I wondered if I was going to now catch Kalpesh hiding in her place. "Thomas," Deborah said, pulling open the front door and leaning on it. "How nice to see you. Come in. Come in."

She was in a skirt, stocking feet, and a beige blouse. Her face was slightly flushed, as if she'd been running around tidying. Or hiding a man in the back room. As usual, she was vivacious to the point almost of caricature.

"Have a seat. Oh, I got a call," she said, picking up her cell off a table. She gave me a mischievous look. "It's from you."

"I wanted to see you in person, anyway."

"Sure. What is it?" As comfortable as a cat in the sun, she tucked her legs beneath her on a love seat. I sat across from her on the sofa.

"There are things going on in these two campaigns that aren't right. We talked about it the other day."

Deborah's smile produced a dimple in her cheek. "Why do I get the feeling you're about to chew me out?"

"The other night I tracked Kalpesh to your doorstep. He's the Sheffield leak, isn't he?"

Deborah resettled herself on the love seat as if I'd knocked her off balance. "Whew. I wasn't expecting that."

"You denying it?"

"You mean am I denying that he was at my place the other night? Or am I denying he's spying for us?"

"Are you denying he was feeding, or is feeding, you information from the Sheffield campaign?"

"I don't understand how this affects you."

"A plane with eleven people on board went down. Since I've been asking about it, I've been warned off by the FBI and the NTSB. There are men parked in front of my house in a government vehicle. A reporter who was looking into it with us is in the hospital. Her husband is dead. Now tell me I'm wrong about you receiving information from Kalpesh."

She came off the love seat and sat next to me, followed by a draft of warm air that was suffused with her scent, like fresh-cut apples and peach blossoms. Her voice grew soft. "Thomas, you're the only straight shooter in our whole office. And I feel awful for what you've gone through." She was sagging against me on the sofa so that I could feel the side of her thigh against mine. She touched my hand, her fingers shorter and bonier than I'd expected. "I thought you were going off the deep end with these accusations when we spoke before, but I've had a chance to mull it over and now I'm not so sure. Do you really think the Sheffield crash was not an accident?"

"It was murder."

"I respectfully disagree, and I'm sure most everyone else you run into is going to disagree, too."

"You guys were all so certain Maddox was going to win. Why?"

"Good Lord! Thomas, if we'd had any inkling anybody was going to get hurt . . . You can't believe that, can you?" She was wheedling now, scooting closer. I remembered enough of the single life to know what she was leading up to. She believed Kathy was out in the ocean and I was a widower, so it was possible she was working her way up to offering a mercy fuck. Or maybe Deborah just liked to have her fun where she found it. I didn't know her well enough to say either way.

"I believe you knew something. The polls had Maddox down by fifteen, eighteen, even twenty points, but you were all cocky as hell about winning."

"Cocky? I wouldn't use that word. We were—"

"Conceited."

"Confident. Thomas, I'll never admit this in public, but there were . . . notions being passed down. I guess, we knew *something* was going to happen. I thought it was going to be fairly innocuous, like vote rigging."

"Vote rigging is innocuous?"

"Maybe it's not exactly innocuous, but it's not eleven people dead, either."

"Tell me about it."

"They've got these new electronic ballot counters, and there have been rumors circulating that the people supplying and running them favor Maddox, and that . . . well, maybe they'd be inclined to push a certain button enough times to put Maddox in the lead."

"You thought the election was rigged?"

"Only that it was a possibility."

"Holy crap."

She flinched, gave me a look meant to be playful, and leaned against my arm. "Don't get worked up about it. We didn't engineer it. We weren't even sure it was going to happen. It was just cocktail-party rumors."

"You realize what you're saying here? You suspected there

was going to be election fraud, and you didn't go to the authorities?"

"We heard a rumor. How many rumors have we heard this fall?"

"Did you hear a rumor there was going to be a plane crash?"

"Of course not."

"Why not go to the authorities about the vote rigging?"

"Thomas, you don't actually believe Sheffield's husband would make a better senator than James, do you?"

"You're not going to give me an ends-justifies-the-means talk, are you? Because it's beginning to sound like you believe it's okay to subvert the democratic process if things aren't going your way."

"We're getting kind of intense here. Tell you what." She bounded off the sofa, strode across the room, made two drinks, and brought them back, handing one to me. "I know you don't drink. Ginger ale. It'll cheer you up."

All I could think about was the numbing depression that descended on me the last time I ate the meal she prepared for me, and Bert's ridiculous warning to not accept food or drink from anyone. Not that I thought she was poisoning me . . . or that my earlier depression was related to anything I'd eaten or drunk . . . but then . . . I put the glass to my lips and pretended to imbibe.

"Deborah, tell me everything you know about Kalpesh's activities."

She frowned.

"Listen to me. Somebody told me the plane was going down three days before it happened. Obviously I didn't believe him or I would have tried to stop the flight. Because somebody knew it was going down before it did, I have to think there was some sort of plan involved, that it was not an accident. Right now there are people in Seattle whose job it is to make sure none of this comes to light. They're murdering people."

"You think they put that reporter in the hospital?"

"Yes. Her husband's dead."

"Thomas, you're scaring me." She put her drink on the

table and came into my arms. After a bit, I realized she was crying. And then, before I could figure out how to put a halt to it, she was kissing me, her lips as salty as Kathy's had been an hour earlier. My first thought was that she was a good kisser—excellent, in fact—but my second thought was that this wasn't a contact I wanted, and for a split second I tried to think of what the appropriate response would be if Kathy were still out of the picture, because any other response might give away too much. My hesitation was just enough that she took it as encouragement and began to slip off my sport coat.

"Whoa. Whoa," I said, disentangling myself and standing beside the couch. "This is too soon. It's too soon."

She smiled in a manner that was half lascivious and half calculating, looked at my trousers, and said, "Are you sure?"

"You're not going to tell me what you know, are you?"

"This isn't something I can just hand out like Halloween candy. I have to think about it."

"People are dying."

"All right. You've got me scared. But I need a day to think it over."

"Do me a favor, will you? Don't tell Kalpesh we talked."

"Of course not."

═══ FORTY-FOUR ═══

IT WAS TEN-THIRTY in the morning, and the doctors were considering whether to discharge me from the hospital. I wasn't ready for tackle football on the lawn, but the worst was over. I'd been up often enough to know I could do considerably more than people gave me credit for, and my brain was beginning to function normally, even if my stomach wasn't; funny how a flagpole through your intestines can disrupt digestion. Most of my memory from the night of the bombing had returned. Home care meant I could battle the aches with pain pills instead of the intravenous morphine drip.

Having later recognized me and made all the connections, Dorothy MacDonald, the nurse from Naselle, had gone to an Oregon newspaper with her story of caring for one of the supposed Sheffield crash victims after the accident. Clearly, nobody believed her or it would have made the national news.

In the days after finding Kathy, I spotted Snake on the street and, thinking he was Bert, followed him into a grocery store and demolished a good portion of two aisles in a demented endeavor to tear him to shreds. We fled before the cops arrived.

A lot of things had happened since Kathy's return. For two days I tailed Kalpesh. I slapped an illegal tap on his landline at his condo, but still wasn't able to track down his contact. I interviewed him, told him what I knew, and begged him to give me a name, but he resolutely denied passing information to anybody. Maybe he was telling the truth. There were a lot of people working for Sheffield. I couldn't pick on him just because he was the only one I knew well. Snake and I speculated that it was possible the campaign offices had been bugged and the killers had gotten their timetables from that source—it wasn't like campaign headquarters hadn't been bugged before.

A few days after I brought Kathy back to Seattle, Kalpesh resigned from the Sheffield campaign and signed on with James Maddox. It was about the last thing I, or anybody else, had expected. After all, the Sheffield ticket was probably going to win the election. Kalpesh claimed that, although he had supported Jane Sheffield wholeheartedly, he had some major conflicts with Sheffield's husband. The defection was highlighted on the front page of both local papers, and Kalpesh gave several interviews designed to make the reshuffled Sheffield team look weak and the Maddox team robust. Still, the polls continued to favor Sheffield, albeit not by the landslide predictions of earlier days.

After spending a full day with Kathy, filling her in on the events subsequent to her death, getting reacquainted as one could do only with a wife who had come back from the grave, I went back to work for the Maddox campaign. Since Deborah Driscoll and Kalpesh were now working in the same office, it was the best way to keep an eye on both of them. People thought I was still in torment over the loss of my wife, so I couldn't go around looking as jubilant as I felt. Nor did anybody give me anything more challenging to do than licking stamps and running errands. They treated me almost as if I were retarded, which suited me fine. In my spare time, which I had a lot of, I kept notes on Deborah's contacts, Kalpesh's phone calls, tracked who they met, and monitored their day-to-day activities. I was hoping to catch Kalpesh contacting somebody outside the organization, not that the killers would necessarily still be in contact. He did make some secretive calls, but when I tracked them, they were to friends at the Sheffield headquarters, personal stuff.

Bert kept in touch using stolen cellphones, while I—at Bert's direction—rotated through various phones borrowed from friends or co-workers. Bert continued to insist all our communications be on the phone, claiming he had his hands full shadowing NTSB investigators and trying to cultivate somebody else from the media as an ally. I knew Snake had warned him about the beating he'd taken in his stead. Neither the FBI nor the NTSB investigators had made any major announcements; the official plane crash investigation had not been completed. No matter how much I implored, Bert refused to divulge how he knew the plane was going to go down.

The week prior to the bombing saw multiple phone and email threats against James Maddox. Probably because they thought I was still in serious mourning, I was left out of the loop when it came to investigating the threats. A few days before the bombing at Garfield High School, Winston Seagram from the FBI began spending time with Maddox. It wouldn't do to have both senatorial candidates from Washington State offed, would it? Not that anybody important believed the Sheffield flight was murder. Even so, an assassination on top of an accident was going to pull down unwelcome attention.

The threats to Maddox put everybody on alert. We brought in new security grunts, several of whom had formerly worked either for the Secret Service or local police departments. Maddox even brought in people from his own security company, Protection Dot Com. The ex–Secret Service guys had all kinds of ideas for screening people and processing different venues, but underneath it all, what impressed me most about the commotion was that Maddox actually seemed scared. He hadn't shown much emotion over Sheffield's crash, but these threats to his own life? With more ardor in his voice than I'd heard in a while, he grumbled, "I don't mind serving in the goddamned Senate for six years, but I do mind getting my head shot off because I'm trying to do a public service."

Because of our precautions, the explosion at the Garfield High School gymnasium came as a surprise, nobody more surprised than me.

It had been a long day. Meetings all morning. A five-hundred-dollar-a-plate luncheon in Bellevue. A talk at the University of Washington at three. A dinner with special donors and a few of the cognoscenti in downtown Seattle, and straight from there to the speaking engagement at Garfield. It wasn't until afterward when Maddox and his followers filed out to the foyer that Kalpesh approached me. "Thomas, we're having a hard time tracking down that briefcase James always carries. Have you seen it?"

"Nope."

"I wonder if you might go back and check the podium?"

"Sure."

I didn't appreciate the way Kalpesh had managed to weasel himself into Maddox's camp and become my boss, or the way he seemed to be treating me like a servant. I didn't much like anything about Kalpesh anymore. Just when they needed him most, he'd gone AWOL from the campaign Kathy had died for—or almost died for. He was one of those guys who, once you started hating him, you couldn't stop. Either that, or I was going a little nutso myself; maybe more of the latter than the former. Ruth Ponzi was out of the hospital but not back at work. Including the bombing, there would be fifteen dead in all, though how much of it was connected, I could not say.

When I went back into the gymnasium, the crowd had dispersed to the point where there were only about thirty people, many shuffling toward the exits. On the way into the gym, I received a call from Bert Slezak.

"Where are you?" Bert asked.

"Garfield High School. Maddox just made a speech."

"We have to talk. You and me. But I don't want to meet you if you're going to beat the hell out of me."

"I'm not making any promises one way or the other. Half the time, I don't know what I'm going to do anymore."

"So now you know how my life is."

"I'm not that twitter-pated yet."

Because my phone reception was cutting in and out, I began heading for an outside door on the far side of the building. I would fetch the briefcase in a minute. It wasn't going anywhere. "Where do you want to meet?"

"How about in front of a police station?"

"Funny. Hey, listen. The phone reception is really crappy in here, so I'm—"

And then my ears were ringing, and it felt as if somebody had tried to rip my jacket off. My balls hurt, and when I tried to move, there was only blinding pain. It took a few minutes to orient myself. The phone was gone. One shoe was missing. So was most of my coherent thought. I was straining to figure out what had happened, watching the wounded straggle out, the firefighters and other rescue personnel maintaining their distance because of the threat of a second bomb. I was standing with a rod through my torso; it had pinned me to the bleachers. Then the woman crawled over and gave me a list of messages for her family.

I was slowly bleeding to death and I knew it. But then, against orders, chased by two firefighters in full gear, James Maddox burst into the gym. Maddox had a look on his face I can still remember vividly, a look that said, "Hey, this can't go on. People are hurt. Time to do something." Somewhere along the line I must have lost consciousness, because I woke up on the floor with Maddox hovering over me, the spike still protruding from my abdomen. It hurt like hell, and I let out a caterwauling I'm ashamed of to this day. The two firefighters who'd come in behind him brushed Maddox aside and picked me up. I heard one of them say, "Scoop and run."

They carried me out so quickly Maddox was only able to get a hand on one of my legs, but that was how the news photographer captured it, and that was the photo that went around the world, no firefighters in sight, just a cropped photo of the senatorial candidate rushing out of the bombed-out building with my bloody torso and my upside-down head in the foreground. The thrust of the accompanying story was that Maddox was loyal to his people, not a man who brooked red tape or impractical regulations when lives were on the line.

Overnight Maddox's poll numbers climbed, putting him three points ahead of Sheffield instead of twelve behind. He was leading for the first time all autumn. That single gutsy action had revealed to the world what he was made of; it had brought all of Maddox's history as a police officer to the foreground and forged a new people's hero.

Earlier on the same day they released me, James Maddox stood with a film crew outside my hospital room discussing whether or not they would be allowed inside to film. I didn't want anything to do with it. I'd inadvertently become the symbol that restored Maddox's campaign hopes, but I didn't want to be the instrument that propelled Maddox into office, not if I could help it.

Outside my room, Snake and one of my doctors squabbled with Deborah Driscoll, Maddox, and Kalpesh, all of whom argued in favor of the photo op. Deborah kept peeking in, giving me a wink as if we were co-conspirators.

"Thomas?" Maddox said, striding into the room and touching my shoulder affectionately. I noticed Snake was keeping the cameraman out in the hall. "I'm glad you made it."

"Me too."

"I've been up to visit a couple of times, but you were asleep."

"I must have thought you were here to give a speech," I said, grinning.

He didn't find my comment amusing. Deborah stood beside him, chewing her lip, her weight on one leg, giving me the look she gave to men, the one that made each of us feel she had a special thing going for us. She had fixed on my ideology and realized I wasn't exactly thrilled with the thought of Maddox becoming our next senator.

"What we're going to try to do here is get some film of you and me greeting each other," Maddox said. We'd already gone through this charade—he'd made the request, I'd said no, and Snake had taken them out into the corridor to say no again.

"I told you how I feel about that."

"Christ, Thomas. I saved your life."

"I know, and I'll figure out a way to repay you, but not like this."

"It's little enough to ask."

"Yes, it is, but it's not going to happen. I was wondering about the bomb. Did they ever figure out why it didn't go off when you were on the podium?"

There was something in the tone of my comment that made Maddox step back. He didn't say anything. Neither did anybody else. I had the feeling that people around him didn't speak much about the bombing. He leaned forward and turned on his speechifying voice. "It's been a tragedy for a lot of people, but especially for America. Anytime anarchists try to take away the democratic process, we all lose. Just give me the goddamned photo op."

Behind him, Deborah saw the glint of temper in my eyes.

"Who placed the bomb?"

"The FBI's working on it."

"Are they still staking out my house?"

"What? Who?"

"The FBI. They were staking out my house. Somebody was."

"I don't know anything about your house. This was probably a radical fringe group. There's some speculation they may have rigged the Apple flight to take me down, and got Jane Sheffield instead."

"The FBI's saying the plane crash was an assassination?"

"There's been speculation in that direction. This is all hush-hush. Remember, before we canceled we had booked that same airline. When they finally arrest some of these people and question them, we'll know more. But remember, we're not sure these people are involved with the plane crash. At this point, it's all conjecture."

"They were after *you* the whole time?"

"Possibly. It's beginning to look like somebody can't stand the thought of me in the Senate."

"Yeah," I said. "A little over half the voters in the state."

If he'd been angry before, he was furious now. As a way of exculpation, Deborah said, "Don't worry about it. He's on drugs. He doesn't know what he's saying."

Apropos of nothing, Maddox said, "There's talk we might never catch the bombers."

How odd, I thought, that Maddox, who, back in his SPD days, had carried a reputation for abject cowardice, had shown such outstanding disregard for his own safety the night of the bombing. Could it have been because he was virtually certain there was no second bomb? Could it have been that while the firefighters and other rescue personnel were waiting for the second bomb to go off, the old tried-and-true tactic of terrorists, Maddox had foreknowledge that it wasn't there?

"A horrible thing," Maddox said. "Horrible, horrible. But in the end, what with all the favorable news footage we've been getting, it was actually lucky for the race."

"You're running just about the luckiest campaign anybody ever ran, aren't you?"

Maddox gave me a flat look that assured me he didn't know whether I was being sarcastic or was just hell-bent on getting myself fired. The flunkies behind him turned and headed for the door. There was no doubt in their minds, or in Deborah's, that I'd turned on him. Maddox was the only one who didn't seem sure of it. Or maybe he was just so intent on getting the photo op that he didn't want to let it sink in. Deborah shook her head almost imperceptibly, then smiled, again almost imperceptibly. Maddox said nothing as he left. Deborah lagged behind.

"You going to use those?" I asked.

"What? Use what?"

I nodded at the cellphone in her hand, with which she'd been surreptitiously taking pictures of my meeting with Maddox.

"If you were in my place, would you?" she asked.

"I'm not in your place."

"If you were?"

"Part of the reason I'm not in your place is I never would have snapped those pictures."

"I wouldn't be judging others too harshly if I were you."

"What do you mean by that?"

"You were spying on Kalpesh and me in my apartment."

I had no reply for that because it was true. By the time my face cooled off, she was gone. She was right, though. There were times when I felt the ends justified the means and acted on it just as often as anybody else. As much as I wanted to hold other people's feet to the fire, I needed to own up to my share of guilt, too.

FORTY-FIVE

FOR ALMOST HALF A MINUTE after Kathy opened the front door to Delilah's house I couldn't do anything but stand like a dummy and drink her in. In our entire relationship, we'd never had a moment quite like it. Our first real reunion since her death and resurrection and my bombing. In some ways seeing Kathy in that doorway was like seeing her for the first time. She was almost a stranger but in other ways was as familiar as an old shoe under the bed, though quite a bit prettier. We both knew our relationship would never be the same, that there would always be a before and an after. Before she died—after she died. Before the bomb—after the bomb. It didn't mean our relationship would be any worse or better or weaker or stronger, but we would have befores and afters.

We had both spent time under a doctor's care. We had both been drugged for days on end. We had both been scared out of our wits at the bedside of the other. Today I was the quasi-invalid and Kathy was the healthy one. Despite her regained health, I could see that hiding out was gnawing at her sanity. Kathy was a people person who needed to be out in the world. She thrived on social interaction, and this enforced isolation and idleness was withering her spirit.

After we finished staring at each other, Kathy ran sliding across the floor in her socks and kissed me exuberantly. "It's so good to have you back." We soon found ourselves in a large, overstuffed chair in the living room, her bottom squarely in my lap. "Glad to see you're still alive, buster."

"Glad to see *you're* still alive, sister."

"I guess this is how we're going to greet each other from now on."

"You talking about the woody?"

"Uh . . . no. I was glad to see you're alive."

"Oh, right. That's what I meant. I am alive."

She laughed, and the kissing lasted longer than the first round. She sat back and said, "So how long am I going to have to hide out? Not that Delilah isn't a wonderful host, but this isn't my house and I need to get back to work. Hell is being trapped in another woman's house because maybe a cabal of renegade government ops will maybe want to kill you if you maybe leave. This whole thing is so screwed up."

"Bert saved your life once. We have to respect his judgment on this, crazy as it sounds. Have you heard from him?"

"Not a peep. And you're right. I think. It's just that I've got cabin fever."

"Snake tells me they've talked, but he still doesn't have a clue where Bert is. He went out to their grandmother's place in Enumclaw, but as far as she knew Bert hadn't been there. I'm going out to check again in a few minutes."

"Why not wait for Elmer?"

"I'll be okay by myself."

"After Enumclaw, what?" She kissed me.

"We'll see where that leads."

"And then what?" She kissed me again.

"And then . . . Oh, I get it. Well, that might be a while. I'm still beat all to hell. But keep your motor revving, sister. I'll get my strength back shortly."

"I'm so glad you're doing better. I never did give a rat's ass for Maddox, but he saved your life, and I'll be forever grateful to him for that."

"Bert saved yours. What do you think about turning him over to the police for kidnapping?"

"If the police get hold of him he'll clam up like a . . . well, like a clam, and he's the truest link you have to whoever brought that plane down. *If* somebody brought it down."

"I keep thinking he's going to confess to having a part in it."

"I'm still having a hard time believing it was taken down on purpose."

"Of course you are. It means a U.S. senator was murdered right out in front of God and our drying laundry, and if a federal agency is working to cover it up, it means the feds are in on it, too. Who wants to believe our government is that corrupt?"

"You're right. It's about what you're willing to believe."

"In the hospital I had a lot of time to think. Kalpesh steered you onto that airplane, and after he began working for Maddox, he steered me into that gym."

"Don't go blaming this on Kalpesh."

"He sent me right to the bomb. If I hadn't accidentally detoured, I would be in a thousand pieces, just like that poor janitor."

"Thomas, you don't know he's involved in anything other than a love affair."

"He switched allegiances pretty fast."

"That's true. He was the last person I expected to jump ship."

"You remember anything else about that day with Bert?"

"Not much. I got in his car, opened a bottle of water, and basically the next thing I knew, I was here at Delilah's. I've been thinking he put something in that water."

"I was thinking the same thing."

I showered and changed into some clean clothes Snake had procured for me while I was in the hospital, and then I left just as Snake came in. To confuse whoever might be triangulating on my phone, Snake and I swapped cellphones, which we had been doing ever since I'd discovered I was being followed. Kathy had been at Delilah's almost six days. A total of sixteen days had elapsed since the crash. The news on the car radio said the NTSB had completed their report on the matter of the Sheffield plane crash and there would be an official pronouncement the following morning. I was halfway to Enumclaw when Snake's cellphone in my pocket chimed. "Thomas?"

"Yeah?"

"I just got a call for you. That redhead, Deborah Driscoll. The hot one."

"What did she say?"

"She was on her way to a meeting. Said she's been thinking about your discussion in the hospital and wants to talk to you in private about Ruth Ponzi and some other stuff. Said you could find her at her place."

"When?"

"All she said was 'later.' "

"Thanks."

ENUMCLAW WAS WET AND COLD, clouds scudding across the sky in eighteen shades of gray. I could see Mount Rainier today, its snow-covered presence looming to the south like the backdrop to a fairy tale.

I parked in the same spot we'd used the other day and hiked across the property. When I got close to the small trailer Bert lived in, I heard what sounded like a Christian radio station blaring from one of the barns. Bert's little pickup truck was parked in front of his trailer, the engine cold. In the back was an unfurled tarpaulin and ropes tied to the tie-downs on the side of his truck. There was a small swatch of blood on the sidewall. I wondered if Bert could have been poaching deer. Or maybe I was looking at my future. I hadn't brought a weapon and didn't have a plan. Beating the hell out of Snake in the mistaken belief he was Bert had taken some of the starch out of my anger. The morphine I'd been on had taken more.

Still, when he answered the door, there was something about the way he said "Hey, man" that annoyed me more than it should have. Without giving it a whole lot of thought, I swung, got a solid poke in, and sent him flying backward. I'd more or less promised myself this wouldn't happen, but what the hell. When I went inside, he was reaching for something under the bed. I kicked him in the ass and sent him sprawling. He hit his head on the end wall of the trailer and bounced back, coming at me unexpectedly like a whirlwind. Despite his training, I'd like to think under normal circumstances he wouldn't have had a chance, but he managed to get a knee into my stomach, which was still bandaged and already aching from the exertion of hitting him. I went down hard on my back, Bert on top of me, grasping for something off to my right, probably a weapon. The quarters were so tight I began to believe I would never get him off me. I managed to grab his right arm and chomped down hard until he screamed. At the same time my left hand reached out for anything that might serve as a weapon.

All I found was a cat's litter box. When his mouth was at its widest, at the apex of his scream, I scooped up a handful of litter and shoved it into his mouth. For a few moments as I watched him choke and claw at his mouth, I thought I might have killed him. Then he gagged and rolled off me.

All I could think about was Kathy, drugged into a stupor in that miserable rented farmhouse in Naselle while I thought she was dead. I stood up, groping around in the shadows until I found the weapon he'd been reaching for. It was a Taser, a stun gun designed to emit powerful but nonfatal electric impulses. I'd been Tased before and knew how much it hurt and how quickly it put most people out of commission. The thought that he'd been willing to inflict that much pain on a man who'd just gotten out of the hospital riled me enough that I switched it on and touched his shoulder with it. It jolted him off his knees and onto his back, where he twittered like a hooked Dolly Varden.

He still hadn't cleared all the cat litter out of his mouth and was trying to spit, his eyes turning into moons of panic. Coughing and hacking, he crawled out of the trailer and into the wet yard, where he stood up and tried to get water from the garden hose. "Why are you doing this?" he gasped, speaking through puffy lips.

"Why am I doing this? Could it be because you kidnapped and drugged my wife? Because you immobilized her with plaster casts and head wraps for ten days? Could that be the reason?"

"I saved her life."

"You let ten other people fly off to their deaths." I smacked him, but he rebounded almost immediately, after which I hit him again. My knuckles hurt. The violent activity had ripped the stitches in my side. I would be lying if I said I was proud of what I was doing, because I wasn't, though I felt helpless to stop myself.

I could feel blood running down the inside of my shirt. I

knew if I continued, I was going to kill him and maybe my-self. I didn't want to kill him. Hell, I didn't want to kill any-body. I knew from experience, unlike most types of personal pain that eventually fade away or get reasoned out of exis-tence, the pain of killing a man never faded. There was some-thing else going on, too. Bert apparently was willing to take any amount of punishment. It was almost as if he wanted me to beat him to death. He had a certain amount of masochism built into his psyche, as did his brother. As boys they'd taken so much punishment from their father, they now prided themselves on their ability to withstand brutal treatment. It was one of the reasons Elmer had been such a standout on the rodeo circuit. Part of him liked getting hurt.

I could hear the stitching in his shirt rip as I began drag-ging him across the yard toward my car. "What are you go-ing to do with me?"

"I don't know."

"They wouldn't have listened. Even Kathy didn't listen. I started to tell her the plane was going to go down, and she looked at me like I was freaking out, so I gave her that bull-shit about killing somebody and being wanted by the police."

"How did you get to the airfield so fast that day? You had to have been in the area already. You were following us, weren't you?"

"I'm telling you, I was worried about Kathy's safety even before I knew she was going to take that flight. So what if I was following the two of you? It saved her life, didn't it?"

"You drugged her for ten days. What was the plan? Going to sell her on the black market?"

"Hell, no. I love . . . *like* Kathy too much to ever let any-thing happen to her. I was going to tell her everything, but when I went out there and let her get most of the stuff out of her system, she wouldn't buy it. You did, though. You were in the perfect mood to help me run down these bastards. I *was* going to tell you about Kathy."

"When?"

"I don't know." I hit him again. He shook it off and didn't lose his footing. "I have to warn you, if you kill me, my pris-oner will end up dying, too."

"Who?"

"My prisoner. He's going to die if I don't get back to him. You'll never find him without my help, either."

"Your prisoner? What the hell are you talking about?"

"I'll show you. Afterward, if you still feel like taking me in, I'll go without a hassle."

"Where is this prisoner?"

Bert started walking. Wary of trickery, I followed. I'd hurt him badly, so the chance of him pulling off any unexpected gymnastics was only fair to middling, but still, the possibility existed. He led me to the barn where I'd heard the music earlier, pulled open a large door that dragged against the dirt floor, and escorted me to the back, where there was a kerosene lantern hanging on a post. The space was largely empty, the sky showing through the roof in at least two spots, one wall canting inward to the point that the next moderate earthquake would likely bring the whole structure tumbling down. Bert turned the sound on the portable radio down but not off. In the rear of the barn, in what must have at one time been a horse stall, a chesty man sat on a rickety wooden chair, his arms bound behind his back, his legs duct-taped to the chair. A strip of duct tape had been pulled across his eyes in a way that was going to be painful to remove. His nose was flattened and bleeding. He looked as badly beaten as Bert did.

"Who is it?" I said.

"See for yourself," Bert whispered. "But don't talk out loud. As long as he doesn't get a fix on our voices, he won't know who we are."

"He doesn't know who you are?"

"I got him from behind, then got the tape on his face before he could recover. Even if he'd caught a glimpse, I was wearing a ski mask. He's clueless."

It was one thing to postulate about bad guys running around the country doing evil; it was another to kidnap one of them and hold him hostage. At least I assumed the prisoner had something to do with the alleged Sheffield conspiracy. While I struggled with it, Bert stood to one side and crossed his arms, his bruised lips curled into a snarl.

By the time I figured out who the bloodied man was, Bert

had sidled over to a cubbyhole in the dark and come out with what I was slow to recognize as a beanbag gun, a riot-control device that, at this range and given my condition, might well be lethal. For a gun lover, he certainly collected a lot of odd-ball weapons that weren't technically guns. The man on the chair was Timothy Hoagland, the lead investigator for the National Transportation Safety Board. Hoagland wore suit trousers, brown wingtip shoes, a patterned ochre tie, and an off-white shirt spattered with his own blood. His jacket was missing. "This is insane," I said. "You can't keep him."

"Is somebody there?" asked Hoagland, who could barely hear us over the music. "Who's there?"

Bert pivoted and fired the riot-control weapon. The bean-bag struck me in the chest, knocking me onto the straw floor. I felt as if I'd been hit by a cannonball. I'd been warned by the doctors that until I was completely healed I wasn't to take any sharp blows: no motorcycle riding, boxing, mountain biking, skateboarding, or what have you. I'm sure the doctor would have included getting knocked down by a riot gun if he'd known there was a chance I might run into Bert Slezak.

FORTY-SIX

BY THE TIME I GOT BACK to my feet, Bert was in the stall smacking Hoagland. The pain I was feeling in my gut was as bad as the day of the bombing, maybe worse. I was pretty sure I was bleeding internally. Hoagland was beginning to feel pain, too, and wasn't shy about verbalizing his displeasure, though the radio was turned loud enough to muffle his screams.

Bert had retrieved the Taser from my jacket pocket while I was writhing in the straw, so I had no weapon now.

"Stop hitting him," I said.

"Why? Because it's not nice? Look at this, pal." He pushed his own face in my general direction.

"You deserved it."

"Think he doesn't?"

"There's somebody else here, isn't there?" Hoagland was hearing bits of our conversation over the squalling radio, but because of the tape across his eyes, he couldn't see either of us.

"Of course there's somebody here, asshole." Bert whacked him across the side of the face with an open palm.

"Stop it," I said.

"Whoever you are, please, please get this brute—" Bert hit him so hard both man and chair capsized into the straw. I wouldn't have thought Bert had the capability to generate that much force. He walked around and laboriously pulled the entire package upright. I wish I'd had the energy or presence of mind to rush him when he turned his back, for the opportunity wasn't likely to arise a second time, but I was still stunned and hurting badly from the beanbag gun.

"You've gone crackers," I said.

"Don't you see? The report was written before he got to town. Everything he's been doing here is a sham."

"You've got to let him go."

"Like hell." Addressing Hoagland, whose face was in shadows cast by the kerosene lantern, Bert yelled, "Tell my friend here what you told me."

"I didn't tell you anything. You—"

Touching the Taser to his thigh, Bert zapped Hoagland, who hollered and jerked. The Taser explained how a small man like Bert had managed to get somebody of Hoagland's girth and weight off his feet, off the street, and into that chair. When Bert Tased him again, I moved forward to stop him, but before I could accomplish my objective, Bert casually swung around and shot me in the hip with the beanbag gun. The blow spun me into the straw.

"Those are supposed to be used at a distance," I moaned.

"Hurts, don't it?"

"You planning to kill us both?"

"You're not paying attention. You're on my team here."

"Am I? Then give me that gun."

As I struggled to my feet, Hoagland began talking. "Okay. It's all true. I worked for the CIA for eighteen years and then for shell organizations that contracted for the Company. I've done my share of misdeeds, but it was always for God and country. All I know about this plane crash is what I told you. It was explained to me that there might be some unpatriotic speculation concerning whether or not it was an accident, so I was to handle the press relations and write a report that clarified things."

"You were told this before the plane went down?" Bert asked.

"After, of course."

"You were told prior."

"Have it your way."

"So you knew a plane was going down with a senator on it a week before it happened? What exactly were you told to clarify in this report?" Bert asked.

"That it was an accident."

"Even if it wasn't?"

"Even if it wasn't. You realize you're in serious trouble. They're probably looking for me right now."

"Maybe, but unless you got a locator shoved up your ass, they're not going to find you. Do you have a locator shoved up your ass?"

Hoagland didn't reply. I could see he was more frightened than he wanted to let on, because, while his face remained as impassive as it had the day I saw him at Boeing Field, his legs quivered. It has been repeatedly demonstrated that under torture, people say whatever it is they think their interrogators want to hear, so it didn't seem to me there was any quick way to verify Hoagland's confession. There was no guessing what clues Bert had given him before my arrival.

Bert said, "It wasn't an accident, was it?"

"No."

I was standing now, moving closer while Bert stepped away from Hoagland. Though weary and beaten, I sensed that despite everything I knew about torture's ultimate ineffectiveness, Hoagland was telling the truth.

"Who told you to whitewash the investigation?" I whispered into Hoagland's ear, knowing it would be almost impossible later to identify a whisper.

"That's not how it works."

"How *does* it work?"

"Somebody calls and tells me how it's going to be. They don't give names."

"I know you have at least one name."

"I don't."

Bert looked at me and shook his head. Apparently he'd pursued this line of questioning earlier without success. It was weird. Bert and I had been antagonists moments earlier, and now, without even knowing how it had happened, I was assisting in the torture of a fellow human. "You ever get a call like that before?"

"A few times."

"From whom?"

"Fuck you."

"When?"

This he was reluctant to answer until Bert touched his back with the Taser. He didn't push the button, probably because I was close enough to punch him if he did, but nonetheless

Hoagland replied. "Couple of crashes. You remember Jameson?"

"No."

"Wellstone?"

"I remember. The question on the table is, who brought the Sheffield flight down?"

"I don't know. That's not my end of it."

"Who do you think?"

"Could have been two or three different outfits. They do stuff in South America. Sometimes we bring them up here and let them work."

"Who ordered it?"

"I don't know. I really don't."

"Your end of it is to whitewash the investigation so everybody agrees it was an accident?" Hoagland hesitated. "Who else knew about this? Any local authorities?"

"God, no."

"FBI?"

"Not all of them."

"Which?"

"Winston Seagram. I'm not sure how many others."

"But there *are* others?"

"There would have to be."

"And as far as you know, Senator Sheffield was the target?"

"Obviously. Everybody else on that plane was riffraff."

He was beginning to show some attitude. I had been suspicious of what he was saying before, but the attitude was more believable than anything else he'd conveyed. It was the attitude of a predator, not a victim. Even as a prisoner, he found it difficult to drop the arrogance that came with power the way spare buttons came with a suit. "Why assassinate a senator?"

"Why do you think? There's a key election coming up, or don't you read the papers?"

"Why kill eleven people to get one?" I whispered.

"Easier for the masses to believe it was an accident."

"It's easier to put across a big lie than a little one?"

"Right. Can I have some water?"

Bert nodded at a pint bottle of water near the kerosene

lantern. I uncapped it and tipped it to Hoagland's lips. "How was the plane brought down?"

"Look, I don't know who brought the plane down or even how. There are lots of methods. Lots of ways. Just like you boys are going to die. Oh, there won't be any arrests or handcuffs. You boys are simply going to disappear. They'll ask you questions, too. And you'll give answers. After they're finished, you'll vanish. If they don't get you today, they'll put teams on you and get you tomorrow."

"You must think your cellphone is somewhere close by, huh?" Bert whispered. It was clear from the way Hoagland tipped his head to hear better that he had been counting on it. "Your cellphone? So they can triangulate on us? It's riding back and forth across Puget Sound on a ferry." Hoagland did a good job of not looking disappointed, but even so, I could see something in his slack facial muscles had changed.

Bert gestured for me to follow him toward the door of the barn. When we were a sufficient distance from Hoagland and the radio, he said, "I think we squeezed this plum about dry. I been workin' him most of the day, and that's all I got. And don't look at me like that. You were askin' questions, too." Bert was grinning and I could see some of the same bravado and insanity Elmer displayed when he found himself in a bind. He was proud of his achievements here but knew he'd handed himself an enormous problem.

"You kidnapped him and now you don't have anything to show for it."

"The hell I don't. He as well as admitted the plane was brought down by a government agency. That the NTSB report is a cover-up."

"He didn't say the government brought it down."

"He's working for a federal agency, and they're covering it up. It was the government. You heard him."

"What I heard was a man tied to a chair telling you what you wanted him to say." Bert was right. I did believe the confession, but I had to play devil's advocate, because everything we'd heard was not only inadmissible in a court of law but also in the court of public opinion.

"I didn't prompt any of that. That all came out of his own brain."

"I'm to take your word for that?"

"The week before that plane went down I saw this asshole meet with James Maddox. That's how I knew it was going to happen."

"Hoagland and Maddox?"

"That's how I knew to get Kathy out of there. I knew Timothy has been specializing in plane crashes."

"That's it? You saw him with Maddox?"

"Well, I didn't exactly see them together. But they were in the same hotel. I ended up saving Kathy's life because of it. I would have saved them all if I could have. I would have run my truck into the plane, but all that would have done was put them into another plane. Which would have gone down. I'd be locked up and they'd be dead. Kathy included."

"How was it you came to catch him in Maddox's vicinity?"

"It was just . . . I was just there."

"Why?"

"Thomas, you know if we let him go, he'll sic a team of agents on us. They'll spare no expense to track us down. I once saw them spend four million government dollars tracking down a clerk they thought needed to die, and he'd done a hell of a lot less than what we've been doing here. Whether you like it or not, you're in this up to your neck."

"And if we turn him over to the local police?"

"You give him to them, you'll have to turn me in, too. He knows there's two of us. You can't tell them you found him tied to a chair in some field." Bert grinned, then handed me the beanbag gun and the Taser. "I guarantee this. You turn me over to the cops, I'll be dead inside of two days. Suicide, burst appendix, brain aneurism, whatever. And your hunt for whoever tried to kill your wife and murdered all those others will hit a brick wall. He doesn't know who you are now, but he will as soon as you turn him over. Their cleanup squad will take you out; and Elmer, too. Kathy. Maybe even your paper boy and the guy does your taxes. That's how they work."

Hoagland had been eerily calm while threatening us, and if he was connected to people ruthless enough to take down a plane with eleven people on board, there would be no hesitation to eliminate a pest like Bert Slezak. Hoagland's threats had been matter-of-fact, a dull business transaction contemplated by a dull man. I'd seen his kind before and I trusted my gut. He'd threatened us because he thought we were lightweights and hoped to panic us into making a mistake, but the threats were genuine. We couldn't let him go. But we couldn't murder the man, either. And if we ever revealed who we were, we would eventually end up dead.

"Tell me about seeing Hoagland and Maddox before the crash," I said. It was the one piece out of all this information that stuck in my craw. James Maddox, my ex-boss, my friend, the man I'd felt beholden to for so many years, had taken a meeting with an individual who'd come to town to cover up a multiple murder—including the murder of my wife—and had taken that meeting prior to the Sheffield crash. I wanted to believe Bert was lying, but I couldn't. Hoagland said he'd been contacted about the crash investigation before the plane went down. I believed Hoagland. I also believed he was going to make sure we died if we gave him the chance.

"A week or so before the crash I saw one of Hoagland's flunkies at the Renaissance in Seattle," Bert said. "The guy was an operative I knew from a job we did together years ago. Hoagland came down to the lobby to talk with him. I hung around long enough to see Maddox come in, without his normal entourage. He walked right past them, like they didn't know each other, but you could tell they did. They had a meeting. Trust me on this. Or ask him yourself."

I went back and whispered the question in Hoagland's ear, and he jumped. Because of the cacophony of the radio, he hadn't expected me to be so close. "What?" he asked.

"You have a meeting with Maddox before the plane crash? Here in Seattle?"

"We're old friends. I met him in D.C. when he was in the House of Representatives. His company worked with mine."

"What did you talk about?"

"The weather. I told you. We're old friends."

"Did he know the plane was going down?" I touched the Taser to his shoulder but didn't fire it.

"If you're going to hurt me, he knew. Otherwise, he didn't."

I'd reached a wall I couldn't get through. Bert had mouse-trapped me. While he held the riot gun, I'd had no choice but to go along with the program, but now that I was holding the weapons, I could untie Hoagland, let him go free, drive him back to his hotel, and apologize—get Bert and me both killed. Or take him to the police and help him swear out a complaint against Bert—get Bert and me both killed.

There was little doubt Bert had committed a crime, but I hardly believed it a crime he should die for. Hoagland, on the other hand, had implicated himself in an ongoing felony per-petuated against the whole country, a plot to influence an election by removing one of the candidates. Power brokers in D.C. wanted Sheffield out of the Senate. In order to achieve that end, they'd murdered her and nine other people.

There was an underlying question even more basic than what I was asking. Did I trust Bert Slezak?

He'd saved Kathy's life.

He'd also kept her drugged for ten days and told her I was dead.

He'd called me at the gym seconds before the bomb went off. We still hadn't talked about that.

"The bomb," I said, walking back toward Bert.

"It was meant for you all along. They knew you were ask-ing questions. Don't you see? Make it look like it was Mad-dox they were after, when they were really trying to nail you. If people are setting bombs for Maddox, it turns him into a saint of sorts. Isn't that how they're playing it to the press now?"

"That bomb was meant for *me*?"

"How hard is it to fix a bomb so it goes off during a forty-minute speech? You can't tell me they screwed that up. If you can build a bomb, you can work a timer. I can't believe you haven't thought of this before."

"I've been on morphine."

"You on morphine now?"

"I've taken some pills, but I'm okay."

"Maddox worked a variation on what I think was the original plan by running in to get you. The public thought he was risking his life, but it was like betting on a two-headed nickel. He knew there was no second bomb."

"Why save me if they were trying to kill me?"

"Why not ask why he didn't go in right away?"

"You've got a point. Waiting for me to bleed out?"

"He'd save you, but not until he thought you were going to die anyway. Except he mistimed it and you survived."

I looked across the barn at Hoagland, who was struggling with his bonds. Bert followed my eyes and said, "In the old days, bombs used to be one of his specialties."

"You ask him about it?"

"I've asked, but you're welcome to give it a shot."

Thinking about how close I'd come to pulling the trigger on the Taser a moment earlier, I said, "No. I want this to end."

"How do you propose to do that?"

"I'm thinking."

"Kind of like holding a wolf by the ears, isn't it?"

"Your brother used that phrase a few days ago."

"You realize if the situation were reversed, we'd both be dead already."

═══ FORTY-SEVEN ═══

WE WERE ON INTERSTATE 90, Bert and I in the front seat of my Taurus, our package in the trunk. I'd already passed two state troopers parked alongside the road. An hour from now we could get stopped and nothing short of a dog team would find anything suspicious, but if we got pulled over now, we were going to end up in prison. Normal citizens didn't drive around with federal officials hog-tied in the trunks of their cars. Hoagland's condition wasn't going to make things any better for us.

"They'll find him up here," said Bert, who had argued vociferously that we dump Hoagland down a well or sink him in the ocean with weights anchored around his neck. "He had a bad rep in the Company. Even people who worked with him were scared of him."

"Are you saying you're scared of him?"

"Hell, yes. And you would be too if you had an ounce of common sense."

"If I had an ounce of common sense I would have called the police the minute you gave me the Taser back."

We drove up into the clouds toward the closed ski areas.

At this time of year there was often a light dusting of snow on the highest peaks, but the clouds had come in low enough to obscure them. Traffic was light except for big trucks laboring on the final grade at the summit, their stacks smudging the late afternoon with sooty diesel smoke. The peaks around us were dappled with alpenglow. We were heading for a place called Cabin Creek, about ten miles on the other side of Snoqualmie Pass. I'd cross-country skied there in the winter, when it was splendid, but any other time of year it was nothing more than an old unpaved road. When we pulled off the interstate and took the overpass into Cabin Creek, patches of blue sky appeared overhead. It was a typical weather pattern for the area, wet and rainy on the west side of the Cascade Range, dry and warmer on the east.

As I drove across the overpass and onto the rutted gravel road, Bert scanned the area for official vehicles, state, federal, or otherwise. "I think it's clear," he said.

There were no other cars on the dirt road, and it didn't look as if there had been for a while. The color of blue in the sky and the absence of sun indicated it would be dark soon. A quarter mile down the road, we stopped next to a gated side road. Bert and I looked at each other, then went around to the trunk, opened it, and considered the motionless lump inside the tarpaulin. Together we picked it up and lugged it west along a narrow path I remembered as a ski trail in the winter. We walked almost two hundred yards, well out of sight of the road, before we put him down. I leaned over and tried to catch my breath; Bert likewise. My stomach wound was still aching and bleeding from the beanbag hits. When some time had passed, Bert whispered, "I hear a car on the road."

"Crap!"

"Quick," Bert said. "Go back and shut the trunk. They see it open, they'll know we dumped something. They'll come back in here to see what it was."

There wasn't a lot of time to think about it. I jogged back to the road, but if there had been another vehicle roaming the vicinity, it was gone by the time I got there. I slammed the trunk, and by the time I turned around to go back, Bert was running down the slope toward me carrying a bunched-up canvas tarp against his chest.

"Hurry," he yelled. "Let's get the hell out of here."

"I want to check on Hoagland."

"Forget it. He's right behind me."

"You were supposed to loosen things. Not set him free."

"I cut one rope and he jumped up at me. He must have been playing possum."

"Christ."

"I know. I barely got out of there."

"Did he recognize you?"

"He didn't see me. He didn't have the tape all off his face, but it was close."

I reversed the car up the road, then turned it around and drove back the way we'd come, checking the rearview mirror repeatedly to see if Hoagland was chasing us on foot, but he wasn't anywhere in sight. Should he get disoriented, it could easily take Hoagland hours to make his way out of these woods. However, a smart man would hear the freeway and head toward the white noise of fast-moving cars and trucks and be safe within minutes. He would figure out where he was by the road signs.

WE CRAWLED THROUGH rush-hour traffic on the 520 bridge, a mass of clouds and occasional points of sunlight needling us from the fading sunset over the Olympic Mountains in the west. As was often the case at this time of day, even Seattle's side streets were jammed. I let Bert out in Montlake amid a massive traffic tie-up. "Sure you want me to let you out here?" I asked.

"This is fine. I got things to do."

"Keep in touch."

"You don't seem too happy about this, Thomas."

"Like he said, they're never going to stop looking."

It was a creepy feeling to realize I needed to be looking over my shoulder for federal agents over the next few weeks, or maybe the rest of my life. And then, of course, the niggling doubts began to ooze in. I was convinced I hadn't given my identity away to Hoagland, nor had Bert, but that didn't mean Bert wouldn't do something else patently illegal and get arrested for it. I began thinking of small details I should have considered earlier. For instance, had we left tire prints at Cabin Creek? If we had, there was a possibility they could track the make and model of my car. Had Bert left fingerprints on the duct tape he'd used to truss up Hoagland?

I drove to Capitol Hill and found Deborah's building, the front door unlatched; I went in and knocked on her door in the first-floor hallway. Nobody answered.

It was an old building with carpets in the hallways, recently refurbished but still smelling old. Except for the faint sound

of music emanating from one of the units on the first floor,
the hallway was silent. I called Deborah's cellphone and left
a message when she didn't answer. The events of the afternoon had put me into a depression, my first since Kathy
turned up alive. I started thinking about all the things I'd
done wrong in my life and how much of it had been done in
the past few hours. I wondered what the hell I was going to
tell Kathy. Hey, baby, bet you'll never guess who I kidnapped
today? That's right, we beat up a federal official and dumped
him in the next county after wrapping him in a tarp. Just to
make sure he was really pissed, we shocked him with a Taser.

Deborah had called my cellphone when Snake had it and
said she wanted to talk to me. Was she beginning to suspect
the truth of what I'd been claiming, that Sheffield's death was
murder? While I strongly suspected Deborah had been ac-
cepting privileged information from the Sheffield campaign,
there wasn't any room in my mind for thinking she had taken
it any further than that. After hearing about Ruth Ponzi's
accident, maybe she was getting scared. She *should* be scared.
We should all be scared. It was a dangerous business. Everybody in the damned country should be scared.

As I paced the hallway, I thought I heard music again and
realized it was coming from Deborah Driscoll's living room.
I knocked on the door again. This time the door popped open
of its own accord. Apparently, it had been barely latched,
same as the front door to the building. Somebody had been
in a hurry. I pushed it wide with my fingertips.

"Hello? Hello?" Emmylou Harris was singing "The Pearl"
in her plaintive voice. There was no sign of an occupant, although the lights were on. "Deborah?" The bathroom door
was closed, and I could see a light beneath it. A small puddle
of water was spreading from under the bathroom door onto
the hardwood floor like an inkblot test. The unlocked front
door worried me, but the water worried me more. I knocked.
I couldn't hear anybody. The door was locked. I put my
shoulder against it and muscled it open.

The room was full of warm moisture, the shower curtain
stretched across the tub enclosure. "Deborah!" I said. "Deborah?"

I stepped into the puddle. None of the towels had been disturbed, but there were shoe prints on the sopping wet throw rug. I called her name one more time and pulled the shower curtain aside.

Deborah Driscoll lay on her back, half floating and half submerged, her pretty face above the surface. She was dead, her long red hair spread out around her bare shoulders like seaweed. Her eyes bulged. Except for her face, her skin was even paler than I remembered. There were no obvious marks indicating foul play, so the story wasn't immediately clear. This could be an accidental drowning, a suicide, or a homicide. I searched for the petechial hemorrhaging around her eyes that would indicate strangulation but didn't see it. The stupidest thought came to me right then, that everybody had been right about her hair being dyed.

She wasn't stiff yet, so rigor mortis hadn't set in. I rolled her partway over to look at her buttocks—lividity had colored them, which meant the blood had had time to settle—and she was well beyond saving. Gently, I put her back as she had been. I turned the dribbling water off.

I walked to the hallway. Once the police arrived, I knew I wouldn't be allowed to look at anything, but three or four minutes of delay in reporting the death wouldn't hurt. In stocking feet, I padded around the condo. I found Deborah's cellphone in the kitchen. Her number list in the phone included me, dozens of professional contacts, as well as her mother in Portland, and a woman I presumed was a sister in Scotland. Timothy Hoagland's name and number were in her phone, but taking into account her position in the Maddox campaign, that was to be expected. A search of all of her recent outgoing calls revealed she'd called Maddox, then Kalpesh, then me, except she'd gotten Snake, who had my phone.

The kitchen was tidy. A peek in the garbage under the sink revealed one empty wine bottle and some frozen-dinner packaging. Nothing else. The bedroom was at the end of the hallway beyond the bathroom. As I proceeded toward it, I realized the killer might still be here. I hadn't exactly done a thorough check. Nor was I up to par for meeting a panicky killer hell-bent on covering his tracks. The front door had been unlocked, and while Deborah had been dead for a while, it was still possible I'd surprised somebody inside.

I pushed the bedroom door open slowly, then looked through the crack to make sure nobody was behind it. I peeked under the bed. In the closet. None of the windows were unlocked. The bed was mussed. A set of her clothing, presumably from that day, was laid across a chair: panties and bra on top, shoes neatly lined up under the chair. Deborah told me once she'd gone to an all-girls boarding school and this looked like one of the habits she'd learned there. There was nothing under the bed except a small discarded tin-foil wrapper that had once held a condom. No dust balls and no unfinished books. On the other side of the bed I spotted the prophylactic that went with the wrapper. She had had sex with somebody in this bed not long ago. While it wasn't a mini condom, I was relatively certain it was the sort of exotic brand Kalpesh would carry.

I didn't spend a lot of time in each room, just enough to be satisfied I hadn't overlooked anything obvious. I was looking for any hint as to what Deborah had been planning to tell me, or an indication of who else she might have told about our meeting. Had Kalpesh killed her to conceal his own involvement in the death of a senator, or had somebody else come into the building after he exited? Was it possible Deborah had more than one lover and the condom wasn't Kalpesh's at all? Unless other factors intruded, the first suspect in a murder was usually the last known person with the victim. I had every reason to believe that person was Kalpesh, but the DNA evidence under the bed would eventually give the police the right name.

I went back into the bathroom and sat on the closed lid of the toilet, looking around the room for anything I'd missed. I needed to think about this for a few minutes before I called anyone else in. The bathroom door had swung closed on its own.

I'd only known her five weeks, but they were weeks filled with chitchat, business, and turmoil. I recollected her kindness in driving me to Sheffield's funeral and making dinner for me, remembering I'd treated her shabbily afterward. She'd been a smart, ambitious, hard-driving woman with a streak of kindness and fun underneath. She was about the same age as Kathy and similar to her in many respects. They both commanded a room when they entered it; they both turned men's heads. Both were committed to a political credo. They had something else in common, too: They'd both died by homicide. Adults didn't drown in the bathtub. It was a shame Deborah wouldn't come back to life the way Kathy had.

FORTY-EIGHT

"YOU SURE THERE WAS a loaded condom in here fifteen min-utes ago?" asked Hampsted, who was the shortest police officer I'd ever met.

"I saw it."

"It's not there now."

"You said that before. I don't see how that's possible."

"Unless *you* took it."

"Like I put it in my collection? You're welcome to check my pockets." I'd zipped my jacket up over the blood-streaked shirt I'd rumpled while tousling with Bert.

"Don't get snippy with me."

"Don't accuse me of putting a used condom in my pocket."

"You say you've been in the apartment for twenty, twenty-five minutes, that as far as you know, nobody else was here, and yet that condom vanishes into thin air. Are we supposed to think it got up and walked away by itself?"

"You ask the first officers who came in?"

"They didn't see it. You think there was a possibility the killer was in here and took it when he left? Could you have missed him?"

The thought that somebody had been hiding in the condo, tiptoeing around the apartment while I'd been there alone, spooked me. I knew from my struggles with Bert that I was in no condition to ward off an attack. I was even weaker and more beat-up now than in that barn with Bert.

"She's a big girl," said Hampsted. "There aren't any signs of a struggle. The shower curtains haven't been torn down."

"Right. But a strong man, catching her unaware, could hold a woman under in the tub and drown her before she knew how to stop him."

"Maybe. Tell me something, Black. Did you have a sexual relationship with the victim?"

"No."

"You sure?"

"I would remember."

"With that lady? Who wouldn't? Did you want to have a relationship with her?"

"I'm married."

"I own a couple of horses, but that doesn't keep me from wanting to ride the neighbor's horse."

"I didn't want a relationship with her." I wondered how long it would take for him to figure out my wife was dead, or was supposed to be dead.

All I could figure was somebody had reentered the condo after I went into the bathroom to sit with Deborah's body. I hadn't timed it, but I'd probably been in there five or six minutes. I'd been in a funk and my hearing was compromised from the bomb, so it was possible somebody had come in the front door and walked past the partially closed bathroom door without alerting me. How bold would you have to be to come back to a murder scene after the body had been discovered? Maybe the owner of the condom hadn't known I was there. Or found out only as he was passing the bathroom. It was unnerving: If he'd had a gun and we'd run into each other, the police could well be looking at two bodies instead of one.

If he was as implicated in feeding information from the Sheffield camp to outside sources as I thought he was, Deborah's meeting with me wouldn't have pleased Kalpesh. But would he have killed her over it? Not unless he was in a lot deeper than I suspected. In all likelihood, I didn't have a clue—supposing that he'd killed her—why he might have done it. For a myriad of fatuous, imagined, and real reasons, lovers killed loved ones every day. They'd had sex. Maybe they'd quarreled about her planned meeting with me. She decided to take a bath. He waited until the tub was full, then stepped into the bathroom and pushed her under, keeping his weight on her head until she stopped struggling. It would have been a ghastly but relatively simple operation.

On the other hand, Kalpesh may have been gone when she was killed. Hoagland comes up missing—his spooks go out and start tying up loose ends. Was Driscoll a loose end for them? If that was the case, they might be out to kill Kalpesh, too. Or maybe they already had. Bert and I might be next on the list. Even if they didn't know who'd taken Hoagland, we'd spoken to Ponzi. We'd asked questions. I'd made allegations, maybe too many allegations. Bert had caused a scene at Cape Disappointment and gotten himself arrested.

Hampsted and a tech were in the bedroom poking around. I could tell Hampsted didn't completely believe my story, but as long as he couldn't think of a reason for me to be lying, he was going to bide his time. "She have a dog?" he asked.

"Not that I know of. Why?"

"Dogs'll eat anything."

Following me through the condo to the doorway, Hampsted looked up at me and said, "You're not the guy who got blown up at the Maddox rally, are you?"

"One of them."

"Shouldn't you be in the hospital?"

"I got out today."

"Shit. First the bomb, and then you walk in on this. You lead an adventurous life, Mr. Black."

"So I've been told."

"Wait a minute. If you're the guy from the bomb blast . . . your wife died in the plane wreck, didn't she?"

"So I've been told."

"You said you weren't going to sleep with the lady in the tub because you're married?"

"No, I said I wasn't interested in a relationship with her."

"Because you're married."

"That plane went down, what? Fifteen, eighteen days ago? Give me a break."

He mulled it over, trying to find something wrong with it. Finally, he said, "I'd like you to go out and write a statement. After that you can go. Oh, yeah. One thing. Do you know anybody who had any reason to harm her?"

"No."

I was lying, of course. There was a consortium who wouldn't

want her talking to me, but I didn't know who they were, and my only evidence that they existed was the testimony of a petty criminal and the tortured words of a man who would deny everything and who wanted to kill me, hardly evidence I could present to Hampsted. What was more, I didn't know what Deborah had been planning to tell me. I couldn't very well tell him I thought a group of professional assassins was running around trying to tidy up after the murder of a senator, not if I wanted him to believe anything else I said. The missing condom had done enough damage to my credibility.

By the time I finished my statement, the medical examiner's people had removed the body. Hampsted met me outside Deborah's front door. He was still overwhelmed by the dead woman's looks. Poor Deborah. Even in the afterlife she had the ability to addle men's brains.

"She have a boyfriend?" Hampsted asked. "Somebody who might have belonged to that condom you said you saw?"

"His name is Kalpesh Gupta. Used to work for Jane Sheffield, but after the plane crash, he went over to work with Maddox."

"Funny. Since we last spoke I've been on the phone with one of her co-workers, and she swears the dead woman wasn't seeing anyone."

"So why ask me?"

"Cross-checking."

"She was sleeping with Kalpesh Gupta."

"That a secret?"

"I think so."

"So how come you know about it?"

"I saw him here one night."

"And you were . . . what? Visiting her yourself? I thought you weren't interested in the lady. Or were you just waiting outside to see if you might get lucky?"

"I was working on something."

"Something you weren't going to tell me about?"

"It turned out to be nothing."

"And that didn't make you happy, did it?"

"What do you mean?"

"I mean, a guy puts the moves on a lady and she doesn't reciprocate. He watches her and sees her with some other guy, so he watches her closer. Catches her in her bath and drowns her out of spite. Calls us. That guy could have been you."

"You want to give me a lie detector test?"

"Forget it. For now let's just say you weren't involved. Was she having sex with more than one guy?"

"I only knew about Kalpesh."

"But it was possible?"

"Anything's possible."

"It's even possible she got in the tub and drowned by accident, isn't it?"

"No. That's not possible. She's thirty years old. Not three."

FORTY-NINE

IT WAS DARK by the time I got into the car and used the cell-phone. Bert answered right away. "Bert. Deborah Driscoll is dead."

"Who's Deborah Driscoll?"

"She works for Maddox. *Worked* for Maddox."

"Was she giving information to somebody?"

"I don't think so. I do think she was receiving confidential information from Kalpesh Gupta, who worked in the Sheffield camp. We'd set up a meeting. I think she was going to tell me about it."

"There was a mole in the Sheffield camp? I was right, wasn't I?"

"He was feeding information to Deborah, but I suspect he was feeding it to someone else as well."

"Gupta, huh? I think I've seen him on the news. That Indian dude?"

"You leave him alone."

"You might not feel that way a week from now. Especially if more people you know turn up dead. This Deborah Driscoll? You fond of her?"

"You could say that."

"I'm sorry. You tell the police?"

"They're not holding me, if that's what you're worried about."

"Christ. You know what this is, don't you? They're cleaning up. It was triggered when I took one of their key players off the table, maybe their top man for all I know. It would be just like them to send the guy who planned the crash to head up the investigation. That's why he was here early. Damn!"

"You really think Hoagland was in charge?"

"If he was, he was lying through his teeth and we were

buying it hook, line, and sinker. Bastard. I know one thing. Once their cleanup starts, it's not going to stop. They'll be watching your house. You need to get out of town. You got cash squirreled away somewhere?"

"Some."

"Don't use any plastic, or they'll be on you like white on rice. Where are you going? Never mind. I don't want to know."

"How long do you think we need to hide out?"

"I don't know. We're moving into territory I've never visited before. We may have to hide forever."

"That's not going to happen."

"Why not?"

"Kathy won't stand for it. Hell, she wants to go back now."

"Just lay low for a while. I may be able to work some of the old Slezak magic."

"Bert?" But he'd already signed off.

When I arrived at the tiny house in north Seattle, Delilah was in the kitchen scarfing down dinner, already running late for her karate class. Kathy was in the bedroom with the door closed. Snake was on his computer, a set of well-oiled pistols on the table beside him. There were four voice mails on my cellphone when Snake handed it back to me. The first three were from Deborah Driscoll. It was eerie listening to her voice now that she was dead. "Thomas? Come over late this afternoon or this evening, and I'll try to connect some of the dots for you." She didn't sound frightened in the least. The next message showed a little more reserve. "Thomas? Deborah again. I haven't heard back, but I'll assume you're coming. I'm afraid I have some negative points to make about James in relation to that plane crash. It's kind of scary now that I'm thinking it through. We'll talk." The third message: "Deborah again. Just reminding you I'll be here all evening." The earlier calls had come from a relatively calm woman, but in the last her voice was muffled under a scrim of tension. I wondered if she'd had an inkling of what was in store for her.

When Kathy came out of the bedroom she wore deck shoes, shapeless polyester slacks, and a cotton jacket she must have gotten at the Goodwill. She wore a bad brown wig and had on a pair of thick glasses and freckles she'd applied with makeup. She was good at making her face go dead, too. With her new posture and attitude, she was the kind of woman nobody would look at twice. When she saw the look on my face, she burst into laughter. "What's up, buster?"

"You new in town, sister?"

"Just fell off the turnip wagon."

"I think your own mother would walk right past you."

She stepped across the room and hugged me. "I've been reading all that material you left and . . . damn it . . . there are things a lot of people know but nobody will talk about. Things that need talking about."

"Last time we spoke, you seemed to think I was a nutcase."

"I didn't say 'nutcase.' You're not a nut. Well, you are, but not that kind. Somebody murdered Jane and those others. Bert knew something. That meant others must have, too."

"Bert saw Hoagland in town before the flight. He thinks he was contacting Maddox."

"You're kidding, right?"

"No joke. That's what he said."

"You think Maddox knew about the crash before it happened?"

"I'm beginning to wonder."

"Thomas, the official version comes out tomorrow, but they're already calling it an accident. Do you think . . . ?"

"Bert says if you start trying to convince people, you'll be making yourself a target. After talking to Hoagland, I tend to agree. Oh, and Deborah Driscoll was killed this afternoon."

"Oh, God."

I told her about it. When I finished and she'd asked all the pertinent follow-up questions and I'd answered them, I added, "I think we need to get out of town. Maybe make one stop on the way out."

"And go where?"

"We'll figure it out. I always think better when I'm holed up in a motel with a sexy farm girl. Are you wearing sexy lingerie and garters?"

"Of course."

"There's at least that." I kissed her.

From the other room, Snake said, "You guys can cut out the mush."

"Give me a break here," I said. "She was dead until last week."

KALPESH STOOD OPENMOUTHED in the doorway to his plush downtown condominium. After greeting me, he stared at Kathy without recognizing her. It was amazing. At the other end of the hallway, two workmen in coveralls puttered with an exit sign. "Why don't we step inside?" I said.

"Yes, of course. Both of you, come in." Once we had the door closed behind us, Kalpesh looked at Kathy as if he thought he might recognize her, then gave up on it.

"My cousin," I said. "Carol."

"Sure. Glad to meet you."

Every time I'd seen him around the Maddox camp he'd been leery of being left alone with me. I could tell by the way he kept staring that he thought there was a possibility I was here to blame him once again for Kathy's death. "That plane was taken down," I said.

"That's ridiculous, and you know it."

"It isn't."

"Who would take a plane down? A terrorist?"

"Government sponsored," I said.

"The Saudis? Pakistan?"

"Us. *Our* government."

When he realized how invested I was in the concept, he stepped back and invited us to sit down. The living room was immaculate as it had been during my first visit. Over Puget Sound, we could see streaks of rain drifting in above the city lights.

Earlier, Snake had gone to my house to check on things and pick up his belongings. He'd reported via cellphone that my house was still being watched and that the neighbors were reporting visits by men in civilian clothing who, judging from their haircuts and bearing, were military. I was beginning to wonder what we'd gotten ourselves into. I was beginning to get angry, too, knowing that in front of me was the man who maybe had helped start the chain of events that led to all this.

Whether he'd known what he was doing or not, Kalpesh, I was sure, had been the mole in the Sheffield camp. I was hoping that now, with Deborah's death, I might be able to shake him up enough to get something out of him.

"I want to know who you were talking to when you worked for Jane Sheffield."

"We've been over this ground before. I wasn't spying."

"But you were. For Deborah and probably for somebody else. I just want to know who that somebody else was."

"Did she tell you that?"

I wasn't sure if he knew about her death. Obviously, if he'd killed her he knew, but I couldn't be sure he'd killed her. If he did know Deborah was dead, he didn't necessarily realize I knew. It had only been a couple of hours. "Did Deborah tell you I was giving her information?"

"Yes."

He looked disappointed, as if he hadn't expected her to rat on him. Or, as if this whole line of questioning was tiresome. "I didn't give her any information. Not as such. True, we were seeing each other when I was working with Jane, and we had a number of telephone conversations pursuant to that relationship. She may have extrapolated from some personal things I said, but anything of a political nature she took away from those conversations was strictly accidental."

"I don't believe you."

An uncomfortable silence ensued, and after it had dragged on awhile, I said, "Kalpesh, why did you change camps?"

"Beliefs change. Circumstances change. We all have to make our decisions."

"How long have you known you were going to switch camps?"

"I . . . really don't see how that is any of your business."

"Answer the question and we'll go away."

Without replying, Kalpesh walked to the front door and put his hand on the knob. As we left, he said, "It was nice to meet you, Carol."

As we left, the two workmen were still monkeying around at the end of the corridor. When they saw us, one of them put a walkie-talkie to his mouth and spoke into it, turning his back on me when he saw me watching. It may have been an innocent work radio, but then, I was beginning to lose my belief in innocence.

"Think you should have mentioned Deborah Driscoll's death?" Kathy asked.

"I'd like to be there when the police show up and ask him if he was sleeping with her. I'm guessing he thinks that was a secret."

"Won't they find his fingerprints all over her place?"

"Maybe."

"He didn't recognize me, did he?"

"Not even close."

The elevator arrived and we stepped into it. "They're spies," Kathy said, as we descended to street level.

"Who?"

"Those two guys at the end of the hall. They had feds written all over them."

"Maybe. Maybe not."

"Geez. I'm beginning to sound like Bert."

FIFTY

ONCE AGAIN WE DROVE to the coast in the rain, this time in my car with its powerful engine and beefed-up drivetrain. Ecology be damned; we were worried about our lives here. I had rejected the idea of bringing along a weapon, although Snake volunteered to lend me one of his .44 Magnums and three boxes of cartridges, a generous offer considering he thought of his guns the way others thought of their children. Kathy and I wanted to be free, but we didn't want to hurt anybody doing it. Mired in our own thoughts, we didn't say much on the drive. Nor did we listen to the radio or play music. During the past two weeks we'd been thrust into another world, one that the plane crash, our own research, and Bert's harebrained actions had shattered into a million pieces. It was as if we'd stepped into *The Matrix*.

We used up an hour in Tacoma, eventually locating my man in a pool hall on Pacific Avenue. Tommy had been peripherally involved in a massive theft from a construction company but had begged me to forget he was implicated and for reasons too complex to go into, I granted his plea. In return, he'd promised anything but his firstborn. It was time to collect. "Give me your cellphone," I said. "Take mine to Mount Rainier and hide it somewhere in the inn where nobody will find it for a couple of days. Get out of there yourself. Do not stay near it. Can you do that?"

"I'll have to go AWOL at work for a day, but you got it. Is this going to make us even?"

"Even Steven. Under no circumstances are you to tell anybody about this. No fingerprints."

"Got it. You in some sort of trouble, man?"

"You don't want to know."

Tommy was a Finnish immigrant with a pins-in-his-mouth

accent, and a penchant for small-time goof-ups and big-time theft. He was in his early forties and had a pregnant girlfriend who had just turned nineteen. It was the first time, he told me, he'd ever been truly in love, and this would be his first child. "My kid is not going to want for anything," he told me once. "I was an orphan, but I'm going to take care of this kid." Maybe I shouldn't have, but I believed him.

Tommy walked to the back of the pool hall and brought me four cellphones. "They all work," he said. "Use one until you don't feel comfortable with it, then toss it. Keep them in the trunk or something. You don't want brain cancer from all those microwaves."

"These all yours?"

"More or less."

"They're stolen, huh?"

"More or less."

We had reached the coast before we finally turned on the car radio. It was just before midnight, the odd headlights zooming at us from the opposite direction, once in a while a pair of luminescent eyes staring at us from the roadside. One item in the newscast jumped out at me: "In breaking news, the body of National Traffic Safety Board supervisor Timothy Hoagland was found late this evening east of Seattle near Interstate 90. Cause of death was not immediately disclosed. Hoagland had been in Seattle to head up an investigation into the crash of a light plane two weeks ago in which Senator Jane Sheffield and ten others were killed. State patrol officials say there will be an autopsy tomorrow morning. Police declined to say whether they think his death is linked to the now-concluded Sheffield investigation. Results of the Sheffield investigation were slated to be announced at a news conference tomorrow morning, but officials are now stating that the announcement may be indefinitely delayed. In other news—"

I got Bert Slezak on the line the first time I tried him. "You bastard! You killed him after I left."

"I didn't."

"That's why you didn't want me going back to check. What did you do, drug him so he would die of exposure? Or did you knock him in the head with a rock?"

"I didn't do nothin'. I only heard about it an hour ago myself. They must have been tailing us."

"Why would they kill Hoagland? He was masterminding the cover-up."

"Maybe they thought Hoagland was going to talk. No matter what he told them, they would assume he spilled at least part of it. It's not illogical that they would kill him. These people are colder than Eskimo spit. These are the same assholes who wanted to set off a nuclear suitcase bomb in San Francisco so they could declare war on the entire Mideast. Wiping a major city off the map meant about as much to them as changing the channel does to you."

"You killed him."

"Maybe he had a heart attack. We didn't exactly treat him according to the Geneva Conventions."

"Oh, now it's 'we'?"

"You were asking questions, too. I swear on my grandmother's grave the man was breathing when I last saw him."

"Your grandmother is aboveground."

"My *other* grandmother. He must have gone out to the highway and got hit by a truck. Or had a heart attack. You've got to believe I didn't kill him. You know this isn't even the United States government chasing us. This all comes from the Bilderberg Group. World financial powers. They're behind this. They're the ones on our tails."

"The Bilderberg what?"

"There's three cabals of rich folks giving orders to every government on earth. Bill Clinton met with them in Germany before he ran for president. Both Bushes are members. The Rockefellers. This is why nothing is ever going to change. Don't you see? They control everything. You don't think so, pop your head up, call a news conference, and see if you and Kathy wake up for breakfast."

"Yeah, yeah, yeah," I said, and hung up, disgusted with the turn of events and Bert's ever increasingly paranoid, off-the-wall theories. I'd bought into so many of them, too. Kathy looked across at me in the darkness and said, "What did you two do to Timothy Hoagland?"

"It's a long story."

"Good, because we have a lot of time."

I was still feeding her details when we checked into a dark little motel on the ocean. The motel was on the beach and not far from the last one we'd stayed at. The lulling roar of a high tide accompanied our arrival. By the time I'd finished explaining everything and we'd turned on the crummy television to catch the late-night news, neither of us was in the mood for anything romantic. Kathy was furious with me for not turning Hoagland over to the police the minute I had the power to do so, and even more furious for holding on to the story until now.

"He threatened to have us murdered," I said. "If I turned him over, he would know my name. We released him out in the woods, where he would be safe and free and we might be, too."

"But he wasn't safe, was he?"

"Maybe not, but Bert swore letting Hoagland know who we were was the same as signing our own death warrants."

"After everything that's happened, how could you trust Bert?"

"Because he saved your life."

"But you helped torture a man."

"I believed Hoagland when he said he was part of the conspiracy. He was in town before the plane went down. He collaborated in the murder of ten people. Eleven if you count Ruth Ponzi's husband. Twelve when you include Deborah Driscoll. Fourteen if you count us."

"We're not dead."

"No, but you *were*. And I *almost* was. And we still might be."

"You think the bomb had anything to do with the rest of it?"

"I don't know. You look around the country, you don't see any other Senate races like this."

"We need to work by the rule of law here. Go to the authorities. Bring this all out into the open. Get the newspapers involved."

"The newspapers are not going to do anything but repeat the official line. If we're arrested, the newspapers will treat us as criminals. Anything and everything we say after that will be suspect. And Bert threw the rule of law out the window when he saved you from riding that plane into the ocean. That was the start."

"If you're going to act outside the law, we can't expect the law to come to our rescue."

"So far the law hasn't had anything to do with this."

Kathy blamed me for not taking the high road and turning Hoagland over to an ambulance crew the minute I saw him, and Bert over to the police. She even blamed me for getting gulled by Bert at Cabin Creek. On all counts, I was forced to agree with her. Bert had always been sneaky, and I should have taken that into account.

Twenty minutes after we doused the lights, Kathy said, "Thomas?"

"What?"

"I hate to say this, but if that man is guilty of half of what we think he is, he deserved what Bert did to him."

"Maybe so, but we're not the judge and jury. The last thing I want to do is be responsible for somebody's death. Even his."

"When was the last time anybody in the intelligence community in this country was prosecuted . . . for anything? *You* might go to prison. Bert might. But they won't. I'm sorry I got so upset. You think there's any chance we'll get our lives back?"

"No." That was when she started crying.

Two days passed. We walked on the beach. We talked. We drove around talking to locals and trying to figure out if anybody else had experienced any kind of electromagnetic interference on the day of the crash. That was our real reason for hiding at the beach, to do some more investigation. Later in the week, I would contact my friend in the Coast Guard and see if he'd heard any rumors about EMI. We went to a local grocery store and stocked up on popcorn and magazines. We watched the Seattle news for more information on Hoagland's death, but there was nothing new. I phoned Snake about it, and he called back half a day later and said that as far as he could tell, Hoagland's death had been ruled a homicide, and because of his position as a federal investigator the FBI was handling the case. It was unusual but not unheard of for the FBI to look into homicides. While he was calling around trying to scare up news about Hoagland, he'd spoken to one of his contacts at the King County Medical Examiner's Office and learned that Deborah Driscoll's death had been ruled accidental. "Accidentally drowned in a bathtub?" I said.

"Don't holler at me. I'm not the one who called it. My buddy in the ME's office wouldn't come out and say it, but I got the feeling there was some pressure for the verdict. She had some wine in her system. They're saying she fell asleep and drowned."

"And nobody's questioning it?"

"The ME's office is not a debate society."

Later I phoned Ruth Ponzi at her house, expressed my sorrow at her husband's death, and tried to find out how much work she'd done on the Sheffield tragedy before the car accident put her out of commission. I wanted to know how much dust she'd stirred up before her car accident. She refused to talk to me. She didn't sound offended or confused. She was firm, and when I tried to push it, scared. "Did they ever catch the guy who hit you?" I asked.

"No," she said, and hung up.

Several times I contacted Bert by cellphone, and each time he continued to deny he'd had anything to do with Hoagland's death. He said he thought agents were on his trail and he didn't have long before they would murder him. I was certain he was exaggerating, but there was never any way to be sure with Bert. Later that day and all the next he was unreachable.

I asked Snake to go out to his grandmother's property and see if his brother was holed up in the trailer. Snake told me he would call back with a report.

We switched motels each day, always using phony names. My wounds began to heal. Perhaps it was the salt air or the feeling of relative security that concealment endowed on us. Rain or shine, mostly rain, Kathy and I walked the beach, talking, speculating, and wondering if either of us had any kind of grip on reality. "After reading all that stuff on the Internet," Kathy said, "election fraud, all the problems with the 9/11 report, the campaign finance problems, I wonder why I wasn't aware of all of it before. It's all public information."

"It's human nature to ignore what's wrong. It's the reason people don't want an X-ray that might show cancer. What if they have it?"

"I'm now wondering if any of the last three national elections were legitimate, and so are millions of others. When was the last time in this country this many people felt our elections were rigged?"

"Not in our lifetimes."

"Even if they weren't rigged, all those people believing it represents a massive failure of the system. The collective paralysis in refusing to recognize that we've lost our focus in this country boggles the mind. Hell, it took a death and a near-death experience to wake me up."

"I got news for you. Until your average American can't watch football, buy another beer, and turn on the lights, everything's fine."

Around sunset of our second evening at the beach, Snake called and said that it looked like Bert had vanished. When he went out to his grandmother's property to check on Bert's trailer, all he found was a hole in the ground. All the barns and outbuildings had been blown down or obliterated by a massive explosion that the local authorities had chalked up to teenagers with stolen dynamite, but Snake said his grandmother had recently been visited by gentlemen with military-style haircuts and ill-fitting civilian clothes who'd asked harsh questions about both her grandsons and about a man named Black.

"So where's your brother?" I asked. "Did he blow up with the trailer?"

"They didn't find any body parts. I think he's hiding. I'm thinking you and Kathy should disappear permanently."

"I refuse to throw my life away because some thugs, government-sponsored or not, are trying to run me out of town," said Kathy, when I relayed Snake's suggestion. We were walking on the beach, the only figures on the sand for miles. We might as well have been the last two people on earth.

FIFTY-ONE

IT WAS OUR FOURTH AFTERNOON in hiding, and Kathy and I decided we would drive to Cape Disappointment, which was just down the coast from where we'd been staying and was the locus for any search for the maybe phantom EMI device that may or may not have taken down the Sheffield flight. In retrospect, I think Kathy wanted to see the farmhouse where she'd been held for so many days, but the Cape was as close as she dared suggest. In her mind there was still something terrifying and otherworldly about those missing ten days and that farmhouse.

The Pacific Ocean was enjoying a series of the lowest tides of the decade, but the swells were rambunctious and at one point we saw a whale spouting off the coast. The weather forecasters said another serious storm would roll in by morning. We met with my Coast Guard friend, Hutchins, then talked to locals about electronic problems, if any, on the day the plane went down. We learned that two fishing boats had reported trouble with electronic equipment around the time of the crash.

Then, at loose ends, we did all the touristy things one does at the Cape: visited the lighthouse, checked out the World War II bunkers constructed to defend against a Japanese invasion that never arrived—as if the Japanese could only hit the coast at that one spot—and strolled through the Lewis and Clark Interpretive Center hand in hand. We had never been more in love or more uncertain about our future.

By closing time at the interpretive center, we'd had a long day. Still, instead of tramping out to the parking lot with the remaining patrons, we walked along the bluff trail and watched the roiling ocean below. It didn't take long before even the docents had left and we were alone.

We found a great depression in the bluff, a grassy swale that sloped steeply down to the water two hundred feet below. At the top of the depression was a bench with a donor's name engraved on a metal plate. We sat on the bench and waited for the sunset to color ten miles of gray between us and the horizontal strip of blue sky that was just beginning to turn orange at the far side of the storm front. "This is going to be great," Kathy said.

"Spectacular."

"Look at us. We're reduced to living in the moment."

"Something we should try more often."

"Planning for tomorrow and worrying about yesterday overloads your brain."

"Fries the circuits."

"Maybe the moment's all you've got." The voice belonged to a man behind us. Because of the wind and the susurrus of the ocean below, he had closed in before either of us noticed. I kicked myself for being unalert enough that somebody could sneak up on us.

He was a tall man with a broad torso, wearing a rumpled suit and holding a chrome-plated revolver in his bandaged right hand. When I stood up, he pointed the revolver at my stomach. Kathy didn't know him, but I did. "Mr. Hoagland," I said.

"Mr. Black."

"Reports of your death have been exaggerated."

"We're not here about my death. It's yours we're going to see about."

"The whole world thinks you're dead."

"They're going to think you're dead, too. Except, in your case, it will be true."

"You barely know me. Why would you want to do me harm?"

He gave me an appraising look, as if trying to determine if he'd heard my voice before or if maybe he'd ridden in the trunk of my car, if I'd carried him in a tarpaulin. "You've been all over the state asking questions about the plane wreck, doing your best to prove I'm doing something inappropriate. You've become a nuisance. Hell, when we get the laws changed, your

Internet records alone should be enough to get you thrown in prison."

"For what?"

"Treason."

"Since when does reading different opinions constitute treason? And how do you know what I've been doing on the Internet?"

"We've got logs. You get on every morning and check Velonews for the latest cycling, and then you read your treasonous sites—9/11 conspiracy theories, CIA operations in Central America. All that crap."

"I'm just a guy, man."

"You're a guy who buddies up to Bert Slezak, is what you are."

"I know the man. A lot of people do."

Somehow he'd figured, or assumed, or guessed that Bert had been his captor, and because of it he'd blown up Bert's trailer, or ordered it blown up, and now he was after me.

Kathy walked around one end of the bench while I walked around the other. Hoagland stepped back a pace but kept the pistol fixed on my belly.

"Get over there with him," he said, gesturing with the weapon.

"Don't do it," I said.

"Get over there."

"Screw you," said Kathy. I made a slight feint, just enough so that he was reluctant to take the pistol off me. I knew from my police training, as no doubt he did, too, that holding a gun on someone who was only nine feet away wasn't much protection. Human reaction times were such that somebody inside a ten-foot range had an excellent chance of jumping the gun holder. But then, I was still convalescing from my wounds, so my reaction time would be slower than normal. Also, if we engaged in hand-to-hand combat, Hoagland would have the advantage of outweighing my one-eighty by at least fifty pounds. He'd worked for the CIA and had probably had hand-to-hand combat training. All I had going for me was desperation and knowing how to fight dirty. Bert had tortured him three days ago, and while he carried marks from that experience on his face and his bandaged hand, I couldn't be certain it had weakened him the way the bomb and my hospital stay had weakened me.

"Let her go," I said. "She doesn't have anything to do with anything. We just met in a bar in Portland."

"You don't drink, so I doubt you spent any time in a bar. And you haven't been to Portland in a year. Don't carry a gun, either. You have an aversion to them. In fact, you're pretty much of a sitting duck."

"Is that how you look at it? Anybody who doesn't carry a gun is a sitting duck?"

"That's right."

"How do you know all this about me?"

"We keep tabs. And this woman is your wife."

"Why me?"

"Don't be disingenuous, Mr. Black. You and Bert Slezak have been dogging me since I arrived in state. I should have had somebody take him off the playing board that first week, but I mistakenly thought he had been rendered harmless by years of alcoholism."

"How did you find me?"

"We traced your cellphone to Mount Rainier. Guy had it tried to play tough, but we managed to get him into our van in the parking lot. It took eight minutes to break him down. From there, it was a cinch to triangulate on the cellphones he'd given you. We had to be patient, though, because you only turned them on sporadically. We picked you up outside your motel this morning actually, and followed you here. Nice of you to hang around until everybody else was gone."

"I don't see any *we*."

"Rest assured, I'm not alone. Where is Bert Slezak?"

"I don't know."

"If you want, I can kneecap your wife. But I *will* get some answers here." He made as if to swing the gun toward Kathy. I took a step forward, and he brought it back to me. Recognizing what I was doing, Kathy made a move, too, so he wasn't sure where to point the weapon.

"Why are you doing this?" Kathy asked.

"Don't be blaming this on me," Hoagland said. "I was

tending my own business when somebody decided to make it personal. People get personal with me—I get personal back. Your friend Slezak attacked me. I just want to know what you know about it." He chuckled, but there was no mirth in it. When I didn't reply, he continued, "I think you were involved, too."

"I wasn't."

"Oh, but you were."

"What did you do to Tommy?"

"Who's Tommy?"

"The man who had my cellphone."

"He's in a quiet place where he will remain."

"Until what?"

"Until the animals carry away his bones."

I couldn't think about anything but Tommy's pregnant girlfriend and my stupidity in putting him at risk.

"I'll give you one last chance to come clean. You do, maybe I'll spare you. It's a long shot, but right now all you have are long shots. I was taken up into the mountains by a couple of bastards who thought they were going to get away with it. One was tall . . . like you . . . and smelled of medicine. He was also disabled, as you seem to be." I was still moving with a slight limp from the bombing. "The other was Slezak."

"I have friends. They'll find out what happened here."

"Slezak's brother, Elmer? We're removing him from the equation tomorrow. And this? This is going to look like just another unfortunate drug-related crime. Even if they don't buy it, they'll never look for me. I'm dead, and dead men can do whatever they want. Ironic, isn't it?"

"Look. You've scared us plenty. Now let us go."

Hoagland laughed, and I noticed he had a habit, when he laughed, of tipping his head back and for just a fraction of a second, closing his eyes. I remembered his trademark guffaw from our first meeting at Boeing Field. He'd done the head-tipping thing back then, too. If I'd known it was coming I might have used that moment to rush him. It would have given me just the head start I needed. It would have been chancy; he might have gut-shot me anyway, but it was a glimmer of hope, and a glimmer was more than I'd had up until now.

"My name is Kathy Birchfield," Kathy said. "You might have seen my name on the passenger list from the Sheffield flight. The world thinks I was on the plane. When they find me here, there's going to be a lot of interest."

"What makes you think you'll be found?"

Kathy turned so pale that I had to jump in, both to distract him and to distract her. I said, "I have proof you were involved in taking down that plane." Hoagland turned to me, and for the first time I saw a note of alarm in his impassive features. "The proof's with an attorney. You were in state and talking about it before it went down. You were part of it."

"I came out to see my nephew."

"And met with Maddox prior to the accident."

He gave me a long look, trying to figure out where I'd gotten my information. One way would have been if I'd been involved in the interrogation in Bert's barn. "You don't have crap on me."

"But I do. For one thing, I met the mechanic who rigged the plane." He was even more amused than I'd dare hope for. His dead eyes lit up. "Your mechanic gave me every detail of how he did it."

Hoagland surveyed my face for a moment. I knew why he was entertained. The plane hadn't been rigged; they'd found some other way to take it down, probably the EMI device Bert was so keen on. My assertion was hokum and he knew it. Once again he threw his head back and roared—and when he did he closed his eyes for a fraction of a second.

I went in low and fast, grabbing his gun hand and turning it toward his torso, using my full body weight and momentum to bowl him over, at the same time putting a foot behind him to make sure he tripped and went down. He landed heavily, I on top of him, the revolver between us. My quickness had startled him. It had startled me, too. Thinking about getting murdered and watching your wife get murdered alongside you jacks up the adrenaline. He had the gun by the handle, while I had it by the barrel. He tried to pull the gun out of my fist, but

I had a death grip on it. He tried to pull the trigger, but I was holding the cylinder so that it wouldn't revolve. I was weaker than I'd reckoned, but still I maintained my hold on the weapon as we rolled on the gravel pathway.

"Run, Kathy. Get the hell out of here."

For half a minute we rolled in the gravel, neither gaining an advantage. I found his bulk and weight difficult, if not impossible, to direct, and for a few seconds it seemed as if he was going to maneuver his way on top and hold me down, but I wriggled out of it and we rolled again.

We rolled off the path and down onto the grassy slope, picking up speed, the two of us locked together. I gouged his eye. I bit him. And then, somewhere in all the rolling, I got my left elbow into his throat and hit him hard. I hit him again, this time in the face. Blood spurted from his nose, and he stopped fighting just long enough for me to pull the gun out of his limp fist. I stood over him while he rose up on one knee and tried to reach out for me, but I danced to one side and clubbed him across the forehead with the gun. When he got up and tried to rush me, I clubbed him again. Scalp wounds bleed a lot, and soon most of his face was coated in scarlet. He balanced on one knee, teetering this way and that, trying to regain his footing and equilibrium while I stepped back and scanned the hillside for Kathy, who was on the trail where I'd left her. Despite my urging, she hadn't deserted me.

"Walk up there," I said to Hoagland. We were thirty yards below the bench on the steeply sloping hillside. It seemed to take him forever to get to his feet and stumble up the grassy hill. It was steeper than it looked, and the grasses and undergrowth were wet and slippery, causing him to skid several times. Out over the ocean the sunset had turned glorious, shafts of brilliant light piercing the clouds and brightening the various shades of green on the hill below us. The ocean sounded close, though the path extended a good two hundred feet below the bench, and it was maybe a fifty-foot drop to the water after that.

Walking like a drunk, Hoagland managed to stagger up the hill and lean against the back of the bench with one hand. It was the second time in as many days that he'd become my prisoner, and once again I didn't know what to do with him other than to leave him here and run. But that didn't seem right or practical. He'd find us again, and next time maybe we wouldn't be so lucky. While the three of us were trying to figure out what should happen next, something small and fast whizzed erratically off the cinder path twenty feet in front of us. Simultaneously I heard a distant pop. When I looked up, a man in a light blue suit stood eighty yards away, aiming in my direction what I assumed from the sound was a 9 mm pistol. A second bullet whirred off the cinder path, this one somewhat closer than the first. He was either a bad shot, or these were warning rounds. Even at this distance I was pretty sure I knew who he was. It was an odd feeling of wanting to believe it and not wanting to believe it at the same time. Tying these two men together so blatantly was something I'd been attempting and failing to do for a week, and now they'd done it for me.

Hoagland grinned at me, his teeth limned with blood that had run down his face and into his mouth. "You're dead, fucker," he said. He turned toward the man in the distance. "Shoot him. Keep shooting. Kill both these motherfuckers."

"Run, Kathy."

"Not on your life."

"Then get behind me."

"Are you crazy?"

"Make his target smaller. Do it. Help me out here." She stepped behind me, while I put both hands into the air as a gesture of peace. As angry and driven and frightened as I was, the last thing I wanted to do was to kill a man. Or even to shoot at him. The figure in the distance walked toward us, pistol braced in a two-handed law enforcement shooting posture everybody knew from the movies. He fired a third time.

"What are we going to do?" Kathy asked.

"I don't know."

He fired again. I heard the bullet in the air, closer this time. I'm not sure why I didn't raise the pistol I'd confiscated from Hoagland. Perhaps, given his first attempts, I didn't believe the shooter could hit us at that range. Or perhaps I was paralyzed with indecision. He was walking toward us, closing fast, and soon would be within range of his skills. Most people, even good shots, were not very accurate at eighty yards. Even seventy or sixty yards was long for most pistol shooters, but he was down to fifty now. An expert could hit a man at fifty yards every time, though I doubted this shooter could.

"Is that who I think it is?" Kathy asked.

"I think so."

"Jesus. What's he doing? He's . . ."

"Out of his mind?"

"He must be."

Even the worst shooter could get lucky, and I was painfully aware that the next shot might kill or cripple one of us. For my part, even wielding a short-barreled revolver, I knew I had retained the great bulk of my former shooting skills.

"Shoot!" Hoagland screamed. "Kill these fuckers!"

The figure in the distance yelled something, but with my still-compromised hearing, it took me a few seconds to figure out what. He said, "You promised he wouldn't have a gun."

"He's afraid of guns. Just shoot him. Shoot them both like we talked about." The man in the distance continued to walk toward me. When he'd gotten inside of forty yards, he stopped, raised his 9 mm, and sighted. I lifted my .38 and slowly squeezed the trigger. I aimed at and hit his left leg.

The bullet spun him around, and as he whirled in a semicircle, he fired off rounds almost like a machine gun, the pistol swinging at the end of his wildly swinging arm, bullets spraying all over the place. As he began to fall and reached out to stop himself, the last round from his gun somehow hit him in the torso. He flopped onto his back and lay motionless, legs splayed, pistol on the ground beside him. It took a moment to mentally process the bizarre scene we'd just witnessed. Below us on the scree, Hoagland stood, mouth agape, waiting for his partner to rise back up and kill me, but the fallen man did not move.

When it became clear that our gunfight had come to a standstill, Hoagland barreled up the hillside like a huffing stallion. In one fist he carried a large rock I hadn't seen him pick up. When he got close, he swung it at my skull. Kathy had already stepped back away from me. I ducked and pushed him away. "You lucky bastard," he growled, rushing me a second time.

The hate in him was so palpable you could almost see it rising off his red face in waves. I stood waiting while he interrupted his second charge in order to catch his breath. When he felt sufficiently recovered, he charged. You had to give him credit. He was a man with a rock trying to overpower a man with a gun, who'd just made a forty-yard pistol shot. Then it occurred to me that he must have thought my shot was an accident. As he rushed me, I stepped to one side and clubbed him across the temple with the .38. His reaction was so sudden and comical I thought for a fraction of a second he was making a joke. He stood straight up, eyes rolling back in his skull, and before I could catch him, he fell onto his side and began rolling down the hill. It didn't seem possible that physics wouldn't arrest his fall, but each time I thought he was going to come to a stop he twitched or crumpled and continued rolling, and at one point he even broke into a cartwheel of sorts. He skidded and slid the full two hundred feet down the steep slope, then hesitated on the lip before disappearing. Although I couldn't see all of it, I knew he'd dropped the remaining fifty vertical feet into the ocean.

Kathy and I stared at each other for a second, the shock and horror evident on our faces. The fall, we both knew, was not anywhere near survivable. Taking a deep breath, I walked up the pathway toward the man I'd shot. When I got to him he was alive, his dark brown eyes open to the dimming sky. His right hand was groping for something, clawing at the gravel. I assumed Kalpesh Gupta was trying to get hold of his gun so he could finish killing me.

Kalpesh was in pain, that was clear enough. The wound to his thigh was bleeding profusely and I knelt, removed his belt, and cinched it around his leg, pushing a handkerchief under the belt as a dressing. The bullet had gone into his side just above the belt line. I pulled his shirt up and hoped it wasn't too serious. The glazed look in his eyes told me different, that he'd probably hit one or more vital organs and was bleeding internally and rapidly going into shock. "Did you know it was us?" Kathy asked.

Kalpesh stared past my shoulder at Kathy and tried to speak twice before he could force the words out of his parched throat. "Just tying up loose ends. Or maybe it was you tying up loose ends." He chuckled at the irony. Though it was cool outside, he was perspiring, his face and hair wet, his shirt soaked with perspiration and, now, blood. I tried to stanch the bleeding from his side.

"We've got to call for help," Kathy said.

"Don't be a fool," Kalpesh said. "I'll be dead in a minute. You let anybody official know where you are and what happened here, you'll both be dead, just like me."

"You're not going to die," Kathy said. "We'll call somebody."

"Out here? Help's gotta be half an hour away. You listen to me. Nobody's going to believe any of it. You two want to live, hide the bodies. Trust me on this."

"Why did you come with him?"

"Don't be dense. You get in the way of a steamroller, you get squashed. I always liked you, Kathy. I didn't want it to be this way. Not Deborah, either. I almost couldn't go through with that. I came so close to letting her go."

He tried to swing his eyes back from Kathy but he got about halfway through the motion when all cognition left his face. His eyes went blank. His breathing ceased.

"Oh, God," said Kathy. "Is he dead?"

"Yes."

"I can't bear this."

"We were lucky. I shouldn't have waited so long."

"How did he shoot himself like that?"

"Adrenaline. The question now is, what are we going to do? We have a couple of choices. We could leave him here and call the authorities. Let them investigate things as they lie. Hope they believe our story. Or we could exit stage left and cross our fingers that this doesn't get traced to us, knowing that if it does, because we left the scene, we will be presumed guilty."

"How many people do you think are looking for us right now?"

"I don't know. Maybe just these two. If it's more, and we turn ourselves in . . . they'll try to kill us. I doubt they'll try like these two did. There won't be any talking. They'll just do it."

"What's your idea, Thomas?"

"If I was alone, I might push him into the ocean behind Hoagland and get rid of their car."

"That would be illegal. Covering up a shooting."

"Illegal or dead. I figure those are our choices."

"We'd be circumventing the law."

"Or we'd be dead."

"But we'd be circumventing the law."

"You're the law-and-order person. I'm the bad boy. Tell you what. I'm going to defer to your call on this. You decide."

"You're being mean."

"If we do this, it's a secret we'll carry for the rest of our lives and that's going to be as hard for you as it will be for me. I don't want to be the one to put that on you. Your call."

FIFTY-TWO

WHEN I DRAGGED KALPESH down to the bluff, removed his identification, cellphone, and keys, and rolled him into the surf fifty feet below in the same spot where Hoagland had gone over, Kathy's tears weren't faked and neither was her ghostlike complexion. She was weeping for him, but she was weeping for us, too. What we'd become. His worries had ended. So had Hoagland's. Ours were just beginning. Even though we'd made the decision, I had to think about it for several minutes more before I rolled the corpse off the bluff. Did we want to live the rest of our lives with this godawful secret hanging over us? As I pondered the options and cast about for others, I looked out to sea. Hoagland's body had already drifted several hundred yards out and appeared to be headed toward Japan, probably following the same path the unclaimed bodies from the Sheffield wreck had taken. There was no way to be certain, but it was unlikely either body would be retrieved.

I tried to imagine convincing the authorities that, unprovoked, Timothy Hoagland and Kalpesh Gupta had attacked us. It bothered me that I didn't know for certain how closely Kalpesh had worked with Hoagland. I still didn't know for certain if either had taken part in bringing down Sheffield's plane, but I strongly suspected both had. The big question was, if we got caught now, would anybody believe our story? Kalpesh's gun would show evidence of having been fired, and one of the two bullets in his body would have come from it, and if they looked hard enough they would find shell casings in the grass, showing that he'd done a lot of shooting, but it was still possible somebody would conjecture I'd shot him and then fired his gun to make it look like a gunfight. There was only one living witness, and she was on my side and everybody knew it. There would be even more suspicion over the fact that I'd been with my supposedly dead wife. Once we were implicated in Kalpesh's death, nobody would believe our reasons for not bringing Kathy forward. Nobody was going to believe much of anything we had to say. The world believed that Hoagland had been dead for five days. Another thought came to me. Once I got arrested for killing Kalpesh, they might reopen the Driscoll case with the idea of charging me with her death. Wouldn't that be ironic?

It was with all these regrets and not a few misgivings that I dumped Kalpesh fifty feet into the surf. A few minutes later as we stood in the grass trying to grasp the enormity of what we'd done, he bobbed into view, face up, and we watched his body begin the slow journey out to sea behind Hoagland's. I had the two guns in my pockets, along with an extra clip for the 9 mm. We still weren't sure there wasn't somebody else coming for us, but even so, Kathy and I stood on the bluff until darkness had thoroughly cloaked our crime. We were both in the daze that comes after you do something very wrong and realize you're going to have to live with it. We weren't watching the sunset as it changed colors; we were both silently tracing the path of the bodies as they worked their way out to sea.

It was dark when we located Hoagland's vehicle in the parking lot—a large four-door American car, government issue with government plates. I put on gloves, found the key on the fob that had been in Kalpesh's pocket, and drove it while Kathy took my Ford. It was pitch-dark when we abandoned Hoagland's car at a picnic area near a beach-access road not far from our motel. After taking extensive notes on Kalpesh's calls in and calls out, I walked out to the beach, turned off both phones I'd found on Kalpesh, and sent them into the waves sealed in a plastic bag I'd knotted at the mouth. There was a hole in the bag and I guessed it would sink two or three miles out.

At one in the morning, just before the tide was at its lowest, Kathy drove me back to Hoagland's government car. Neither of us had slept. The storm clouds were starting to billow, but the tide was as far out as I'd ever seen it. I lowered all the windows and drove out onto the beach. I didn't use headlights for fear an insomniac, illicit lovers, or a crabbing vessel might spot me. Not far away was a small stream that fed into the ocean, and now, with the tide out, the flats beside the stream would extend for a good two hundred yards beyond the high-tide mark. It was an area where the beach was like quicksand and where many a car had been sunk forever. I sped into the water, knowing that after the car bogged down, it would keep sinking. Losing cars on this beach was a running joke among the locals.

I managed to get the vehicle a hundred and fifty yards past the tide line before it stalled and I crawled out through the open window and swam ashore against a riptide. The water was cold enough to numb my extremities, and I was shivering uncontrollably as I jogged up the beach to where Kathy waited in the Ford, the heater running full blast. Swimming had been a bad idea. All of it had been a bad idea.

Back at the motel I took a long shower and climbed into bed, but I was still cold. "I can't believe we did that," Kathy said.

"We have a choice?"

"Half my clients think they didn't have a choice. That's what makes me feel so sick about all this. I feel like one of my clients."

"What were we supposed to do?"

"I don't know. I don't know if I can stand to be this anxious for the rest of my life, either. I want my old life back, the one where I wasn't worried about getting arrested, just murdered."

"It could be worse."

"How? How could it be worse?"

"We could be the ones floating toward Japan."

"Hold me."

SHORTLY AFTER DAWN I heard a tapping on our patio door. Kathy was still in bed trying to catch a few winks after a sleepless night. Shoeless and shirtless, I was in the kitchenette rummaging through our bags in search of breakfast. The patio slider opened to a plot of tall beach grasses, which gave way to a hundred yards of dry, soft sand and beyond that, although unseen, the foamy white line where the ocean had run up during the night to finger the hard-packed sand. The tapping came again.

I couldn't think of anybody it might be except the motel manager or maybe the local police. For a moment a shiver of trepidation ran through my bones. I was still trying to get used to the idea that I'd been involved in the deaths of two men and had disposed of their bodies, had been trying to wrap my brain around it all night. Eventually I would deal with it, but I knew it was going to take at least a few weeks to accept that it had happened and maybe even a few months to stop reliving every second of the event every hour on the hour.

Our visitor turned out to be Bert. "What the hell?" I asked, pulling the slider open four inches.

"You gotta let me in."

"Why?"

"He's coming for you."

"Who?"

"Timothy Hoagland and whoever else he's working with."

"Hoagland's dead."

"No, he's not. He's been alive all along. He was just pretending to be dead. I don't know why he did it, but it's just his kind of stunt. Maybe he needs to disappear for some other reason. I don't know."

"You're only saying he's alive so I won't think you killed him."

"I swear to God he's alive."

"What makes you think he's coming for me?"

"I have an inside source."

"Inside what?"

"Inside his organization."

"Have you had this inside source the whole time?"

"Yeah, but I didn't know he was trustworthy until just this last day or two. I'm telling you, they're coming for you. They know Kathy's alive, and they want you both out of the picture."

"Why?"

"Maybe because of your association with me. But he's going to kill you."

"Why would this so-called inside source be friendly to you?"

"We used to work together."

"Who is it?" Kathy asked, from the other room.

"Your favorite client." I turned back to the patio slider. "How did you find us?"

"My friend said they'd traced you to the coast, but they were waiting for you to turn on a cellphone or some fool thing. They were tracking you by your phone. I've been driving past motels for two days looking for your car. I'm guessing they're doing the same thing. You don't have much time."

Wrapped in a cotton gown she'd purchased on one of our day trips into Hoquiam, Kathy stepped around me, let Bert in as if he were a long-lost cousin, kissed his cheek, and said, "That's for saving my life."

If there had been any doubt he was in love with my wife, it was eliminated when I witnessed him turn into Dopey after the kiss from Snow White: all glowing and pink cheeked, like a giant dumpling. Just as it began to wear off, she hauled back and slapped him across the opposite cheek. She hit him hard. The impact made a sound like a slammed door.

"Gawd! What's that for?" he yelled.

"For drugging me with that bottle of water and telling me Thomas was dead."

"I had to do that. I had—"

She slapped him again, this blow even harder than the first. "All you had to do was tell me the plane crashed."

"Jesus, Kathy . . . I just—"

"From now on you can call me Ms. Birchfield."

"Yes, ma'am. Christ almighty."

I'd been pretty sure all along he wanted her to think I was dead because he had some screwy pipe dream that if I was out of the picture the path would be clear for him.

Kathy stomped across the small room, gathered up some clothes in the bedroom, and headed into the bathroom to change. Bert kept his eyes on her until the door closed, hoping, I think, to catch a glimpse of forgiveness. When that failed, he turned to me. "Did you know she was going to do that?"

I bobbled my eyebrows in amusement. "Think you were followed?" I asked.

"No."

"Sure?"

"Relatively sure. I got here a couple hours ago and waited down the road until I thought you'd be awake. They caught some dude with your phone and killed him. That's what my friend told me. For about a day there I thought it was you. Come on, man. We have to move."

Kathy came out dressed for an early-morning walk and said, "Let's talk about this on the beach." In the yard, Snake was waiting—standing guard, actually, armed and grim. I noticed a large pistol in Bert's waistband, too.

From our motel you could walk maybe three miles on the beach in either direction before finding an impediment to your progress; to the south it was the small river running into the ocean, where I'd ditched Hoagland's car. The ocean was creeping inland every year, reclaiming land, so the car was only going to burrow deeper and deeper.

"You don't seem to get it," Bert said, when we were a quarter mile down the beach. "They could be training an M-82 on us right now." For effect, he glanced around, but there was nothing except windblown ocean on one side and sand dunes and bluffs on the other; not even any boats on the water, at least none that I could see. "They're coming to kill you two. And me. And my brother. And anybody who knows us. They're going to place drugs all over hell to make it look like a cocaine deal gone crazy." It made sense. When I'd searched Hoagland's car, there had been some suspicious-looking packages in the trunk. And it matched the spirit of what Hoagland told us. But I didn't say anything to either brother. Kathy and I had made a pact never to talk about what had happened yesterday.

"You have a friend who's part of this?" I asked.

"A support member. He doesn't know much."

"And you're not going to tell us his name?"

"So they can torture it out of you when they find you and then kill him? I don't think so. All this is on a need-to-know basis. He swears Hoagland is planning to kill you. Taking some FBI guy along or maybe a political operative. He's promised this guy a high-paying job in Homeland Security after they do the deed. No arrest, man. Just a plain old assassination." He turned and looked at his brother, who was fifty yards away and out of earshot, standing sentry duty. "Elmer and I are going to see if we can't find a safe place to hide out until this blows over. I would advise you two do the same. Me? I'm going to keep after these bums."

"What does that mean?" Kathy asked.

"It means I'm going to find out who was responsible and rectify things."

"How?"

"I don't know how I'll find them, but there's only one way to rectify."

"For God's sake, don't go on a rampage," Kathy said, glancing at me for confirmation. Bert was a government-trained sniper. He knew these people. He'd worked with them or others like them. He knew their mind-set and their tactics. If he thought some of them needed to be wiped off the map—after what had happened last night, after the plane crash, after Deborah's murder and Ponzi's husband's and now Tommy's—I wasn't so sure I wanted to rein him in. In fact, unleashing Bert on these people seemed almost like a reasonable solution. Immoral, illegal, and just plain wrong, but somehow viscerally satisfying.

"Tell me what happened those last minutes you had with Hoagland," I said.

"Up there in the woods after you left? I won't mince words. I thought about killing him. I cut him loose thinking he was unconscious, but he wasn't. He started to rip the duct tape off his eyes, and I ran, man."

"Did he recognize you?"

"I didn't think so at the time, but he must have, because somebody blew my trailer all to hell."

"And he's after me because he knows we were hanging together?"

"That'd be my guess. I doubt his superiors have authorized any of it. He's gone rogue, Thomas."

"Because you tortured him."

"He deserved it."

"Nobody deserves it."

"And now he's on a killing spree. Anybody he can get his hands on who might have been involved. Me. You. He's going to get away with it. Hell, the FBI's backing him up."

"What about Deborah Driscoll? Anybody talking about who killed her?"

"These guys don't talk about stuff after it happens. They just say we've got a problem, and a day later the problem is missing or dead or in a plane wreck."

"The driver who killed Ponzi's husband?"

"They'll never find him. Come on. You two need to start running."

Bert headed up the beach, where he and his brother walked side-by-side, twenty yards of sand between them, treating this as if it were a military operation. I peered down the beach in the direction of the Cape. The mist on the beach kept visibility to less than half a mile, but I kept looking anyway.

"You think they're going to find the bodies?" Kathy asked in a low voice.

"I think that storm last night is carrying them straight to Tokyo."

"It's a creepy feeling to know somebody could knock on your door and . . ."

"It is, indeed."

As they drove away, it occurred to me that we might not see either Bert or Elmer again. Ever. Or, that they might be the survivors and that they might not see us again. Ever.

FIFTY-THREE

KATHY AND I WERE IN her office when two FBI agents came to visit—the tall one and the weird one, as we later dubbed them. It had been almost five weeks since we bid adios to Bert and Elmer, and to date we hadn't heard a peep from either of them. Whether they were dead or still in hiding or spending the last of their pesos in a Mexican whorehouse was anybody's guess. We'd come to the slow conclusion that Hoagland and Kalpesh hadn't told anyone where they were going the day they disappeared. Once his disappearance became public knowledge, it was stated in the papers that Kalpesh's last known interaction was when he bought gas at a south Seattle Arco station. A month later his car was found in a Costco parking lot. After our stay on the coast, one storm after another pounded the Washington shoreline, so I had a feeling anything that was going to be found would have been found by now.

The FBI visitors wore nondescript suits. The tall one introduced himself as Agent Miller and did all the talking. His hair was clipped short to deaccentuate his bald spots, and he had the soft, pink skin of somebody who rarely spent time outdoors. The weird partner had bulging eyes, pretended to be bored, and stroked his chin as if enjoying the touch of his own smooth skin, as if he'd just shaved off a beard. It wasn't until weeks later that I began to wonder if they were authentic. When I phoned the local FBI office, they wouldn't tell me anything.

There had been surprisingly little public hoopla concerning the disappearance of one of the key figures in the Maddox campaign. I could only guess that Maddox and company had squelched what might have turned into an uproar. *The Seattle Times* ran an article about Kalpesh Gupta on the front page, but after that he was relegated to the back of the paper.

A severe winter storm had struck the day we came back from the ocean, raking the coast and taking out power for thousands of Washingtonians, blotting up most of the headlines for the next few days. As soon as we'd recovered from the storm, the state held the elections, and they took up most of the headline space. To everyone's astonishment, James Maddox won the race and became a U.S. senator from Washington State. I was both flummoxed and heartbroken, and for half a day Kathy didn't speak to me.

Some of the behind-the-scenes speculation about Kalpesh's disappearance ranged from suicide, to carjacking and murder, to some sort of freak automobile accident. As far as we could tell, nobody was officially looking for Hoagland. After all, he'd been reported dead before our contretemps at the Cape.

When we got back to Seattle we announced publicly that Kathy had missed the Sheffield flight and immediately afterward was involved in an automobile accident that had rendered her incommunicado for weeks. Our story wasn't far off the truth and seemed to satisfy most of her friends, even if a few of them looked at us askance when we told it. We were patiently waiting to see what the FBI would think of it.

Agent Miller sat down in the closet I used for an office while his bug-eyed pal blocked the doorway. I was at my computer. It turned out Kathy was the last thing he was interested in. "We understand you are acquainted with a Bert Slezak," Miller said, his delivery so droll and deadpan it was comical.

"He was a client of my wife's."

"But you were friends?"

"Acquaintances."

"When was the last time you heard from him?"

"A month or so, I guess."

"You guess?"

"You want me to look at my calendar and figure it out?"

The agents exchanged looks. "You know what Slezak was involved in?"

"I know he once got caught stealing women's panties off a clothesline."

"Do you know what he was doing before he left town?"

"I didn't know he left town. If he did, he probably had women's panties with him."

We all stared at one another for a while. I knew what they were here for and they knew I knew; they were trolling to see if they could provoke a reaction, if they could see whether I was a confederate or just an acquaintance. "All right then," I continued. "You want to know what was on his mind? He thought the Sheffield flight was taken down on purpose."

Neither of them registered anything like surprise. "Were you two investigating this?"

"We talked about it before my wife turned up alive."

"Your wife. We'll want to talk to her later."

"She's in the next room."

"We know. Did Slezak ever say anything about doing injury to anyone in the government?"

"Not that I recall."

"He talk about overthrowing it?"

"The United States government? No."

"What was the nature of his thinking?"

"He said certain elements were subverting democracy."

"Which elements would that be?"

"I never found out."

"But he thought somebody shot down Senator Sheffield's flight?"

"Brought it down somehow. He wasn't always specific."

"That was ruled accidental."

"He didn't believe the ruling."

"Do you?"

"Is this a personal question, or do you want to know for some official reason?"

"I'm going to tell you something, Mr. Black. I want you to keep it in confidence."

"Sure."

"We're reviewing the Sheffield crash. We know you and Slezak were doing the same thing. Plenty of people have pointed out discrepancies in the NTSB report. We would appreciate it if you and your friends leave it alone until we come to our own determination."

"When will that be?"

"It will take some time."

"Okay."

"So you won't look into it?"

"Not for a while."

"You ever meet Kalpesh Gupta?"

"Of course. He worked with my wife on the Sheffield campaign."

"And what was the nature of your relationship?"

"We weren't close friends if that's what you mean."

"Had you met Timothy Hoagland?"

"I met him at Boeing Field at a press conference."

"And what did you talk about?"

"I still thought my wife was dead at the time. I don't remember any of it."

"You never saw Hoagland after that?"

"Not that I recall."

"What else can you tell us about Slezak's investigation?"

I told him about the death of Ruth Ponzi's husband and Deborah Driscoll. He appeared familiar with both incidents. "You were a friend of this woman?" he asked, referring to Driscoll.

"We worked together."

"And what was Slezak's interest in these deaths?"

"Bert thought they were killed to intimidate anybody who might have been digging for information on the Sheffield crash. Deborah Driscoll called me and was going to tell me something I wasn't supposed to know about the campaign."

"And what was that?"

"I don't know. She died before she could tell me."

"You think two people were murdered to keep your friend Bert Slezak from continuing his investigation?"

"Basically."

"Sounds a little far-fetched."

"It does, doesn't it?" A senator's plane diving into the ocean for no discernible reason sounded far-fetched, too, but I didn't bring it up. An NTSB investigator dying the day before his report came out sounded far-fetched, but I didn't mention that, either.

"Mr. Black, I'm going to be frank. I've been instructed to try to make a deal with you. If it were up to me, I wouldn't be telling you any of this." He sighed. "We're after a black bag group. Rogue operatives, some of whom may at one time have worked for the government. We believe they may have committed treason."

"Treason? As in shooting down an airplane with ten people on board?"

"We're not at liberty to reveal any more than that. Our plan is to take the group apart, but that's going to take some time and a lot of patience. We think you may have tangled with them."

"In what way?"

"We're not sure. All we know is you were on their hit list."

"Am I still on it?"

"They seem to have disbanded. However, we have an offer for you. Keep your nose out of our investigation, and we'll stay out of your life. How does that sound?"

"Like a threat."

"Don't mistake our intentions. All we want is to work without distractions. If we're going to catch these people, we need to be left alone. We don't want the general populace to find out about this. In fact, we'll deny everything said here if you repeat it. Are you following me?"

"How do I know you're going after them? How do I know you're not part of it yourselves?"

"We're the FBI. We're on your side."

"Information is what feeds a democracy. If there's monkey business afoot, the populace needs to know the details."

"You're taking an unreasonable attitude, Mr. Black."

"Anybody can tell you, that's the attitude I usually take."

"If you're contacted by Bert Slezak, you better get in touch with our office. He's committed crimes, and we're going to bring him in. It would be a pity if we had to name you as a co-conspirator."

"What crimes?"

"Just stay out of it."

THEY SPENT A LONG TIME in Kathy's office. At one point, I heard her laughing through the door, so I knew it wasn't all business.

"They give you a hard time?" I asked after they'd left.

"They worked hard at being gracious."

"Not with me."

"They said you copped an attitude."

"Me?"

"You really think it was smart to get sarcastic with the FBI?"

"I was just trying to be myself."

"Apparently you succeeded. You think they're really trying to bring the black bag boys to account?"

"I think they're part of the cleanup operation. They were here to intimidate us into dropping it. Nothing else."

"I thought the same thing. Thomas, you're not going to keep looking into this, are you?"

"Jane Sheffield and the others were murdered. Maddox is a United States senator today because of that murder. I'm not even sure the election was straight. What do you want me to do?"

"I think you and I can go on with our lives, if that's what we choose. It's a matter of what we decide to do."

"Don't I know it."

═══ FIFTY-FOUR ═══

TWO WEEKS AFTER THE ELECTION I set up a meeting with James Maddox. I knew he routinely traveled with a posse, so I specified he show up alone. I'd spent a lot of time analyzing the phone numbers I'd taken off Hoagland. Maddox's number had shown up five times, both incoming and outgoing. I could think of several reasons why Hoagland would be talking to Maddox on the day he drove out to kill me and Kathy, none of them good.

From time to time I employed the services of a technical whiz just out of high school. I had him fix up a cheap cellphone I'd acquired so that calls emanating from it appeared to be emanating from Timothy Hoagland's old number. One phone company technician told me it was impossible, but my boy genius arranged it without much difficulty. Then, knowing my incoming call would show up as one from Hoagland and that the sound quality would be mediocre on my cellphone, I phoned Maddox doing little to disguise my voice. "We need to meet."

"I thought . . . Is this . . . ? What happened to you? We knew you were playing dead, but then you really disappeared. Everybody's looking for you."

"I'm only going to be in town a few hours. Something has come up that you need to know about."

"Tim? Your voice sounds funny."

"I've been traveling."

"I haven't heard from you. I didn't—"

"Shut up and write this down." It was pretty obvious he was used to taking orders from Hoagland.

We met in West Seattle on California Avenue at a tiny roadside park overlooking Elliott Bay, the lights of downtown Seattle, and the shipping terminals on Harbor Island. I arrived

forty minutes early and concealed myself in the brush, waiting
for Maddox or his confederates to arrive early and set up an
ambush, but Maddox showed up alone five minutes before the
appointed time and, motor running, waited in his Mercedes. I
called him again on the dummied-up phone and told him to
turn his engine off and walk out to the overlook. "Why the
cloak-and-dagger?" he asked.

"If you can't guess, I'm not going to say it on the phone."

"I just don't know why—"

"Think about the last person who had your seat in the Senate. Think about it real hard."

He shut off his motor and walked to the overlook. Even
though nobody was around and he was only traveling thirty
feet, he locked his car. I let him stew in the cold wind for ten
minutes and then sneaked up behind him. "I suppose I should
call you 'Senator' now."

He jumped. "Black?"

"Happy to see me?"

"You'll have to leave. I'm meeting somebody."

"Yeah? Who?"

"It's private. What are you doing here, anyway?" Maddox
looked around for more surprises.

"I thought all along you were too damn confident about
winning the election."

"What do you mean?"

"You knew you were going to win even when the rest of
the world thought you were screwed."

"Confidence. It's a valuable asset to a politician. To anybody, really. You should try it."

"Baloney, it was confidence. Kalpesh was working in the
Sheffield camp, feeding information to Deborah. You guys
knew everything they were going to do before they did it.
When that didn't turn the trick, you brought in the big guns
and had her plane taken down."

"Are you insane?"

"And you're here to meet one of those big guns, aren't
you?"

"Who would I be meeting that possibly—?"

"Timothy Hoagland."

The name coming out of my mouth surprised him as much as my arrival had. "Hoagland's dead."

"Then why are you meeting him? And how did you know that plane was going down before it happened?"

"My friend, paranoia is a one-note symphony. It bores people. Try to vary it a little."

"You guys had it in the bag and knew it."

"We had information, sure. Somebody from the other camp volunteers it . . . for whatever reason. Maybe they're looking for a job after the election. Maybe they're just a disgruntled employee. Get used to it. Everybody does it."

"Does everybody conspire to murder their rival?"

"I don't have to listen to this."

"You still haven't told me why you're out here in the cold waiting for a dead man."

"He called."

"Hoagland called? I thought you said he was dead."

"Somebody called from his phone. Now get the hell out of my way."

"I think you were involved in a conspiracy to commit murder. A murder that would have included my wife if she hadn't had a stroke of luck."

"I saved your life, you ungrateful wretch."

"Thanks for reminding me about the bomb. The question there is, was it set to get you or was it set to get me?"

"Don't inflate your own importance."

"There's no inflation here. I'm just thinking it through."

"You really have gone over the edge."

"And Deborah? Who gave the order to get rid of her?"

"You need help."

"Sooner or later, I'm going to prove this. Or enough of it to put you in jail."

We glared at each other for a few seconds, during which he put on a show of righteous indignation. A few weeks ago it might have worked; I might have doubted the conspiracy existed, doubted a U.S. senator was capable of such things, that there were black bag organizations in our country perpetuating outrageous travesties, but not now. For a few moments I thought about exacting justice on my own. I could slam the heel of my hand into his windpipe and have him on the ground in seconds. He'd be gasping for air, and I'd be standing on his throat. I could do it. I had the rage, the strength, and the cunning. I'd recovered from the bombing and was lifting weights again. He was a desk jockey. It was dark and nobody would see. Nobody would hear his cries, if he even had time to cry out. I would roll his silver-haired body down the hillside into the brush and drive his car to another city.

Instead, I watched him flounce back to his car and lock the doors behind him. Maybe he knew how close I'd come to assaulting him. Maybe it showed on my face. He knew the bomb had been meant for me, and he'd known it before it went off. Thinking back on how he'd treated me that day, it was easy to see that now. They killed four innocent bystanders in their attempt to get me, nine others when they killed Jane Sheffield. Add to the list Ponzi's husband. And Deborah. Tommy. It was maddening to know all this and not be able to prove it. It was even more maddening to watch him drive away and know he would soon be in Washington, D.C., preparing to rule the country.

FIFTY-FIVE

FROM TIME TO TIME over the next months I experimented by telling parts of my story to relative strangers. When I went to Spokane on business I braced a cabdriver, telling her what I believed happened to the Jane Sheffield flight and all the rest of it. I tried my theories out on strangers in coffee shops. At a New Year's Eve party given by one of the law firms trying to recruit Kathy, I tested it on a couple of office temps. Once, when he and I were the only people on board, I laid out the story for a bus driver. Except for a homeless guy on the street who said, "Right on, brother," the reactions were virtually the same: bewilderment, then a polite attempt to hide disbelief, and efforts to change the subject or separate from me as soon as possible. I'd become one of those dim-witted provocateurs who walk around telling people how both Kennedys were assassinated by J. Edgar Hoover and how Nixon was in on it.

The way my thinking had changed was scary. For a lot of reasons it was the scariest thing that had ever happened to me.

Early one morning, in the middle of an extraordinarily warm and sunny April, I walked into the office and found Ruth Ponzi waiting for me. It had been almost seven months since her husband's death and as long since I'd spoken to her. In the past year I'd seen a lot of relatives of the dead and, while she looked somewhat revitalized, she still had traces of the look I once thought I'd carry for the rest of my life. She'd colored her hair darker and was doing something new with her makeup, toned it down, I believe. She looked better and worse at the same time; better physically, but there was a hurt deep in her eyes, a hurt I sensed might never dissipate. In addition, there was something about the cut of her jib that alerted me to the fact that she was filled with purpose now.

"You have a minute?" she asked.

"All the time in the world." I escorted her into my cubicle and closed the door, noting the look Beulah gave me from the other room. Beulah clearly thought something momentous was about to happen, though as far as I knew, she'd never met Ponzi before. But then, Beulah was good that way. My own thoughts ran more toward Ponzi blaming me for her husband's death.

"I'd like to know where I can find the Sinclair Lewis twins," she said.

"You're talking about Bert and Elmer? I don't know where to find them. I wish I did. I'd like to know they're okay."

"They're in hiding?"

"I think so."

"In lieu of that, maybe you can tell me what happened last fall."

"You're talking about the election?"

"I'm talking about the dirty dealing surrounding the election. I'm talking about campaign workers who ended up dead or missing. About that plane crash and your wife's miraculous survival. About my husband's death. For a long time I didn't know what to do, but now I have a plan."

"And that plan is?"

"Right now I'm just here to listen. I want to know everything you can tell me."

"You're sure?"

"I've never been more sure of anything in my life."

"The information I give you might be . . . unhealthy."

"I've been in the hospital. I lost my husband. I'm not worried about my health." She sat back in the chair, waiting. It took over an hour to lay out all of Bert's theories, a few of mine, and to explain without giving away too much that I believed the deaths of Hoagland and the disappearance of Kalpesh Gupta were intertwined. I kept my participation in the tale to a minimum. Even as I spoke, it occurred to me that she'd been recruited by one police agency or another to get me to open up. I didn't really think so, but it was a possibility. Since last fall, my paranoia knew no bounds. In any case, I couldn't withhold the facts from this woman and I didn't.

She asked penetrating questions, and when I was finished answering, she said, "Are you game to get back to this?"

"You're going to write an exposé?"

"Yes, but I'm going to need help."

"I need time to think about it."

"I figured that would be your answer. I'll be working on it, and I won't stop until I get to the bottom of everything that happened. You call me whenever you're ready to help."

During the next weeks I continued to earn a living as a private investigator, chipping away at the Sheffield incident in my spare time. I did not bother any of my clients with my theories. I networked with an ex-government employee in South Carolina who'd put up a website exposing various government conspiracies and who said he was interested in the Sheffield crash; I took enormous satisfaction in knowing that Kathy and I and the Slezak twins weren't the only believers on the planet.

Elmer returned from wherever he'd been and was immediately questioned by the FBI. They didn't learn much from him, nor did they arrest him. Our dog returned, too, looking even better fed than when he left and doing his best to pretend he'd never been away. I eventually was able to remember all the messages the woman in the gym gave me before she died, and I delivered them in a sorrowful meeting with her family. It was embarrassing, because they treated me like a hero and I felt like a murderer. I felt even worse about putting Tommy in harm's way and getting him killed. I located his girlfriend, wanting to help her out, but she had another boyfriend by the time I got there and he ran me off. Kalpesh Gupta's disappearance remained a mystery. Timothy Hoagland was still classified as having died somewhere in the Cascade Mountains off Interstate 90. No official cause was ever given for his death.

Soon after he came back to the Northwest, Elmer resumed his drinking career, engaging in a long bender before he went back to the clinic to straighten out. When I visited him in the clinic he told me what the FBI had asked about me, and it was immediately clear they knew stuff they could only have found out by eavesdropping on my phone conversations.

In June, Snake received a postcard from Argentina without

a message, just the stamp and Snake's address. "What's this mean?" I asked, when he showed it to me.

"It means he's all right."

"You think they're monitoring your mail?"

"They're monitoring everything."

"When are they going to stop?"

"I don't know. Six months. A year. When they get bored."

Late that month Bert phoned me. "I'm coming home," he said. "Be there in a couple of days."

"Are you still . . . ?"

"There's nobody after me. Nobody after you, either."

"How do you know?"

"A little birdie told me. Everything's been rolled up. They're on to other things."

"You sure we're safe?"

"As safe as we'll ever be in this country."

"What about Sheffield? Is anybody ever going to know the truth?"

"People don't want the truth."

When I told Kathy about my conversation, she said, "I hope Bert didn't kill somebody to make this go away."

"If he did, let's hope they were guilty."

"We're all guilty."

It had been twelve months fraught with disappointment. Disappointment that my wife had died and that my brain had unraveled so completely. I'd learned more about myself than I needed to know. Disappointment that Maddox was considerably less than even my worst evaluations had given him credit for. Most of all, disappointment that there were enough misguided Americans around to make something as ghastly as the Sheffield crash come off without a hitch, enough complacency among the throngs that nobody was thinking much about it.

Like every other voter, I was confronted with citizenship choices every day. I could carry on as usual, hoping dirty politics and the attendant illegal shenanigans wouldn't crop up again, hoping the great machine I'd seen running amok didn't run over anybody else's toes the way it did with Sheffield and her co-workers and Ponzi's husband and Deborah and the four people who died in the Garfield gym. And my friend

Tommy. Hoping everything would turn out okay in the end. I could use my talents to help swing things back to the way our founding fathers envisioned them, or I could wait for somebody else to do it. It was my choice, and I was painfully aware of my own reluctance to stick my neck out again. Still, late in the afternoon on a Friday when everybody else was rushing home to buy beer for the weekend I picked up the phone and dialed Ruth Ponzi.